DAVID MORRELL

DESPERATE MEASURES

WARNER BOOKS

A Time Warner Company

WARNER BOOKS EDITION

Cover design by Jesse Sanchez
Cover photography by Herman Estevez

Warner Books, Inc.
1271 Avenue of the Americas
New York, NY 10020

Visit our Web site at
www.twbookmark.com

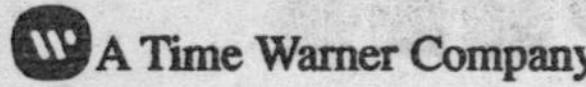
A Time Warner Company

Printed in the United States of America

Originally published in hardcover by Warner Books
First Printed in Paperback: July 1995
Reissued: May 2001

10 9 8 7 6 5 4 3 2

RAVES FOR *DESPERATE MEASURES* AND DAVID MORRELL

"UTTERLY COMPELLING, AS SWIFT AS A RUNAWAY TRAIN, FULL OF EXCITEMENT AND EMOTION. . . . DAVID MORRELL'S BEST BOOK SINCE *FIRST BLOOD*."

—Dean Koontz

"HIGH-VOLTAGE ENTERTAINMENT THAT GUARANTEES TO LEAVE READERS BREATHLESS."

—Copley News Service

"A HITCHCOCKIAN ROLLER-COASTER RIDE, with the extra depth few thrillers possess."

—*Tribune Newspapers* (AZ)

"EXTRAORDINARY . . . INTELLIGENT, MINDBENDINGLY INVENTIVE, UTTERLY SUSPENSEFUL, AND THOUGHT PROVOKING . . . *DESPERATE MEASURES* had me in its grip. I just couldn't stop reading it."

—Thomas Gifford, author of *The Wind Chill Factor* and *First Sacrifice*

"MORRELL WRITES IN A LUCID AND CINEMATIC STYLE, and his works can be read and re-read many times without losing suspense."

—Associated Press

more . . .

"MORRELL STANDS HEAD AND SHOULDERS ABOVE MOST OF HIS CONTEMPORARIES. . . . He may well be the writer who finally succeeds in raising the suspense novel to a level of literary respectability long ago realized in England but never quite achieved here." —***National Review***

"MORRELL IS A MASTER. . . . His fans won't be disappointed by the complex but hurtling plot." —***Publishers Weekly***

"MORRELL'S BEST BOOK EVER . . . flows with thrills and gut-wrenching excitement . . . beautifully organized and nearly impossible to put down . . . a must for any Morrell fan and any fan of the intrigue/thriller genre."

—***Cedar Rapids Gazette***

"FEW THRILLER WRITERS BRING AS MUCH IMAGINATION TO THEIR CRAFT AS DAVID MORRELL. In these days of recycled plots through prequels, sequels, and serials, he puts a shine of originality on each new effort. . . . Both plausible and satisfying, not to mention immensely intriguing . . . the story hits the ground running and never pauses while racing from one hairsbreadth escape to the next." —***Lexington Herald-Leader* (KY)**

"MORRELL IS AT THE TOP OF HIS CRAFT. The in-depth characterization, believable and unpredictable plot developments, and psychological depths will draw all readers."

—***Library Journal***

"THE ABSOLUTE MASTER . . . the craftsman so many of us look to for guidance."

—**Andrew Vachss**

"MORRELL IS IN FINE FORM IN *DESPERATE MEASURES*, a book that moves fast and furiously."

—***Dayton Daily News***

"MORRELL IS A GOOD WRITER, SIMPLE, BITING, TERSE."

—***Hartford Courant***

"ANYONE WHO ENJOYED THE FUGITIVE WILL RELISH *DESPERATE MEASURES* . . . Morrell at his very best. The action races like a burning fuse to a dynamite ending."

—***New City* (IL)**

"ANOTHER HIGH-SPEED THRILLER . . . GRIPPING."

—***Kirkus Reviews***

"MORRELL'S WRITING STYLE IS CRISP AND TOUGH, and he knows how to grab a reader and hold him well past bedtime."

—***Life***

ALSO BY DAVID MORRELL

Fiction

First Blood (1972)

Testament (1975)

Last Reveille (1977)

The Totem (1979)

Blood Oath (1982)

The Hundred-Year Christmas (1983)*

The Brotherhood of the Rose (1984)

The Fraternity of the Stone (1985)

The League of Night and Fog (1987)

The Fifth Profession (1990)

The Covenant of the Flame (1991)

Assumed Identity (1993)

The Totem (Complete and Unaltered) (1994)*

Extreme Denial (1996)

Double Image (1998)

Black Evening (1999)

Burnt Sienna (2000)

Nonfiction

John Barth: An Introduction (1976)

Fireflies (1988)

***Limited edition. With illustrations. Donald M. Grant, Publisher, Hampton Falls, New Hampshire.**

To Mel Parker,
who is what every author dreams of:
a talented editor who is also a friend.

ONE

1

The pistol, a Colt .45 semiautomatic, was capable of holding seven rounds in its magazine. But at the moment, it held only one, which Pittman fed into the firing chamber by pulling back the slide on top of the weapon. The well-oiled metal made a smooth snicking sound. Fourteen years earlier, when Pittman had written his first newspaper story, it had been about a retired policeman who had committed suicide. Pittman had never forgotten a conversation he had overheard, the respectful tones with which two patrolmen at a coffee machine in their precinct headquarters had referred to their former comrade's death.

"Poor bastard, couldn't stand retirement."

"Drinking problem."

"Wife left him."

"Went out with style. Used his backup gun—a semiautomatic, Colt .45. Just one round in it."

The reference had puzzled Pittman until he did some research and learned that when fired, a semiautomatic pistol ejected the used empty cartridge and chambered a new one. The hammer recocked itself. This feature made rapid firing possible during an emergency. But the retired policeman who had shot himself had evidently considered it unethical to leave a loaded, cocked weapon next to his body after his suicide. There was no way to predict who would find his body. His landlady perhaps, or her ten-year-old son, who might foolishly pick up the gun. So, to avoid the danger that someone might later get hurt, the retired policeman had put only one round in the weapon. He knew that after the bullet was discharged, the slide would remain back, the firing chamber empty, the weapon completely safe.

"Went out with style."

Thus, Pittman, too, put only one round in his pistol. Weeks earlier, he'd applied for a permit to have a firearm in his apartment. This afternoon, after the authorities had determined that Pittman wasn't a felon, had never been in a mental institution because of violent behavior, et cetera, he had been allowed to go to the sporting-goods store and take possession of the pistol, a .45, the same as the retired policeman's. The clerk had asked how many boxes of ammunition he wanted. Pittman had responded that one would definitely be more than sufficient.

"I guess that means you're just going to keep it at home for protection, huh?"

"Yes, protection," Pittman had said.

(From nightmares, he had silently added.)

In his small third-floor apartment, with the door locked, he now sat at his narrow kitchen table, studied the cocked pistol, and listened to the din of evening traffic outside. The clock on the stove made a whirring sound, one of its mechanical numbers changing from 8:11 to 8:12. He heard dehumanized laughter from a television situation comedy vibrate through the wall behind him. He smelled fried onions, the odor seeping under his door from an apartment down the hall. He picked up the weapon.

Although he had never been trained to handle firearms, he

had done his customary research. He had also read about the anatomy of the human skull, its soft spots. The temples, the hollows behind the ears, and the roof of the mouth were the most obviously vulnerable. Pittman had read about would-be suicides who had shot themselves in the head, only to give themselves a lobotomy instead of killing themselves. Although infrequent, it most often happened when the barrel was aimed toward the side of the forehead. Squeezing the trigger evidently caused the barrel to move slightly away from the temple. The bullet struck and was deflected by the thick plate of bone above the eyebrows. The would-be suicide became a vegetable.

Not me, Pittman thought. He meant to do this completely. The retired policeman whose example he followed had chosen to place the barrel of his gun inside his mouth—no way of flinching and moving the barrel away from its target—and he had chosen an extremely powerful handgun, a .45.

Pittman had gotten a drink at a bar on the way to the sporting-goods store and at two other bars on the way back home. He kept a bottle of Jack Daniel's in the cupboard next to the refrigerator, but he had not had anything to drink since he had locked his door behind him. He didn't want anyone to think, on the basis of a medical examiner's report, that drunkenness had led him to behave irrationally. More, he wanted to be clearheaded. He wanted to approach his last act with maximum focus.

A question of procedure occurred to him. How could he justify the mess he would make? By process of elimination, he had decided that his self-inflicted death would have to be by means of a bullet. But here at the kitchen table? His blood on the wood, the floor, the refrigerator, possibly the ceiling? Pittman shook his head, stood, held the .45 carefully, and walked toward the bathroom. He concentrated to maintain his balance, climbed into the bathtub, pulled the shower curtain closed, sat down in the cold white tub, and now he was ready.

The .45's gun oil smelled sweet as he brought the pistol toward his mouth. He opened his lips, felt a moment's revulsion, then placed the hard, greasy barrel within his mouth. The barrel was wider than he had anticipated. He had to stretch the corners of his mouth. The bitter-tasting metal scraped against his bottom front teeth, making him shiver.

Now.

He had thought about nothing except his suicide ever since he had applied for the permit to buy his gun. The waiting period had given him a chance to test his resolve. He had exhausted every argument for and against. He had been in such emotional agony that every portion of his brain screamed for release, for an end to his pain.

He tightened his finger on the trigger, but the trigger's resistance was more than he had expected. He had to squeeze harder.

The phone rang.

He frowned.

The phone rang again.

He tried to concentrate.

The phone rang a third time.

Pittman wanted desperately to ignore it, but as the phone persisted, he reluctantly realized that he would have to answer it. This decision had nothing to do with second thoughts, a need to give himself time to change his mind. Rather, it was a need to be thorough. A man of principle, he had promised himself that he would leave no loose ends—no debts unpaid, no favors unreturned, no slights unapologized. His will was in order, his slim assets going to his ex-wife, along with a note of explanation. His work obligations had ended yesterday, the conclusion of the two weeks' notice he had given his employer. He had even arranged for his funeral.

Then who would be phoning him? he wondered. A wrong number? A salesman? What if there was some final detail to which he had not attended? He had done his best to round off his life.

The phone kept ringing. He got out of the tub and went into the living room, grudgingly picking up the phone.

"Hello?" It was such an effort to speak.

"Matt, this is Burt." There wasn't any need for Burt to identify himself. His cigarette smoke–ravaged throat made his distinctive voice constantly hoarse and gravelly. "You took so long, I wasn't sure you were home."

"In that case, why did you let the phone keep ringing?"

"Your answering machine wasn't on," Burt said.

"Even when it's on, I'm sometimes home."

"Well, how would I know that if you never answered?"

Pittman felt detached from the conversation, as if drugged. "What do you want, Burt?"

"A favor."

"Sorry. Can't do it."

"Don't turn me down till you hear the favor."

"It doesn't make a . . . Burt, we're even. We don't owe each other anything. Let's leave it at that."

"You make it sound like just because you quit, we'll never see each other again. Hey, we'll keep owing each other plenty. Yesterday was your last day, so you probably haven't heard. They gave us the word this morning. The *Chronicle* will close its doors a week from Friday."

Burt's voice seemed to come from far away. Pittman felt groggy. "What?"

"We realized the newspaper was in bad shape. Not this

bad, though. Bankrupt. Couldn't find a buyer. In-depth stories can't compete with TV news and *USA Today*. So the owners are liquidating. Nine days from now, after a hundred and thirty-eight years, the final issue hits the stands."

"I still don't . . ."

"I want you to come back to work, Matt. We were understaffed to begin with. Now . . . Look, I've spent thirty years of my life on the *Chronicle*. I don't want it to go out like it's garbage. Please, come back and give me a hand. It's just nine days, Matt. The obit department's as important as any department we've got. Next to the comics and the sports, that's what most readers turn to first. I don't have time to break in a new guy, and I couldn't find one anyhow, not when we're going to be out of business a week from Friday and some bastards are taking off work, looking for other jobs. Be a buddy, Matt. If not for me, for the paper. Hell, you worked here fourteen years. You must have *some* feeling for this place."

Pittman stared at the floor.

"Matt?"

Pittman's muscles cramped from emotional pain.

"Matt? Are you there?"

Pittman studied his gun. "Your timing's lousy, Burt."

"But will you do it?"

"You don't know what you're asking."

"Sure I do. For you to be my friend."

"Damn you, Burt."

Pittman set down the phone. In anguish, he waited for it to ring again, but it stayed silent. He set down the pistol, went over to the bourbon bottle next to the refrigerator, and poured himself a drink. No ice, no water. He quickly drank it and poured himself another.

2

Under the circumstances, it struck Pittman as ironic that he worked in the obituary department of a dying newspaper. His desk, one of many, separated by waist-high partitions, was on the fourth floor, across from and midway between the elevator and the men's room. Although the *Chronicle* was understaffed, movement and noise surrounded Pittman, people walking, phones ringing, reporters answering, computer keyboards being tapped. Arts and Entertainment was behind him, Home Tips on his left, the Community Service Calendar on his right. He felt a gray haze distance him from everything.

"You look awful, Matt."

Pittman shrugged.

"You been sick?"

"A little."

"What's happening to the *Chronicle* will make you even sicker."

"Yeah, so I heard."

The tubby man from Business placed both hands on the front of Pittman's desk and loomed down. "Maybe you also heard the damned pension might be in trouble. And . . . But how *could* you have heard? I forgot you quit two days ago.

Saw it coming, huh? Gotta give you credit. Hope you made a deal, a few weeks' extra pay or . . ."

"No." Pittman cleared his throat. "Actually I didn't know anything about it."

"Then why . . . ?"

"I just got tired."

The man looked blank. "Tired. What are you doing back here?"

Pittman was having grave difficulty concentrating. "Came back to help. Only a week from tomorrow. Everything will be over then." Already the time felt as if it would be an eternity.

"Well, if I were you and I had money in the bank— which I assume you must have or you wouldn't have quit— I wouldn't be wasting my time here. I'd be looking for another job."

Pittman didn't know what to say to that.

The tubby man leaned so close to Pittman's desk that his open sport coat covered the phone, which suddenly rang. In surprise, the man peered down toward the hidden source of the ringing. He straightened.

Pittman picked up the phone.

The call, from what sounded like a middle-aged woman, her voice strained with emotion, was about a seventy-five-year-old man (Pittman guessed it was the woman's father) who had died at his home.

Pittman reached for a form and wrote down the deceased's full name. "Did you wish to specify the cause of death?"

"Excuse me?" The woman sounded breathy, as if she'd been crying. "This has been such a strain. What do you mean 'specify'?"

"Did you wish to be exact and say why he died, ma'am?

Perhaps you wish to say 'after a lengthy illness.' Or perhaps you don't wish to give any cause of death at all."

"He had cancer."

The statement struck Pittman as if an icy blade had knocked him off balance. Unprepared, he suddenly had mental images of Jeremy. Robust, with thick, long, windblown red hair, playing football. Frail, hairless, dead in an equipment-crammed room in a hospital intensive-care unit.

"I'm sorry."

"What?"

Pittman's throat constricted. "I lost a son to cancer. I'm sorry."

An awkward pause made the line seem to hum.

"A lengthy illness," the woman said. "Don't say he had cancer."

Other details: surviving relatives, former occupation, time and place for the funeral.

"Donations?" Pittman asked.

"For what? I don't understand."

"Sometimes close relatives of the deceased prefer that, instead of flowers, a donation be sent to a favorite charity. In this case, perhaps the Cancer Society."

"But wouldn't that be the same as saying he had cancer?"

"Yes, I suppose it would."

"A lengthy illness. My father died from a lengthy illness. I don't want to get involved in the rest of it. If I mention the Cancer Society, every charity in town will be calling me. Is that all you need? Don't forget to mention he belonged to the East Side senior citizens bowling team."

"I've got it," Pittman said.

"In that case . . ."

"I'll need your address."

"But I already told you where my father lived."

"No, I need *your* address, so the *Chronicle* can send you a statement for printing the obituary."

"Statement?"

"Yes, ma'am."

"You mean a bill?"

"Yes, ma'am."

"The newspaper doesn't print obituaries as a community service?"

"No, ma'am."

"Shit."

3

It had been a mistake, Pittman realized. He hadn't imagined the intense effort that it would take for him to go through the motions, to pretend to be committed to his job. Even the simplest gestures, picking up his phone, writing notes, required an exertion of will that left him as exhausted as the marathons he used to run before Jeremy became ill.

He took four more calls, each requiring a greater effort, each more draining. Death by car accident, drowning, hanging, and old age. Hanging had been a method Pittman had considered. When he'd been a reporter, research on one of his stories had taught him that in males, hanging was rumored to have erotic side effects, its victims producing erections. Hanging also had the advantage of being less messy than a death by gunshot. But the trouble was, it wasn't instantaneous. It didn't guarantee results. The rope might slip, or someone might find you in time to resuscitate you. Then you'd have to go through the pain all over again.

Someone coughed.

Glancing up, Pittman saw a stocky, craggy-faced man in his fifties with a brush cut and bushy eyebrows. The man had his navy blazer draped over his shoulder, his muscular upper arms bulging against his rolled-up shirt sleeves. His striped tie was loosened and the top shirt button was open, exposing his bull-like neck. He gave the impression that he was out of uniform, that he belonged in the military. But like Pittman, Burt Forsyth had never been in the military. Burt had worked for the *Chronicle* since he'd gotten out of college, eventually becoming its editor.

"Glad you could make it." Burt's voice was even more gravelly than it had sounded last night.

Pittman shrugged.

"You look beat."

"So people keep telling me," Pittman said.

"I'd have thought your day off would have made you look rested."

"Well, I had a lot of things to do."

"I bet." Burt's gaze was piercingly direct.

Does he suspect? Pittman wondered.

"Considering how busy you are, I appreciate your making time for the *Chronicle*."

"For you," Pittman said.

"The same thing."

When Jeremy had gotten sick, when Jeremy had died, when Pittman had collapsed, Burt Forsyth had always been there to provide reinforcement. "Need to go to the hospital to see your boy? Take all the time you need. Need to stay with him in intensive care? As long as you want. Your job? Don't worry about it. Your desk will be waiting for you." Burt had visited Jeremy in the hospital. Burt had arranged for the most valuable National Football League player to phone Jeremy. Burt had escorted Pittman to and from the mortuary. Burt had gotten drunk with Pittman. Although Pittman had tried to convince himself that he had paid back every debt, the truth was that Burt could never be repaid. Of all those who might have called last night, Burt was the one person Pittman could not refuse.

Burt studied him. "Got a minute?"

"My time is yours."

"In my office."

What now? Pittman thought. Is this where I get the lecture?

4

The *Chronicle* had a no smoking policy. Pittman could never understand how Burt managed constantly to have the recent smell of cigarette smoke on him. His office reeked of it, but there weren't any ashtrays, and there weren't any cigarette butts in the wastebasket. Besides, Burt's office had glass walls. If he was breaking the rule and smoking in here, the reporters at the desks outside would have seen him.

A big man, Burt eased himself into the swivel chair behind his desk. Wood creaked.

Pittman took a chair opposite the desk.

Burt studied him. "Been drinking too much?"

Pittman glanced away.

"I asked you a question," Burt said.

"If you were anybody else . . ."

"You'd tell me it was none of my business. But since I'm the one asking . . . Have you been drinking too much?"

"Depends," Pittman said.

"On?"

"What you call too much."

Burt sighed. "I can tell this isn't going to be a productive conversation."

"Look, you asked for nine days. I'm giving them to you. But that doesn't mean you can run my life."

"What's left of it. You keep drinking as much as I think you have and you'll kill yourself."

"Now that's a thought," Pittman said.

"Drinking won't bring back Jeremy."

"That's another thought."

"And killing yourself won't bring him back, either."

Pittman looked away again.

"Besides, I'm not trying to run your life," Burt said. "It's your job I'm trying to run. I've got something different I want you to do, a special kind of obituary, and I want to make sure you're up to doing it. If you're not, just say so. I'll keep you on the desk, answering obit calls and filling out forms."

"Whatever you want."

"I didn't hear you."

"I came back to work because you asked. If there's something you need, I can do it. What kind of special obituary?"

"The subject isn't dead yet."

5

Pittman changed positions in the chair. Of course, it wasn't any surprise to him, although it generally was to what Pittman called "civilians," that some obituaries were written before the subject's death. Aging movie stars, for example. Celebrities of one sort or another who were mortally ailing or in extremely advanced years. Common sense dictated that since they were going to die soon and since they were famous, why not prepare the obituary sooner rather than later? On occasion, the subjects were remarkably resilient. Pittman knew of one case where a lengthy obituary had been written for an elderly comedian—twenty years earlier—and the comedian in his nineties was still going strong.

But Pittman judged from Burt's somber expression that he hadn't been summoned here just to write something as ephemeral as an obituary for a not-yet-dead movie star. Burt's brows were so thick, they made his eyes seem hooded—dark, intense.

"All right." Pittman gestured. "The subject isn't dead yet."

Burt nodded.

"But evidently you're convinced that he or she *will* be dead within nine days."

Burt's expression didn't change.

"Otherwise, the obituary won't be any good," Pittman said, "because the *Chronicle* will be dead a week from tomorrow, and I never heard of other newspapers buying freelance obituaries."

"It's my gift to you."

"Gosh. I don't know what to say. How generous."

"You're not fooling anybody," Burt said. "You think I haven't figured out what you're planning to do?"

Pittman showed no reaction.

"Ellen phoned yesterday," Burt said.

Pittman felt sudden heat in his stomach, but he didn't allow himself to show any reaction to that either, to the mention of his ex-wife.

"She says you've been acting strangely," Burt said. "Not that I need her to tell me. I've got eyes. In fact, anybody who thinks of you as a friend has noticed. You've been going around making a point of paying back favors, money you borrowed, whatever. You've been apologizing for any harm you caused, and I know it's not because you're cleaning house as part of joining AA, not the way you've been drinking. That car accident three weeks ago. Three A.M. A deserted road in Jersey. A bridge abutment. What the hell were you doing out driving at that hour? And even as drunk as you were, I don't see how you couldn't have avoided that big an obstacle. You *meant* to hit it, and the only reason you didn't die is that your body was so loose from the booze, you bounced like a rag doll when you were thrown from the car."

Pittman touched a still-healing gash on the back of his hand but didn't say anything.

"Don't you want to know what Ellen wanted?" Burt asked.

Pittman stared at the floor.

"Come on," Burt demanded. "Quit acting like you're already dead."

"I made a mistake."

"What?"

"Coming back to work. I made a mistake." Pittman stood.

"Don't," Burt said. "Let me finish."

A reporter appeared in the doorway.

"In a minute," Burt said.

The reporter assessed the two men, nodded somberly, and went away. Other reporters, seated at their desks, were glancing toward the glass walls of Burt's office. Phones rang.

"What Ellen wanted was to tell you she was sorry," Burt said. "She wants you to call her."

"Tell me about this obituary."

"Give her a chance."

"Our son died. Then our marriage died. There's plenty to be sorry about. But I don't want to talk about it. I'm through talking about it. Nine—correction: Since I promised last night, if we count today, it's *eight* more days, Burt. That's all the time I'm willing to give you. Then we're even. Tell me about the obituary."

6

Assessing Pittman, Burt didn't blink for quite a while. At once he shrugged, sighed, then picked up a folder on his desk. "Jonathan Millgate."

Pittman felt a spark speed along his nerves.

"That name ought to sound familiar from when you were working on the national affairs desk, before . . ." Self-conscious, Burt let the sentence dangle.

"Before I cracked up, you mean? Or fell to pieces, or . . . What's the euphemism these days?"

"Needed a rest."

"I'm not so fuzzy-minded that I wouldn't remember the name of one of the grand counselors."

Burt raised his thick eyebrows.

From the forties, from the beginning of the Cold War onward, a group of five East Coast patricians had exerted a continuous influence on American government policy by acting as major advisers to various Presidents. At first they had been cabinet members and ambassadors, later private consultants, mostly to Republican Presidents, but not exclusively. During the Democratic administration in the late seventies, Carter was supposed to have consulted with them about the Iran hostage situation. It was rumored that on their advice he authorized the failed hostage-rescue attempt and in effect opened the way for Ronald Reagan to get into the White House. Eventually, as they aged, they acquired the status of legends and became known as the grand counselors.

"Jonathan Millgate would be about eighty now," Pittman said. "Mother a society maven in Boston. Father a billionaire from investments in railroads and communications systems. Millgate graduated at the top of his class, with a law degree from Yale. Nineteen thirty-eight. Specialty: international law, which came in handy during the Second World War. Went to work for the State Department. Moved upward rapidly. Named ambassador to the USSR. Named ambassador to the United Nations. Named secretary of state. Named national security adviser. Tight with Truman. Jumped parties to become a Republican and made himself indispensable to Eisenhower. Not close to Kennedy. But despite the party differences, Johnson certainly relied on Millgate to help formulate policy about Vietnam. When the Republicans came back into office, Nixon relied on him even more. Then Millgate suddenly dropped out of public view. He retreated to his mansion in Massachusetts. Interestingly, despite his seclusion, he continued to have as much influence as a high-level elected or appointed official.

"He had a heart attack this morning."

Pittman waited.

"Here in town," Burt said.

"But apparently not a fatal attack, because you said the subject of the obituary wasn't dead yet."

"Since the *Chronicle*'s dying anyhow, we can afford to experiment. I want the obit long, and I want it dense. With facts, with intelligence, with style. A cross between the front page and the editorial page. That used to be your specialty."

"You're gambling he won't last until a week from tomorrow, that *he'll* die before the *Chronicle* does."

"What I'm really gambling," Burt said, "is that you'll find the assignment interesting enough to make you want to do others like it, that you'll get committed to something besides grief, that you and the *Chronicle* won't die together."

"Gambling's for suckers."

"And working on obituaries too long can make a person morbid."

"Right," Pittman said dryly. "It's not like reporting on national affairs can make you morbid." He turned to leave.

"Wait, Matt. There's one other thing."

7

Pittman glanced back and saw the envelope Burt was holding. His chest felt cold.

"The guy who subbed for you yesterday found this in your desk drawer." Burt opened the envelope. "It's addressed to me, so he figured he'd better deliver it." Burt set a sheet of paper on the desk. "I guess I got it earlier than you wanted. Pretty impersonal, don't you think, given all we've been through?"

Pittman didn't need to read the typed note to know what it said.

> *Matthew Pittman, 38, West 12th St., died Wednesday evening from a self-inflicted gunshot wound.*
>
> *A memorial service will begin at noon on Saturday at Donovan's Tavern, West 10th St. In lieu of flowers, memorial donations may be made to the children's cancer fund at Sloan-Kettering in the name of Jeremy Pittman.*

"It was all I could think of."

"Brevity's a virtue." Burt tapped the sheet of paper. "But

so is thoroughness. You didn't mention that you worked for the *Chronicle*."

"I didn't want to embarrass the newspaper."

"And you didn't mention that you were survived by your ex-wife, Ellen."

Pittman shrugged.

"You didn't want to embarrass her, either?" Burt asked.

Pittman shrugged again. "I got writer's block when it came to calling Ellen by her new last name. I finally decided to hell with it."

"I wish you could ignore your other problems as conveniently. Eight more days, Matt. You promised me eight more days."

"That's right."

"You owe me," Burt said.

"I *know*," Pittman said with force. "I haven't forgotten what you did for—" To interrupt the confrontation, he glanced at his watch. "It's almost noon. I'll get started on Millgate's obituary after lunch."

8

The tavern had three things to recommend it: It was out of the way, it didn't do much business, and the little business it did wasn't from staff members of the *Chronicle*. Pittman could drink in peace, knowing that he wouldn't be interrupted—not in this place. Its only reason for existing was for the coming and going of numbers runners. When Pittman had come in and asked for a drink, the bartender had looked shocked to be having a legitimate customer.

Pittman nursed two Jack Daniel's on the rocks while he did his newspaper's crossword puzzle. Anything to occupy his mind. Burt had been trying to do that, as well: to distract him. And Burt's tactic had been effective. Because the crossword puzzle *wasn't* effective. The only words that kept coming into Pittman's mind were *Jonathan Millgate*.

Pittman had once worked on a story about Millgate, back when he had been at the national affairs desk. Before Jeremy's death. Before . . . Seven years ago, Jonathan Millgate had been rumored to be involved as a middleman in a covert White House operation whereby munitions were illegally supplied to right-wing governments in South America in exchange for the cooperation of those governments in fighting the war against drugs. It was further rumored that Millgate had received substantial fees from those South American governments and certain weapons manufacturers in exchange for acting as a go-between in the secret exchange.

But Pittman had found it impossible to substantiate those rumors. For a man who had once been so much in the public eye, Millgate had become a remarkably private, guarded person. The last interview he'd given had been in 1968 after the Tet offensive against American forces in Vietnam. Millgate had spoken to a senior reporter for the *Washington Post*, expressing strong sympathy with the Nixon administration's policy of sending considerably more U.S. soldiers to Vietnam. Because Millgate was respected so much, his statement was interpreted to represent the opinion of other conservative political theorists, especially Millgate's fellow grand counselors. Indeed, the implication was that Millgate was endorsing a policy that he and the other four grand counselors had themselves formulated and privately urged the Nixon White House to adopt: heightening America's involvement in the Vietnam War.

By the time Pittman became interested in Millgate because of the possible munitions scandal, Millgate's effect on presidential attitudes was so discreet and yet powerful that his reputation for diplomacy had achieved mythic status. But no government source could or would say anything about him. As a consequence, Pittman (full of energy, motivated, in his prime) had gone to Burt Forsyth and requested permission to investigate Millgate's legend.

Pittman's telephone log eventually recorded one hundred attempts to call Millgate's business and government associates. Each executive had declined to be interviewed. Pittman had also contacted Millgate's law office in an attempt to make an appointment to interview him. Pittman was put on hold. He was switched from secretary to secretary. He was told to call numbers that were no longer in service. Pittman had phoned the Justice Department, hoping that the team investigating Millgate would give Pittman an idea of how *they* stayed in contact with him. He was told that the Justice Department had no need to remain in contact with Millgate, that the rumors about his receiving kickbacks because of his alleged involvement in a munitions scandal had been proven to lack substance, and that the investigation had been concluded in its early stages.

"Can you tell me which attorney represented him in your initial discussions?"

After a long pause, the man had answered, "No. I can not."

"I didn't get your name when you picked up the phone. Who am I speaking to, please?"

The connection had been broken.

Pittman had gone to a computer hacker, about whom Pittman had written what the hacker considered to be a fair story about the hacker's motives for accessing top secret Defense Department computer files. "I wanted to show how easy it was, how unprotected those files were," the hacker had insisted. But despite his pleas that he'd been motivated by loyalty to his government, the hacker had gone to prison for three years. Recently released, bitter about how the government had treated him, delighted to see his defender again, the hacker had agreed to Pittman's request and, with greater delight, had used a modem to access telephone company computer files in Massachusetts.

"Unlisted number? No problem. As a matter of fact, check this—your dude's got four of them."

Pittman had looked at the glowing computer screen and begun to write down the numbers.

"Forget the pen-and-paper routine. I'll print out the dude's whole file."

That was how Pittman had learned not only Millgate's private numbers but the addresses for his Boston mansion and his Martha's Vineyard estate, as well. Determined, he had phoned each of Millgate's private numbers. Each person on the other end had treated Pittman with deference until with shock they realized what he wanted.

"I demand to know how you learned this number."

"If you'd just let me speak to Mr. Millgate."

"What newspaper did you say you worked for?"

Fifteen minutes after Pittman's final attempt, he'd been summoned to Burt Forsyth's office.

"You're off the Millgate story."

"This is a joke, right?"

"I wish it was. I just got a call from the *Chronicle*'s publisher, who just got a call from somebody who must have a hell of a lot of influence. I'm under strict orders to give *you* strict orders to work on something else."

"And you're actually going to give me those orders?"

Burt had squinted at the smoke he blew from his cigarette—in those days, smoking in the building had not been forbidden. "You've got to know when to be rigid and when to bend, and this is a time to bend. It's not as if you had anything solid. Admit it, you were on a fishing expedition, *hoping* you'd find a story. To tell the truth, you were taking more time than I'd expected. And there's something else to be considered. It's been suggested that you broke the law in the way you obtained Millgate's telephone numbers. Did you?"

Pittman hadn't answered.

"Work on this story instead."

Pittman had been angry at Burt for several days, but the

object of his anger had shifted when there turned out to be a certain synchronicity between the police-brutality assignment Pittman was given and what happened next. On his free time over the weekend, Pittman had gone to Boston, intending to stake out Millgate's mansion in the hope that he would see Millgate leave. Pittman's plan was to follow Millgate's limousine until he could find a place that allowed him to approach Millgate with questions. One minute after Pittman parked on the mansion's tree-lined street, a police car stopped behind him. One hour later, he was being questioned as a burglary suspect at police headquarters. Two hours later, he was in a holding cell, where two prisoners picked a fight with him and beat him so badly that he needed a thousand dollars' worth of dental work.

Visiting Pittman in the hospital, Burt had shaken his head. "Stubborn."

The wires that secured Pittman's broken jaw had prevented him from answering.

9

Pittman finished his second Jack Daniel's and glanced across the almost-deserted tavern toward the bartender, who still seemed startled that he'd actually had a legitimate customer. A man carrying a bulging paper bag came in, looked around the shadowy interior, raised his eyebrows at the sight of Pittman, got a shrug and a nod from the bartender, and proceeded toward a room in the back.

Pittman considered ordering another bourbon, then glanced at his watch and saw that it was almost 1:30 in the afternoon. He'd been sitting there brooding for longer than he'd realized. He hadn't thought about Millgate in quite a while—years—since well before Jeremy had become ill. Pittman's jaw had healed. He'd pursued other assignments. Millgate had managed to make himself invisible again. Out of sight, out of mind. The only reminder had been periodic twinges in Pittman's jaw during especially cold weather. Sometimes when he fingered the line where his jaw had been broken, he would recall how he had tried to investigate the two prisoners who had beaten him. They'd been admitted to his cell a half hour after he'd been placed there. The charges against them had been public drunkenness, but Pittman hadn't smelled any alcohol on their breath when they had beaten him. Subsequent to the beating, they had been mistakenly released from jail, a mix-up in paperwork. Their names had been common, their addresses temporary, and Pittman had never been able to contact them or investigate their backgrounds to find out if Millgate had been responsible for the beating.

As he left the murky bar, his head aching from the harsh assault of afternoon sunlight, Pittman felt searing anger intrude on his cold despair. He had always resented aristocrats and their supposition that money and social stature made them the equivalent of royalty. He resented the disdain with which they felt themselves unaccountable for their actions. During his peak as a national affairs reporter, his best stories had been exposés of criminal activity by those in high places, and Jonathan Millgate would have been the highest target Pittman had ever brought down.

I should have been more persistent.

Pittman's flare of anger abruptly died. Ahead, at a noisy intersection where pedestrians were stopped for a red light, he noticed a tall, lanky boy with long hair, slight shoulders, and narrow hips moving his feet slightly to the beat of imagined music. The boy looked to be about fifteen. He wore a rumpled denim jacket that had an emblem of a rock star. His jeans were faded. His running shoes, high-topped, were dyed green and had names written on them. From the back, the boy reminded Pittman so much of Jeremy that he felt as if a hand had squeezed his heart. Then the boy turned his head to speak to a companion, and of course, the boy looked nothing at all like Jeremy, whose jaw had not been as strong as this boy's and whose complexion hadn't been as clear and whose teeth had needed braces. Imperfect physically, but perfect as a son. It wasn't just that Jeremy had never gotten into trouble, or that his grades had been excellent, or that he had been respectful. As important as these things were, what

Pittman missed most about Jeremy was his captivating personality. The boy had been blessed with a wonderful sense of humor. He had always been so much fun to be around, never failing to make Pittman feel that life was better because of his son.

But not anymore, Pittman thought.

The brief angry fire he'd felt when thinking about Millgate no longer had significance. That was from another time, another life—before Jeremy had become ill. Pittman resented what Burt was trying to do. It was an insult to Jeremy's memory for Burt to assume that an assignment about Jonathan Millgate could distract Pittman from his grief.

I ought to tell him to stuff it.

No. Keep your word. When you end this, it has to be cleanly. You can't be obligated to anyone.

10

In the old days, Pittman would have gone to the area, formerly in the basement, where back issues of the newspaper were stored on microfilm. The master index would have contained file cards for "Millgate" and "Grand counselors," and from them, Pittman would have learned which issues and pages of the newspaper to read on microfilm. That section of the newspaper where the microfilm was kept had been traditionally called the morgue, and although computer files had replaced microfilm, death was so much on Pittman's mind that he still thought of himself as entering a morgue when he sat at his desk, turned on his computer terminal, and tapped the keys that would give him access to the newspaper's data files.

Given Millgate's secretive lifestyle, it wasn't surprising that there wasn't much information: only a few small items since Pittman had researched Millgate seven years earlier. Millgate and the other four grand counselors—still retaining immense political power, even though they no longer had direct ties with the government—had been feted at a White House dinner, where the President had given Millgate the Medal of Freedom, America's highest civilian honor. Millgate had accompanied the President on *Air Force One* to an international conference on world economics in Geneva. Millgate had established an institute for the study of post-Communist reconstruction in Russia. Millgate had testified before a Senate confirmation committee about his high regard for a Supreme Court nominee, who also happened to be the son of one of the grand counselors.

The phone rang.

Pittman picked it up. "Obituaries."

A fifty-two-year-old woman had been killed in a fire, he learned. She was unmarried, without children, unemployed, not a member of any organization. Aside from her brother, to whom Pittman was speaking, there weren't any surviving relatives. Thus, the obituary would be unusually slight, especially because the brother didn't want his name mentioned for fear people to whom his sister owed money would come looking for him.

The barrenness of the woman's life made Pittman more despondent. Shaking his head, dejected, he finished the call, then frowned at his watch. It was almost three o'clock. The gray haze that customarily surrounded him seemed to have thickened.

The phone rang again.

This time, Burt Forsyth's gravelly voice demanded. "How's the Millgate obit coming?'

"Has he . . . ?"

"Still in intensive care."

"Well, there isn't much. I'll have the obit finished before I go home."

"Don't tell me there isn't much," Burt said. "We both know better. I want this piece to be substantial. Seven years ago, you wouldn't have given up so easily. Dig. Back then, you kept complaining about how you couldn't find a way to see Millgate. Well, he's a captive interview this time. Not to mention, there'll be relatives or somebody waiting at the hospital to see how he's doing. Talk to them. For Christ sake, figure out how to get into his room and talk to *him*."

11

Pittman stood across from the hospital for quite a while. The building was soot gray. The mid-April day had been warm, but as the sun descended behind skyscrapers, cool shadows made Pittman cross his arms and hug himself.

This was the same hospital where Jeremy had died. Pittman had come to the corner across from the Emergency entrance, the same corner where he had often stood late at night after visiting Jeremy. From this corner, he had been able to see the window of Jeremy's room on the tenth floor. Gazing up through the darkness for several hours, he had prayed that Jeremy wouldn't be wakened by the need to vomit because of his chemotherapy.

Amid the din of traffic, Pittman now heard a siren. An ambulance veered from the busy street and rushed to a stop beneath the portal at the Emergency entrance. Attendants leapt out and urgently removed a patient on a gurney. Pedestrians glanced toward the commotion but kept walking swiftly onward.

Pittman swallowed, squinted up toward what he still thought of as Jeremy's window, and turned away. Jonathan Millgate was in that hospital, in the adult intensive-care ward that was just down the sixth-floor hallway from the children's intensive-care ward, where Jeremy had died. Pittman shook his head. He couldn't tolerate going into the hospital, couldn't make himself go up to that floor, couldn't bear exposing himself to the torment on the faces of people waiting to hear about their loved ones. It would be all he could do not to imagine that he was one of them, not to sit down with them and wait as if for news of Jeremy.

It would be far too much.

So he went home. Rather than take a taxi, he walked. He needed to fill the time. As dusk increasingly chilled him, he stopped for several drinks—to fill the time. The elevator to his third-floor apartment creaked and wheezed. He locked himself in his apartment, heard laughter from a television show vibrate through thin walls from the apartment next to him, and had another drink.

To fill the time.

He sat in darkness. He imagined what it would have been like if Jeremy had lived. With basketball playoffs approaching, he would have spent the coming Saturday afternoon playing one-on-one with Jeremy. Afterward they'd have gone for pizza and a movie, or maybe to Tower Records—whatever they wanted to do. The future would have been theirs.

Pittman wept.

He turned on the kitchen light, opened the drawer where he'd put the .45, and took out the pistol.

Vaguely conscious that the time was 8:00 P.M., because the sitcom next door had ended and another was starting, he continued to stare at the .45. His eyes became like the lenses of a microscope, focusing intensely on the gleaming blue metal, magnifying the trigger, the hammer, the opening in the barrel from which the bullet would . . .

The next thing he was aware of, a new sound disturbed

him, the smooth deep voice of a man who spoke in formal cadences. The voice came from the apartment next door. The voice was . . .

A television news announcer? Frowning, Pittman turned his gaze from the .45 and fixed it on the stove's mechanical clock. Its numbers whirred, 10:03 becoming 10:04. Pittman frowned harder. He had so absorbed himself in the gun that he hadn't been conscious of so much time passing. Hand trembling, he set down the .45. The news announcer on the television next door had said something about Jonathan Millgate.

12

"Haven't seen you in a while, Matt." The heavy man, an Italian, had gray hair protruding from the bottom of his Yankees baseball cap. He wore a Yankees baseball jersey as well, and he held a ladle with which he'd been stirring a large steaming pot of what smelled like chicken-noodle soup as Pittman came into the diner.

The place was narrow, with Formica-topped tables along one side, a counter along the other. The overhead fluorescent lights made Pittman blink after the darkness of the street. It was almost 11:00 P.M. As Pittman sat at the counter, he nodded to the only other customer, a black man drinking a cup of coffee at one of the tables.

"You been sick?" the cook asked. "Is that why you haven't been in?"

"Everybody keeps saying . . . Do I look sick?"

"Or permanently hungover. Look at how loose your clothes are. How much weight have you lost? Ten, fifteen pounds? And judging from them bags under your eyes, I'd say you haven't been sleeping much, either."

Pittman didn't answer.

"What'll it be for tonight?"

"To start with, a favor."

The cook appeared not to have heard as he stirred the soup.

"I wonder if you could store this for me."

"What?" The cook glanced at the counter in front of Pittman and sounded relieved. "That box?"

Pittman nodded. The box had once held computer paper. Now it concealed the .45 and its container of ammunition. He had stuffed the box with shredded newspaper so that the gun wouldn't shift and make a thunking noise when the box was tilted. He had sealed the box many times with tape.

"Just a place to store this," Pittman said. "I'll even pay you for . . ."

"No need," the cook said. "What's in it? How come you can't keep it at your place? There's nothing funny about this, is there?"

"Nah. It's just a gun."

"A *gun*?"

Pittman smiled at his apparent joke. "I've been working on a book. This is a copy of the printout and the computer discs. I'm paranoid about fires. I'd ask my girlfriend to help, but she and I just had a fight. I want to keep a duplicate of this material someplace besides my apartment."

"Yeah? A book? What's it about?"

"Suicide. Let me have some of that soup, will you?"

Pittman prepared to eat his first meal in thirty-six hours.

13

He'd packed the gun and left it with the cook at the diner because his experience of losing time while he stared at the weapon had taught him there was every chance he might shoot himself before he made good on his promise to work for Burt Forsyth until the *Chronicle* died. The effort of getting through this particular day, the bitterness and emptiness he had felt, had been so intense that he couldn't be certain of his resolve to keep himself alive for eight more days. This way, in the event of overwhelming despair, he would have a chance of regaining control by the time he reached the diner, got the box, and went to his apartment.

For now, he had to do what Burt Forsyth intended—to distract himself. Jonathan Millgate meant nothing to him. Pittman's career meant nothing. The *Chronicle* meant nothing. But Burt Forsyth *did*. In honor of Jeremy, Pittman felt compelled to keep the promise he had made. For eight more days.

Despite his reluctance, he went back to the hospital. This time, he took a taxi. Not because he was in a hurry. After all, he still had a great deal of time to fill and would have preferred to walk. But to get to the hospital, he would have had to pass through several neighborhoods that became dangerous at this hour. He found it bitterly ironic that in doing his best to postpone his death for eight more days, he had to be extra careful about not dying in the meanwhile.

He returned to the hospital because of the television announcer's reference to Millgate. Through the thin walls of his apartment, he had listened to the news report. Pittman's expectation was that Millgate had died and a brief summary of his public-service career was being provided. Burt Forsyth would be annoyed about that—Millgate dying before Pittman finished the obituary in time for tomorrow morning's edition of the newspaper. But the TV news story had not been about Millgate's death. To the contrary, Millgate was still in intensive care, as the announcer had pointed out.

Instead, the story had been about another possible scandal in Millgate's background. To the government's dismay, a copy of a Justice Department special prosecutor's report had been leaked to the press this evening. The report, a first draft never intended for publication, implicated Millgate as a negotiator in a possible covert attempt—unsanctioned by Congress—to buy nuclear weapons from the chaos of governments in what used to be the Soviet Union.

An unsubtantiated charge against him. Solely an in-house assessment of where the Justice Department's investigation might eventually lead. But the gravity of the news announcer's voice had made the grave allegation sound like established fact. Guilty until proven innocent. This was the second time in seven years that Jonathan Millgate had been implicated as a go-between in a major arms scandal, and Pittman knew that if he failed to investigate this time, if he didn't at least make an attempt to get a statement from Millgate's people, Burt Forsyth would accuse him of reneging on his bargain to do his best for the *Chronicle* during the brief time remaining to it. For Burt and what Burt had done for Jeremy, Pittman forced himself to try.

14

Pittman stood on the corner across from the hospital's Emergency entrance. It was after midnight. A drizzle intensified the April night's chill. He buttoned his wrinkled London Fog topcoat and felt dampness even through the soles of his shoes. The drizzle created misty halos around gleaming streetlights and the brighter floodlights at the Emergency entrance. By contrast, the lights in some of the hospital rooms were weak, making Pittman feel lonely. He stared up toward what had been Jeremy's window on the tenth floor, and that window was dark. Feeling even more lonely, he crossed the street toward the hospital.

At this hour, traffic was slight. The Emergency area was almost deserted. He heard a far-off siren. The drizzle strengthened, wetting the back of his neck. When Jeremy had been sick, Pittman had learned about the hospital in considerable detail—the locations of the various departments, the lounges that were most quiet in the middle of the night, the areas that had coffee machines, the places to get a sandwich when the main cafeteria was closed. Bringing Jeremy to the hospital for chemotherapy, he had felt uncomfortable at the main entrance and in the lobby. The cancer had made Jeremy so delicate that Pittman had a fear of someone in a crowd bumping against him. Given Jeremy's low blood-cell counts, a bruise would have taken a considerable time to heal. In addition, Pittman had felt outraged by the stares of people in the lobby, who seemed shocked to see a skinny, bald fifteen-year-old, his face gaunt, his hairless scalp tinted blue from blood vessels close to the surface. Terribly sensitive about his son's feelings, Pittman had chosen an alternate route, in the back, a small entrance around the corner to the left of the Emergency area. The door was used primarily by interns and nurses, and as Pittman discovered, the elevators in this section were faster, perhaps because fewer people used them.

Retracing this route created such vivid memories that he sensed Jeremy next to him as he passed a private ambulance parked outside this exit. It was gray. It had no hospital markings. But through a gap in curtains drawn across the back windows, Pittman saw a light, an oxygen unit, various medical monitors. A man wearing an attendant's white coat was checking some equipment.

Then Pittman was beyond the ambulance, whose engine was running, although its headlights were off. He noticed a stocky man in a dark suit drop the butt of a cigarette into a puddle and come to attention, seeing Pittman. *You must really have needed a cigarette,* Pittman thought, *to stand out here in the rain.*

Nodding to the man, who didn't nod back, Pittman reached for the doorknob and noticed that the light was out above the entrance. He stepped inside, went up four steps to an echoey concrete landing, and noticed another stocky man in a dark suit, this one leaning against the wall next to where the stairs turned upward. The man's face had a hard expression with squinted, calculating eyes.

Pittman didn't need the stairs; instead, he went forward, across the landing, through a door to a brightly lit hospital corridor. The pungent, acrid, too-familiar odors of food, antiseptic, and medicine assaulted him. When Pittman used to come here daily to visit Jeremy, the odors had been constantly present, on every floor, day or night. The odors had stuck to Pittman's clothes. For several weeks after Jeremy's death, he had smelled them on his jackets, his shirts, his pants.

The vividness of the painful memories caused by the odors distracted Pittman, making him falter in confusion. Did he really want to put himself through this? This was the first time he'd been back inside the hospital. Would the torture be worth it just to please Burt?

The elevator doors were directly across from the door through which he had entered the corridor. If he went ahead, he suspected that his impulse would be to go up to the tenth floor and what had been Jeremy's room rather than to go to the sixth floor, where Millgate was and where Jeremy had died in intensive care.

Abruptly a movement on Pittman's right disturbed him. A large-chested man stepped away from the wall next to the door Pittman had used. His position had prevented Pittman from noticing him when he came toward the elevators. The man wore an oversized windbreaker.

"Can I help?" The man sounded as if he'd swallowed broken glass. "You lost? You need directions?"

"Not lost. Confused." The man's aggressive tone made Pittman's body tighten. His instincts warned him not to tell the truth. "I've got a sick boy on the tenth floor. The nurses let me see him at night. But sometimes I can barely force myself to go up there."

"Sick, huh? Bad?"

"Cancer."

"Yeah, that's bad."

But the man obviously didn't care, and he'd made Pittman

feel so apprehensive, his stomach so fluttery, that Pittman had answered with the most innocent, believable story he could think of. He certainly wasn't going to explain his real reason for coming to the hospital to a man whose oversized windbreaker concealed something that made a distinct, ominous bulge on the left side of his waist.

Footsteps made Pittman turn. He faced yet another solemn, stocky man, this one wearing an overcoat. The man had been standing against the wall on the opposite side of the door from where the man in the windbreaker had been standing. Neither man had rain spots on his coat. The rain had started fifteen minutes previously, so they must have been waiting in this corridor at least that long, Pittman thought. Why? Recalling the man who'd been smoking outside and the man in the stairwell, he inwardly frowned.

"Then you'd better get up and see your boy," the second man said.

"Right." More uneasy, Pittman reached to press the elevator's up button when he heard a ding and the doors suddenly opened. Loud voices assaulted him.

"I won't be responsible for this!"

"No one's *asking* you to be responsible. He's *my* patient now."

The elevator compartment was crammed. A man on a gurney with an oxygen mask over his face and an intravenous tube leading into his left arm was being quickly wheeled out by two white-coated attendants. A nurse swiftly followed, holding an intravenous bottle above the patient. A thin, intense young man was arguing with an older red-faced man who had a stethoscope around his neck and a clipboard with what looked like a medical file in his hand.

"But the risk of—"

"I said he's *my* responsibility."

The young man surged from the elevator just as Pittman felt hands behind him grab his arms and pull him back out of the way. The gurney, the two attendants, the nurse, and the young man hurried past him toward the door to the stairwell. As the man with the stethoscope charged out, trying to stop them, two dark-suited, solemn, well-built men—they also had been in the elevator—veered ahead of him and formed a blockade.

"Damn it, if you don't get out of my way—"

"Relax, doctor. Everything's going to be fine."

Pittman squirmed, pained by the force of the hands that gripped him from behind. Through the window in the stairwell door, he saw the man who'd been waiting on the landing dart forward to open the door. The attendants pushed the gurney through, then lifted it, hurrying with it down the stairs to the exit from the hospital. Although restrained, Pittman was able to turn his head enough to see the man who'd been smoking in the rain yank the outside door open.

The attendants rushed with the gurney, disappearing into the night along with the nurse and the thin, intense man. The somber, stocky men retreated, letting go of Pittman, moving swiftly into the stairwell, down the stairs, through the outside door.

The man with the stethoscope trembled. "By God, I'll phone the police. They can't—"

Pittman didn't stay to hear the rest of his sentence. What he heard instead were repeated thunks as doors to the private ambulance outside were opened and closed. He ran down the stairs. Peering out toward the drizzle-misted darkness, he saw the private ambulance pull away, a dark Oldsmobile following.

Immediately he lunged into the chilling rain. Seeing frost come out of his mouth, he raced through puddles toward the street corner opposite the Emergency entrance. From having come to the hospital so often with Jeremy, he knew the easiest places to hail a taxi late at night, and the corner across from Emergency was one of the best.

An empty taxi veered around a curve, almost striking Pittman as he ran across toward the corner.

"Watch it, buddy!"

Pittman scrambled in. "My father's in that private ambulance." He pointed toward where, a block ahead, the ambulance and the dark Oldsmobile were stopped at a traffic light. "He's being taken for emergency treatment to another hospital. Keep up with them."

"What's wrong with *this* hospital?"

"They don't have a machine he needs. Hurry. *Please.*" Pittman gave the driver twenty dollars.

The taxi sped forward.

Pittman sat anxiously in the backseat, wiping rain from his forehead, catching his breath. What the hell was going on? he wondered. Although the oxygen mask had concealed the face of the patient on the gurney, Pittman had noticed the man's wrinkled, liver-spotted hands, his slack-skinned neck, and his wispy white hair. Obviously old. That wasn't much to go on, but Pittman had the eerie conviction that the man on the gurney was Jonathan Millgate.

15

"I thought you said they were taking your father to another hospital," the taxi driver said.

"They are."

"Not in New York City, they ain't. In case you haven't noticed, we just reached New Rochelle."

Pittman listened to the rhythmic tap of the taxi's windshield wipers. As tires hissed on wet pavement, he concentrated to provide an explanation. "The ambulance has a two-way radio. Maybe they called ahead and the hospital they were going to didn't have the machine they needed."

"Where I live over on Long Island, they've got plenty of good hospitals. I don't know why they didn't head there What's wrong with your father, anyhow?"

"Heart disease."

"Yeah, my brother has a bad ticker. Thirty years of smoking. Poor bastard. Can hardly walk across the room. You better hope your father's strong enough to hang on, because it doesn't look like the ambulance is gonna stop here in New Rochelle. Christ, at this rate, we'll soon be in Connecticut."

Headlights gleamed in the rain.

"I'd better let my dispatcher know what's going on," the driver said. "Listen, I'm sorry about your father and all, but buddy, this long a trip needs special arrangements. If we end up in Stamford or some damned place like that, I won't be able to get a fare to come back to the city. I'm gonna have to charge you both ways."

"I'll pay it."

"How?"

Rain tapped the roof.

"What? I'm sorry . . . I wasn't listening."

"How are you gonna pay me? You got the cash? Rough estimate—we're talking over a hundred bucks."

"Don't worry. You'll get paid."

"But I do worry. I need to know if you've got the cash to— Wait a second. Looks like they figured out where they're going."

The sign at the turnoff heading north said SCARSDALE/ WHITE PLAINS.

16

"What's all those trees to the right?"

"Looks like a park," Pittman said.

"Or a damned forest. Man, we're way out in the country. I *knew* I shouldn'ta done this. How am I gonna find a fare back to the city from way out here?"

"We're not in the country. Look at those big houses on your left. This is some kind of expensive subdivision. There's a sign up ahead. Yeah. SAXON WOODS PARK AND GOLF CLUB. I told you we're not in the country."

"Well, either the guys in that ambulance plan to take your father golfing or— Hold it. They're slowing down."

So did the taxi driver.

"They're turning off," Pittman said. "There, to the right."

The driver kept going, passing a high stone wall and a gated driveway. As the red taillights of the ambulance and the Oldsmobile receded into the darkness, the gate—tall, made of wrought-iron bars—swung electronically back into place.

"Funny how these days they make hospitals to look like mansions," the driver said. "What the hell's going on, buddy?"

"I haven't the faintest idea."

"What?"

"I honestly don't know. My father's really sick. I expected . . ."

"Say, this isn't about drugs, is it?"

Pittman was too confused to answer.

"I asked you a question."

"It's not about drugs. You saw the ambulance leave the hospital."

"Sure. Right. Well, I don't plan to spend the rest of the night driving around Scarsdale. At least I think that's where we are. Ride's over, buddy. You've got two choices—head back with me or get out right now. Either way, you're paying both ways."

The driver turned the taxi around.

"Okay, let me out where they left the road," Pittman said.

The driver switched off his headlights, stopping fifty yards from the gate. "In case it's not a good idea to advertise that you followed them."

"I'm telling you, this isn't about drugs."

"Yeah. Sure. You owe me a hundred and fifteen bucks."

Pittman groped in his pockets. "I already gave you twenty."

"What are you talking about? That's supposed to be my tip."

"But I don't have that much cash."

"*What?* I asked you earlier if—"

"I've got a credit card."

"That's useless to me! This cab ain't rigged to take it!"

"Then I'm going to have to give you a check."

"Give me a break! Do I look like the trusting type? The last time I took a check from a guy, it—"

"Hey, I told you I don't have the cash. I'd give you my watch, but it isn't worth *fifteen* dollars."

"A check," the driver muttered. "This fucking job."

After Pittman wrote the check and gave it to him, the driver studied the address at the top of the check. "Let me see your driver's license." He wrote down Pittman's Social Security number. "If this check bounces, buddy . . ."

"I promise it won't."

"Well, if it does, I'm gonna come to your apartment and break both your legs."

"Just make sure you cash it before a week from Saturday."

"What's so special about a week from Saturday?"

"I won't be around." Pittman got out of the car, thankful that the rain had lessened to a mist, and watched the taxi pull away in the darkness. A distance down the road, the driver switched his headlights on.

17

In the silence, Pittman suddenly felt isolated. Shoving his hands in his overcoat pockets for warmth, he walked along the side of the road. The shoulder was gravel, its sandy bed sufficiently softened by the rain that his shoes made only a slight scraping sound. There weren't any streetlights. Pittman strained his eyes, but he could barely see the wall that loomed on his left. He came to a different shade of darkness and realized that he'd reached the barred gate.

Without touching it, he peered through. Far along a driveway, past trees and shrubs, lights glowed in what seemed to be a mansion.

What now? he thought. It's two o'clock in the morning. It's drizzling. I'm cold. I'm God knows where. I shouldn't have gone to the hospital. I shouldn't have followed the ambulance. I shouldn't have . . .

As his eyes adjusted to the darkness, he studied the top of the gate, then shook his head. He was fairly certain that he could climb over it, but he was even more certain that there'd be some kind of intrusion sensor up there. Before Jeremy's death and Pittman's nervous breakdown, he had worked for a time on the newspaper's Sunday magazine. One of his articles had been about a man whom Pittman had nicknamed "the Bugmaster." The man was an expert in intrusion detectors and other types of security equipment—for example, eavesdropping devices, otherwise known as bugs, ergo the Bugmaster. Enjoying Pittman's enthusiasm about information, the Bugmaster had explained his profession in detail, and Pittman's prodigious memory for facts had retained it all.

A place this size, Pittman knew, was bound to have a security system, and as the Bugmaster had pointed out, you never go over a wall or a gate without first scouting the barriers to make sure you're not activating a sensor. But at this hour, in the dark, Pittman didn't see how he could scout anything.

So what the hell are you going to do? You should have gone back to Manhattan with the taxi driver. What did you think you'd accomplish by hanging around out here in the rain?

Through the bars of the gate, a light attracted Pittman's attention.

Two of them. Headlights. Approaching along the driveway from the mansion. Pittman watched them grow larger, thought about hurrying along the road and hiding past the corner of the wall, then made a different decision and pressed himself against the wall right next to the gate.

He heard a smooth, well-tuned, powerful engine. He heard tires on wet concrete. He heard a buzz and then a whir. The gate's motor had been activated by remote control. The gate was swinging open toward the inside of the estate, its sturdy wheels scraping on concrete.

The engine sounded louder. The headlights flashed through the open gate. Sooner than Pittman expected, the dark Oldsmobile that had escorted the ambulance surged through the opening, turned to the left in the direction the taxi had taken to go back to the city, and sped into the night.

Pittman was tempted to remain motionless until the car's lights disappeared down the road. But he had something more immediate to occupy him, for abruptly he heard another buzz, another whir. The gate was closing—faster than he expected—and he sprinted to get through the opening before it was blocked.

The sturdy gate brushed past his coat. The lock snapped into place. The night became silent again.

18

Pittman found that he was holding his breath. Despite the expansive grounds ahead of him, he felt a spasm of claustrophobia. The darkness seemed to smother him. At once the cold drizzle sharpened his senses, bracing him. He inhaled and glanced around, reassured that no threat emerged from the shadows.

You expected guards?

No, but . . .

Dogs maybe?

Right.

Wouldn't they have followed the car? Wouldn't you have seen them by now?

Maybe. Maybe not. They might be trained not to follow cars.

So what's the worst that can happen? If there *are* dogs, they'll find you and corner you and bark until somebody comes. You'll be charged with trespassing. That's no big deal for a guy who's planning to kill himself eight days from now.

But what if the dogs are trained to attack?

This isn't a top secret military installation. It's a Scarsdale estate. Relax. And anyway, so what if the dogs are trained to attack? Do you think being killed by a couple of Dobermans would be any worse than shooting yourself with a .45?

Yes.

What standards you have.

Chilled by the rain, Pittman moved forward. At first he was tempted to approach the mansion through the cover of the trees. But then he decided there wasn't any need—the night and the gloomy weather provided him with sufficient cover. Following the murky driveway, he came around a shadowy curve and discovered that he was closer to the mansion than he expected.

Next to a sheltering fir tree, he studied his destination. The building was high, wide, made of brick, with numerous gables and chimneys. There were several lights in windows on the ground floor, less on the second story. From this angle, he could see a five-stall garage on the left. The garage had a sundeck on top, with two sets of French doors leading off the deck into a second-story room that was lit, although Pittman couldn't see what was in there. Mostly what attracted his attention was the private ambulance, parked, its lights off, apparently empty, in front of the stone steps that led up to the mansion's large front door.

Now what? Pittman thought.

He shrugged. With eight days to live, what difference did it make? In an odd way, he felt liberated. After all, what did he have to lose? Knowing when he was going to die gave him a feeling of immunity.

He stepped from the fir tree and concentrated to maintain his balance on wet, slippery grass as he crept down a dark slope toward the mansion. Moving cautiously toward the lights of the mansion, taking advantage of shrubs, a fountain, a gazebo to give him cover, he came closer to the illuminated windows. The drenched grass had soaked his shoes and socks, chilling his feet, but he was too involved in studying the windows to care. Curtains had been drawn, forcing him to cross the driveway where it ran parallel to the front of the mansion. He felt exposed by the drizzle-shrouded glare of arc lights as he darted toward bushes beneath the front windows.

Moisture dripped from the branches onto his overcoat. Again in shadows, he crouched tensely, moved through an opening in the bushes on the left side of the front doors, then warily straightened, able to see through a gap in the curtains at one window. He saw a portion of a luxuriously appointed oak-paneled living room. The room didn't seem occupied. Quietly he shifted toward the next window, moving closer to the front door.

The next window's curtains were open. He showed as little of his head as possible while he peered in. Immediately he realized that this window was part of the same living room that he'd just seen through the other window. But why would curtains in one window be closed, while the other curtains were not? He eased down out of sight, remembered the ambulance behind him in front of the mansion, and suspected that someone must have been waiting anxiously for the ambulance to arrive. When it had, that person had hurried from the room, too preoccupied to bother closing the curtains.

But where had that person gone? A detail that Pittman had seen in the room now acquired significance. On a carved mahogany table in front of a fireplace, there had been several teacups and coffee mugs. Okay, not one person. Several. But where . . . ?

Pittman glanced to his right toward the mansion's front steps. They were wide, made of stone. A light blazed above impressive double doors and revealed a closed-circuit camera aimed toward the steps and the area in front of the entrance. If there were other closed-circuit cameras, Pittman hadn't seen them, but he had no intention of revealing himself to this one.

The best way to proceed, he decided, was to double back, to go left instead of right, and circle the mansion in the reverse direction from the one in which he'd intended to go. The method would eventually lead him to the windows on the right side of the entrance, but without forcing him to cross the front steps.

He turned, stayed low, close to the mansion's wall, and shifted past the moisture-beaded shrubs, ignoring the two windows that he'd already checked. He came to a third window, the drapes on this one completely closed. After listening intently and hearing no sounds, he concluded that the room was empty and moved farther along, rounding a corner of the mansion.

Arc lights caused the drizzle to glisten. The lights were mounted on the side of the mansion and beneath the eaves of the sundeck that topped the multistall garage. Hugging the wall, Pittman crept ten feet along the side of the mansion, then reached the large garage, where it formed a continuation of the building. There weren't any windows, so Pittman didn't linger. Coming to the corner of the garage, he checked around it and saw that all five garage stalls were closed.

Past the garage, he faced the back of the house. There, fewer arc lights illuminated the grounds. But they were bright enough for Pittman to see a large, covered, drizzle-misted swimming pool, a changing room, fallow flower gardens, more shrubs and trees, and, immediately to his right, stairs that went up to the sundeck on top of the garage.

There had been lights beyond the French doors that led

from the sundeck into an upper-story room, he remembered. Deciding that he'd better inspect this area now rather than come back after checking the windows on the ground floor, he started up the wooden steps.

19

The sundeck was disturbingly unilluminated. Pittman didn't understand. Crouching in the darkness on top, he wondered why the other parts of the building had outside lights, while the sundeck did not.

The room beyond the two sets of French doors was well lit, however. Past substantial ornate metal furniture upon which cocktails and lunches would be served when the weather got warm, Pittman saw bright lamps in a wide room that had a cocktail bar along the left wall in addition to a big-screen television built into the middle of the right wall.

At the moment, though, the room was being used for something quite different from entertainment. Leather furniture had been shifted toward the television, leaving the center of the room available for a bed with safety railings on each side. A long table beyond it supported electronic instruments that Pittman recognized vividly from the week when Jeremy had been in intensive care: monitors that analyzed heartbeat, blood pressure, respiration rate, and blood-oxygen content. Two pumps controlled the speed with which liquid flowed from bottles on an IV stand into the right and left arm of a frail old man who lay covered with sheets on the bed. The two male attendants whom Pittman had seen at the hospital were making adjustments to the monitors. The female nurse was taking care that there weren't any kinks in the oxygen tube that led to prongs inserted in the old man's nostrils.

The oxygen mask that had obscured the old man's face when he was taken from the hospital now lay on top of a monitor on the table beyond the bed. Pittman couldn't be totally sure from outside in the darkness, but what he had suspected at the hospital insisted more strongly: The old man bore a resemblance to Jonathan Millgate.

The intense young man who had been in charge of getting the old man out of the hospital had a stethoscope around his neck and was listening to the old man's chest. The somber men who had acted as bodyguards were standing in the far-left corner.

But other people were in the large room, as well. Pittman hadn't seen them at the hospital, although he definitely had seen them before—in old photographs and in television documentaries about the politics of the Vietnam War. Four men. Distinguished-looking. Dressed in conservative custom-made dark three-piece suits. Old but bearing a resemblance to images of their younger selves.

Three wore spectacles. One had a white mustache. Two were bald, while the other two had wispy white hair. All had stern, pinched, wrinkled faces and drooping skin on their necks. Their expressions severe, they stood in a row, as if they were on a dais or part of a diplomatic receiving line. Their combined former titles included ambassador to the USSR, ambassador to the United Nations, ambassador to Great Britain, ambassador to Saudi Arabia, ambassador to West Germany, ambassador to NATO, secretary of state, secretary of defense, national security adviser. Indeed, several of these positions had been held by all of these men at various times, just as they had all at various times belonged to the National Security Council. They had never been elected to public office, and yet in their appointed roles they had exerted more influence than any but the most highly placed politicians. Their names were Eustace Gable, Anthony Lloyd, Victor Standish, and Winston Sloane. They were the legendary diplomats upon whom Presidents from Truman to Clinton, Republican and Democrat, had frequently relied for advice, their shrewdness having earned them the nickname "the grand counselors." Four of them. Which suggested that the old man in the bed was, in fact, the fifth grand counselor: Jonathan Millgate.

20

The intense young man with the stethoscope said something that Pittman couldn't hear. The nurse said something in response. Then the two male attendants spoke. Again Pittman was too far away to make out what they were saying. The man with the stethoscope turned toward the grand counselors and seemed to explain something. One of the elderly diplomats, a gaunt-cheeked man with a white mustache, Winston Sloane, nodded wearily. Another, his narrow face pinched with wrinkles, Eustace Gable, asked a question. The man with the stethoscope answered. A third elderly diplomat, Anthony Lloyd, tapped his cane on the floor in a gesture of frustration. Although their faces were pale, their ancient eyes were fiery. With a final comment, Eustace Gable left the room. His associates solemnly followed.

The nurse approached the draperies. When she pulled a cord on the side, the draperies moved, then stopped. She pulled harder, but something prevented her from closing them all the way. From the deck, Pittman studied the room with increasing confusion. The four bodyguards went after the counselors, as did the two ambulance attendants, leaving only the man with the stethoscope and the female nurse. The latter dimmed the room's lights, and now Pittman understood why there weren't any arc lamps illuminating the sundeck. The group didn't want the glare of the outside lights intruding on the room after it was put into comparative darkness. The red lights on the monitors were almost as bright as the muted glow of the lamps. In the dusky atmosphere, the patient was being encouraged to rest. But that was about all Pittman did understand, and as he crouched in the darkness beside the metal deck furniture, he wiped rain from his face, shivered from the cold, and asked himself what he should do.

You proved your suspicion. That *was* Jonathan Millgate they took from the hospital. You don't know why, but you do know where they took him, and that's all you can do for now. It's time to go. You'll get pneumonia if you stay in this rain much longer.

That final thought made Pittman smile with bitterness. You almost killed yourself tonight, and now you're worried about catching pneumonia? Not yet. Your time isn't up for another eight days.

And it won't be pneumonia that kills you.

He watched the man with the stethoscope leave the dusky room. As the nurse continued inspecting Millgate's monitors and tubes, Pittman turned toward the stairs that led down from the sundeck. He heard a noise that paralyzed him.

21

It came from directly below him, a combination of a drone and a rumble. The roof of the sundeck vibrated beneath Pittman's wet shoes.

One of the motorized garage doors was being opened. Pittman's heartbeat quickened. He crouched lower, making certain that he wouldn't be a silhouette against the roofline. Nonetheless, he was able to see light spill from the garage, revealing raindrops on dark puddles as the door opened higher, then stopped, its motor becoming silent.

In the unnerving quiet, varied only by the hiss of the drizzle, Pittman suddenly heard the scrape of footsteps on concrete, the creak of car doors being opened, the echo of voices.

". . . priest," an elderly man's brittle voice said, taut with emotion.

"Don't worry," a second elderly voice said. "I told you the priest never arrived. Jonathan never spoke to him."

"Even so."

"It's been taken care of," the second aged voice emphasized, reminding Pittman of the rattle of dead leaves. "It's safe now. Secure."

"But the reporters . . ."

"Have no idea where Jonathan is. Everything is under

control. The best thing we can do is separate and get back to a pretense of normalcy."

Throughout, Pittman heard the sound of people getting into a vehicle. Now he heard the thunk of car doors being closed, the sudden roar of an engine.

Headlights blazed. A dark limousine surged out of the garage and sped along the murky driveway, past trees and shrubs and toward the gate that led from the estate.

Pittman's bent legs cramped. He began to stand, then flinched when he heard further voices.

"The taxi," another aged voice said.

"If you're correct that we were followed . . ." This voice was crusty, yet filled with phlegm.

Pittman couldn't make out the rest of the sentence. What he heard instead was a louder rumbling drone as a second garage door rose. Other lights gleamed into the drizzle-misted night.

When the noise of the garage door stopped, Pittman strained to listen, hoping that the voices would continue.

". . . a coincidence. A late commuter coming from Manhattan."

"But in a taxi?"

"Perhaps the trains don't run this late. There might be several explanations. Until we know for certain, I refuse to become alarmed."

"But we saw the headlights go past the gate as we drove toward the house."

"You heard me send Harold to look into the matter. If it *was* the same taxi, it had less than a minute's head start before Harold went after it. And if the taxi came from Manhattan, it would be one of few, if any, in the area at this hour. Its city of origin would be marked on the vehicle. I'm certain that Harold would intercept it well before it reached the thruway."

"You'll keep me informed."

"Of course. Relax. Look at how your hands are shaking. Be calm, my friend. You didn't use to worry this much."

"I didn't have as much to lose."

"Nor did we all."

"Good night, Eustace."

"Good night, Anthony."

Despite the worry in their voices, the tone of the old men was strikingly affectionate.

Car doors thunked shut. An engine roared. Another dark limousine sped from the garage and along the murky driveway.

22

From above, crouching in the darkness of the sundeck, Pittman watched the taillights recede, then disappear, the sound of the limousines fading into the silence of the night. With a final droning rumble, all the garage doors descended, cutting off the lights inside. The gloom in the area intensified.

Pittman slowly straightened. His legs were stiff. His calves prickled as blood resumed its flow through arteries that had been constricted. He turned toward the French doors for a final look at Jonathan Millgate helpless in his bed, surrounded by monitors, bottles, and tubes.

Pittman's pulse faltered.

Through the gaps in the draperies, what he saw seemed magnified by the glass panes in the French doors. At the same time, he felt as if he watched helplessly from a great distance. The nurse had left the room, leaving Millgate alone. She had shut the door. Millgate had not been asleep, contrary to what she evidently believed. Instead, he was attempting to raise himself.

Millgate's features were twisted, agitated. The oxygen prongs had slipped from his nostrils. His IV tubes had become disengaged from the needle in each of his arms. He pawed with both hands, trying to grasp the railings on his bed with sufficient strength to raise himself. But he wasn't succeeding. His face had become an alarming red. His chest heaved. Abruptly he slumped back, gasping.

Even at a distance, through the barrier of the French doors, Pittman thought he heard Millgate's strident effort to breathe. Before Pittman realized, he stepped closer to the window. The warning buzzer on the heart monitor should have alerted the nurse, he thought in dismay. She should have hurried back by now.

But as Pittman stared through the window, he was close enough that he knew he would have been able to hear an alarm, even through the glass. Had the sound been turned off? That didn't make sense. He studied the pattern of blips on the monitor. From so many days of watching Jeremy's monitors and insisting that the doctors explain what the indicators said, Pittman could tell from Millgate's monitor that his heartbeat was far above the normal range of 70 to 90 per minute, disturbingly rapid at 150. Its pattern of beats was becoming erratic, the rhythm of the four chambers of his heart beginning to disintegrate.

A crisis would come. Soon. Millgate's color was worse. His chest heaved with greater distress. He clutched at his blankets as if they were crushing him.

He can't get his breath, Pittman thought.

The oxygen. If he doesn't get those prongs back into his nostrils, he'll work himself into another heart attack.

The son of a bitch is going to die.

Pittman had a desperate impulse to turn, race down the steps, surge toward the estate's wall, scurry over, and run, keep running, never stop running.

Jesus, I should never have done this. I should never have come here.

He pivoted, eager to reach the stairs down from the sundeck. But his legs wouldn't move. He felt as if he were held in cement. His will refused to obey his commands.

Move. Damn it, get out of here.

Instead, he looked back.

In agony, Millgate continued to struggle to breathe. His pulse was now 160. Red numbers on his blood-pressure monitor showed 170/125. Normal was 120/80. The elevated pressure was a threat to anyone, let alone an eighty-year-old man who'd just had a heart attack that placed him in intensive care.

Clutching his chest, gasping, Millgate cocked his head toward the French doors, his anguished expression fixed on the windows. Pittman was sure Millgate couldn't see him out in the darkness. The dim lights in the room would reflect off the panes and make them a screen against the night. Even so, Millgate's tortured gaze was like a laser that seared into Pittman.

Don't look at me like that! What do you expect? There's nothing I can do!

Yet again Pittman turned to flee.

23

Instead, surprising himself, Pittman reached into his pants pocket and took out his keys and the tool knife—similar to a Swiss army knife—that he kept on his key ring. He removed two pieces of metal from the end of the knife. He was fully prepared to shoot himself to death in eight days. But there was no way he was going to stay put and watch while someone else died—or run before it happened and try to convince himself that he didn't have a choice. Millgate was about to go into a crisis, and on the face of it, the most obvious way to try to prevent that crisis was to reattach his IV lines and put the oxygen prongs back into his nostrils.

Maybe I'm wrong and he'll die anyhow. But by God, if he does, it won't be because I didn't try. Millgate's death won't be my responsibility.

Thinking of the .45 in the box at the diner, Pittman thought, *What have I got to lose?*

He stepped to the French doors and hesitated only briefly before he put the two metal prongs into the lock. The tool knife from which he had taken the prongs had been a gift from a man about whom Pittman had once written an article. The man, a veteran burglar named Sean O'Reilly, had been paroled from a ten-year prison sentence, one of the conditions being that he participate in a public-awareness program to show homeowners and apartment dwellers how to avoid being burglarized. Sean had the slight build of a jockey, the accent of an Irish Spring commercial, and the mischievously glinting eyes of a leprechaun. His three television spots had been so effective that he'd become a New York City celebrity. That was before he went back to prison for burglarizing the home of his attorney.

When he had interviewed him at the height of his fame, Pittman had suspected that Sean would end up back in prison. In elaborate detail, Sean had explained various ways to break into a house. Pittman's enthusiasm for information had prompted Sean to elaborate and dramatize. The interview had lasted two hours. At its end, Sean had presented Pittman with a gift—the tool knife he still carried. "I give these to people who really understand what an art it is to be a burglar," Sean had said. What made the knife especially useful, he explained, was that at the end of the handle, past miniature pliers, screwdrivers, and wire cutters, there were slots for two metal prongs: lock-picking tools. With glee, Sean had taught Pittman how to use them.

The lesson had stuck.

Now Pittman worked the prongs into the lock. It was sturdy—a dead bolt. It didn't matter. One prong was used to free the pins in the cylinder, Sean had explained. The other was used to apply leverage and pressure. Once you did it a couple of times, the simple operation wasn't hard to master. With practice and Sean watching, Pittman had learned how to enter a locked room within fifteen seconds.

As he freed one pin and shoved the first prong farther into the cylinder to free the next, Pittman stared frantically through the French door toward Millgate's agonized struggle to breathe.

Pittman increased his concentration, working harder. He had worried that when he opened the door, he would trigger an alarm. But his worry had vanished when he'd noticed a security-system number pad on the wall next to the opposite entrance to the room. From his interview with the Bugmaster, Pittman remembered that owners of large homes often had their security company install several number pads throughout their homes. These pads armed and disarmed the system, and it made sense to have a pad not just at the front door but at all the principal exits from the dwelling.

But in this case, the security company had installed the pad in the wrong place—within view of anyone who might be trying to break in through the French doors. From Pittman's vantage point, as he freed another pin in the cylinder of the lock, he could see that the illuminated indicator on the number pad said READY TO ARM. Because so many visitors had been coming and going, the system had not yet been activated.

Pittman felt the final pin disengage. Turning the second metal prong, he pivoted the cylinder, and the lock was released. In a rush, he turned the latch and pulled the door open.

The opposite door was closed. No one could hear Pittman as he hurried into the dusky room. Millgate was losing strength, his effort to breathe less strenuous. Pittman reached him and eased the prongs for the oxygen tube into Millgate's nostrils.

The effect was almost magical. Within seconds, Millgate's color had begun to be less flushed. His agitation lessened. A few more seconds and the rise and fall of Millgate's chest became more regular, less frenzied. Throughout, Pittman was in motion. He grabbed the IV tubes that Millgate had inadvertently jerked from the needles in his arms. As Pittman inserted the tubes back onto the base of each needle, he noticed that liquid from the tubes had trickled onto the floor. How would the nurse account for that when she came back into the room? he wondered. Then he noticed the water tracks that he had brought in from the rain, the moisture dripping off his overcoat.

I have to get out of here.

A final look at the monitors showed him that Millgate's blood pressure, respiration rate, and heartbeat were becoming less extreme. The old guy's going to make it a while longer, Pittman thought. Relieved, anxious, he turned to leave the room.

But he was shocked as an aged clawlike hand grabbed his right wrist, making him gasp. Pittman swung in alarm and saw Millgate's anguished eyes staring at him.

Pittman clutched the old man's fingers and worked to pry them off, surprised by the ferocity of the old man's grip.

Jesus, if he yells . . .

"Duncan." The old man spoke with effort, his voice thin and crackly, like cellophane being crumpled.

He's delirious. He doesn't know who he's talking to.

"Duncan." The old man seemed to plead.

He thinks I'm somebody else. I've been in here too long. I have to get out.

"Duncan." The old man's voice thickened, now sounding like crusted mud being stepped upon. "The snow."

Pittman released the old man's fingers.

"Grollier." The old man's throat filled with phlegm, making a grotesque imitation of the sound of gargling.

To hell with this, Pittman thought, then swung toward the French doors.

He was suddenly caught in a column of light. The entrance

to the room had been opened. Illumination from the hall spilled in, silhouetting the nurse. She stood, paralyzed for a moment. Abruptly she dropped a tray. A teapot and cup crashed onto the floor. She screamed.

And Pittman ran.

24

Pittman's brief time in the room had made him feel warm. As he raced onto the sundeck, the night and the rain seemed much more chilling than they had only a few seconds earlier. He shivered and lunged through puddles, past the dark metal patio furniture and toward the stairs that led down from the deck. At once he was blinded, powerful arc lamps glaring down at him from the eaves of the mansion above the sundeck, reflecting off puddles. The nurse or a guard had switched on the lights. From inside the building behind him, Pittman heard shouts.

He ran harder. He almost lost his balance on the stairs. Gripping the railing, flinching from a sliver that rammed into his palm, he bounded down the wooden steps. At the bottom, he almost scurried in the direction from which he had come, toward the tree-lined driveway and the gate from the estate. But he heard shouts from the front of the house, so he pivoted toward the back, only to recoil from arc lights that suddenly blazed toward the covered swimming pool and the flower gardens. There, too, he heard shouting.

With the front and rear blocked to him, Pittman charged to the side of the house, across concrete at the entrance to the large garage, over spongy lawn, toward looming dark fir trees. Rapid footsteps clattered down the stairs from the sundeck.

"Stop!"

"Shoot him!"

Pittman reached the fir trees. A needled branch pawed his face, stinging him so hard that he didn't know if the moisture on his cheeks was rain or blood. He ducked, avoiding another branch.

"Where the—?"

"There! I think he's over—!"

Behind Pittman, a bough snapped. Someone fell.

"My nose! I think I broke my fucking—!"

"I hear—!"

"In those bushes!"

"Shoot the son of a bitch!"

"Get him! If they find out we let somebody—!"

Another branch snapped. Behind him, Pittman's hunters charged through the trees.

Just in time, Pittman stopped himself. He'd come to a high stone wall, nearly running into it at full force. Breathing deeply, he fiercely studied the darkness to his left and then his right.

What am I going to do? he thought in a frenzy. I can't assume I'll find a gate. I can't keep following the wall. Too obvious. They'll listen for the sounds I make. They'll get ahead of me and behind me and corner me.

Turn back?

No! The police will soon arrive. The house has too many outside lights. I'll be spotted.

Then what are you going to . . . ?

Pittman hurried toward the nearest fir tree and started to climb. The footsteps of his pursuers thudded rapidly closer. He gripped a bough above him, shoved his right shoe against a lower branch, and hoisted himself upward along the trunk. Bark scraped his hands. The fir tree smell of turpentine assaulted his nostrils. He climbed faster.

"I hear him!"

Across from the top of the wall, Pittman reached out along a branch, let his legs fall away from the tree trunk, and inched hand over hand toward the wall. The branch dipped from his weight. Dangling, he kept shifting along. The bark cut deeper into his hands.

"He's close!"

"Where?"

Moisture dropped from the fir needles onto Pittman. Even greater moisture dropped from the branch to which he clung. Water cascaded onto the ground.

"There!"

"That tree!"

Pittman's shoes touched the top of the wall. He swung his legs toward it, felt a solid surface, no razor wire or chunks of glass along the top, and released his grip, sprawling on the top of the wall.

The gunshot was deafening, the muzzle flash startlingly bright. A second shot was so dismaying that Pittman acted without thinking, flipping sideways off the top of the wall. Heart pounding, he dangled. The rough wall scraped against his overcoat. He didn't know what was below him, but he heard one of his pursuers trying to climb the tree.

Another man shouted, "Use the gate!"

Pittman let go. His stomach swooped as he plummeted.

25

Exhaling forcefully, Pittman struck the ground sooner than he anticipated. The ground was covered with grass, mushy from rain. He bent his knees, tucked in his elbows, dropped, and rolled, trying desperately to minimize the impact. That was the way a skydiver he had once interviewed had explained how parachutists landed when they were using conventional equipment. Bend, tuck, and roll.

Pittman prayed it would work. If he sprained an ankle, or worse, he would be helpless when his pursuers searched this side of the wall. His only hope would be to hide. But where? As he had swung toward the top of the wall, his impression of the dark area behind it had been of unnerving open space.

Fortunately he had an alternative to being forced to try to hide. Using the momentum of his roll, he surged to his feet. His hands stung. His knees felt sore. But that discomfort was irrelevant. What mattered was that his ankles supported him. His legs didn't give out. He hadn't sprained or broken anything.

On the other side of the barrier, Pittman's hunters cursed and ran. Noises in a tree suggested that one of them continued to climb toward the top of the wall.

His chest heaving, Pittman charged forward. The murky

lawn seemed to stretch on forever. In contrast with the estate from which he'd just escaped, there weren't any shrubs. There were hardly any trees.

What the hell *is* this place?

It felt unnatural, eerie. It reminded him of a cemetery, but in the darkness, he didn't bump into any tombstones. Racing through the drizzle, he noticed a light patch in the lawn ahead and used it as a destination. At once the ground gave away, a sharp slope that caused him to tumble in alarm, falling, rolling.

He came to a stop on his back. The wind had been knocked from him. He breathed heavily, wiped wet sand from his face, and stood.

Sand. That explained why this section of the ground had been pale. But why would . . . ?

A tingle ran through him. My God, it's a golf course. There'd been a sign when the taxi driver brought him into the subdivision: SAXON WOODS PARK AND GOLF CLUB.

I'm in the open. If they start shooting again, there's no cover.

Then what are you hanging around for?

As he oriented himself, making sure that he wasn't running back toward the wall, he saw lights to his left. Specterlike, they emerged from the wall. Pittman had heard one of his pursuers talk about a gate. They'd reached it and come through. His first instinct was to conclude that they had found flashlights somewhere, probably from a shed near the gate. But there was something about the lights.

The tingle that Pittman had felt when he realized that he was on a golf course now became a cold rush of fear as he heard the sound of motors. The lights were too big to come from flashlights, and they were in pairs like headlights, but Pittman's hunters couldn't be using cars. Cars would be too heavy, losing traction, spinning their wheels until they got stuck in the soft wet grass. Besides, the motors sounded too small and whiny to belong to cars.

Jesus, they're using golf carts, Pittman realized, his chest tightening. Whoever owns the estate has private carts and access to the course from the back of the property. Golf carts don't have headlights. Those are handheld spotlights.

The carts spread out, the lights systematically covering various sections of the course. As men shouted, Pittman spun away from the lights, darted from the sand trap, and scurried into the rainy darkness.

26

Before Jeremy's cancer had been diagnosed, Pittman had been a determined jogger. He had run a minimum of an hour each day and several hours on the weekend, mostly using the jogging path along the Upper East Side, next to the river. He had lived on East Seventieth at that time, with Ellen and Jeremy, and his view of exercise had been much the same as his habit of saving 5 percent of his paycheck and making sure that Jeremy took summer courses at his school, even though the boy's grades were superior and extra work wasn't necessary. Security. Planning for the future. That was the key. That was the secret. With his son cheering and his wife doing her best to look dutifully enthusiastic, Pittman had managed to be among the middle group that finished the New York Marathon one year.

Then Jeremy had gotten sick.

And Jeremy had died.

And Pittman and Ellen had started arguing.

And Ellen had left.

And Ellen had remarried.

And Pittman had started drinking heavily.

And Pittman had suffered a nervous breakdown.

He hadn't run in over a year. For that matter, he hadn't

done any exercise at all, unless nervous pacing counted. But now adrenaline spurred him, and his body remembered. It didn't have its once-excellent tone. It didn't have the strength that he'd worked so hard to acquire. But it still retained his technique, the rhythm and length and heel-to-toe pattern of his stride. He was out of breath. His muscles protested. But he kept charging across the golf course, responding to a pounding in his veins and a fire in his guts, while behind him lights bobbed in the distance, motors whined, and men shouted.

Pittman's effort was so excruciating that he cursed himself for ever having allowed himself to get out of shape. Then he cursed himself for having been so foolhardy as to get into this situation.

What the hell did you think you were doing, following the ambulance all the way out here? Burt wouldn't have known if you hadn't bothered.

No. But *I'd* have known. I promised Burt I'd do my best.

For eight more days.

What about breaking into that house? Do you call that standard journalistic procedure? Burt would have a fit if he knew you did that.

What was I supposed to do, let the old man die?

As Pittman's stiffening legs did their best to imitate the expert runner's stride that had once been second nature to him, he risked losing time to glance back at his pursuers. Wiping moisture from his eyes, he saw the drizzle-haloed spotlights on the golf carts speeding toward him in the darkness.

Or some of the carts. All told, there were five, but only two were directly behind him. The rest had split off, one to the right, the other to the left, evidently following the perimeter of the golf course. The third was speeding on a diagonal toward what Pittman assumed was the far extreme of the course.

They want to encircle me, Pittman realized. But in the darkness, how can they be sure which way I'm going?

Rain trickled down his neck beneath his collar. He felt the hairs on his scalp rise when he suddenly understood how his pursuers were able to follow him.

His London Fog overcoat.

It was sand-colored. Just as Pittman had been able to see the light color of the sand trap against the darkness of the grass, so his overcoat was as obvious to his pursuers.

Forced to break stride, running awkwardly, Pittman desperately worked at the belt on his overcoat, untying it, then fumbling at buttons. One button didn't want to be released, and Pittman yanked at it, popping it loose. In a frenzy, he had the coat open. He jerked his arm from one sleeve. He freed his other arm. His suit coat had been somewhat dry, but now drizzle soaked it.

Pittman's first impulse was to throw the overcoat away. His next impulse, as he entered a clump of brush, was to drape the coat over a bush to provide a target for the men chasing him. That tactic wouldn't distract them for long, though, he knew, and besides, if . . . *when* . . . he escaped, he would need the coat to help keep him warm.

The brushy area was too small to be a good hiding place, so Pittman fled it, scratching his hands on bushes, and continued charging across the murky golf course.

Glancing desperately back over his shoulder, he saw the glare of the lights on the carts. He heard the increasingly loud whine of their engines. Rolling his overcoat into a ball and stuffing it under his suit jacket, he strained his legs to their maximum. One thing was in his favor. He was wearing a dark blue suit. In the rainy blackness, he hoped he would blend with his surroundings.

Unless the lights pick me up, he thought.

Ahead, a section of the golf course assumed a different color, a disturbing gray. Approaching it swiftly, Pittman realized that he'd reached a pond. The need to skirt it would force him to lose time. No choice. Breathing hard, he veered to the left. But the wet, slippery grass along the slope betrayed him. His left foot jerked from under him. He fell and almost tumbled into the freezing water before he clawed his fingers into the mushy grass and managed to stop himself.

Rising frantically, he remembered to keep his overcoat clutched beneath his suit jacket. With an urgent glance backward, he saw a beam of light shoot over the top of the slope down which he'd rolled. The whine of an engine was very close. Concentrating not to lose his balance again, Pittman scurried through the rainy darkness.

He followed the rim of the pond, struggled up the opposite slope, and lunged over the top just before he heard angry voices behind him. Something buzzed past his right ear. It sounded like a hornet, but Pittman knew what it was: a bullet. Another hornet buzzed past him. No sound of shots. His hunters must have put silencers on their handguns.

He scurried down a slope, out of their line of fire. To his right, through the rain, he saw lights trying to overtake him. To his left, he saw the same. His legs were so fatigued, they wanted to buckle. His heaving lungs protested.

Can't keep this up much longer.

He fought to muster energy.

Have to keep going.

Too late, he saw the light-colored patch ahead of him. The grass dropped sharply. Unable to stop, he hurtled out into space, flailed, and jolted down into another sand trap. The impact dropped him to his knees. He struggled upright, feeling the heaviness of wet sand clinging to his trousers.

Spotlights bobbed, speeding nearer. With a final burst of energy, he struggled across the sand trap. His shoes sank into the drizzle-softened sand. He left a deep, wide trail. Jesus, even if they don't have my overcoat as a target, they'll know from my tracks which way I went when I reached the grass, he thought.

Tracks. Pittman's skin prickled as he realized that this might be his only chance to save himself. The instant he raced out of the sand onto the grass, he reversed his direction and hurried through the darkness along the edge of the sand trap toward the top of the slope from which he had leapt. As he ran through the drizzle, he yanked his balled overcoat from beneath his suit jacket.

The whine of an engine sounded terribly close. Spotlights bobbed above him. He came to where the grass dropped sharply toward the sand. Careful not to disturb this section, he eased over the edge and lay sideways where the sand met the almost-vertical, sharp downward angle of the earth. There, he spread his sand-colored overcoat across his head and suit jacket. He felt its weight on his lower thighs, almost covering his knees. He bent his legs and drew them toward his body, tucking them under the hem of the overcoat. His breathing sounded hoarse. He strained to control it.

Please, he kept thinking. Please.

With his overcoat covering his head, he heard drizzle patter onto him. He heard the whine of engines—close. The whine diminished abruptly, as if the carts had come to a stop.

Vapor from Pittman's breath collected under the overcoat. Dank moisture dribbled along his chin. The wet chill made him shiver, although he compacted his muscles and struggled not to tremble.

Can't let them notice me.

He shivered for another reason, anticipating the impact of a bullet.

Isn't that what you wanted? If they shoot you, they'll be doing you a favor.

But I want it to be *my* idea.

He silently prayed: If only his overcoat blended with the sand. If only the men stared straight ahead instead of looking down at—

"There!"

Pittman's heartbeat lurched.

"Tracks in the sand!"

"Toward that section of grass!"

Something made an electronic crackle: a walkie-talkie.

"Alpha to Beta! He's headed in your direction! He's reached the northeast quadrant!"

A garbled voice responded. The walkie-talkie made an electronic squawk. The whine of the engines intensified. Beneath the smothering, moisture-laden overcoat, Pittman heard the carts speed away past the sand trap, toward the continuation of the grass.

His clothes soaked from the wet sand he lay upon, Pittman waited, not daring to move. Despite the stifling buildup of carbon dioxide beneath the overcoat, he forced himself to continue to wait. At last he relented, slowly moving the coat. As he inched it off his face, inhaling the fresh, cool air, he squinted toward the darkness, afraid that he would see a man above him grin and aim a pistol.

But he saw only the slope of the earth above him, darkness, and drizzle pelting his eyes. After the cloying stale air beneath the coat, the rain made him feel clean. He eased upward, came to a trembling crouch, and saw the lights of the carts receding in the murky distance. Careful to bunch his overcoat beneath his suit coat, he crept from the sand trap and headed in the direction from which the carts had come. He was soaked, chilled. But for all his discomfort and apprehension, a portion of his mind was swollen with exultation.

Nonetheless, he still had to get out of the area, off this golf course, away from the estate. The carts might return at any time. Although his legs were unsteady, he managed to lengthen his stride and increase its frequency.

Enveloped by the night and the rain, he almost faltered with increased dread when it occurred to him that without a way to keep his bearings, he might wander in a circle until his pursuers came upon him. Immediately, in the distance to his left, he saw moving lights, but not those on the carts. These were larger, brighter. Their beams probed deeper through the rain. The headlights of a car, or maybe a truck. They moved parallel to him, then disappeared.

A road.

TWO

1

"Car trouble."

"Man, look at you shiver," the motel clerk said.

"Got soaked finding a pay phone to call a tow truck. The garage says my car won't be ready till the afternoon. I need a place to get dry."

"I guess you're not from around here." The clerk was paunchy, in his forties. He had thick red beard stubble and strained features from working all night.

Pittman shook his head. "I'm on the road a lot, selling college textbooks. Left New Haven last night for a meeting in New York."

"Looks like you're not going to make it."

"I didn't have to be at the meeting till Monday. Figured I'd spend the weekend having a good time. Shit."

Pittman gave the clerk his credit card and filled out the registration form, making sure to claim a New Haven address. He felt strange lying, but he knew he had to. The clerk needed a reasonable explanation for Pittman's drenched appearance, and the truth certainly wasn't acceptable.

"Here's your card back. Here's your key."

Pittman sneezed.

"Man, you need to get out of those wet clothes."

"That's all I've been thinking of."

2

The name had been appealing: Warm Welcome Motel. Pittman had found it among several other motels a half hour after he'd hurried, shivering, from the golf course area. Houses had been dark, streetlights widely separated. Whenever he saw headlights, he had darted toward the shelter of bushes or a backyard before he could be seen. He'd had a vague idea of which way the thruway was. Fear had spurred him.

Now, as he locked the motel door behind him, the last of his energy drained from him. He sank into a lumpy chair and sipped the cardboard cup of bitter but wonderfully hot coffee that he'd bought from a noisy machine at the end of the concrete-block hallway. The room's carpet was green and worn. He didn't care. The walls were an unappealing yellow. He didn't care about that, either, or about the hollow beneath the dingy orange cover of the mattress on the bed. All he cared about was heat.

Need to get warm.

His teeth chattered.

Need a hot bath.

He turned the room's thermostat to seventy-five, then stripped off his wet clothes. After arranging his trousers, shirt, and suit coat on hangers, he left the closet door open in hopes they would dry. He put his soaked shoes near the baseboard radiator, draped his socks and underwear over the back of a chair, and twisted the hot-water faucet on the bathtub.

For an instant, he was afraid that the water would be only tepid. Instead, it sent steam billowing around him. He leaned over the gushing tap, luxuriating in the heat. Only when the tub was nearly full did he add any cold water, just enough so he wouldn't scald himself as he settled into the exquisitely hot bath. He slid down until the steaming water came up to his chin. The tub was so full that water trickled into the overflow drain. By shifting sideways, he managed to tuck his knees under so he was almost completely submerged.

He exhaled with pleasure and felt heat penetrate his skin, his muscles, his bones, dissipating the heavy chill that had gathered at his core. Gradually his arms and legs stopped quivering. He closed his eyes and realized that he hadn't enjoyed a physical sensation so much since . . .

His mind balked but finally permitted the thought.

. . . since the night Jeremy had died. He had felt so guilty being alive while Jeremy was dead that he hadn't been able to tolerate even the simplest, most basic of pleasures. The taste of a good meal had become repugnant—because Jeremy would never again be able to enjoy that sensation. The soothing feel of clean sheets, the freshness of a morning breeze, the comfort of sunlight streaming through a window: Any positive sensation was abhorrent—because Jeremy would never be able to share them.

And one of the sensations that had made Pittman feel especially guilty was the warmth of a shower. Jeremy had enjoyed spending what had seemed to Pittman (before Jeremy got sick) an undue amount of time in the shower. After Jeremy's funeral, Pittman had suddenly discovered that he felt repelled by the thought of a shower. Since he needed to clean himself, he had moderated the problem by keeping the temperature of the water as neutral as he could manage. Just because he had to bathe didn't mean that he had to enjoy it.

Now, for the first time since Jeremy's death, Pittman was surprised to discover that he was allowing himself to experience a pleasurable sensation. He told himself that the sensation was necessary, that he absolutely needed to get warm. After all, he had once done a story about participants in a wilderness survival course, and one of the dangers that the instructors had kept emphasizing was that of becoming wet and chilled and dying from hypothermia. So, yes, he could grudgingly allow a positive sensation under this circumstance.

But the truth was, his enjoyment wasn't just tolerated; he relished it. For the first time in longer than he cared to remember, he appreciated the feelings of his body.

But thoughts of Jeremy caused a black pall of gloom to sink over his mind again. He found it bleakly ironic that despite his eagerness to commit suicide, his escape from the estate had prompted him to endure such intense fear for his life.

You should have let them do you a favor and shoot you.

No. Pittman angrily echoed a thought from a few hours earlier. It has to be *my* idea, not theirs. When I go out, it'll be *my* way, at a time and place of my own choosing. I've got my own deadline, eight days from now, and I damned well intend to stick to it. Not sooner.

His anger became melancholy as he remembered the reason that he hadn't already killed himself. I promised Burt. For what Burt did for Jeremy.

Then melancholy became confusion as thoughts about Burt reminded Pittman of why he had followed the ambulance.

He imagined the questions that Burt would demand answers for.

Why had Millgate been taken from the hospital? Why had he been driven to the estate in Scarsdale? Why had the guards at the estate not just pursued Pittman but instead tried to kill him?

As soon as Pittman was off the property, the risk the guards thought he posed would have been at an end. Pittman could understand them wanting to capture him and turn him over to the police. But to want to kill him? Something was very wrong.

After draining the tub and refilling it with more hot water, Pittman finally felt that the chill within him had been smothered. He pulled the plug and got out of the tub to towel himself vigorously. Again he caught himself enjoying a sensation and checked the impulse. After wrapping himself with a blanket, he turned off the lights and peered past the blind on the room's window. It looked out onto the motel's rain-puddled parking lot. He saw a car come in and worried that it might be the police, who, alerted by the guards at the estate, would be out looking for him.

But the car didn't have any dome lights on its roof and it wasn't marked. Pittman wondered then if the car might belong to the estate, that this might be some of the guards searching the area for him, talking to clerks at various motels. Only when he saw a woman get out of the car and enter a room on the other side of the parking lot did his tension ease.

The police. At the golf course, he hadn't heard any sirens. Did that mean the police had not been alerted? he wondered. How would the guards have explained shooting at a prowler after the prowler had reached a public area?

And the guards, would they still be hunting him? They might check the local motels, sure. But wasn't it more logical for them to assume that their quarry would want to get as far away as possible?

Besides, they don't know who I am or what I look like.

Pittman's knees buckled from fatigue. Shivering, he crawled into bed and gradually became warm again. He told himself that he would sleep for a couple of hours. Burt usually got to the newspaper around eight. Pittman would call, tell Burt what had happened, and get instructions.

I'd better tell the desk clerk to wake me around eight, Pittman thought. In the dark, he reached for the telephone. But his arm felt weighted down. He drifted.

3

Pittman woke slowly, groggily, his eyelids not wanting to open. At first he thought it was the bright sunlight through the room's thin blind that had wakened him. Then he suspected it was the din of thruway traffic rattling the window. Sore from his exertion the night before, he sat up and rubbed his legs. Finally he left the warmth of the bed and relieved himself in the bathroom. When he returned to the bed, wrapping a blanket around him, he felt sufficiently awake to phone Burt. But when he reached toward the bedside phone, he noticed the red numbers on the digital clock beside it: 2:38.

Jesus, he thought, straightening. It's not morning. It's Friday *afternoon*. I slept almost ten hours.

The discovery made him feel out of control, as if he'd lost something—which he had, one of his remaining days. He hurriedly picked up the phone, read a card next to it that told him to press 9 for a long-distance call, then touched the numbers for the *Chronicle*.

The line made a faint crackling sound. The phone at the other end rang, and fifteen seconds later, the newspaper's receptionist transferred the call to Burt's office.

As usual, Burt's crusty smoker's voice was instantly recognizable. He didn't need to announce as he always did, "Yeah, Forsyth here."

"It's Matt. Listen, I'm sorry I didn't get in today. Something weird happened last night. I was at—"

"I can't talk right now. I'm in a meeting."

Pittman heard a click as the call was interrupted.

What the . . . ?

Pittman frowned and slowly set down the phone.

Burt's never that abrupt, he thought. Not to me. Man, he must really be pissed. He figures I let him down by not coming in.

Pittman picked up the phone again. He couldn't tolerate the misunderstanding. Once more the receptionist transferred the call.

"Forsyth here."

"This is Matt. Look, I said I was sorry. I swear to you it's not my fault. I've got something I need to tell you about. Last night—"

"I don't have time for that. I'm with some important people."

For a second time, Burt broke the connection.

Pittman's head throbbed. Frowning harder, he replaced the phone.

Yeah, he's pissed all right. Important people. I get the point. For letting him down, he's telling me as far as he's concerned, *I'm not* important.

Pittman debated about calling a third time but reluctantly decided not to. Whatever's bugging him, it's obvious he isn't going to let me settle it over the phone.

Troubled, aching, Pittman stood and reached for his clothes. They were damp but at least no longer soaked. Because he had hung his slacks, shirt, and suit coat on hangers, there were less wrinkles than he feared. Another plus was that the mud on them had caked; he was able to brush off most of it. His overcoat was a mess, however: torn and grimy. He crammed it into the wastebasket. Then he wet his rumpled sandy hair and combed it. Although he definitely needed a shave, the motel didn't supply a shaving kit, so that would have to wait. Hungry but in a hurry, he remembered that he'd seen a McDonald's down the street. No bags to pack. All he had to do was grab his key and leave.

Opening the door slightly, he peered out to see if anyone was watching his room. No one as far as he could tell. As he crossed the parking lot toward the motel's office, he discovered that the air was chilly despite the bright sun. His damp socks and underwear made him uncomfortable.

4

Important people. During the Metro ride into the city, Pittman kept assessing what Burt had told him. The clack-clack-clack of the train on the rails became like a mantra and helped Pittman to focus his concentration. Important people.

Maybe Burt had been telling the truth. A week from today, the *Chronicle* would close its doors. There had to be all kinds of complicated arrangements to make. It was possible that the owner and the publisher and God knew who all were in Burt's office discussing the direction the newspaper should take in its final days.

But wouldn't people that important make Burt go to their office rather than want to meet in his?

Pittman reversed the direction of his thoughts and again suspected that Burt was angry at him.

In rush-hour traffic outside Grand Central Station, Pittman couldn't find an empty cab, so he decided to use the subway. His intention had been to go to the *Chronicle*, but his watch now showed eight minutes after five. The sun was low behind skyscrapers. The air had turned cold, and Pittman's damp clothes made him shiver again. Burt wouldn't be at the office now anyway, he thought. He'd be on his way to the bar where he always went after work.

I'm not going to sit in that bar and have my teeth chatter all the time I'm trying to explain. What I need first are dry clothes.

Pittman got out of the subway at Union Square, still couldn't find an empty cab, and walked all the way to his apartment on West Twelfth Street. The air was colder, the light paler as he hurried along. He unlocked the door to the vestibule of his building. Then he unlocked the farther door that allowed him past the mailboxes into the ground-floor corridor of the building itself.

As usual, the smell of cooking assailed him. Also as usual, the elevator wheezed and creaked, taking him to the third floor. As usual, too, the television was blaring in the apartment next to his. He shook his head in discouragement, unlocked the door, stepped in, shut and locked the door, and turned to discover a man sitting in his living room, reading a magazine.

5

Pittman's heartbeat faltered. "What the . . . ?"

The man set down the magazine. "Is your name Matthew Pittman?"

"What the hell do you think you're . . . ?"

The man was in his late thirties. Thin, he had short brown hair, a slender face, a sharp chin. He wore a plain gray suit and shoes with thick soles. "I'm with the police department." He opened a wallet to show his badge and ID. He stood, his expression sour, as if he'd much sooner be doing something else. "Detective Mullen. I'd like to ask you a few questions."

"How did you get in here?"

"I asked the super to let me in."

Pittman felt pressure in his chest. "You can't just . . . You don't have a right to . . . Damn it, have you got a warrant or something?"

"Why? Have you done something that makes you think I'd need a warrant?"

"No. I . . ."

"Then why don't you save us both a lot of time. Sit down. Let's discuss a couple of things."

"*What* things? I still don't . . ."

"You look cold. Your clothes look like they've been wet."

Pittman hurriedly thought of an acceptable explanation. "Yeah, a waiter spilled water on my jacket and pants and . . ."

The detective nodded. "Same thing happened to me two weeks ago. Not water, though. Linguini. You'd better change. Leave the door to your bedroom open a bit. We can talk while you get dry clothes. Also, you look like you could use a shave."

"I've been trying to grow a beard," Pittman lied. In the bedroom, listening to the detective's voice through the slightly open door, he nervously took off his clothes, threw them in a hamper, then grabbed fresh underwear and socks from his bureau drawer.

He had just put on a pair of brown slacks when he saw the detective standing at the door.

"I wonder if you could tell me where you were last night."

Feeling threatened, his nipples shrinking, Pittman reached for a shirt. "I was home for a while. Then I went for a walk."

The detective opened the door wider, making Pittman feel even more threatened. "What time did you go for the walk?"

"Eleven."

"And you came back . . . ?"

"Around one."

The detective raised his eyebrows. "Kind of dangerous to be out walking that late."

"I've never had any trouble."

"You've been lucky. Anybody see you?"

Pittman almost mentioned the cook at the diner, but then he realized that if the detective talked to the cook, the cook would mention the box Pittman had left, and the detective might find the handgun. Pittman's permit allowed him to keep the .45 only in his apartment. It would look suspicious that he had hidden the weapon somewhere else.

"Nobody saw me."

"Too bad. That makes it difficult."

"For what? Look, I don't like your barging in here, and I don't like being questioned when I don't know what this is all about." Pittman couldn't hide his agitation. "Who's your superior at your precinct? What's his telephone number?"

"Good idea. I think we ought to talk to him. Matter of fact, why don't we both go down and talk to him in person?"

"Fine."

"Good."

"After I phone my lawyer."

"Oh?" the detective said. "You think you need a lawyer now?"

"When the police start acting like the gestapo."

"Aw." The detective shook his head. "Now you've hurt my feelings. Put on your shoes. Get a coat. Let's take a ride."

"Not until you tell me what's going on." Pittman couldn't get enough air.

"You didn't go for a walk last night. You took a taxi up to an estate in Scarsdale and broke in."

"I did *what*? That's crazy."

The detective reached into his suit coat pocket and brought out an envelope. He squinted at Pittman, opened the envelope, and removed a sheet of paper.

"What's this?"

"A Xerox of a check," the detective said.

Pittman's stomach cramped when he saw that it was a copy of the check he had written to the taxi driver the previous night. How the hell had the police gotten it?

The detective's expression became more sour as he explained. "An ambulance driver heading from Manhattan to the Scarsdale estate last night says a taxi followed him all the way. He got suspicious and wrote down the ID number on the light on the taxi's roof. So after we were contacted about the break-in at the estate, we tracked down the cabbie. He says the guy who hired him to drive up to that estate wrote a check to pay for the ride. *This* check. With your signature at the bottom. With your name and address printed at the top."

Pittman stared at the copy of the check.

"Well, are you going to admit it, or are you going to make me go to the trouble of bringing you and the cabbie face-to-face so he can identify you?"

Pittman exhaled tensely. Given what he intended to do seven days from now, what difference did it make? So I broke into a house to save an old man's life, he thought. Is that so big a crime? What am I trying to hide?

All the same, he hesitated. "Yes. It was me."

"There. Now don't you feel better?"

"But I can explain."

"Of course."

"After I call my lawyer."

Pittman passed the detective at the door to the bedroom and entered the living room, heading for the telephone.

"We're not going to have to go through that, are we?" The detective stalked after him. "This is a simple matter."

"And I want to keep it simple. That's why I want to call my lawyer. So there aren't any misunderstandings."

Pittman picked up the phone.

"I'm asking you not to do that," the detective said. "I have just a few questions. There's no need for an attorney. When you were with the old man, did he say anything?"

Pittman shook his head. "I don't understand."

"Did he say anything?"

"What's that go to do with . . . ? So what if . . . ?"

The detective stepped closer, his face stern. "Did . . . the . . . old . . . man . . . say . . . anything?"

"Gibberish."

"Tell me."

Pittman continued to hold the phone. "It didn't make any sense. It sounded like Duncan something. Then something about snow. Then . . . I don't know . . . I think he said Grollier."

The detective's features tightened. "Did you tell anybody else?"

"Anybody else? What difference would . . . ? Wait a minute. This doesn't feel right. What's going on here? Let me see your identification."

"I already showed you."

"I want to see it *again*."

The detective shrugged. "This is all the identification I need."

The detective reached beneath his suit coat, and Pittman stiffened, his pulse speeding at the sight of the gun the detective pulled out. The gun's barrel was unusually long. Pittman suddenly realized that it wasn't a barrel but a silencer attached to the barrel.

Policemen didn't carry silencers.

"You meddling shit, you give me any more trouble and I'll put a goddamn bullet up your nose. Who else did you tell?"

The tip of the silencer snagged. As the man's gaze flickered down toward his suit coat, Pittman reacted without thinking, a reflexive response. Despite his self-destructive intentions, he had no control over his body's need to defend itself against sudden fear. Startled, in a frenzy, he swung the phone with all his might, cracking its plastic against the man's forehead.

The man lurched backward. Blood streaked his brow. He cursed, struggling to focus his vision, raising the pistol.

Terrified, Pittman struck again, smashing the man's nose. More blood flew. The man fell backward. He walloped onto a coffee table, shattered its glass top, crashed through, and slammed against the floor, his upturned head ramming against the metal rim of the table.

Staring at the pistol in the man's hand, Pittman raised the phone to strike a third time, only to discover that he'd stretched the extension cord to its limit. Trembling, he dropped the phone and searched desperately around for something else with which to hit the man. He grabbed a lamp, about to throw it down at the man's head, when at once he realized that the man wasn't moving.

6

The man's eyes were open. So was his mouth. His head was propped against the far metal rim of the coffee table. His legs, bent at the knees, hung over the near rim.

Holding the lamp high, ready to throw it, Pittman stepped closer. The man's chest wasn't moving.

Dear God, he's dead.

Time seemed to have accelerated. Simultaneously Pittman felt caught between heartbeats, as if time had been suspended. For seconds that might have been minutes, he continued to stare down at the man with the gun. Slowly he set the lamp back on its table. He knelt beside the man, his emotions in chaos.

How did . . . ? I didn't hit him hard enough to . . .

Christ, he must have broken his neck when he smashed through the glass. His head hid the metal side of the table.

Then Pittman noticed the blood pooling on the floor under the man—a lot of it.

Afraid that the man would spring into motion and aim the gun at him, Pittman touched the corpse's arm and shifted the body. He swallowed bile when he saw that a long shard of glass had been rammed into the man's back, between his shoulder blades.

Pittman's face felt clammy.

He was thirty-eight years old. He had never been in the military. Apart from the previous night and the Saturday seven years earlier when the two men had broken his jaw, his only experience with violence had been through people he had interviewed who were acquainted with violence, either as victims, criminals, or police officers.

And now he had killed a man. Appalled by the blood on the telephone, he gingerly set it on its receptacle.

What am I going to . . . ?

Abruptly he worried that somebody had heard the crash. He swung toward the wall behind which the neighbor's television blared—people laughing, an announcer saying something about a trip to Jamaica, people applauding, a game show. He expected to hear urgent footsteps, the neighbor pounding on the door.

Instead, what he heard was the TV announcer giving out a prize on the game show. No matter the noise from the television, his apartment seemed eerily quiet.

What if I was wrong and he really *is* a policeman?

Breathing with effort, Pittman opened the man's suit coat and took out the police identification that the man had shown him. A card next to the badge said that the detective's name was William Mullen. The photograph on the ID matched the face of the dead man. But as Pittman examined it, he was unnerved to discover that the photograph had been pasted over another photograph, which didn't look anything like the corpse. Pittman checked the man's wallet, and in addition to almost four hundred dollars, he found a driver's license in the name of Edward Halloway, residence in Alexandria, Virginia. Pittman had never heard of any New York City policeman who lived several states away. This definitely wasn't a cop.

What the hell was he, then?

7

The phone rang.

Pittman stared.

The phone rang a second time.

Who would—?

The phone rang a third time.

Should I—?

The phone rang a fourth time.

Suppose it's Burt.

Pittman picked it up. Listening, he said nervously, "Hello."

Pause.

Click.

Jesus.

8

In a rush, Pittman entered his bedroom, grabbed a brown sport coat, and pulled his suitcase from his closet. Instantly he put the suitcase back and took out the gym bag he had used when he had still been a runner. He had once interviewed a security specialist, who was an expert in blending with a crowd. One of the hard things, the expert had said, was to find something that would hold weapons or equipment but not be conspicuous. A suitcase was too bulky, and besides, anybody who carried a suitcase into any public building other than a transportation terminal attracted attention.

Conversely, while a briefcase looked more natural, especially if you were well dressed, it wasn't big enough. But a reasonably attractive gym bag was ideal. Enough people went to exercise after work that a gym bag appeared natural, even if the person carrying it wore a suit, although casual clothes were obviously better.

And a gym bag held a lot.

Trembling, Pittman put a fresh pair of underwear and socks into the bag. He shoved in an extra shirt, a tie, his black sweat suit, his running shoes, his electric razor, a toothbrush, toothpaste, and shampoo.

What else?

This isn't summer camp you're going to. You have to get out of here fast. That phone call was probably from someone working with the gunman.

Pittman hurried into the living room, frowned down at the corpse, and almost took the four hundred dollars from the dead man's wallet.

That would look great to the police. After you killed him, you thought why not steal from him, too?

What about his gun?

What about it?

Do I take it?

Who do you think you are? John Wayne? You know enough about guns to shoot yourself, not anybody else.

9

As the phone started ringing again, Pittman grabbed his spare overcoat, opened his apartment door, peered out, saw no one, went into the dimly lit corridor, and locked the door behind him.

In his apartment, the phone kept ringing.

He hurried toward the elevator. But the moment he reached it, extending his right hand to press the down button, not yet touching it, he heard a buzz.

Creaking, the elevator began to rise from the ground floor.

Pittman felt pressure behind his ears.

He headed down the stairs but froze as he heard footsteps scraping far below him, coming up the concrete steps, echoing louder as they ascended from the ground floor.

Invisible arms seemed to pin his chest, squeezing him. One man in the elevator, another on the stairs. That would make sense. No one could come down without their knowing.

Pittman backed up, straining to be silent. Again in the corridor, he analyzed his options and crept up the stairs toward the next floor.

Out of sight, he heard the elevator stop and footsteps come out. They hesitated in the corridor. Other footsteps, those in the stairwell, came up to the third floor and joined whoever had gotten out of the elevator.

No one spoke as both sets of footsteps proceeded along the corridor. They stopped about where Pittman judged his apartment would be. He heard a knock, then another. He heard the scrape of metal that he recognized as the sound of lock-pick tools. A different kind of metallic sound might have been the click of a gun being cocked. He heard a door being opened.

"Shit," a man exclaimed, as if he'd seen the corpse in Pittman's apartment.

Immediately the footsteps went swiftly into a room. The door was closed.

I can't stay here, Pittman thought. They might search the building.

He swung toward the elevator door on the fourth floor and pressed the down button. His hands shook as the elevator wheezed and groaned to his level.

Part of him was desperate to flee down the stairs. But what if the men came out and saw him? This way, he'd be out of sight in the elevator—unless the men came out in the meantime and decided to use the elevator, stopping it as it descended, in which case he'd be trapped in the cage with them.

But he had to take the risk. Suppose the men had left someone in the lobby. Pittman needed a way to get past, and the elevator was it. His face was slick with sweat as he got in the car and pressed the button for the basement. As the car sank toward the third floor, he imagined that he would hear a buzz, that the car would stop, that two men would get in.

He trembled, watching the needle above the inside of the door point to 3.

Then the needle began to point toward 2.

He exhaled. Sweat trickled down his chest under his shirt.

The needle pointed toward 1, then B.

The car stopped. The doors grated open. He faced the musty shadows of the basement.

The moment he stepped out, the elevator doors closed. As he shifted past a furnace, the elevator surprised him, rising. Turning, he watched the needle above the door: 1, 2, 3.

The elevator stopped.

Simultaneously, via the stairwell, he heard noises from the lobby: footsteps, voices.

"See anybody?"

"No. Our guys just went up."

"Nobody came down?"

"Not that I saw. I've been here only five minutes. Somebody took the elevator to the basement."

"Basement? What would anybody want down there?"

"A storage unit maybe."

"Check it out."

Pittman hurried beyond the furnace. In shadows, he passed locked storage compartments. He heard footsteps on the stairs behind him. He came to the service door from the basement. Sweating more profusely, he gently twisted the knob on the dead-bolt lock, desperate not to make noise. The footsteps reached the bottom of the stairs.

Pittman opened the door, tensed from the squeak it made, slipped out into the night, shut the door, and broke into a run. The narrow alley, only five feet wide, led each way, to Twelfth Street or past another apartment building to Eleventh Street. Reasoning that the men who were chasing him would have a car waiting in front of his building on Twelfth Street, he darted past garbage cans toward Eleventh Street.

At the end, a stout wooden door blocked his way. Clumsy with fright, he twisted the knob on another dead bolt and tugged at the door, flinching when he heard a noise far along the alley behind him. He surged out onto Eleventh Street, straining to adjust his eyes to the glare of headlights and streetlights. Breathing hard in panic, he turned left and hurried past startled pedestrians. His goal was farther west, the din of traffic, the safety of the congestion on Seventh Avenue.

And this time, he did find an empty taxi.

10

Burt Forsyth wasn't married. He considered his apartment a place only for changing his clothes, sleeping, and showering. Every night after work, he followed the same routine: several drinks and then dinner at Bennie's Oldtime Beefsteak Tavern. The regulars there were like a family to him.

The bar, on East Fiftieth Street, was out of tone with the expensive leather-goods store on its left and the designer-dress store on its right. It had garish neon lights in its windows and a sign bragging that the place had a big-screen television. As Pittman's taxi pulled to a stop, several customers were going in and out.

Another taxi stopped to let someone off. Pittman studied the man, then relaxed somewhat when the man went into the bar without looking in Pittman's direction. After using the last of his cash to pay the driver, Pittman glanced around, felt somewhat assured that he hadn't been followed, and hurried toward the entrance.

Pittman's gym bag attracted no attention as he stood among patrons and scanned the crowded, dimly lit, noisy interior. It was divided so that the beefsteak part of the bar was in a paneled section to the right. A partition separated it from the serious drinking part of the establishment, which was on the left. There, a long counter and several tables faced a big-screen television that was always tuned to a sports channel. Pittman had been in the place a couple of times with Burt and knew that Burt preferred the counter. But when he studied that area, he didn't see Burt's distinctly rugged silhouette.

He stepped farther in, working his way past two customers who were paying their bill at a cash register in front. He craned his neck to check the busy tables but still saw no sign of Burt. Pittman felt impatient. He knew he had to get in touch with the police, but his sense of danger at his apartment had prompted him to run. Once he escaped, he had planned to use a pay phone to contact the police. As soon as he'd gotten in the taxi, though, he'd said the first words that came into his mind: "Bennie's Tavern." He had to sort things out.

He had to talk to Burt.

But Burt wasn't in sight. Pittman tried to encourage himself with the thought that Burt might have made an exception and chosen to eat in the restaurant part of the bar. Or maybe he's late. Maybe he's still coming. Maybe I haven't missed him.

Hurry. The police will wonder why you didn't get in touch with them as soon as you escaped.

Feeling a tightness in his chest, Pittman turned to make his way into the restaurant and caught a glimpse of a burly, craggy-faced man in his fifties with a brush cut and bushy eyebrows. The man wore a rumpled sport coat and was visible only for a moment as he passed customers and descended stairs built into the partition between the two sections of the building.

11

At the bottom of the hollow-sounding wooden stairs, Pittman passed a coat room, a pay phone, and a door marked DOLLS. He went into a door marked GUYS. A thin man with a gray mustache was coming out of a toilet stall. The man put on a blue suit coat and stepped next to a long-haired young man in a leather windbreaker at a row of sinks to wash his hands. The burly man whom Pittman had followed downstairs was standing to the left at a urinal, his back to Pittman.

"Burt."

The man looked over his shoulder and reacted with surprise, a cigarette dangling from his mouth. "What are *you* doing here?"

Pittman walked toward him. "Look, I can explain why I wasn't at work today. There's something I need to talk to you about. Believe me, it's serious."

The other men in the rest room listened with interest.

"Don't you realize it isn't safe?" Burt said. "I tried to tell you on the phone today."

"Safe? You sounded like you were giving me the brush-off. A meeting. Important people. Sure."

Urgent, Burt pulled up his zipper and pushed the urinal's lever. As water gushed into a drain, he threw his cigarette into the urinal and pivoted. "For your information, those important people were—" Burt noticed the two men standing at the sinks, watching him, and gestured. "Come on, let's get out of here."

Impatient, Pittman followed him out the door and along the hallway. They stopped at its end, a distance from the rest rooms and the stairs that led down.

Burt whispered hoarsely, "Those important people were the police."

"What?"

"Looking for you."

"What?"

"Haven't you listened to the radio? You didn't see the evening news?"

"I haven't had time. When I got back to my apartment, a man—"

"Look, I don't know what you did last night, but the cops think you broke into a house in Scarsdale and murdered Jonathan Millgate."

"WHAT?" Pittman stepped backward against the wall.

The man with the leather windbreaker came out of the men's room, glanced curiously at Pittman and Burt, then went up the stairs.

Frustrated, Burt waited until the man disappeared. "Look," he said quietly, sternly to Pittman, "we can't talk here. The police might be watching me in case you try to get in touch. In fact, I have a hunch one of them's at a table next to mine."

"Where then? When can we talk?"

"Meet me at eleven o'clock. Madison Square Park. The

entrance on Fifth Avenue. I'll make sure I'm not followed. Damn it, what did you get yourself into? I want to know what's going on."

"Believe me, Burt, you're not the only one."

12

Pittman was so disoriented that only when he was out on the shadowy street did he realize that he should have asked Burt to lend him some money. The Metro ride from Scarsdale into Manhattan and the taxi from his apartment to the restaurant had used all his cash. He had his checkbook, but he knew that the stores open at this hour would accept checks only for the amount of purchase. That left . . .

Pittman glanced nervously behind him, saw no sign that anyone was following him, and walked quickly toward Fifth Avenue. There, a few blocks south, he came to the main office of the bank he used. The automated teller machine was in an alcove to the left of the entrance. He put his access card into the slot and waited for a message on the ATM's screen to ask him for his number.

To his surprise, a different message appeared. SEE BANK OFFICER.

The machine made a whirring sound.

It swallowed his card.

Pittman gaped. What the . . . ? There's got to be some mistake. Why would . . . ?

The obvious dismaying answer occurred to him. The police must have gotten a court order. *They froze my account*.

Burt was right.

"Haven't you listened to the radio? You didn't see the evening news?" Burt had demanded. Pittman walked rapidly along a side street, checking several taverns, finding one that had a television behind the bar. Since the *Chronicle* and all the other New York City newspapers came out in the morning, they wouldn't have had enough time to run a story about anything that happened to Jonathan Millgate late last night.

The only ready source of news that Pittman could think of was a cable channel like CNN. He sat in a shadowy, smoke-filled corner of the tavern and in frustration watched the fourth round of a boxing match. He fidgeted, not sharing the enthusiasm of the other patrons in the bar about a sudden knockout.

Come on, he kept thinking. Somebody put on the news.

He almost risked drawing attention to himself by asking the man behind the bar to switch channels to CNN. But just as Pittman stood to approach the counter, news came on after the fight, and Pittman was stunned to see his photograph on a screen behind the reporter. The photo had been taken years earlier when Pittman had had a mustache. His features had been heavier, not yet ravaged by grief. Nonetheless, he immediately receded back into the shadows.

"Suicidal obituary writer kills ailing diplomat," the reporter intoned, obviously enjoying the lurid headline.

Feeling his extremities turn cold as blood rushed to his stomach, Pittman listened in dismay. The reporter qualified his story by frequently using the words *alleged* and *possibly*, but his tone left no doubt that Pittman was guilty. According to the Scarsdale police, in cooperation with the Manhattan homicide department, Pittman—suffering from a nervous breakdown as a consequence of his son's death—had determined to commit suicide and had gone so far as to write his own obituary. Newswriters who had desks near Pittman characterized him as being depressed and distracted. He was said to be obsessed with Jonathan Millgate, an obsession that had begun seven years earlier when Pittman had become irrationally convinced that Millgate was involved in a defense-industry scandal. Pittman had stalked Millgate so relentlessly for an interview that Millgate had considered asking the police for a restraining order. Now, in his weakened mental state, Pittman had again become fixated on Millgate, apparently enough to kill him as a prelude to Pittman's suicide. Warned of the danger, Millgate's aides had taken the precaution of moving the senior statesman from a New York hospital where he was recovering from a heart attack. Pittman had managed to follow Millgate to an estate in Scarsdale, had broken into Millgate's room, and had disconnected his life-support system, killing him. Fingerprints on the outside door to Millgate's room as well as on Millgate's medical equipment proved that Pittman had been inside. A nurse had seen him flee from the old man's bedside. A check that Pittman had given to a New York City taxi driver who drove him to the estate had made it possible for the police to narrow their investigation to Pittman as their main suspect. Pittman was still at large.

Pittman stared at the television and strained to keep from shaking. His sanity felt threatened. Despite the differences, surely everyone in the tavern must know it was *his* photograph they'd just been shown. He had to get onto the street before someone called the police.

The police. Pittman walked in alarmed confusion from the bar, keeping his head low, relieved that no one tried to stop him. Maybe I'm wrong. Maybe I ought to *go* to the police. Tell them they're mistaken. I tried to *help* Millgate, not kill him.

Sure. And what about the man you killed in your apartment? If he's still there, if his buddies haven't moved him. Do you expect the police will take your word about what happened? As soon as they get their hands on you, they'll put you in jail.

Is that so bad? At least I'll be safe. The men at my apartment won't be able to get at me.

What makes you sure? Seven years ago, two men broke your jaw while you and they were in custody in Boston. Security might fail again. And this time what happens to you could be lethal.

13

When Pittman entered the diner, he watched to see if anyone looked suspiciously toward him. No one seemed to care. Either they hadn't seen the story about him on TV or else they didn't make the connection with him. After all, no one here knew him by name, except for the cook who was usually on duty at this hour, and the cook knew Pittman only as Matt.

"How you doing, Matt?" the cook asked. "No show for several weeks, and now you're back two nights in a row. We'll get some weight back on you quick. What'll it be tonight?"

Still dismayed that the police had arranged for his bank's automated teller machine to seize his card, Pittman said, "I'm low on cash. Will you take a check for a meal?"

"You've always been good for it."

"And an extra twenty dollars?"

"Hey, you don't appreciate my cooking that much. Sorry."

"Ten dollars?"

The cook shook his head.

"Come on."

"You're really that low?"

"*Worse* than low."

"You're breaking my heart." The cook debated. "Okay. For you, I'll make an exception. But don't let this get around."

"Our secret. I appreciate this, Tony. I'm starved. Give me a salad, the meat loaf, mashed potatoes, plenty of gravy, those peas and carrots, a glass of milk, and coffee, coffee, coffee. Then we'll talk about dessert."

"Yeah, we *will* get some weight back on you. You sure that's all?"

"One thing more."

"What is it?"

"The box I gave you last night."

14

Outside the diner, Pittman sought the cover of a nearby alley. Crouching in the darkness with his back to the street, he opened the box, took out the .45 and the carton of ammunition, and placed them in his gym bag.

He heard a threatening voice behind him. "What ya got in the bag, man?"

Looking over his shoulder, Pittman saw a street kid, tall, broad shoulders, steely eyes, late teens.

"Stuff."

"*What* stuff?" The kid flashed a long-bladed knife.

"*This* stuff." Pittman aimed the .45.

The kid put the knife away. "Cool, man. Damned good stuff." He backed off, hurrying down the street.

Pittman put the gun back in the gym bag.

15

Madison Square Park was the site of Pittman's favorite Steichen photograph, an evocative early-twentieth-century depiction of the Flatiron Building, where Broadway intersects with Fifth Avenue. The photograph showed a winter scene with snow falling on horse carriages, and to the left, taking up only part of the photograph but seeming to dominate the photo as much as the Flatiron Building did, were the bare trees of Madison Square Park.

Pittman positioned himself on Fifth Avenue about where he assumed that Steichen had stood with his tripoded camera. Although it was spring and not winter, the trees were still not fully leafed, and Pittman used the night to imagine that he'd been taken back in time, that the muffled clop of horses' hooves had replaced the busy roar of traffic.

He had gotten to the park a half hour early. There'd been no other place to go. Besides, although the meal at the diner had given him back some energy, he was still tired from the exertion of the previous night and the considerable walking he'd done all day. Despite his fears, his body felt more fit than it had in over a year. His muscle aches were almost a pleasure. Even so, he had pushed his body to its limit. He needed to sit.

But not in plain view. After briefly pretending that he was Steichen, he left where he thought that the great photographer had placed his camera and retreated toward the trees, walkways, and benches of the park. At night, he became only one of the park's many indistinct visitors, most of them homeless, lounging on the benches.

He thought, and he waited.

On schedule at eleven o'clock, Burt Forsyth got out of a taxi on Fifth Avenue. As the taxi drove away, merging with the headlights of traffic, Burt paused just long enough to light a cigarette, the glow from his lighter possibly intended as a beacon, something to attract Pittman's attention and help Pittman recognize him.

Then Burt walked into the park, passing the war memorial flagpole. Obviously, Pittman thought, I'm supposed to go over to him. He doesn't know where I am.

After staring behind Burt to see if anyone was following, Pittman stood from his shadow-obscured bench.

But as he approached, Burt's expression intensified. He shook his head slightly, firmly in what seemed a warning. He gestured unobtrusively ahead and continued past Pittman.

Pittman did his best not to call out to Burt. I'm supposed to follow, is that it? In case we've got company? To be extracautious?

As casually as he could make it seem, Pittman took a path that ran parallel to the one Burt had chosen. Burt crossed the park, went up to Twenty-sixth Street, and proceeded to the right along it. Following, Pittman walked by a white marble court building, turned east onto Twenty-sixth Street, ignored the darkened expensive shops on his right, and concentrated on Burt ahead of him.

Halfway along the block, Burt abruptly stepped out of sight beneath a makeshift roof that protected the sidewalk in a construction area. When Pittman hurried to catch up to him, he saw that Burt was waiting in the shadows behind two Dumpsters and a jungle of metal scaffolds.

Pittman veered toward him.

"I don't know what to do, Burt. The television news makes me look like a maniac."

"I told you it was bad. *What happened?* How did you get into this mess?"

"I didn't kill Millgate."

"Then why were you seen running from his room?"

"There's an innocent explanation."

"Innocent? Your fingerprints are on his life-support system. What were you doing in—?"

"Burt, you have to believe me. This is all a big mistake. Whatever caused Millgate's death, I had nothing to do with it."

"Hey, *I* believe you. But I'm not the one you have to convince. How will you explain to the police about—?"

A sudden shadow made Burt turn from the scaffolding toward the sidewalk. Hearing a noise, Pittman glanced in that direction as well, seeing a man loom into view. The man was silhouetted by a streetlight, so Pittman couldn't see his face, but he could see the oversized windbreaker the man wore.

The man made a gesture, pulling something out.

No! Pittman stumbled back. Trapped, he bumped against garbage cans.

Cornered, seeing the pistol the man was aiming, Pittman had no other defense except to raise his gym bag, preparing to throw it.

When the man fired, the pistol's silencer reduced the sound of the shot so that it wasn't any louder than a fist against a pillow.

The bullet hit the gym bag, bursting through, missing Pittman as he lost his balance, falling among garbage cans, striking concrete.

The gunman came into the shadows. Pittman stared up at him in panic, expecting the next bullet to be between his eyes. But a metallic clatter startled the gunman and made him swing toward Burt, who had stumbled against a section of scaffolding. The gunman shot him in the chest.

Gasping, Burt lurched back.

By then, Pittman was frantically yanking at the zipper on his gym bag.

As the gunman returned his attention to Pittman, Burt collided against the bars of the scaffolding and rebounded off them, pawing at the air, involuntarily grabbing the first thing in front of him: the gunman. Finding Burt's arms around his shoulders, the gunman pulled them away, spun, and shot him again, this time in the face.

Pittman had the gym bag open.

The gunman pivoted toward him and raised the pistol.

Pittman gripped the .45, cocked it, and pulled the trigger. The unsilenced .45 made a roar that seemed all the worse because it contrasted with the three previous muffled shots. The roar felt like hands slamming against Pittman's ears. It echoed, amplified by the narrow confines. Pittman's ears rang as he fired and fired again.

Then he stopped.

Because he didn't have a target. The man was no longer there.

The confinement had helped Pittman's aim. The gunman was on his back, blood spewing from his chest, throat, and left eye.

Pittman retched, tasting bile. But he couldn't allow himself to give in. Burt. He had to help Burt. He scrambled toward him, felt for a pulse, but he couldn't find one. No! Burt!

Despite the torturous ringing in his ears, he suddenly heard shouting, a siren in the distance. He felt paralyzed with shock. His eyes stung as he took one last look at his friend. Then, with the siren wailing nearer, his paralysis broke. He rushed to grab the gym bag, shoved the .45 into it, and charged away from the scaffolds.

As a woman screamed on the opposite side of the street, Pittman raced east along Twenty-sixth Street in the direction of Park Avenue. God help me, he kept thinking.

But he and God weren't on the best of terms. Because God had allowed Jeremy to die. So Pittman pleaded to the only element of an afterlife of which he was certain.

Jeremy, listen carefully. Please. Son, please. You have to help your father.

16

How long do I have before the police come after me? Pittman thought.

An inward voice urged him to run, to keep running, never to stop. But another inward voice, which reminded Pittman of Jeremy, warned him that running would attract attention. Slow down. Act like nothing's wrong.

Behind him, in the distance, Pittman heard sirens. The police would find the bodies. They'd talk to the woman who had screamed when she heard the shots and saw Pittman scramble out of the construction area. They'd start searching for a man with a gym bag who'd run along Twenty-sixth Street toward Park Avenue.

Get rid of the gym bag, the inward voice said, and again Pittman thought it sounded remarkably like Jeremy.

Get rid of it? But the bag has my clothes, the gun.

Hey, what good will the clothes and the gun do you if you're in jail?

Walking, trying not to show his tension and his impulse to hurry, Pittman crossed Park Avenue. On the other side, along Twenty-sixth Street, cars and pedestrians thinned. He came to another construction area. Hearing more sirens, he glanced around him, saw no one looking in his direction, and dropped the gym bag into a Dumpster.

He turned south on Lexington Avenue. Sweating, still forcing himself to walk slowly, he skirted Gramercy Park, which was locked for the night. Continuing south, then heading west, hoping he didn't attract attention, he eventually came to Union Square Park and was struck by how much his life had changed in the six hours since he'd gotten off a subway here and had walked to his apartment.

But he couldn't go to his apartment now, that was sure, and he didn't know where else he could go. The police would be watching friends he might ask for help. Hotels would be warned to watch for anyone using his credit card. What the hell am I going to do?

17

"Hey, what's all them sirens about?" a stoop-shouldered, beard-stubbled man asked. He was slumped on a metal bench, holding what was obviously a pint of alcohol concealed in a paper bag. His overcoat had no elbows. His hair was mussed. He had two missing front teeth. Pittman had the sense that the man, who looked sixty, was possibly thirty.

"Damned if I know." Exhausted, Pittman sat next to him.

The man didn't respond for a moment. "What?"

"The sirens."

"Huh?"

"You asked about the sirens, what was causing them."

"They're disturbin' my peace 'n' quiet."

"Mine, too."

"Hey, I din't say you could sit there."

Siren wailing, dome lights flashing, a police car raced around the park and sped north on Broadway.

"Another one," the man said. "Disturbin' my . . . Damn it, you're still sittin' there." The man clutched his bottle. "My bench. I din't say you could . . ."

Another police car wailed by.

"Take it easy," Pittman said.

"Yur tryin' to steal my bench," the man said louder.

"I told you, take it easy."

"Where's a policeman?"

"I'll pay rent."

"What's 'at?"

"I'll pay rent. You're right. This is *your* bench. But I'll pay to share it with you. How does ten dollars sound?"

"Ten . . . ?"

"And I'll trade you my overcoat for yours."

The woman who had screamed when Pittman scrambled from the bodies would tell the police that the man with the gym bag had been wearing a tan overcoat. The coat that Pittman wanted to trade for was dark blue.

"Trade?"

"I want to share the bench."

The man looked suspicious. "Les see your money."

Pittman gave him the ten-dollar bill he'd gotten from the cook at the diner, the last cash he had, except for a few coins.

"And the coat."

Pittman traded with him. The man's coat stank of perspiration. Pittman set it beside him.

Switching his bottle from hand to hand, the man struggled into the coat. "Nice."

"Yep."

"Warm."

"Yep."

"My lucky day." The man squinted at Pittman, raised the bottle to his lips, upended it, drank the remainder of its contents, and dropped the bottle behind him onto the grass. "Goin' for another bottle. Guard the bench."

"It'll be here when you get back."

"Damn well better be."

The man staggered from the park, heading south on Broadway.

As another police car wailed by, Pittman slumped lower on the bench, hoping to blend with the park's other residents. The night's chill in combination with the aftermath of adrenaline made him hug himself, shivering. Urgent thoughts assaulted his mind.

Burt had said he suspected a detective was watching him from a table in the restaurant. Maybe it wasn't a detective, Pittman thought. Maybe it was the gunman, who followed Burt from the restaurant, hoping I'd be in touch with him.

But the gunman didn't need to kill Burt. Burt wasn't a threat to him. In the darkness, Burt wouldn't have been able to identify him.

Pittman felt colder. In the shadowy park, he hugged himself harder. The son of a bitch, he didn't have to kill Burt!

A movement to Pittman's right distracted him. Still slumped on the bench, he turned his head, focusing sharply on two figures moving toward him. They didn't wear uniforms. They weren't policemen, unless they were working under cover. But they didn't move with the authority of policemen. They seemed to creep.

Predators. They must have seen me give money to the guy who was on this bench. Now they want money, too.

Pittman sat up. The figures came closer.

If there's trouble, I'll attract the police.

Pittman stood to walk away, but the shambling figures reached him. He braced himself for an attack.

"Goddamn it," a slurred voice said. "Git away from him. He's mine. I foun' him. He's rentin' my bench."

The figures glared at the man in Pittman's overcoat, who was coming back with a bottle in a paper bag.

"Din't you hear me? Git." The man fumbled in his grimy pants and pulled out a church key–style bottle opener. He jabbed its point at them. "Move yur asses away from my bench. 'S mine. Mine and his."

The sullen figures hesitated, then shifted back toward the shadows from which they had risen.

"Bastards." The man slumped onto the bench. "They'da taken my bench in a minute. Gotta keep watchin'."

"That's the truth."

The man drank from his bottle. "Lie down."

"What?" Pittman asked suspiciously.

"Git some sleep. You look beat."

Pittman didn't move.

"I won't let those bastards git to you. I always stay up, guardin' my bench."

18

Pittman woke with a start. The shadows were gone. The air was pale, the sun not yet risen over the city's buildings. Traffic was sporadic.

As he became fully alert, his memories from the previous night made him flinch. He sat upright. The man to whom he'd given his trench coat was no longer on the bench.

But someone else was—a well-dressed, slender, gray-haired man who wore spectacles. Pittman had the sense that the man, who seemed to be in his fifties, had nudged his knee.

"Did you sleep well?"

Skin prickling, Pittman had no idea if this was a policeman or a pervert. He debated what to answer. "No, not really."

"That's understandable. When *I* slept on a bench like this, I always woke up with back trouble."

"When *you* did?"

"Before I reformed. You look like you're recently down on your luck. Fairly good clothes. But that overcoat. Where on earth did you get that overcoat?"

Pittman realized that the grungy blue coat was draped across his lap. The man to whom he'd given his own coat must have covered Pittman when, despite all his effort not to, he drifted off to sleep. That would have been about 3:00 A.M.

"I got it from a friend."

"Certainly. Well, no doubt you wonder what I'm doing here."

Pittman didn't respond.

"My name is Reverend Thomas Watley. I come here every morning to see if the park has any new occupants. The other residents are quite familiar with me. In fact, at the moment, they've gone to my church. Every morning at six, a free, although modest, breakfast is available. There's also a place to shower, shave, and relieve oneself. Would you care to join us?"

Pittman still didn't respond.

"I do conduct a religious service, but your attendance is not required, if that's what worries you."

Pittman kept staring.

"Well, then." The man shrugged. "I must get back to my guests." He held out his hand.

At first Pittman thought that the man wanted to shake hands, but then he realized that the man was trying to give him something.

"In case you decide not to join us, here's five dollars. I know it isn't much, but sometimes it takes only a little boost to raise a person back to where he was. Remember, whatever caused your downfall, it's not irremediable. The problem can be solved."

"Reverend, I very much doubt that," Pittman said bitterly.

"Oh?"

"Unless you can raise the dead."

"You lost your . . . ?"

"Son."

"Ah." The reverend shook his head. "You have my sincerest condolences. There is no greater burden."

"Then what makes you think my problem can be solved?"

This time, it was the reverend who didn't respond.

"Thank you for the money, Reverend. I can use it."

19

Wearing the grungy blue coat, Pittman stooped his shoulders and tried to look as defeated as he felt, making himself walk unsteadily up Lexington Avenue. The sun rose above buildings. Traffic increased. Horns blared.

Pittman wanted it to seem that he was oblivious to anything but objects along the sidewalk. Trying to appear off balance, he turned from Lexington onto Twenty-sixth Street. He stooped and pretended to pick up a coin, looked at his palm with satisfaction, then put the pretend coin into his dingy coat.

He risked a glance ahead of him and saw some slight commotion in the next block between Park Avenue and Madison, near Madison Square Park. The dome lights on a stationary police car were flashing. The bodies would have been removed by now. The investigation of the crime scene would be concluding.

Burt. Sickened by what had happened last night, Pittman continued to waver along Twenty-sixth Street. When he came to some garbage cans, he lifted their lids and snooped inside. He moved on. He came to other garbage cans and inspected them as well, ignoring the smell. Then he came to a Dumpster. Trying to look awkward, he struggled up the side of the bin, poked around in it, clutched his gym bag, lurched down, and reversed his direction, heading back toward Lexington. He was far enough away that the police would not have noticed him, especially as disheveled as he looked. After all, he thought caustically, the homeless are invisible.

20

About the only thing in his favor, Pittman decided, was that it was Saturday. The man he needed to contact would more likely be at home than at work. The trouble was that when Pittman looked in a Manhattan telephone directory, he didn't find any listing for the name of the man he was looking for: Brian Botulfson. He called information and asked an operator to see if Brian Botulfson was listed in any of the other boroughs.

In Brooklyn. The operator wouldn't give Pittman the address, though, forcing him to walk to the New York Public Library, where he looked in the directory for Brooklyn and found the address he wanted. He could have phoned Brian, but one of the things he'd learned early as a reporter was that while phone contact had the merit of efficiency, it couldn't compare to an in-person interview. The subject could get rid of you on the phone merely by hanging up, but a face-to-face meeting was often so intimidating that a subject would agree to talk.

Pittman had met Brian only a couple of times, mostly in connection with Brian's arrest for using his computer to access top secret Defense Department files. The last occasion had been seven years ago when Brian had done Pittman a favor, obtaining Jonathan Millgate's unlisted telephone numbers. Now Pittman needed another favor, but there was a chance that Brian either wouldn't remember their previous conversations or wouldn't care—at least on the phone. The contact had to be one-on-one.

Pittman dumped his grungy coat in a waste can. After using some of Reverend Watley's five dollars to buy orange juice and a Danish from a sidewalk vendor, he boarded a subway train for Brooklyn, took his electric razor from his gym bag, made himself look as presentable as he could, stared out the window, and brooded.

21

The last time Pittman had seen him, Brian Botulfson lived in a run-down apartment building on the Lower East Side. Surrounded by expensive computer components that hid the cockroaches on the dingy walls, Botulfson had obviously enjoyed the glamorized image of an impoverished student. But now his apartment building was quite respectable—clean, made of brick, with large, glinting windows, in an attractive neighborhood, the Park Slope section of Brooklyn.

Pittman nodded to a man coming out of the well-maintained building. Then he climbed steps, paused in the vestibule, studied the names on the buzzer directory, and pressed the button for 4 B.

When he didn't get an answer, he pressed again.

One-on-one contact? Great. But what if nobody's home? Damn it, I came all this way for nothing.

He was about to press the button a third time when a nasally male voice spoke from the tinny microphone. "Yes? Who is it?"

"Brian?" Pittman asked. "Is that you?"

"Who am I talking to?"

"Matt Pittman. Do you remember me, Brian? When you

had that trouble about hacking some years ago, I did a couple of stories about you in the *Chronicle*."

The intercom became silent.

"Brian?"

"What do you want?"

"To talk, Brian." Pittman liked to use a person's first name as often as seemed natural. It established a bond. "Quite a while since we saw each other. I thought I'd catch up, find out what you've been doing."

The intercom became silent again.

"I need to talk to you about something, Brian."

"What is it?"

"I feel a little awkward down here, with my face against this intercom. Unlock the door, will you, Brian? I'd like to come up."

A further silence.

"Brian?"

To Pittman's relief, he heard a buzzer at the side of the door electronically freeing its lock.

He quickly turned the knob, pushed the glass-paneled door open, and entered the building's recently painted, fresh-smelling, white lobby. The comparison between this and Pittman's own dingy apartment building was striking. Brian must have a job that paid well, Pittman decided.

An elevator took him to the fourth floor, where he went to 4 B, heard a child crying beyond it, and knocked. Even though Brian was now expecting him, ten seconds elapsed before the door was opened.

Pittman was surprised by Brian's appearance. Seven years ago, Brian had preferred sneakers, torn sweatshirts, and jeans with the knees ripped out. He'd had two shark's-tooth earrings. His scraggly hair had hung down over his shoulders. All in all, he'd looked more like a candidate for a heavy-metal rock group than the computer fanatic he actually was.

Now he wore black Bass loafers, gray slacks, and a blue button-down oxford-cloth shirt. The earrings were gone, as were the holes through which the jewelry had been attached. His brown hair was cut so short that it didn't touch his ears. He had wide-rimmed bifocal glasses. His very conventional appearance drew attention to his short, slight stature and his weak chin, which a thin mustache did nothing to hide.

"What do you want?" Brian blocked the doorway.

Pittman glanced past him and saw an infant in a high chair at a kitchen table.

"Is that your child, Brian? Things certainly have been happening. You've got to fill me in."

Pittman made a move to enter, but Brian didn't budge.

"What do you want?" Brian repeated.

"Brian, this isn't very sociable of you. I come all this way to see you, and you don't even want to catch up on old times."

In addition to the cries from the infant, Pittman heard an announcer.

"Watching TV while you feed your baby?"

"The news." Brian's expression was sober. "CNN."

"Ah."

Brian's expression becamc even more solemn.

So he knows, Pittman thought. "Anything interesting? Seems to me I heard something about Jonathan Millgate. That reminds me of seven years ago when you helped me get his unlisted telephone numbers."

Brian's eyes narrowed. Inwardly he seemed to flinch. "What do you want?" he asked a third time.

"A favor."

"Why?"

"Isn't it obvious? Why does anybody ask a favor? I need help."

"That's not what I meant. Why should I do you a favor?"

"That's a tough one, Brian. I guess because you're a human being. Incidentally, your child's starting to climb out of that high chair."

Brian swung, saw that the baby was in danger of falling, and hurried to grab it. The baby cried harder.

Pittman stepped in and shut the door. "Boy or girl?"

"Hey, I didn't say you could—"

"What have you got there? A jar of apricot baby food? Let me help feed . . . Boy or girl?"

"Boy. But I didn't say you—"

"How old?"

"Almost a year. But—"

"Wonderful-looking boy. What's his name?"

"Daniel. Now, look, I—"

"Brian, I'm in trouble, okay? From the expression in your eyes, I think you know I'm in trouble. I think you just heard something about it on CNN. I bet you said to yourself, 'No, that can't be the same guy who interviewed me. It can't be the same guy I did a favor for and got him Jonathan Millgate's unlisted telephone numbers. Matthew Pittman. Yeah, that was his name.' And then all of a sudden, here I am knocking on your door. A lot to adjust to, isn't it?"

Brian held the baby and looked nervous.

"Are you married, Brian? Where's your—?"

"She's gone for groceries."

"Well, I look forward to meeting her." Pittman set down his gym bag. "I wasn't kidding. Let me help feed your son."

Holding the baby, Brian stepped slightly backward.

"Brian, I think you misunderstand. I'm not here to make trouble. All I need is a small favor, and then I'm out of here."

Suspicion fought with hope. "Do what?"

"Nice apartment. Love the plants. Clean. Roomy." Pittman opened a door and found what was obviously Brian's workroom. "Ah. I see you still keep up your interest in computers."

"I'm a programmer for Nintendo."

"And how about hacking, Brian? Do you still do any of that?"

"That was years ago. Since I met Gladys, I . . . Wait a minute. You're asking me to . . ."

"And then I'm gone."

Brian's cheeks quivered with tension. "Nintendo would fire me if they found out I was hacking. Gladys would have my nuts."

"They wouldn't know. All I need is one piece of information, Brian. Then I promise I'm out of here. With luck, before Gladys gets back."

The baby squirmed. Brian eased him into the high chair. When he tried to spoon some of the pureed apricots into his mouth, the baby knocked the spoon and sprayed apricots onto Brian's clean shirt.

"Here, I was always good at this." Pittman made a face at the baby and immediately got its attention. He crouched so that his eyes were even with the baby's. He leaned forward so that his nose touched the baby's, but he kept his eyes open, noticing that the baby did the same. He pulled back and opened his mouth.

The baby opened his mouth.

He spooned the apricots into his mouth.

"How the hell did you do that?" Brian asked. "Strangers always make him cry, but you . . ."

"I had lots of practice." The baby reminded Pittman of how Jeremy had looked as a child. He suddenly felt melancholy.

"They say you killed him," Brian said.

"Millgate? No. That isn't true."

"And a man in your apartment, and your boss at the paper."

"The man in my apartment pulled a gun on me. We scuffled. He fell and broke his neck. As for my boss . . ." Pittman hesitated, his throat tight with grief. "No, I didn't do anything to Burt. It was someone else."

"And they say you're hysterical, out of control. That you're planning to kill yourself and you don't care who you take with you."

"No. That isn't true either, Brian." Depression overwhelmed him. "I don't want anybody to get hurt."

"Then you're not suicidal?"

Pittman looked at the baby.

"Well?" Brian asked.

"That's about the only thing that *is* true."

The kitchen became silent, even the baby.

"They say your son died."

Pittman swallowed and avoided the issue. "I really need this favor, Brian. I'm in a lot of trouble that I don't deserve, and I want to set it right."

"Why? I don't see why it should matter if you're planning to kill yourself."

"Yes. I've been asking myself that a lot. . . . I think"—he swallowed again—"it's because all along I planned to go out cleanly. But suddenly everything has gotten very messy."

Feeling pressure in his throat, Pittman spooned more apricots into the baby's mouth.

Brian stared at him. "What the hell happened?"

Pittman frowned toward the floor. Then he told Brian everything.

22

Brian kept shaking his head, alternately bewildered and dismayed. "This is . . ."

"I swear to you, it's the truth."

"Look, you can't do anything about this on your own. You have to go to the police. Tell them what you just told me."

"If you have trouble believing me, would *they*?"

"But you don't have a choice."

"No. I don't think the police could keep me safe."

"Man, oh man, do you realize what you sound like?"

"Who was it said that paranoia was the only sane attitude to have these days?"

Brian looked appalled. "And you expect me to . . ."

"Get me into some computer files that I otherwise wouldn't have access to."

"Like?"

"At my newspaper. I have to show ID and sign in to enter the building. A guard or someone else would recognize me. They'd call the police. But I know the passwords that allow access from an outside telephone."

Brian looked somewhat less threatened. "That's not hard to do. In fact, it's almost a legitimate request. Under other circumstances, it would be legal."

"Yes." Pittman had fed the baby and now was changing its diaper.

"And that's all?"

"Well . . ."

"There's something else?"

"I need to get into the computer system for the city's criminal records."

"Jesus."

"Isn't there a way to route the call through a system of long-distance relays so the call can't be traced before I get the information I need?"

"Yes, but . . ."

Pittman turned as someone opened the door.

The woman—a redhead, severely thin, with stern features—looked alarmed at the sight of Pittman holding the baby. "What are . . . ?"

"Gladys, this is a friend of mine," Brian said.

"Ed Garner," Pittman said, hoping that if he used a different name, she wouldn't associate him with the photographs of him on CNN or in the newspapers.

Gladys marched to a kitchen counter, set down two bags of groceries, and took possession of her baby. Her pinched expression suggested that she felt Pittman wasn't worthy enough to have touched her offspring. "Ed Garner?" She squinted at Brian. "You never mentioned him before."

"Well, I . . ."

"We were buddies in college," Pittman said. "We loved to fool around with computers."

"Computers? You weren't a hacker, I hope." Her voice had the grating sound of a knife being sharpened.

"Never had the nerve."

"Brian had *too much* nerve. He went to prison for it." Her eyes glared.

"Anyway," Pittman said, trying to change the subject, "I heard Brian was living in this area. I've got relatives not far from here, so I figured I'd drop in. Brian was just about to show me some of the stuff he's doing for Nintendo."

Wrinkles developed between Gladys's eyes.

"Weren't you, Brian?" Pittman said.

"If that's all right, Gladys. You can see the baby's been fed and changed."

Gladys narrowed her steely gaze at him. "Just remember, we have to be at my mother's in an hour."

"I couldn't possibly forget."

Brian and Pittman went into the computer room. Brian shut the door. He looked angrily at Pittman.

Pittman worried that the anger was directed at him, then understood its true target.

He had an ally.

23

Furious, Brian turned on the computer, then locked a phone into a modem. His cheeks were flushed. "Which system do you want to access first? Your newspaper's?"

"Criminal records."

Brian didn't react to the change in priorities. Instead, he touched buttons on his telephone.

"You know the criminal-records number by heart?" Pittman asked in amazement.

"No. This is a friend of mine. I don't hack anymore, but I keep in touch with friends who do. This guy's obsessed about eavesdropping on the police. And he never talks on the phone. I always have to go through his computer."

Words appeared on Brian's computer screen.

YOU HAVE REACHED THE STARSHIP *ENTERPRISE*.

"He's also crazy about *Star Trek*." Brian tapped letters on his keyboard.

MR. SPOCK TO CAPTAIN KIRK.

"Spock's my code name," Brian said.

Words appeared in response.

KIRK HERE. WHAT IS YOUR PASSWORD?

Brian typed more letters.

TRIBBLES.

New words appeared on the screen.

PROCEED, MR. SPOCK.

Brian typed:

TOP SECRET MESSAGE FROM STARFLEET COMMAND.
FEAR THAT KLINGONS MAY TRY TO INTERCEPT
TRANSMISSION.

The response came quickly.

ACTIVATE SCRAMBLER.

Brian turned on a machine next to the phone.

SCRAMBLER ACTIVATED.

For the next few minutes, Pittman watched with fascination as Brian tapped his keyboard, read and responded to queries on his screen, and finally wrote down a series of numbers.

"Got it."

MAY YOU PROSPER. SPOCK TO KIRK. OUT.

Brian pressed other numbers on his telephone. "I'm routing this through Fairbanks, Alaska, and Key West, Florida. Even then, the call can be traced. If the criminal-records computer senses an intrusion, I'll have to unplug right away."

"How will you know?"

"That'll tell me." Brian pointed to another machine beside the telephone.

He pressed more numbers and nodded toward the screen. "Okay, we're in. What do you want to know?"

"Access the file for Sean O'Reilly." Pittman spelled the name.

O'Reilly had been the master thief whom Pittman had interviewed some years ago. The tool knife with its lock picks that Pittman had used to get into Jonathan Millgate's room had been a gift from O'Reilly.

"There," Brian said.

Pittman read the screen. Earlier, when he had tried to find Brian's name in the phone book, he had also looked for O'Reillys, with no success. Either O'Reilly was back in prison, had moved to another area, or . . .

"Yes." Pittman picked up a pencil and notepad.

According to O'Reilly's file, he'd been released from prison three months previously—on parole—which meant that he was required to keep the authorities informed about where he was staying.

The address was on the Lower East Side. Pittman quickly wrote it down, tore off the piece of paper, and put it into his pocket.

"Now what other computer files do you want?" Brian asked.

"*I thought so,*" a steely voice said behind them.

Pittman and Brian spun toward the noise.

Gladys must have been listening at the door. She had thrown it open.

She stormed in. "I can't leave you alone for a minute. You can't stay out of trouble."

"Trouble?"

"You *are* hacking. What's the matter with you? Do you like prison so much that you want to go back there?"

"You're mistaken," Pittman said. "I was showing Brian some work I've been doing."

"Get out of my house."

"We accessed my files at—"

"Don't lie to me. Your name isn't Ed Garner. It's Matthew Pittman. CNN just did a story on you. I recognized your picture." Gladys yanked the phone from the modem. "I'm calling the police."

As words vanished from the screen, she raised the phone to her ear and pressed 911.

"Gladys," Brian objected.

From another room, the baby started crying.

"Please," Pittman said.

Gladys spoke to the phone, "My name is Gladys Botulfson. I live at—"

Pittman pressed the disconnect button. "You're doing something stupid, Gladys."

"I don't want any killer near my baby."

"You don't understand."

They stared at each other.

The phone began to ring.

Gladys flinched.

"That'll be the police," Pittman said. "They have an automatic record of the phone number of anyone who calls them."

Gladys tried to pry his hand from the disconnect button.

Pittman used his other hand to grip her wrist. "Don't do it. Think. How would you like your baby's father to go to prison again."

"What?"

The phone kept ringing.

"Aiding a fugitive," Pittman said. "Helping him illegally access computer files. Brian could be put away until your baby starts high school."

Gladys's eyes bulged.

The phone rang again.

Pittman took the receiver away from her and lifted the disconnect button. "Hello? . . . Yes, Gladys Botulfson lives here. . . . I know she called. We were having a bit of a quarrel, I'm afraid. She . . . Here. Let me put her on."

Pittman stared at her, then handed her the phone.

Gladys squinted toward the wailing baby, then toward Brian, finally toward Pittman. Her lips were so pursed that the skin around them was white.

She parted them. "This is Gladys Botulfson," she said to the phone. "I'm sorry for troubling you. What my husband says is true. We were having a fight. I thought I'd scare him if I called the police. . . . Yes, I understand it's a serious offense to abuse the emergency number. It won't happen again. . . . We're calmer now. No, I don't need any help. Thank you."

Gladys set down the phone. She rubbed her wrist where Pittman had gripped it. Her voice was disturbingly flat. "Get out."

Pittman picked up his gym bag. "Brian, thanks for letting me get into the newspaper's computer files." His look toward Brian was direct and meaningful: Don't let her know what files we really accessed.

"Sure."

"I won't tell you again," Gladys said.

"A pleasure to meet you."

Pittman left the apartment and shut the door behind him. When he got in the elevator, he could still hear Gladys's loud, accusing voice from behind Brian's door.

24

Pittman had hoped to borrow money from Brian, but that had obviously been out of the question. With a dollar bill, a dime, and a nickel in his pocket, he proceeded dismally toward where he could catch the train back to Manhattan, although he didn't know why, since he didn't have enough cash to buy a token. The more he walked, the more tired and hungry he became. He felt defeated.

Ahead, cars at a funeral home caused him to suffer the depressing memory of Jeremy's funeral—the closed coffin, Jeremy's photograph in front of it; the mourners, most of them classmates from Jeremy's school; Burt next to Pittman (and now Burt was dead); Pittman's argument with his soon-to-be ex-wife. ("It's your fault," she'd insisted. "You should have taken him to the doctor sooner.")

Pittman recalled how, after the funeral, there'd been a somber reception back at the mortician's, coffee and sandwiches, final commiserations. But Pittman had been so choked with grief that he hadn't been able to force himself to respond to the condolences. He had taken a sandwich that someone had given him, but the rye bread and paperlike sliced turkey had stuck in his throat. He'd felt surrounded by a gray haze of depression.

A similar gray haze weighed upon him now. Instinctive fear had propelled him into motion. Adrenaline had fueled him. The strength and endurance that adrenaline created had finally dwindled, however. In their place were lethargy and despair. Pittman didn't know if he could go on.

He told himself that he'd been foolish to believe that he could disentangle himself from the mess that he had fallen into.

Perhaps I *should* go to the police. Let *them* try to figure things out.

And if someone gets through police security to kill you?

What difference does it make? I'm too tired to care.

You don't mean that.

Don't I? Death would be welcome.

No. You've got to keep trying, a voice inside him said. It sounded like Jeremy.

How? I don't even have enough money to take the train back to Manhattan.

Come on, Dad. All those years of running. Don't tell me you don't have what it takes to do a little more walking.

25

It took three hours. Even though Pittman had switched from his street shoes to the jogging shoes that he'd put in his gym bag, his feet ached and his leg muscles protested. Weak from exertion and hunger, he reached Grand Street on Manhattan's Lower East Side, looking for the address that he'd gotten from Sean O'Reilly's computer file.

He studied the busy street, wary of police surveillance. After all, Gladys Botulfson might have changed her mind. If Brian had said something to infuriate her further, she might have decided to call the police and teach her husband a lesson. Of course, the police wouldn't know where Pittman had gone unless Brian confessed which file he had accessed. But would he? Or would Brian's anger toward Gladys prompt him to defy her?

That wasn't the only thing that bothered him. What if the address Sean O'Reilly had given the authorities was out of date or else a lie? Suppose he wasn't there?

The latter worry intensified when Pittman finally reached the address and discovered that it wasn't an apartment building but a restaurant instead, a sign in the front window announcing PADDY'S.

Shit. *Now* what am I supposed to do?

Needing to get off the street, he did his best to hide his nervousness when, unable to think of an alternative, he entered the restaurant.

He barely noticed its Irish decor—green tablecloths, shamrocks on the menus, a large map of Ireland on one wall. What he did notice was the handful of late-afternoon customers, most of them at the bar.

A few looked in his direction, then returned their attention to their drinks.

Pittman approached the barman, who was muscular, wore a green apron, and stood behind the cash register.

"What'll it be?"

"I'm looking for a friend of mine. Sean O'Reilly."

The barman used a towel to wipe the counter.

"I heard he was staying at this address," Pittman said, "but this is a restaurant. I don't see . . ."

"How?"

"What?"

"How did you get this address?"

"My parole officer's the same as his. Look, is Sean around?"

The man kept wiping the counter.

"Sean and I go back to when he was doing those public-service announcements for the police department," Pittman said. "When he was telling people how to keep their homes safe from burglars."

"So? What do you want him for?"

"Old times. I've got some stories to tell him." Pittman drew his key chain from his pocket and held up the tool knife. "About this."

The bartender watched Pittman remove the lock-pick tools from the end of the knife.

The bartender relaxed. "You've got one of those, too?"

He smiled and pulled out a set of keys, showing his own knife. "Sean only gave these to guys he likes. Yeah, Sean stays here. In a room upstairs. At night, he subs for me."

"But is he around?"

"Ought to be waking up around now. He sure was drunk last night."

A half dozen people came into the restaurant.

"Looks like we're getting busy." The bartender poured tomato juice into a glass, added Tabasco sauce, and dropped in a raw egg. "Stairs through the door in back. Second floor. The room at the end of the hall. He'll be needing this."

26

In a musty upstairs hallway that smelled of cabbage, Pittman knocked on the door. When he didn't get an answer, he knocked again. This time, he heard a groan. His third knock caused a louder groan. He tried the door. It wasn't locked. Pushing it open, he found a sparse room with its shades closed, its lights off, and Sean O'Reilly sprawled on the floor.

"The light, the light," Sean groaned.

Pittman thought that the dim light from the hallway must be hurting Sean's eyes. He quickly shut the door. In darkness, he listened to Sean keep moaning, "The light, the light."

"There isn't any," Pittman said.

"I've gone blind. Can't see anything. The light, the light."

"You mean you want me to turn the lights *on*?"

"Blind. Gone blind."

Pittman groped along the wall, found a light switch, and flicked it. The unshielded yellow light that dangled from the ceiling gleamed and made Sean start thrashing while he pawed at his face.

He wailed, "Blind. You're trying to make me blind."

Oh, for God's sake, Pittman thought. He knelt and pulled one of Sean's hands away from his face, exposing his left eye, which was very bloodshot. "Here. Drink this."

"What?"

"Something the bartender sent up."

Sean clutched the glass and took several swallows, then suddenly made a gagging sound. "What is it? Jesus, Mary, and Joseph, there's no vodka in this."

"Sit up. Drink more of this."

After a struggle, Pittman managed to make Sean empty the glass.

Sean squirmed so that his back was against the side of the bed and scowled. His short stature still reminded Pittman of a jockey. He was as thin as ever. But alcohol had aged him, putting gray in his hair and ravaging his face. "Who are you?"

"A friend."

"Can't remember."

"That's because you need something to eat."

"Couldn't keep it down."

Pittman picked up the phone. "Order something, anyhow."

27

The corned-beef sandwich and dill pickle that the bartender carried up were delicious. Pittman tried to savor them, but his hunger couldn't be controlled. He hadn't eaten anything since the orange juice and Danish this morning. Taking huge bites, he gulped the food down. His empty plate depressed him.

From the bed, Sean looked horrified at Pittman's appetite. "I think I'm going to throw up."

When Sean came back, Pittman had finished the sandwich that the bartender had carried up for Sean.

Sean sat on the bed, scowled at Pittman, and shook his head. "I still don't remember."

"You gave me a crash course on how to break into houses."

"Doesn't ring a bell."

"You said I was a natural."

"Still doesn't ring a . . . Wait a minute. Weren't you a reporter?"

Pittman nodded.

"I gave you . . ."

Pittman held up the tool knife.

"Sure, that's who you are."

"But I've graduated," Pittman said.

"What do you mean?"

Pittman reached inside his gym bag, took out a newspaper that he'd bought on the way to the restaurant, and tossed it over to Sean. "The story under that colorful headline. 'Suicidal Obit Writer on Killing Rampage.' There's an 'alleged' in there someplace, but it doesn't feel sincere."

With a frown, Sean read the article. From time to time, he paused, looked at Pittman, deepened the furrows in his brow, and went back to reading the story.

Finally he set down the newspaper. "It makes you sound very busy."

"Yeah, all that killing. It's almost more work than one man can handle."

"Do I need to be afraid of you?"

"Let's put it this way. Have I done anything to hurt you so far?"

"Then you didn't do what the paper says?"

Pittman shook his head.

"Why did you come here?"

"Because of all the criminals I've met, you're the only one I trust."

"What do you want?"

The phone rang.

Sean picked it up. "Hello?" He listened intensely, then straightened in alarm. "*The police are coming up?* Jesus, they must have found out about the washing machines."

Pittman didn't understand what Sean was talking about.

Sean scrambled toward the window, jerked the curtains apart, yanked the window up, and scurried out onto a fire escape.

Pittman heard heavy footsteps on the other side of the door. He lunged to lock it.

Fists pounded on it.

He grabbed his gym bag and darted toward the open window. Banging his shoulder as he squirmed out onto the fire escape, he cursed and stared below toward where he assumed Sean would be scurrying down the metal stairs. Instead, what he saw were two policemen who stared up, shouted, and pointed.

Footsteps clattered above him. Twisting, craning his neck, he saw Sean rapidly climbing stairs toward the roof. Pittman got to his feet and charged up after him.

"Stop!" he heard a policeman yell from the alley below.

Pittman kept racing upward.

"Stop!" the policeman yelled.

Pittman climbed harder.

"STOP!"

They'll shoot, Pittman thought. But he didn't obey. He reached the top, leapt over a guardrail, and scanned the rooftop for Sean. There! The roofs of all the buildings on this block were connected, and Sean was sprinting past ventilation pipes and skylights toward a door on a roof near the end of the block, his short legs moving in a blur.

"Wait, Sean!"

Pittman raced after him. Behind him, he heard shoes scraping on the fire escape.

Sean reached the door, tugged at it, and cursed when he discovered it was locked.

He was banging his shoulder against it, cursing again, when Pittman caught up to him. "Damn it, I left my keys in my room. I don't have my knife."

"Here." Breathing heavily, Pittman pulled out the knife Sean had given him several years earlier.

With a smile, then a desperate look beyond Pittman toward two policemen who had just climbed onto the roof, Sean yanked the lock-pick tools from the knife, twisted and poked, freed the lock with astonishing speed, and jerked the door open.

As a policeman yelled, Sean and Pittman darted through the doorway. At once, in the dim light of a stairwell, Sean locked the door behind them.

"The washing machines. They know about the washing machines," Sean blurted to himself. "Who the hell told them about the washing machines?"

Fists pounded on the door.

Sean raced down the stairs. Pittman followed.

"Who told them about the washing machines?" Sean kept muttering.

Or are they after me? Pittman wondered.

28

"Don't look behind you. Just keep walking toward the corner."

They rounded it.

"So far so good," Sean said.

He hailed a taxi.

"Don't let the driver think you're in a rush," he told Pittman.

They got in.

"Lower Broadway," Sean told the driver, then started humming.

29

"Here's your knife back."

"Thanks. I'm sorry I couldn't help pay for the taxi."

"Hey, I'm not in jail. That's payment enough."

They were in a loft on lower Broadway. The loft, which seemed to have once been a warehouse, had almost no furnishings, and those were grouped closely together in the middle of what felt like a cavern. Although sparse, the furnishings were expensive—an Italian-made leather sofa, a large Oriental rug, a brass coffee table and matching lamp. Otherwise, in the shadows beyond the pale light from the lamp, there were crates stacked upon crates in every direction.

Sean slumped on the sofa and sipped from a Budweiser that he'd taken from a refrigerator next to some of the crates.

"What is this place?" Pittman asked.

"A little hideaway of mine. You still haven't told me what you want."

"Help."

"How?"

"I've never been on the run before."

"You're telling me you want advice?"

"Last night I slept in a park. It's been two days since I

bathed. I've been scrounging food. I can see how criminals on the run get caught. They finally just get worn down."

"Then I take it you were smart enough not to try to get in touch with your family and friends."

"My only excuse for a family is my ex-wife, and I wouldn't ask her for anything," Pittman said. "As for my friends, well, I have to assume the police will be watching them in case I show up."

"So you came to me."

"I kept asking myself who I knew to get help from but who the police wouldn't know about. Then it occurred to me—all the people I interviewed over the years. Some of them have the kind of expertise I need, and the police would never think I'd go to them."

Sean nodded in approval of Pittman's reasoning. "But I don't know what advice I can give you. There's a bathroom and a shower in back. You can spend the night here. For sure, *I* am. Other than that . . ."

"There has to be something you can tell me."

"If they catch you, you've already got a brilliant defense."

"Oh? What's that?"

"Insanity," Sean said.

"*What?*"

"All that business about your being suicidal. I assume that's another exaggeration."

Pittman didn't respond.

"You mean it's true?" Sean asked in surprise.

Pittman stared at his Coke can.

"Your son died," Sean said, "and you fell apart."

"That's right."

"My sister died when I was twenty-five. She was a year younger than me. Car accident," Sean said.

"And?"

"I nearly drank myself to death. God, I loved her."

"Then you understand," Pittman said.

"Yes. But it's a little different now, isn't it?"

"How do you mean?"

"When you're tired and hungry and scared."

"I feel like I'm being selfish. My son was wonderful. And here I'm thinking about myself."

"I don't presume to tell you how to grieve. But I will tell you this—you can't go wrong if you do what your son would have wanted you to do. And right now, he'd have been telling you to look out for your ass."

30

The shower was primitive, just a nozzle over a plastic stall with a drain in the concrete floor. There wasn't any soap, shampoo, or a towel. Pittman was pleased that he'd had the foresight to put a toilet kit in his gym bag. He found two steel chairs that he put near the shower's entrance, draping his sport coat over one, his slacks over the other. There wasn't any door to the shower, and after he came out to dry himself with his dirty shirt, he discovered that, as he had hoped, the steam from the shower had taken some of the wrinkles out of his jacket and pants. He put on fresh underwear and socks, decided to save his remaining clean shirt by putting on his black cotton sweat suit, and returned to Sean among the crates.

Sean had opened a cabinet, revealing a television, and was watching CNN. "They sure like you."

"Yeah, pretty soon I'll have my own series."

"Well," Sean said, opening another beer. "From the newspaper and now this, I have a pretty good idea of their side. What's yours?" He put his feet on the coffee table.

For the second time that day, Pittman explained.

Sean listened intently, on occasion asked a question, and tapped his fingers together when Pittman finished. "Congratulations."

"Why?"

"I've been a thief since I was twelve. I've spent half my life in prison. I've had to go underground three times because of a misunderstanding with the mob. I've been married to four women, two of them simultaneously. But I have never ever had the distinction of being in as much trouble as you are. And all this happened since two nights ago?"

"Yes."

"Worthy of the *Guinness Book of World Records*."

"At least *you're* amused. I can see I made a mistake coming to you."

"Not so fast. Who sent the gunman to your apartment?"

"I have no idea."

"Why would someone want to make it seem that you killed Millgate?"

"I have no—"

"Damn it, don't you think you'd better *start* having some ideas? As near as I can tell, from the moment you killed that man in your apartment—"

"Accidentally."

"I'm sure that makes a difference to him. . . . Ever since then, you've been running."

"What else was I supposed to do?"

"You wasted time going to this computer expert. Why was it a waste of time? Because your only purpose was to find a way to get in touch with me. Why? Because you want advice on how to keep running. Sorry."

"What?"

"In the first place, you don't need that kind of advice. You've been doing damned well on your own. In the second place, if all you do is keep running, the only thing you'll accomplish is to get tired. Then you'll make a mistake, and they'll grab you."

"But there's no alternative."

"Isn't there? Reverse direction. Hunt instead of being hunted. God knows, you've got plenty of targets."

"Hunt? That's easy enough for you to say."

"Well, I didn't expect you to leap for joy at my advice. From what you've told me, it seems to me that you've been running away since your son died. Running from everything."

The suggestion that Pittman was a coward made his face became hot with anger. He wanted to get his hands on Sean and punch the shit out of him.

"Touched a nerve, did I?"

Pittman inhaled, straining to calm himself.

"I guess you don't like the advice I'm giving you," Sean said. "But it's the only advice I've got. I'm an expert. I've been running from things all my life. Do what I say, not what I do."

Pittman stared, then parted his lips in a bitter smile.

"What's funny?" Sean asked.

"All this talk about running. For twenty years, I ran every day. All that time. Where was I going?"

"To the finish line, pal. And if you're still thinking about killing yourself, if I were you I'd want to go out a winner, not a loser. You can destroy yourself—that's your business. But don't let the bastards do it for you."

Pittman felt his face get hot again. But this time it wasn't because he was angry at Sean. Instead, his fury was directed elsewhere. "Bastards. Yes."

For a moment, he didn't move or speak, didn't breathe. His powerful emotion held him in stasis. Then he squinted at Sean. "When my son died . . ." he began to say, then hesitated.

Sean studied him, obviously curious about what Pittman intended to say.

"When my son died, I can't describe how angry I was—at the hospital, at his doctors. Jeremy's death wasn't their fault. It's just that I desperately needed somebody to be angry at. If somebody had made a mistake, then in a bizarre way Jeremy's death would have made sense. Medical carelessness. The alternative is to accept that Jeremy died because of a cosmic crapshoot, that he was unlucky, that he just happened to get a type of rare, untreatable cancer. That kind of thinking—there's no pattern or point; the universe is arbitrary—can drive a person crazy. When I finally accepted that Jeremy's doctors weren't to blame, I still needed someone to be angry at. So I chose God. I screamed at God. I hated Him. But eventually I realized that wasn't doing any good, either. Because God wouldn't scream back. How could I possibly hurt Him? What good is it to be angry if you can't punish what you're angry at? My anger was useless. It wasn't going to bring Jeremy back. That's when I decided to kill myself."

The reference caused Sean's gaze to narrow, his expression somber.

"Anger." Pittman's jaw muscles hardened. "When I was with Millgate, he said something to me. A name. At least it sounded like a name. 'Duncan.' Millgate said that several times. Then something about snow. Then a while later, he said, 'Grollier.' I didn't know what he meant, and I was too damned busy to ask him. All I wanted was to put Millgate's oxygen prongs back into his nostrils and get out of there. But the gunman who was waiting for me at my apartment sure thought it was important to find out if I'd repeated to anyone what Millgate had said to me. Anger."

Pittman stood. "Stop running away? Hunt them? *Yes*. When Jeremy died, my anger was useless. But this time, it won't be. This time, I've got a purpose. This time, I intend to find someone to blame."

THREE

1

Pittman stood across from the Emergency entrance to the hospital. It was shortly after midnight, and the same as two nights earlier, a drizzle created a misty halo around streetlights. His mind continued to reel from the trauma that so much had happened to him in the brief time since he had last been here. Chilled by the rain, he shoved his hands into the pockets of a wool-lined navy Burberry overcoat that Sean had pulled from a crate. In his right pocket, he touched the .45. It was the only thing that he had taken from the gym bag, which he'd left with Sean at the loft. He peered up toward the pale light in the tenth-floor window of what had once been Jeremy's room. Determination overcame his weariness. Necessity insisted. There were so many things he needed to learn, and one of them was why Millgate's people had taken the old man from the hospital that night. That was when everything had started. After waiting for a gap in traffic, Pittman crossed toward the hospital.

At this late hour, the front lobby was almost deserted. The few people who were slumped in the imitation leather chairs in the lobby seemed to pay no attention as he headed toward the elevators. Nonetheless, he felt exposed.

His nerves troubled him for another reason, for he knew

the memories he would have to fight when he got off the elevator near the intensive-care ward on the sixth floor. He tried not to falter when he glanced toward the large area on his left, the intensive-care waiting room. A group of haunted-looking men and women sat on uncomfortable metal chairs, their faces haggard, their eyes puffy, struggling to remain awake, waiting for news about their loved ones.

Grimly recalling when he had been one of them, Pittman forced himself to concentrate on his purpose. Past the entrance to the children's intensive-care ward, he turned to the right and went down a short corridor to the door for adult intensive care. He had never been in that area, but he assumed that it wouldn't be much different from the children's area.

Indeed, it was virtually identical. After pulling the door open, he faced a pungent-smelling, brightly lit ten-foot-long hallway, at the end of which was a counter on the left and glass cabinets behind it. The counter was covered with reports, the cabinets filled with equipment and medicines. Amid the hiss, wheeze, beep, and thump of life-support systems, doctors and nurses moved purposefully in and out of rooms on the right and beyond the counter, fifteen rooms all told, in each of which a patient lay in urgent need.

Pittman knew the required procedures. Automatically he turned toward a sink on the left of the door, put his hands under a dispenser of disinfectant, and waited while an electronic eye triggered the release of an acrid-smelling red fluid. He swabbed his hands thoroughly, then put them beneath the tap, where another electronic eye triggered the release of water. A third electronic eye activated the hot-air dispenser that dried his hands. He reached for a white gown from a stack near the sink when a woman's grating voice stopped him. *"May I help you? What are you doing here?"*

Pittman looked. A heavyset woman was marching down the hallway toward him. She was in her middle forties, had short gray hair that emphasized her strong Scandinavian features, and wore white shoes, white pants, and a white hospital top.

Pittman couldn't tell if she was a doctor or a nurse. But he understood hospital mentality. If this woman was a nurse, she wouldn't mind being called a doctor. She would correct him, of course, but she wouldn't mind the error. On the other hand, if she was a doctor, she'd be furious to be called a nurse.

"Yes, Doctor, I'm with the team investigating Jonathan Millgate's death." Pittman opened a flip-down wallet and flashed fake police ID that Sean O'Reilly had given him.

The woman barely looked at the ID. "Again? You people were here last night, asking questions, interrupting our schedule."

Pittman noticed that the woman hadn't corrected him when he addressed her as doctor. "I apologize, Doctor. But we have some important new information we have to check. I need to speak with the nurse who was in charge of Mr. Millgate's care at the time he was taken from the hospital."

Pittman tried not to show his tension. Pressured by time, he couldn't be sure that Millgate's nurse would be working this weekend. What he was counting on was that in a hospital, conventional weekends didn't apply. If each nurse took off Saturday and Sunday, no one would be available to watch the patients. So schedules were staggered, some of the staff taking off Monday and Tuesday, others Wednesday and Thursday, et cetera. Conversely, nurses tended to have the same shift for several weeks in a row: seven to three, three to eleven, eleven to seven. That was why Pittman had waited until after midnight—because he needed to speak with the nurse who had been present when, at this time two nights ago, Millgate had been whisked away.

"That would be Jill," the doctor said.

"Is she on duty tonight?"

"Yes."

Pittman didn't show his relief.

"But she's too busy to talk to you right now."

"I understand, Doctor. The patients come first. But I wouldn't be troubling you if this wasn't important. When she takes a break, do you think you could—?"

"Please, wait outside, Mr. . . ."

"Detective Logan."

"When she has a moment, I'll ask Jill to speak with you."

2

It took forty minutes. Leaning against the wall in the corridor outside the intensive-care ward, Pittman identified with the forlorn people in the waiting room. His memory of the stress of that kind of waiting increased his own stress. His brow was clammy by the time the door to intensive care was opened. An attractive woman in her late twenties came out, glanced around, then approached him.

She was about five feet five, and her loose white hospital uniform couldn't hide her athletic figure. She had long, straight blond hair, a beguiling oval face, and cheeks that were so aglow with health that she didn't need makeup.

"Detective Logan?"

"Yes."

"I'm Jill Warren." The nurse shook hands with him. "Dr. Baker said you wanted to ask me some questions."

"That's right. I wonder, could we go somewhere that isn't crowded? There's a coffee machine on the floor below us, near the elevator. Perhaps I can buy you a . . ."

"The floor below us? You sound as if you know this hospital fairly well."

"I used to come here a lot. When my son was in intensive

care." Pittman gestured toward the door to the children's unit.

"I hope he's all right now."

"No. . . . He died."

"Oh." Jill's voice dropped. "What did—?"

"Bone cancer. Ewing's sarcoma."

"Oh." Her voice dropped lower. "I shouldn't have . . . I'm sorry for . . ."

"You couldn't have known. I'm not offended."

"Do you still want to buy me that cup of coffee?"

"Definitely."

Pittman walked with her to the elevator. His tension lessened as they got in and the doors closed. The worst risk he'd taken in coming here was that the doctor who had seen him when Millgate was removed from the hospital would be on duty, recognize him, and call the police.

Now Pittman's brow felt less clammy as he reached the lower floor, which was deserted except for a janitor at the far end of the corridor. Using the last of his change, he put coins in the machine. "How do you like your coffee? With cream? Sugar? Decaffeinated?"

"Actually, I'd like tea." Jill reached past him, pressing a button.

Pittman couldn't help noticing the elegant shape of her hand.

The machine made a whirring sound.

Jill turned to him. "What do you need to ask me?"

Steaming liquid poured into a cardboard cup.

"I have to verify some information. Was Mr. Millgate alert before his associates showed up and took him from the hospital?"

"Associates is too kind a word. Thugs would be more like it. Even the doctor who insisted on removing him."

"Did Millgate object?"

"I guess I'm not making your job easy."

"I beg your pardon?"

"I got off the track right away. I didn't answer your first question. Yes, he was alert. Otherwise—to answer your second question—he wouldn't have been able to object." She sipped from the cardboard cup.

"How's the tea?"

"Scented hot water. These hospital machines. I'm used to it." Her smile was engaging.

"Why did Millgate object? He didn't want to be moved?"

"Yes and no. There's something about that night I still don't understand."

"Oh?"

"The men who came to get him insisted that he had to leave because there'd been a story about him on the late news. They told Millgate they had to get him away before reporters showed up."

"Yes, the story was about a confidential Justice Department report that somehow became public. Millgate was being investigated for being involved in a covert scheme to buy nuclear weapons from the former Soviet Union."

"Nuclear weapons? But that isn't what they said in the newspapers." Jill's eyes were such a pale blue they seemed almost translucent.

"What *who* said?"

"The men who came to get Millgate that night. In the newspapers, they said they took him away because they were afraid this obituary reporter—what's his name?"

"Pittman. Matthew Pittman."

"Yes, in the newspapers they said they were afraid Pittman would kill Millgate if Millgate stayed in the hospital, where Pittman could get at him. But that night, they never said *a word* about Pittman. All they seemed to care about was the news report that Millgate was being investigated."

Pittman felt tense again.

"It's like they changed their story," Jill said.

"And Millgate didn't think the news report about his being investigated was a good-enough reason to take him from the hospital?"

"Not exactly." Pensive, Jill sipped her tea. Her solemn expression enhanced her features. "He was willing to go. Or to put it another way, he was passive. Melancholy. He didn't seem to care about leaving. 'Do whatever you want,' he kept saying. 'It doesn't matter. None of it does. But don't take me yet.' That's what he was upset about. 'Not yet,' he kept saying. 'Wait.' "

"For what?"

"A priest."

Pittman's pulse sped as he remembered that at the Scarsdale estate he had overheard two of the grand counselors talking with concern while he crouched on the roof of the garage.

". . . priest," an elderly man's brittle voice had said.

"Don't worry," a second elderly voice had said. "I told you the priest never arrived. Jonathan never spoke to him."

"Even so."

"It's been taken care of," the second voice had emphasized, reminding Pittman of the rattle of dead leaves. "It's safe now. Secure."

"Tell me about him," Pittman said quickly. "The priest. Do you know his name?"

"Millgate mentioned one priest a lot. His name was Father . . ." Jill thought a moment. "Dandridge. Father Dandridge. When Millgate was brought to intensive care, he was certain he was going to die. He didn't have much strength, but the few words he got out were always about this Father Dandridge. Millgate told business associates who were allowed to visit that they had to send for him. Later he accused them of not obeying. In fact, he accused his son of lying to him about sending for the priest. There's a priest on duty at the hospital, of course. He came around to speak to Millgate. But it seems any priest wasn't good enough. It had to be Father Dandridge. I was on duty early Thursday morning when Millgate begged the hospital priest to phone Father Dandridge at his parish in Boston. I guess the hospital priest did."

"What makes you think so?"

"About an hour after Millgate was taken out of here Thursday night, a priest who called himself Father Dandridge came in to see him. He was very upset about not being able to hear Millgate's confession."

"He came from a parish in Boston? Do you remember the name?"

"I'm afraid not."

Pittman's spirit sank.

"But you don't have to phone Boston to talk to him," Jill said.

"What do you mean?"

"Father Dandridge made a point of telling me that he wasn't returning to Boston. Not until he had a chance to talk to Millgate. If I heard anything, the priest said, I was to call him at a rectory here in Manhattan. St. Joseph's. The priest said he'd be staying for the weekend." Jill glanced at her watch. "Look, I'm sorry, but I've been off the ward too long. I have a patient who's due for his meds."

"I understand. Thank you. You've helped me more than you can imagine."

"If there's anything else you need to know . . ."

"I'll get back to you."

Jill set down the cardboard cup and walked quickly toward the elevator.

It took about twenty seconds for the doors to open, and as she waited, facing the doors, obviously aware that he watched her, Pittman was impressed that she didn't act self-conscious. After she got in the elevator, as the doors closed, for a fraction of an instant she smiled at him. Then she was gone, and the excitement that Pittman felt about what he had learned was replaced by exhaustion that weighed so heavily, his legs bent.

3

Pittman's sudden weakness alarmed him. Light-headed, he feared that he would lose his balance. He leaned against the coffee machine.

What did you expect? he told himself. The past two days, you've had more exercise than you've had all year. You've been running all over Manhattan. You got a few hours sleep on a park bench. You haven't had enough to eat. You've been strung out from fear and adrenaline. It's a wonder you managed to stay on your feet as long as you have.

But I can't collapse. Not *here*. Not *now*.

Why not? he joked bitterly. A hospital's a great place to collapse.

Have to get back to Sean. Have to go back to the loft.

But after Pittman concentrated to steady himself and pushed away from the coffee machine, he discovered that he wasn't steady at all. His legs wavered more disturbingly. His stomach felt queasy. He gripped the wall, afraid that the janitor at the end of the corridor would look in his direction, see that he was in trouble, and call for help.

Have to get away from here.

Sure, and how far do you think you'll get? You're oozing sweat, pal. You're seeing gray. If you go outside, you're liable to collapse on the street. After the police find you, after they see the name on your credit card and find that .45 in your coat pocket . . .

Where, then?

His bitter joke echoed in his mind. A hospital's a great place to collapse.

4

As the elevator rose, Pittman's light-headedness increased. When the doors opened on the sixth floor, he strained to look natural and walked toward the intensive-care area. If Jill Warren came out, or the female doctor he'd spoken to earlier, he doubted that he'd have the strength to explain convincingly why he had returned.

But Pittman didn't have another option. The intensive-care waiting room was the only refuge he could think of that he knew he could get to. Its lights had been dimmed. He veered left from the corridor, passed several taut-faced people trying to doze on the uncomfortable chairs, stepped over a man sleeping on the floor, and came to a metal cabinet in back.

The cabinet contained hospital pillows and blankets, Pittman knew. He had found out the hard way when Jeremy had been rushed to intensive care and Pittman had spent the first of many nights in the waiting room. A staff member had told him about the pillows and blankets but had explained that usually the cabinet was kept locked.

"Then why store the pillows and blankets in the cabinet if people can't get to them?" Pittman had complained.

"Because we don't want people sleeping here."

"So you force them to stay awake in those metal chairs all night?"

"It's a hospital rule. Tonight I'll make an exception." The staff member had unlocked the cabinet.

Now Pittman twisted the latch on the cabinet, found that it was locked, and angrily pulled out the tool knife Sean O'Reilly had given him. His hands trembled. It took him longer than it normally would have. But finally, using the lock picks concealed in the knife, he opened the cabinet.

Dizzy, nauseated, he lay among others in the most murky corner of the waiting room, a pillow beneath his head, a blanket pulled over him. Despite the hard floor, sleep had never come quicker or been more welcome. As he drifted into unconsciousness, he was dimly aware that others in the waiting room groped toward the pillows and blankets in the cabinet that he had deliberately left open.

He was disturbed only once—an elderly man waking a frail woman. "She's dead, May. Nothin' they could do."

5

Daylight and voices woke him. Those who'd remained all night in the waiting room were rousing themselves. Others, whose friends or relatives had evidently just been admitted to intensive care, were trying to acquaint themselves with their new surroundings.

Pittman sat up wearily, concentrated to clear his head, and stood slowly with effort. The combination of the hard floor and his previous day's exertion made his muscles ache. After he folded the blanket and put it and the pillow into the cabinet, he draped his overcoat over an arm, concealing the heavy bulge of the .45 in his right pocket.

A hospital volunteer brought in a cart of coffee, orange juice, and doughnuts. Noticing a sign that said PAY WHAT YOU CAN, Pittman couldn't find any more change in his pockets. Sean O'Reilly had lent him twenty dollars, and Pittman guiltily put in one of those dollars, drank two cups of orange juice, ate two doughnuts, and suddenly was afraid that he would throw up. In a washroom down the hall, he splashed cold water on his face, looked at his pasty complexion in the mirror, touched his beard stubble, and felt demoralized. How can I possibly keep going? he thought.

The suicide that he had almost committed four nights earlier beckoned.

Why bother trying? I'm in so much trouble, I can never get out of it, he thought. Even if I do get out of it, Jeremy will still be dead. What's the point? Nothing's worth what I'm going through.

You can't let the bastards destroy you. Remember what you told yourself—it has to be *your* idea, not theirs. If you kill yourself now, you'll be giving them what they want. You'll be letting them win. Don't let the sons of bitches have that satisfaction.

A short, dreary-looking man whom Pittman recognized from the waiting room came into the washroom, took off his shirt, chose the sink next to Pittman, opened a travel kit, lathered his face, and began to shave.

"Say, you wouldn't have another one of those disposable razors, would you?" Pittman asked.

"Do what I did, buddy. Go down to the shop in the lobby and buy one."

6

St. Joseph's hadn't benefited from the renovation that, thanks to an influx of Yuppies during the eighties, had taken place in other parts of SoHo. Although small, the church's architecture resembled a cathedral, but its sandstone exterior was black with soot, its stained-glass windows grimy, its interior badly in need of painting.

Pittman stood at the rear of the church, smelled incense, listened to an organ that sounded as if it needed repair, and surveyed the impressive amount of worshipers who, unmindful of the bleak surroundings, had come for Sunday Mass. The front of the church wasn't bleak, though. A golden chalice gleamed on the altar. Candles glowed. A tall, intense priest wearing a crimson vestment read from the Gospel, then delivered a sermon about trusting in God and not giving in to despair.

Right, Pittman thought bleakly. He sat in a pew in back and watched the continuation of the first Mass he'd attended in many years. He had never gone to church on a regular basis, but after Jeremy had died, his indifference had turned to rejection. As a consequence, he couldn't account for his impulse when the time came for communion and he followed parishioners toward the altar. He told himself that he wanted to get a closer look at the priest, for an assistant at the church's rectory had told Pittman that Father Dandridge would be conducting this particular Mass.

Coming near to him, Pittman saw that the priest was in his middle fifties and that his strong features had deep lines of strain. He had a jagged scar across his chin, and his left hand was welted from what looked like the consequence of a long-ago fire.

When Pittman received communion, the emptiness inside him felt immense.

The priest ended the Mass. "Go in peace."

Not just yet, Pittman thought.

As the parishioners left, he made his way toward the front of the church, went through a door on the right, and found himself in the sacristy, the room next to the altar where objects needed for Mass were customarily stored.

7

The priest was taking off his vestments, setting them on a counter, when he noticed Pittman enter. Deliberate movements and cordlike sinews visible on the priest's forearms suggested a man who kept his mind and body in condition and control. He became still, watching Pittman approach.

"May I help you?" the priest asked.

"Father Dandridge?"

"That's correct."

"I need to speak to you."

"Very well." The priest waited.

As Pittman hesitated, the priest cocked his head. "You look nervous. Is this a personal matter . . . something for confession?"

"No. Yes. I mean, it *is* personal, but . . . What I need to speak to you about—" Pittman felt apprehensive about the reaction he would get—"is Jonathan Millgate."

The priest's dark eyes assessed him. "Yes, I remember you from the Mass. The anguish on your face as you came up for communion. As if the weight of the entire world were on your shoulders."

"That's how it feels."

"Understandably. If what the newspapers say about you is correct, Mr. Pittman."

Panic. It had never occurred to Pittman that the priest would be able to identify him. Nerves quickening, he swung toward the door, about to flee.

"No," Father Dandridge said. "Please. Don't go. Be calm."

Something in the priest's voice made Pittman hesitate.

"I give you my word," Father Dandridge said. "You have nothing to fear from me."

Pittman's stomach cramped. "How did you know . . . ?"

"Who you are?" Father Dandridge gestured, inadvertently drawing Pittman's attention to his scarred left hand. "Jonathan Millgate and I had a special relationship. It shouldn't be surprising that I would have read every newspaper article and watched every television report I could find to learn more about what happened to him. I have studied your photograph many times. I recognized you immediately."

Pittman couldn't seem to get enough air. "It's important that you believe this. I didn't kill him."

"Important to me or you?"

"I tried to save him, not harm him." Pittman was suddenly conscious of the amplifying echo in the small room. He glanced nervously toward the archway that led to the altar.

Father Dandridge gazed in that direction, as well. The church was almost empty. A few elderly men and women remained kneeling, their heads bowed in prayer.

"No one seems to have heard you," Father Dandridge said. "But the next Mass is scheduled to begin in half an hour. The church will soon be full." He pointed toward two men who entered at the back of the church.

"Is there somewhere we can talk?"

"I ask you again, do you want confession?"

"What I want is what you promised at the end of the Mass. Peace."

Father Dandridge intensified his gaze, then nodded. "Come with me."

8

The priest led the way toward a door at the back of the sacristy. When he opened it, Pittman was amazed to look out toward a garden, its well-kept appearance in contrast with the decay at the front of the church. Neatly mowed grass was flanked by blooming lilacs, their fragrance wafting through the open door. The rectangular area was enclosed by a high brick wall.

Father Dandridge motioned for Pittman to precede him.

When Pittman didn't respond, the priest looked amused. "Suspicious of me? You don't want to turn your back on me? How could I possibly hurt you?"

"Lately, people have been finding ways." Keeping his hand on the .45 hidden in his overcoat pocket, Pittman glanced back through the arch toward the church, which was rapidly being filled. He followed the priest into the garden and shut the door.

The morning sun was warm and brilliant, emphasizing the jagged white scar on Father Dandridge's chin. The priest sat on a metal bench. The sound of the city's traffic seemed far away.

"Why should I believe that you didn't kill Jonathan Millgate?"

"Because if I did, I ought to be on the run. Why would I come to you?"

Father Dandridge raised his shoulders. "Perhaps you're as deranged as the news reports say. Perhaps you intend to kill me, as well."

"No. I need your help."

"And how could I possibly help you? Why would I *want* to help you?"

"In the news reports, Millgate's people claim they took him from the hospital to protect him from me, but that's not true," Pittman insisted. "The real reason they took him is they didn't want to expose him to reporters after the story broke about his supposed connection with trying to buy nuclear weapons from the former Soviet Union."

"Even if you can prove what you say . . ."

"I can."

". . . it's irrelevant to whether or not you killed him."

"It's *very* relevant. Look, I followed him from the hospital, yes. But I wasn't stalking him. I wanted to find out why he'd been taken. At the estate in Scarsdale, the nurse and doctor who were supposed to be caring for him left him alone. He became disconnected from his life-support system. I managed to get into his room and help him."

"But a witness claims it happened the other way around, that you cut off his oxygen and caused him to have a fatal heart attack."

"A nurse came in when I was putting the oxygen prongs into Millgate's nostrils. She heard Millgate tell me something. I think that's what all of this is about. His people were afraid of reporters asking him questions. But *I'm* a reporter, and what Millgate told me may have been exactly what they didn't want anybody to know. They tried to stop me, but I got away, and . . ."

Father Dandridge added, "So they decided to cut off Jonathan Millgate's life-support system, to let him die to prevent him from ever telling anyone else. Then they blamed his death on you so that even if you tried to use what you were told, you wouldn't be believed."

"That's right," Pittman said, amazed. "That's the theory I'm trying to prove. How did—?"

"When you hear enough confessions, you become proficient at anticipating."

"This isn't confession!"

"What did Jonathan Millgate say to you?"

Pittman's energy dwindled, discouragement overcoming him. He rubbed the back of his neck. "That's the problem. It doesn't seem that important. In a way, it doesn't even make sense. But later a man tried to kill me at my apartment because of what Millgate had told me."

"Now you tell *me*."

"A man's name." Pittman shook his head in confusion. "And something about snow."

"A name?"

"Duncan Grollier."

Father Dandridge concentrated, assessing Pittman. "Jonathan Millgate was perhaps the most despicable man I have ever met."

"*What?* But you said that the two of you were friends."

Father Dandridge smiled bitterly. "No. I said that he and I had a special relationship. I could never be his friend. But I could pity him as much as I loathed his actions. I could try to save his soul. You see, I was his confessor."

Pittman straightened with surprise.

"When you saw me in the sacristy, you couldn't help noticing my scars."

"I'm sorry. I didn't mean to . . ."

"It's quite all right. There's no need to worry about my feelings. I'm proud of these scars. I earned them in combat. During the Vietnam War. I was a chaplain in I Corps. A base I was assigned to—close to the demilitarized zone—came under siege. Bad weather kept reinforcements from being brought in. We were under constant mortar bombardment. Of course, as a noncombatant, I wasn't allowed to use a weapon, but I could care for the wounded. I could crawl with food and water and ammunition. I could give dying men the last sacrament. The scar on my chin is from shrapnel. The scars on my hand are from a fire I helped to put out. When I say I'm proud of these scars, it's because they remind me of what a privilege it was to serve beside such brave men. Of two hundred, only fifty survived by the time reinforcements were able to come. None of those who died was older than twenty-one. And I blame Jonathan Millgate for those deaths, just as I blame him for the entire forty-seven thousand men who died in battle in that war. A hundred and fifty thousand men were wounded. Thousands of other lives were destroyed because of the psychological effects of the war. And why? Because Millgate and his four colleagues"—the priest twisted his lips in contempt—"the so-called grand counselors—advised the President and the nation that the domino theory was something worth dying for, that if we didn't keep the Communists out of Vietnam, the rest of Southeast Asia would fall to them. A quarter of a century later, communism is a crumbling philosophy, and Southeast Asia is becoming ever more capitalistic, even though South Vietnam was taken over by the Communists. The war made no difference. But Jonathan Millgate and the other grand counselors became obscenely rich because of their relationship with the arms industry that inevitably profited from the war the grand counselors insisted was necessary."

"And now Millgate was being investigated for a nuclear weapons scandal," Pittman said. "Is that why he wanted so desperately to talk to you before he died? His associates were determined to keep him away from you. They felt you were a threat."

Father Dandridge squinted. "When I came back from Vietnam, I harassed Jonathan Millgate at every opportunity. I organized demonstrations against him. I tried to shame him in every way I could. I believe I was one of the reasons he stopped being a diplomat and retired from public view. Of course, he still manipulated government policy, but at least he was forced to do it from comparative hiding. Then to my surprise, six months ago, he phoned me. He asked permission to come and see me. Suspicious, I agreed, and when he arrived, I discovered that he was having a crisis of conscience. He wasn't a Catholic, but he felt a desperate need to bare his soul. He wanted me to be his confessor."

"His confessor? After all the trouble you'd made for him?"

"He wanted to confess to someone whom he could not intimidate."

"But what was so important that he *needed* to confess?"

Father Dandridge shook his head. "You know I'm bound, at the risk of my soul, never to reveal what I hear in confession."

Pittman breathed out with effort. "Then I came here for nothing."

"Duncan Grollier. Are you sure that's the name you heard?"

Pittman nodded. "Except . . ."

"What?"

"He mentioned Duncan several times. Then snow. Then Grollier. Could Snow be someone's last name?"

"I don't know. But in this case, Grollier isn't. It's the

name of the prep school Millgate went to. That's a matter of public record. I'm not violating any confidence by telling you. In conscience, it's all I *can* tell you. But it ought to be enough."

"What are you talking about? Enough? I don't understand."

9

The bullet struck Father Dandridge's right eye. Pittman was so startled by the sudden eruption of blood and jellylike tissue that he recoiled, gasping. At first he wasn't even sure what had happened. Then stumbling back, he saw the spray of brain and blood that spewed onto the lawn from the rear of Father Dandridge's head.

Pittman wanted to scream, but terror paralyzed his voice. He bumped against a statue and flinched as a bullet blasted chunks from the stone. Although he hadn't heard any shots, it seemed that the bullets were coming from the door through which he and Father Dandridge had entered the garden. Using the statue for cover, Pittman pulled the .45 from his overcoat, tried to control his trembling hands, cocked the pistol, and understood that he'd be foolish to show himself in order to aim at the door.

The garden became eerily silent. The gunman must have used a silencer, Pittman thought. No one in the church knows what happened. No one will send for help.

But another Mass is due to start, Pittman realized. When the priest enters the sacristy to put on his vestments, he'll see the gunman peering out toward this garden.

The priest will call for help—and be shot.

I can't let that happen! I have to get out of here!

Pittman heard a creaking noise as if the door to the garden was being opened wider. His hands were slick with sweat. He clutched the .45 harder.

Shoot!

But I don't have a target!

The noise will bring help.

Not in time.

There weren't any other doors out of the garden. By the time Pittman reached the brick wall and tried to climb it, he knew he'd be shot.

It may have been Pittman's imagination, but he thought he heard a footstep.

He glanced around in a frenzy. His pulse raced. He thought he heard another footstep.

Past a lilac bush on his right, he saw a ground-level window that led to the church's basement. Nauseated by fear, he shot blindly from the side of the statue toward where he thought he had heard the footstep. He lunged toward the opposite side of the statue and fired again and again, this time showing himself but unable to aim steadily. He saw a man dive behind the bench upon which Father Dandridge lay. He saw another man duck back into the sacristy.

And he realized he had only four bullets left. The way he was shaking, he might use them all without hitting either gunman.

Move!

Firing again to cover himself, he charged to his right toward the lilac bush and the window behind it. Chest heaving, he hit the ground, clawed toward the window, and slammed his pistol at the glass, breaking it. The force made the window open. It hadn't been secured. As the window tilted inward on hinges, Pittman thrust himself through the opening. He fell into darkness, twisting, plummeting. With an impact that knocked his breath from him, he landed on a bench, then toppled painfully onto the floor. He winced. Broken glass from the window impaled his left hand, deep, burning. He pulled out the glass, alarmed by the flow of blood and the searing pain, scrambled desperately to his feet, and ran. From the open window, a man shot into the dark room.

Pittman's eyes adjusted to the shadows enough to see a doorway ahead. He fired toward the window, heard a moan, jerked the door open, and surged into a brightly lit room, where he blinked in dismay at a group of women setting out pastries for what looked like a bake sale. Their mouths fell open in shock. A woman dropped a cake. A baby started wailing. Another woman shrieked—but not before Pittman heard noises behind him, the two men climbing down into the room.

"Get out of the way!" Pittman ordered the women. He raised his gun, the sight of which made them scurry. At once he slammed the door behind him, saw that it didn't have a lock, and grabbed one of the tables, dragging it toward the door, hoping to brace the door shut.

A shot from behind the door splintered wood. Pittman fired back. Only one more bullet. As women screamed, he raced toward stairs at the end of the large room. Above him, he heard a commotion in the church.

He reached the stairs, expecting the gunmen to knock the door open and fire at him. But as he hurried up, he risked a glance behind him and saw that the door remained closed. Too many witnesses. They're not taking chances. They're climbing out the window. They're going over the wall.

Hearing numerous hurried footsteps at the top of the stairs, Pittman shoved the .45 into his pocket. Frantic parishioners charged down the steps toward him.

"A man with a gun! Down there!" Pittman showed them the hand that he'd cut on the broken glass. In greater pain, he clutched it, trying to stop the flow of blood. "He shot me!"

"Call the police."

"A doctor. I need a doctor." Sweating, Pittman pushed his way through the crowd.

The crowd began to panic.

"What if he shoots someone else?"

"He might kill all of us!"

Abruptly reversing its direction, the crowd charged up the stairs. The press of bodies made Pittman feel suffocated. Their force carried him up. A door loomed. Someone banged it open. The crowd surged into the street, taking Pittman with them. A few seconds later, he was enveloped by the confusion of hundreds of panicked churchgoers.

As a siren approached, Pittman shoved his bleeding hand into his overcoat pocket. He stayed with a group of frightened men and women who hurried away. By the time the flashing lights of the first police car arrived, he was turning a corner, hailing a taxi.

"What's all the trouble down there?" the driver asked.

"A shooting."

"At a church? God help us."

"*Somebody* better."

"Where do you want to go?"

A damned good question, Pittman thought. In desperation, he told the driver the first nearby location he could think of. "Washington Square."

10

Pittman hoped he seemed just one of many Sunday-morning strollers. In contrast with the week's cool, rainy weather, the day was warm and bright. Joggers and bicyclists sped past street musicians and portrait painters, indigents and street vendors. Near the Washington Arch, students with New York University T-shirts played with a Frisbee while a beard-stubbled man holding a bottle in a paper bag stumbled past them.

Pittman didn't pay attention to any of it. Concealed in his overcoat pocket, his hand continued to throb against a handkerchief that he had wrapped around it to staunch the flow of blood. Obviously he was hurt worse than he'd thought. He felt light-headed again, but this time he was sure it was from the blood he'd lost. He had to get to a hospital. But a hospital wouldn't give him treatment unless he showed ID and filled out an information form. If the receptionist recognized his name or if the police alerted the hospitals to be on the lookout for someone with a bleeding hand . . . No. He had to find another way to get medical help.

And then what? he kept insisting to himself. Where will you go after that? Father Dandridge was supposed to have all your answers, and now he's dead and you don't know anything more than when you started.

Why did they kill him? Pittman thought urgently. If they were after me, why didn't they wait until I left the church?

Because they wanted *both* of us. They must have been watching him. They were looking for any sign that he was going to act on what Millgate had told him in earlier confessions. And when I showed up, they assumed we were working together.

But what did Father Dandridge know that was so important?

Grollier, the prep school Millgate had attended.

It must have *some* significance. Damn it, somebody's worried enough to kill anybody I come in touch with who might know anything about the thoughts that tortured Millgate in his final hours.

Final hours.

Pittman suddenly knew where he had to go next.

11

"Detective Logan," he said to the intercom.

A buzzer sounded, electronically unlocking the outside door.

Pittman stepped through, noting the attractive wood paneling in the Upper West Side apartment building. He took the elevator to the fifth floor. He'd been worried that the woman's phone number wouldn't be listed or that she wouldn't be home after he checked the phone book and came here. As he knocked on the door, he worried as well that she wouldn't be receptive, but when she opened the door, using her left hand to keep her housecoat securely fastened, squinting at him through sleepy eyes, she looked puzzled more than upset.

Silhouetted by sunlight streaming through a living room window behind her, Jill Warren murmured, "Don't you know it's the middle of the night?"

That was something Pittman had hoped for—that instead of going out to enjoy the day, she would be home, sleeping after she finished her night shift at the hospital.

"Sorry," he said. "I didn't have a choice."

Jill yawned, reminding Pittman of a kitten pawing at its face. Although her long blond hair was tangled and her face was puffy from just having been wakened, Pittman thought she was beautiful.

"You need to ask me more questions?"

"A little more than that, I'm afraid."

"I don't understand."

"I need help." Pittman withdrew his bloodstained hand from his overcoat pocket.

"My God." Jill's eyes came fully open. "Hurry. Come in." She gripped his arm, guiding him through the doorway, quickly closing it. "The kitchen's this way. I wondered why you looked so pale. I thought maybe you hadn't gotten any sleep. But . . . Here, put your hand in the sink."

As Pittman wavered, she hurriedly brought a chair from the kitchen table and made him sit beside the sink while she pulled off his overcoat.

The .45 concealed in its right pocket thunked against the chair and made Jill frown.

"Look, I know this is an imposition," Pittman said. "If I'm interrupting anything . . . If someone's here and . . ."

"Nobody."

At the hospital, Pittman had noted that she wasn't wearing a wedding ring. Nonetheless, he'd been concerned that she might be living with someone. Her roommate might have gone out for the day to avoid making noise, to let her sleep.

"I live alone," Jill said. "This handkerchief is stuck to your wound. I'm going to run cool water over it and peel it off. How did you—? Good. It's coming off. Does that hurt?"

"No."

"Sure. That's why your face turned gray. This looks like a cut."

"Broken glass."

"Deep. You should have gone to the hospital instead of coming here."

"Your apartment was closer."

"You need stitches."

"No," Pittman said.

Jill frowned at him, then returned her attention to Pittman's hand. "Which do you object to, the hospital or the stitches?"

Pittman didn't answer.

Jill rinsed the crusted blood off the hand, then directed a gentle flow of water into the cut. "Keep your hand under the water. I have to get bandages and disinfectant."

Then she was gone. Pittman worried that she might decide to run from the apartment.

To his relief, he heard her opening drawers in another room.

He stared at the blood welling from his hand, the water diluting it, pink fluid flowing down the drain. Weary, he looked away, feeling oddly at a distance as he scanned the small, bright, neatly arranged kitchen. A pot holder in the shape of a cat seemed more amusing than it should have been.

"Your face is grayer," Jill said with concern, hurrying back. "I can't imagine what you're smiling about. Do you feel delirious?"

"A little off balance."

"For God sake, don't fall off the chair." Jill put her arms around him, leaning past him, over the sink.

He felt her breasts against his back but was too tired to respond with anything but gratitude that she was taking care of him.

Gently she washed his hand, blotted it with a towel, applied amber disinfectant to the cut, put a dressing on a gauze pad, and wrapped a bandage around the hand. Blood soaked through the first layer. Jill bandaged faster, adding layer after layer.

"You'd better hope this stops the bleeding, or you'll be going to the hospital whether you like it or not," she said.

Pittman stared at the thick padding around his hand. A portion of it turned pink, but it didn't spread.

"One more layer for good luck." Jill wrapped it again. "Now let's get you into the living room and up on the sofa."

"I'm fine," Pittman said. "I can do it myself."

"Yeah, sure, right." Jill lifted him, putting an arm around him as his knees bent.

The sunlit living room turned shadowy for a moment. Then Pittman was on the sofa.

"Lie down."

"Look, I really am sorry."

"Put your feet on this pillow. I want them higher than your head."

"I wouldn't have come here if there was any other way to—"

"Stop talking. You sound out of breath. Lie still. I'm going to get you some water."

Pittman closed his eyes. The next thing he knew, Jill was cradling his head, helping him to drink.

"If you don't feel queasy after this, I'll get you some juice. Do you think you could eat? Would you like something bland like toast?"

"Eat?"

"You make it sound like a new idea."

"The last time I . . . You could say my meals have been irregular."

Jill frowned harder. "Your overcoat's torn. Your pants have dirt on them, as if you've been crawling on the ground. What's going on? How did you get hurt?"

"A broken window."

"You look like you've been in a fight."

Pittman didn't answer.

"We're not going to get anywhere if you're not honest," Jill said. "I'm taking a big chance by helping you. I know you're not a policeman. You're Matthew Pittman, and the police are hunting you."

12

The shock of her statement brought Pittman upright.

"No," Jill said. "Don't try to sit."

"How long have you—?"

"Lie back down. How long have I known? Since about thirty seconds after you started talking to me at the hospital."

"Dear God." This time when Pittman tried to sit up, Jill put a hand on his chest.

"Stay down. I wasn't kidding. If the bleeding doesn't stop, you'll have to go to a hospital."

Pittman studied her and nodded. Adrenaline offset his lightheadedness. "Matt."

"What?"

"You called me Matthew. My friends call me Matt."

"Does that mean I'm supposed to think of you as a friend?"

"Hey, it's better than thinking of me as an enemy."

"And you're not?"

"Would you believe me if I said no?"

"It's not as if you never lied to me before."

"Look, I don't get it. If you knew who I was at the hospital, why didn't you call the police?"

"What makes you think I didn't? What if I told you I played along with your charade because I was afraid of you?

You might have hurt me if I let on I knew who you really were."

"*Did* you phone the police?"

"You don't remember me, do you?" Jill asked.

"Remember? Where would we have . . . ?"

"I'm not surprised. You were under a lot of stress. About as much as anybody can take."

"I still don't . . ."

"It's only in the last six months that I've been working in adult intensive care."

Pittman shook his head in confusion.

"Before that, I worked in the children's section. I left because I couldn't stand seeing . . . I was one of Jeremy's nurses."

Pittman felt as if his stomach had turned to ice.

"I was on duty the night Jeremy died," Jill said. "In fact, I'd been on duty all that week. You'd received permission to sit in a corner of the room and watch over him. Sometimes you'd ask me about the meaning of some of the numbers on his life-support machines. Or you'd get a look at his chart and ask me what some of the terms meant. But you weren't really seeing me. Your sole attention was toward Jeremy. You had a book with you, and sometimes if everything was quiet, you'd read a page or two, but then you'd raise your eyes and study Jeremy, study his monitors, study Jeremy again. I got the feeling that you were focusing all your will, all your energy and prayers, as if by concentrating, you could transfer your strength to Jeremy and cure him."

Pittman's mouth felt suddenly dry. "That's what I thought. Dumb, huh?"

Jill's eyes glistened. "No, it was one of the most moving things I've ever seen."

Pittman tried to sit up, groping for the glass of water on the table beside the sofa.

"Here, let me help." Jill raised the glass to his lips.

"Why do you keep looking at me that way?" Pittman asked.

"I remember," Jill said, "how you helped take care of Jeremy. Little things. Like dipping a washcloth into ice water and rubbing it over him to try to bring down his fever. He was in a coma by then, but all the while you washed him, you were talking to him as if he could hear every word you said."

Pittman squinted, painfully remembering. "I was sure he could. I thought if I got deep enough into his mind, he'd respond to what I was telling him and wake up."

Jill nodded. "And then his feet began curling. The doctor told you to massage them and his legs, to try to keep Jeremy's muscles limber so they wouldn't atrophy."

"Sure." Pittman felt pressure in his throat. "And when his feet *still* kept curling, I put his shoes on him for an hour, then took them off, then put them on in another hour. After all, when Jeremy would finally come out of the coma, when his cancer would finally be cured, I wanted him to be able to walk normally."

Jill's blue eyes became intense. "I watched you every night of my shift all that week. I couldn't get over your devotion. In fact, even though I was due for two days off, I asked to stay on the case. I was there when Jeremy went into crisis, when he had his heart attack."

Pittman had trouble breathing.

"So when I read the newspapers and learned all the murders you were supposed to have committed, I didn't believe it," Jill said. "Yes, the newspapers theorized you were so overcome with grief that you were suicidal, that you wanted to take other people with you. But after watching you for a week in intensive care, I knew you were so gentle, you couldn't possibly inflict pain on anyone. Not deliberately. Perhaps on yourself. But not on anyone else."

"You must have been surprised when I showed up at the hospital."

"I couldn't understand what was going on. If you were suicidal and on a killing rampage, why would you come to the intensive-care ward? Why would you pretend to be a detective and ask about Jonathan Millgate's last night in the ward? That's not how a guilty person would act. But it *is* how a person who's been trapped would act in order to get answers, to try to prove he didn't do what the police said he did."

"I appreciate your trust."

"Hey, I'm not gullible. But I saw the way you suffered when your son died. I've never seen anyone love anybody harder. I thought maybe you had a break coming."

"So you let me pretend I was a detective."

"What was I supposed to do, admit I knew who you were? You'd have panicked. Right now, you'd be in jail."

"Or dead."

13

A knock on the door made Pittman flinch. He frowned toward Jill. "Are you expecting anyone?"

Jill looked puzzled. "No."

"Did you lock the door after I came in?"

"Of course. This is New York."

Again someone knocked.

Pittman mustered the strength to stand. "Bring my overcoat. Put those bandages under the sink in the kitchen. As soon as I'm out of sight in the closet, open the door, but don't let on that I'm here."

The third knock was louder. "Open up. This is the police."

Jill turned toward Pittman.

"The police," he said. "Maybe. But maybe not. Don't tell them I'm here." Apprehension overcame his unsteadiness. He took the overcoat Jill gave him. "Pretend you were sleeping."

"But what if it *is* the police and they find you?"

"Tell them I scared you into lying."

Someone knocked even harder, rattling the door.

Jill raised her voice. "Just a moment." She looked at Pittman.

He gently touched her arm. "You have to trust me. Please. Don't tell them I'm here."

As he hurried toward the closet, he didn't let Jill see the .45 he took from his overcoat pocket. Heart pounding, he entered, stood between coats, and closed the door, waiting in darkness, feeling smothered.

After a moment during which he assumed Jill was hiding any further indication that he had come to the apartment, Pittman heard her put the chain on the main door, then unlock the dead bolt. He imagined her opening the door only to the slight limit of the chain, peering through a gap in the doorway.

"Yes? How can I help you?"

"What took you so long?"

"You woke me up. I work nights. I was sleeping."

"Let us in."

"Not until I see your ID."

Startled, Pittman heard a crash, the sound of wood splintering, the door being shoved open, the chain being yanked out of the doorjamb.

Heavy footsteps pounded into the hallway. The door was slammed shut. Someone locked it.

"Hey, what are you—?"

"Where is he, lady?"

"Who?"

"Pittman."

"Who?"

"Don't look so damn innocent. We know he came up here. One of our men was watching this place and called us. After Pittman went to the priest, we figured he might be making the rounds to anybody else who'd talked to Millgate before he died. And we were right."

"I don't know what you're talking about."

"I checked the bedroom," another voice said. "Nothing."

"Is there a back way out of here, lady?"

"No one in the bathroom," a third voice said.

"Answer me, lady. Damn it, is there a back way out of here?"

"You're hurting me."

"He's not in this closet."

"Check the one in the hall."

"Where *is* he, lady?"

As Jill screamed, Pittman heard footsteps approach the closet.

A heavyset man yanked the door open, exhaled at the sight of Pittman, raised a pistol with a silencer, and lurched back as Pittman shot him.

The gun's report was amplified so loudly by the confines of the closet that Pittman's ears rang fiercely. He surged from the closet and aimed the .45 at two husky men in the living room, one of whom was twisting Jill's arm so severely that she'd sunk to her knees, her face contorted with pain.

They both had silenced pistols, but as they spun, startled, the frenzied look on Pittman's face made them freeze.

"Raise your hands!" Pittman screamed.

Seeing the outraged expression on his face, staring at the .45's barrel, they obeyed. Jill fell away.

"Take it easy," one man said. "The way you're shaking, that gun might go off on its own."

"Right," the other man said. "Don't make it any worse for yourself. We're police officers."

"In your dreams. Keep your hands up. Drop the guns behind you."

They seemed to calculate their chances.

"Do it!" Pittman tensed his finger on the .45's trigger.

The guns thunked onto the floor.

Pittman walked past Jill, picked up one of the silenced

pistols, and shook less violently—because after he'd left the church, there had been only one bullet left in the .45, and he had used it on the man who had opened the closet door. There'd been no time to grab that man's pistol. In order to catch the remaining gunmen off guard, he'd been forced to threaten them with an empty weapon, first making sure to press the lever that closed the .45's ejection slide so they wouldn't realize the weapon was empty, easing it shut so they wouldn't hear a noise.

The men had slammed and locked the main door after they entered.

Now someone else was banging on the door, a frail, worried voice asking, "Jill? Are you all right?"

Pittman frowned at her. "Who is it?"

"The old man who lives next door."

"Tell him you're not dressed or else you'd open the door. Tell him you had the TV too loud."

As Jill moved down the hall, Pittman ordered the men, "Open your jackets. Lift them by the shoulders." Two years ago, he'd done a story about training techniques at the police academy. An instructor had invited him to participate in a session about subduing hostile prisoners. He strained to remember what he'd learned.

When the men lifted their jackets, Pittman walked around them. He didn't see any other weapons. That didn't mean there weren't any, however. "Down on your knees."

"Listen, Pittman."

"I guess you don't think I'd shoot you the same as I shot your buddy."

"No, I'm a believer."

"Then get down on your knees. Good. Now cross your ankles. Link your fingers behind your necks."

As the men assumed that awkward position, Jill returned.

"Did your neighbor believe you?"

"I think so," Jill said.

"Wonderful."

"No. He says when he heard the shot, before he knocked on my door, he called the police."

"Jesus," Pittman said. "You'd better hurry. Put on some clothes. We have to tie these men up and get out of here."

"We?"

"You heard what they said. After I went to the priest, they figured I might go to anyone else who had talked to Millgate before he died."

"What priest?"

"The one you told me about. Father Dandridge. Look, I don't have time to explain. The priest is dead. They killed him. And I'm afraid they think you know too much. You might be next."

"The police will protect me."

"But *these* men said they were the police."

Jill stared at the gunmen on the floor, her eyes wide with understanding.

14

While she dressed quickly, Pittman used bandages and surgical tape to bind the gunmen's arms and legs. Hearing police sirens, he and Jill ran nervously from her apartment. Neighbors, frightened by the gunshot, peered from partially open doors, then slammed and locked the doors when they saw Pittman charging along the hallway.

He reached the elevator but then thought better. "We might be trapped in there." Grabbing Jill's hand, he rushed toward the stairs. She resisted only a moment, then hurried with him. Her apartment was on the fifth floor, and they rapidly reached the third floor, then the second.

On the ground floor, they faltered, hearing sirens approaching.

"Where does that door lead?" Pittman breathed deeply, pointing toward a door at the end of the corridor behind him. It was the only one that didn't have a number on it. It had a red light over it. "Is that an exit?"

"Yes, but—"

"Come on." He tugged at Jill's sleeve and moved quicky along the hallway, through the door, and outside into the shadowy bottom of an air shaft. Garbage cans lined its walls.

"It's a dead end!"

"I tried to tell you." Jill turned to run back into her apartment building. "There's nowhere to—"

"What about *that*?" Pittman pointed toward a door directly across from him. He rushed over to it, twisted its knob, and groaned when he found that it was locked. Doing his best to control his shaky hands, he pulled out his tool knife and used the lock picks, exhaling with relief when he shoved the door open. It led into a hallway in the apartment building behind Jill's. The moment he and Jill were inside, he shut the door and turned the knob on the dead bolt. By the time the police got it open, he and Jill would be out of the area. As they hurried onto Eighty-sixth Street, Pittman imagined the police cars arriving at Jill's apartment building on Eighty-fifth Street.

Two blocks to the east was an entrance to Central Park. Jill's casual clothes—sneakers, jeans, and a sweater—made it easy for her to run. She clutched her purse close to her side. At the hospital, Pittman had sensed from her comfortable, graceful movements that she was an athlete, and now her long legs stretched in an easy runner's rhythm, proving that he'd been right.

They slowed briefly to avoid attracting attention, then increased speed again after they entered Central Park, racing east beyond the children's playground, then south past grown-ups playing baseball on the Great Lawn. Finally, below the Delacorte Theater, Belvedere Lake, and Belvedere Castle, they chose one of the many small trails that led through the trees in the section of the park known as The Ramble.

It was almost two in the afternoon. The sun continued to be strong for April, and sweat beaded Pittman's forehead as well as made his shirt cling to his chest while he and Jill rounded a deserted section of boulders and gradually came to a stop.

In the distance, there were other sirens. Leaning against a tree whose branches were green with budding leaves, Pittman tried to catch his breath. "I . . . I don't think we were followed."

"No. This is all wrong."

"What?"

Jill's expression was stark. "I'm having second thoughts about this. I shouldn't be here. At my apartment, I was scared."

"And you're not scared *now*?" Pittman asked in dismay.

"Those men breaking in . . . When you shot one of them . . . I've never seen anybody . . . The way you were talking . . . You confused me. I think I should have waited for the police to come." Jill drew her fingers through her long blond hair. "*You* should have waited. The police can help you."

"They'd put me in jail. I'd never get out alive."

"Have you any idea how paranoid you sound?"

"And apparently you think it's normal for gunmen to break into your apartment. I'm not being paranoid. I'm being practical. Since Thursday night, everywhere I've gone, people have been trying to kill me. I'm not about to let the police put me in a cell, where I'll be an easy target."

"But the police will think I'm involved in this."

"You *are* involved. Those men would have killed you. You can't depend on the police to keep you safe from them."

Jill shook her head in bewilderment.

"Listen to me," Pittman said. "I'm trying to save your life."

"My life wouldn't have *needed* to be saved if you hadn't come to my apartment."

The remark made Pittman flinch, as if he'd been slapped. Although he heard children laughing on another trail, the trail he was on was suddenly very silent.

"You're right," he said. "I made a mistake."

"I shouldn't have said that. I'm sorry."

Pittman nodded. "I am, too." He walked away. Draped over his left arm was his overcoat, heavy with his .45 and one of the gunmen's pistols with ammunition magazines from the others in his pockets.

"Hey, where are you going?"

Pittman didn't answer.

"Wait."

But Pittman didn't.

"Wait." Jill caught up to him. "I said I was sorry."

"Everything you said was true. The odds are that those men would have left you alone if I hadn't shown up. For certain, Father Dandridge would still be alive if I hadn't gone to see him. Millgate might still be alive, and my friend Burt would be alive, and . . ."

"No. Pay attention to me." Jill grabbed his shoulders and turned him. "None of this is your fault. I apologize for blaming you for what happened at my apartment. You meant no harm. You only came there because you needed help."

Pittman suddenly heard voices, rapid footsteps, what sounded like runners on the trail ahead. He stepped to the side, among bushes, his hand on the pistol in his overcoat pocket. Jill crowded next to him. Three joggers—two young men and a slender woman, all wearing brightly colored spandex outfits—hurried past, talking to one another.

Then the trail was quiet again.

"You'd be safer if you didn't stay with me," Pittman said. "Maybe you're right. Phone the police. Tell them I forced you to go with me. Tell them you're afraid to show yourself because you think the men who broke into your apartment have friends who'll come after you. You might even tell them I'm innocent, not that they'll believe you."

"No."

"You *won't* tell them I'm innocent?"

"I won't tell them anything. The more I think about it, the more I have to agree with you. The police would question me and let me go. But I'd still be in danger. Or maybe I could convince them to put me in protective custody. But for how long? Eventually I'd be on my own, in danger again."

"Then what are you going to do?"

"Stay with you."

"Me?"

"Tell me how I can help."

15

The bank Jill used, Citibank, had a branch south of Central Park, at Fifty-first and Fifth Avenue. As usual on a Sunday afternoon, the avenue wasn't busy. Making sure that passersby didn't overhear him, Pittman explained how the police had arranged for his bank's automated teller machine to seize his card. "But they haven't had time to do anything about *your* card. What's the maximum the bank allows you to take out?"

"I'm not sure. It could be as much as a thousand dollars."

"That much?" Pittman shook his head. "Not that it does us any good. I doubt you've got it in your account."

Jill assumed an odd expression. "I might have."

"Well, I know it's a lot, but this is an emergency. Please, get as much as you can."

They entered the bank's vestibule. Jill shoved her card into the machine and responded to the computer screen's inquiries, pressing buttons. A minute and a half later, she was stuffing a wad of twenties and tens into her purse.

"Don't forget your card," Pittman said. "And here's your transaction printout."

He glanced down, wondering what information might be on it that someone could use if the printout had been left behind. The printout indicated the remaining funds in the account, and Pittman abruptly understood the odd expression on Jill's face when he'd asked her about the size of her account.

"Eighty-seven thousand dollars and forty-three cents?"

Jill looked uncomfortable.

"You've got a fortune in this account."

"That printout is confidential." Her blue eyes flashed.

"I couldn't help looking," Pittman said.

"Surely it occurred to you that I couldn't be living in a large Upper West Side apartment on a nurse's salary."

Pittman didn't answer.

"You mean you had no idea I had money?"

"No. How did—?"

"My grandparents. A trust fund. Some bonds just came due. I'm deciding how to reinvest. That's why there's so much money in the account."

Pittman studied her with wonder.

"Is this going to be a problem?"

"Hell no. If you've got that much money, how about treating a starving man to a decent meal?"

16

The restaurant—on East Seventy-ninth Street—was small and unassuming: a linoleum floor, plain booths, red plastic tablecloths. But the veal scallopini, which Pittman recommended, was excellent, and the modestly priced house Burgundy was delicious.

A few tables had been set out on the sidewalk, and Pittman sat in the sunlight with Jill, enjoying the last of his salad.

"That's your second helping," Jill said. "I didn't think you'd ever get full."

"I told you I was hungry. This is the first decent meal I've had in quite a while. Mostly I've been eating on the run. You didn't like the food?"

"It's wonderful. But the restaurant doesn't exactly announce itself. How on earth did you ever find this place?"

Pittman bit into the final piece of garlic bread. "I used to live around here." The memory made him solemn. "When I was married."

"Past tense?" Jill set down her wineglass.

"Grief and connubial bliss don't seem to go together."

"Now I guess *I'm* the one who's snooping."

"There isn't much to tell. My wife was stronger than I was. That doesn't mean she loved Jeremy less, but after he died, I fell apart. Ellen didn't. I think she was afraid I was going to be like that for the rest of my life. She'd lost her son, and now she was losing . . . I scared her. One thing led to another. She divorced me. She's married again."

Jill almost touched his hand. "I'm sorry."

Pittman shrugged. "She was smart to get out. I *was* going to be like that for the rest of my life. Last Wednesday night, I had a gun in my hand, ready to . . . And then the phone rang, and the next thing . . ."

Jill's eyes widened with concern. "You mean the newspapers weren't exaggerating? You *have* been feeling suicidal impulses?"

"That's a polite way to put it."

Jill's brow furrowed with greater concern.

"I hope you're not going to try to be an amateur psychoanalyst," Pittman said. "I've heard all the arguments. 'Killing yourself won't bring Jeremy back.' No shit. But it'll certainly end the pain. And here's another old favorite: If I kill myself, I'll be wasting the life that Jeremy would have given anything to have. The trouble is, killing myself wouldn't be a waste. My life isn't worth anything. I know I've idealized Jeremy. I know that after his death I've made him smarter and more talented and funnier than he actually was. But Jeremy *was* smart and talented and funny. I haven't idealized him by much. A straight-A student. A sense of humor that never failed to amaze me. He had a droll way of seeing things. He could make me laugh anytime he wanted. And he was only fifteen. The world would have been his. Instead, he got cancer, and no matter how hard the doctors and he fought it, he died. Some gang member with a handgun is holding up a liquor store right now. That scum is alive, and my son is dead. I can't stand living in a world where everything is out of balance that much. I can't stand living in a world where everything I see is something Jeremy will never see. I can't stand remembering the pain on Jeremy's face as the cancer tortured him more and more each day. I can't stand . . ."

Pittman's voice trailed off. He realized that he'd been speaking faster and louder, that some of the customers in the restaurant were looking at him with concern, that Jill had leaned back as if overwhelmed by his emotion.

Spreading his hands, he mutely apologized.

"No," Jill said. "I won't try to be an amateur psychoanalyst."

"Sometimes everything builds up inside me. I say more than I mean to."

"I understand."

"You're very kind. But you didn't need me to dump it all on you."

"It's not a question of being kind, and *you* obviously needed to get it out of you."

"It's not, though."

"What?"

"Out of me. I think . . ." Pittman glanced down at the table. "I think we'd better change the subject."

Jill folded her napkin, neatly arranging the edges. "All right, then. Tell me about what happened Thursday night, how you got into this."

"Yes," Pittman said, his anger changing to confusion. 'And the rest of it."

It took an hour. This time Pittman spoke discreetly, keeping his voice low, pausing when anyone walked by. The conversation continued after Jill paid the waiter and Pittman strolled with her along Seventy-ninth Street.

"A nightmare."

"But I swear to God it's all true," Pittman said.

"There's got to be a way to make sense of it."

"Hey, I've been trying my damnedest."

"Maybe you're too close. Maybe you need someone else to see it from a different angle. Let's think this through," Jill said. "We know Millgate's associates took him from the hospital because a reporter got his hands on a secret Justice Department report that implicated Millgate in a covert attempt to buy nuclear weapons from the former Soviet Union. Millgate's people were afraid of reporters showing up at the hospital and managing to question him."

"They were also afraid of Father Dandridge," Pittman said. "More so. Millgate's people were afraid of something Millgate had told Father Dandridge in confession. Or of something Millgate *might* have told Father Dandridge if the priest had been able to see him Thursday night."

"Then you followed Millgate to the estate in Scarsdale. You got into his room to help him, but the nurse came in unexpectedly and saw you doing it."

"She also heard Millgate tell me something. Duncan. Something about snow. Then Grollier." Pittman shook his head. "But Father Dandridge told me that Grollier wasn't anyone's last name. It was the prep school Millgate went to."

"Why would *that* be important enough to kill anybody?"

They reached Fifth Avenue, and Pittman faltered.

"What's the matter?" Jill asked.

Pittman stared to the right toward a crowd going up and down the steps of the Metropolitan Museum of Art. Vendors, buses, and taxis contributed to the congestion in front. Several policemen on horseback maintained order.

"I guess," Pittman said, "I feel exposed." He glanced down at the weapon-laden overcoat draped over his left arm and guided her back along Seventy-ninth Street. "I want to find out about Grollier prep school."

"How are you going to do that? The only place I can think of with that information is the library. Or someone at a college. But it's Sunday. All those places are closed."

"No, there might be another way."

17

The freshly sandblasted apartment building at the end of East Eighty-second Street overlooked Roosevelt Drive and the East River. Pittman could hear the din of traffic from the thruway below as he and Jill entered the shadows of the cul-de-sac known as Gracie Terrace. The time was almost five in the afternoon. The temperature was rapidly cooling.

Jill peered up at the attractive, tall brick building. "You know someone who lives here?"

"Someone I interviewed once," Pittman said. "When this started and I was trying to figure out how to get help, I realized that over the years I'd interviewed people with all sorts of specialties that might be of use to me. I'm sure the police are watching my friends and my ex-wife to see if I contact them, but they'll never think about people I've met as a reporter."

Nonetheless, Pittman felt nervous. He quelled his emotion and stepped forward.

In the building's shiny, well-maintained lobby, a uniformed doorman greeted them. "May I help you?"

"Professor Folsom. Do you know if he's in?"

"He just got back from his afternoon walk. Is he expecting you?"

Pittman breathed easier. He had been afraid that Professor Folsom might not live here anymore or, worse, that the elderly professor might have died. "Please tell him I'm a reporter. I'd like to talk to him about the Walt Whitman manuscript he discovered."

"Certainly, sir."

They waited while the doorman walked toward a telephone on a counter at the side of the lobby.

"Whitman manuscript?" Jill whispered. "What on earth does Whitman have to do with—?

The doorman came back. "Professor Folsom says he'd be pleased to see you." The doorman gave the apartment number and directed them past a fireplace toward an elevator in a corridor at the rear of the lobby.

"Thanks."

"Whitman?" Jill repeated after they got in the elevator.

"Professor Folsom is an expert on him. He used to teach American literature at Columbia University. He's been retired for about fifteen years. But age hasn't slowed him down. He kept doing research, and five years ago he came across a Whitman manuscript, or what he believes is a Whitman manuscript, in some papers he was examining. There was a controversy about it. Was the manuscript authentic? Was it really a new Whitman poem? Some scholars said no. It seemed a good human-interest story, so I did an article about it. Folsom's quite a guy."

"But won't he remember you? Won't he call the police?"

"Why would he make the connection between a reporter who spoke to him five years ago and a man in the news this week? Besides, he doesn't have a television, and he thought it amusing that I was a newspaper reporter."

"Why?"

"He seldom reads newspapers."

"But how does he get any news?"

"He doesn't. He's a fanatic about history, not current events. He's also an expert in American education. I doubt there's a college or prep school he doesn't know about."

The elevator stopped at the fifteenth floor, and Pittman knocked on Folsom's door.

A tall, slender, stoop-shouldered elderly man peered out. He wore a brown herringbone sport coat, a white shirt, and a striped yellow tie. His skin was pale. His short beard and long hair were startlingly white. His trifocal glasses had wide metal frames, which only partially hid the deep wrinkles around his eyes.

"Professor, my name's Peter Logan. This is my friend Jill."

"Yes. The doorman explained that you were a reporter." Professor Folsom's voice was thin and gentle.

"I'm doing a follow-up on the Whitman manuscript you discovered. At the time, there was a controversy. I'm curious how it was resolved."

"You honestly believe your readers would care?"

"*I* care."

"Come in, please. I always enjoy talking about Whitman." As Professor Folsom led them across a foyer, they passed an immaculately preserved walnut side table. Open doors on each side of the foyer showed similar well-cared-for antiques.

"That's quite a collection," Pittman said.

"Thank you."

They entered the living room, and here there were even more antiques.

"They're exclusively American," Professor Folsom explained with pleasure. "From the mid- and late nineteenth century. That secretary desk was owned by Nathaniel Hawthorne. That hutch was Emerson's. That rocking chair was

Melville's. When my wife was still alive"—he glanced fondly toward a photograph of a pleasant-looking elderly woman on the wall—"we made a hobby of collecting them."

"Nothing that was owned by Whitman?"

"The old fox traveled lightly. But I managed to find several items. I keep them in my bedroom. In fact, the bed itself belonged to him." Professor Folsom looked delighted with himself. "Sit down. Would you like some tea?"

"Tea would be nice," Jill said.

For the next half hour, they discussed poetry and manuscripts with one of the most ingratiating people Pittman had ever met. In particular, the old man's sense of peace was remarkable. Pittman felt envious. Remembering Folsom's reference to his deceased wife, he wondered how it was possible to reach such advanced years and not be worn down by despair.

At last, he was ready to ask his crucial question. As he and Jill stood and prepared to leave, he said, "Thank you, Professor. You've been very kind. I appreciate your time."

"Not at all. I hardly get any visitors, especially since my wife died. She's the one kept me active. And of course, students don't come to visit as they once did."

"I wonder if you could answer something else for me. I have a friend who's looking for a good prep school for his son. Wants him to be on track for Harvard or Yale. My friend was thinking perhaps of Grollier."

"Grollier Academy? In Vermont? Well, if your friend isn't wealthy and doesn't have a pedigree, he'll be disappointed."

"It's that exclusive?" Jill asked.

"Its entire student body is fewer than three hundred. It accepts only about seventy boys as new students each year, and those slots are usually reserved when each student is born. The room, board, and tuition is fifty thousand dollars a year, and of course, parents are expected to contribute generously to the academy's activities."

"That's too rich for my friend," Pittman said.

Professor Folsom nodded. "I don't approve of education based on wealth and privilege. Mind you, the education the academy provides is excellent. Too restrained and conservative for my taste, but excellent nonetheless."

"Restrained? Conservative?"

"The curriculum doesn't allow for individual temperaments. Instead of allowing the student to grow into his education, the education is imposed upon him. Latin. Greek. World history, with an emphasis on Britain. Philosophy, particularly the ancients. Political science. European literature, again emphasizing Britain. Very little American literature. Perhaps that's why my enthusiasm is restrained. Economics. Algebra, calculus. And of course, athletics. The boy who goes to Grollier Academy and doesn't embrace athletics, in particular football and rowing—team sports—will soon find himself rejected."

"By the other students?" Jill asked.

"And by the school," Professor Folsom said, looking older, tired. "The purpose of Grollier Academy is to create Establishment team players. After all, noncomformist behavior isn't considered a virtue among patrician society. The elite favor caution and consensus. Intellectually and physically, the students of Grollier Academy undergo disciplines that cause them to think and behave like members of the special society they're intended to represent."

"It sounds like programming," Pittman said.

"In a sense, of course, all education is," Professor Folsom said. "And Grollier's preparation is solid. Various graduates have distinguished themselves." He mentioned several ambassadors, senators, and governors, as well as a President of the United States. "And that doesn't include numerous major financiers."

"I believe Jonathan Millgate went there," Pittman said.

"Yes, Grollier's alumni include diplomats, as well. Eustace Gable. Anthony Lloyd."

The names were totally unexpected. Pittman felt shocked. "Eustace Gable? Anthony Lloyd?"

"Advisers to various Presidents. Over the course of their careers, they achieved so many diplomatic accomplishments that eventually they became known as the grand counselors."

Pittman tried to restrain his agitation. "What a remarkable school."

"For a particular type of patrician student."

18

Outside the apartment building, the shadows were thicker, cooler. Shivering but not from the temperature, Pittman walked to the end of the cul-de-sac and went up steps to a promenade that overlooked the East River.

"Grollier Academy. Not just Jonathan Millgate, but Eustace Gable and Anthony Lloyd."

"The grand counselors," Jill said.

Pittman turned. "I had no idea. Do you suppose the others went there, as well—Winston Sloane and Victor Standish?"

"But even if they did, what would that prove?"

"Yes." Pittman's forehead throbbed. "What's so important about Grollier Academy that the other grand counselors were willing to kill Millgate and blame me for his murder and kill Father Dandridge and . . . ? All to prevent anyone from knowing why Millgate was fixated on his prep school."

"Or maybe we're completely wrong. It could be Millgate was in fact rambling."

"No," Pittman said emphatically. "I can't believe that. If I did, I'd be lost. I'd have to give up. I wouldn't know how to keep going." He shivered again and put on his overcoat, feeling the weight of the gun in each pocket, repelled by the conditions of his life. "Even as it is . . . what now?

What are we going to do about you? It'll soon be dark. You can't go back to your apartment, and you can't use your credit card to rent a room. The name on your card would help the men looking for you find where you're staying."

"Where were *you* going to spend the night?"

Pittman didn't reply.

"The other nights," Jill asked. "Where—?"

"A park bench and the floor of the intensive-care waiting room."

"Dear God."

"Maybe the police aren't such a bad idea. Call them. Maybe they *can* protect you."

"But for how long? I told you, I'd be terrified that they'd let down their guard. No. I'm staying with you," Jill said.

"In the long run, I'm not sure that would be smart."

"But in the short run, it's the option that scares me the least. Besides, there's something you still haven't figured out about me," Jill said.

"You mean in addition to the fact that you have money?"

"The money's part of it. I don't have to work for a living. The point is, I'm a nurse because I want to be. Because I need to be. And right now . . ."

"Yes?"

"My conscience wouldn't bear what might happen to you if you fail. You need help."

Pittman's chest became tight with emotion. He touched her arm. "Thank you."

"Hey, if I don't hang around, who's going to change the bandage on your hand?"

Pittman smiled.

"You ought to do that more often," Jill said.

Self-conscious, Pittman felt his smile lose its strength.

Jill glanced toward East End Avenue. "I'd better find a

pay phone and tell the hospital that I won't be coming to work. They'll still have time to get a replacement."

But after she made the call and stepped from the booth, Jill looked perplexed.

"What's wrong?"

"My supervisor in intensive care—she said the police had been in touch with her."

"They must have checked your apartment and connected you with the hospital."

"But she said somebody else called her as well, one of my friends, telling her I was all right but that I wouldn't be coming in."

"*What* friend?"

"A man."

Pittman's muscles contracted. "Millgate's people. Trying to cover everything. If you did show up at the hospital tonight, you would never have gotten to the sixth floor. But your supervisor wouldn't be worried enough to call the police when you didn't show up—because your 'friend' told her you were okay."

"Now I'm *really* scared."

"And we still haven't solved our problem. Where are you going to stay?"

"I've got a better idea."

"What?"

"Let's keep moving," Jill said.

"All night? We'd collapse."

"Not necessarily. You need to go to the library, but it won't be open until tomorrow."

"Right." Pittman was mystified.

"Well, they've got libraries in other cities. Instead of waiting until tomorrow, let's use the time. We'll be able to sleep on the train."

"Train?"

"I take the overnight when I go skiing there."

Pittman continued to look perplexed.

"Vermont."

Pittman suddenly, tensely understood. A chill swept through him. "Yes. Where Professor Folsom told us it was. Grollier Academy. Vermont."

FOUR

1

A sleeper car wasn't available. Not that it made a difference—Pittman was so exhausted that he was ready to sleep anywhere. Shortly after the train left Penn Station, he and Jill ate sandwiches and coffee that she had bought in the terminal. She had also been the one who bought the tickets; he didn't want anyone to get a close look at him. For the same reason, he chose a seat against a window in an area that had few passengers. The photo of him that the newspapers and television were using didn't show him as he now looked. Still, he had to be careful.

Soon the rhythmic clack-clack-clack of wheels on rails became hypnotic. Pittman glanced toward the other passengers in the half-full car, assuring himself that they showed no interest in him. Then he peered toward the lights in buildings the train was passing. His eyelids felt heavy. He leaned against the gym bag—he'd retrieved it from Sean O'Reilly's loft—and started to ask Jill how long the trip would take, but his eyelids kept sinking, and he never got the question out.

2

"Wake up."

He felt someone nudging him.

"It's time to wake up."

Slowly he opened his eyes.

Jill was sitting next to him, her hand on his shoulder. Her face was washed. Her hair was combed. She looked remarkably alert, not to mention attractive for so early in the morning. "Guess what?" she asked. "You snore."

"Sorry."

"No problem. You must be exhausted. I've never seen anyone sleep so deeply in such uncomfortable conditions."

"Compared to a park bench, this is the Ritz."

"Do you remember switching trains?"

Pittman shook his head. The car was almost deserted. No one was close enough to overhear them.

"You do a convincing job of sleepwalking," Jill said. "If we hadn't had to board another train, I bet you wouldn't even have gotten up to go to the bathroom."

Pittman gradually straightened from where he'd been scrunched down on the seat. His back hurt. "Where are we?"

"A few miles outside Montpelier, Vermont." Jill raised the shade on the window.

Although the sun was barely up, Pittman squinted painfully at a line of pine trees that suddenly gave way, revealing cattle on a sloping pasture. Across a narrow valley, low wooded mountains still had occasional patches of snow on them.

"What time is . . . ?"

"Six-fifteen."

"I don't suppose there's any coffee left from last night."

"You're dreaming."

"In that case, wake me when this is over."

"Come on," Jill said. "Straighten yourself up. When this train stops, I want to hit the ground running."

"Are you always this energetic so early in the morning?"

"Only when I'm terrified. Besides, when you're used to working the night shift, this is late afternoon, not morning."

"Not for me." Pittman's eyes felt gritty, as if sand had been thrown into them.

"Let me whisper something that might get you going."

"It better be good."

"Breakfast, and I'm paying."

"You're going to have to, since I don't have any cash. But I'll say this—you do have a way with words."

3

"Montpelier? Sounds French."

"The first settlers in this area were French."

"And this is the capital of Vermont?" Pittman sat with Jill at a restaurant table that gave them a window view of New England buildings along a picturesque street. "It doesn't feel as if many people live here."

"Fewer than ten thousand. But then only about six hundred thousand people live in the entire state."

"A good place to hide out."

"Or to send students to a school that's isolated enough that they won't be contaminated by the outside world while they're being taught to be aristocrats."

Pittman sipped his coffee. "Do I detect a little anger?"

"More than a little. My parents tried to raise me that way—to think of myself as better than ordinary people. They're still horrified that I'm a nurse. All those sick people. All that blood."

"I get the feeling your background involves a lot more money than—"

"In polite society, this isn't talked about."

"I was never good at manners."

"Millions."

Pittman blinked and set down his coffee cup.

"I don't know how much," Jill said. "My parents won't discuss it. We're having a difference of opinion about how I should conduct my future. They've been trying to punish me by threatening to disinherit me."

"So that's what you meant about the trust fund from your grandparents."

"They're the ones who earned it. They could handle it without being jerks. But my parents think the money gives them some kind of divine right to look down on people."

"Yes, you *are* angry."

"I told you, I want to help people, not ignore them or take advantage of them. Anyway, my grandparents anticipated all this and let me be independent by establishing the trust fund for me."

"We have a similar attitude. When I was a reporter—"

"Was? You still are."

"No. I'm an obituary writer. But there was a time . . . before Jeremy died, before I fell apart . . . The stories I loved doing the best were the ones that involved exposing the corruption of self-important members of the Establishment, especially in the government. It gave me a special pleasure to help drag them down and force them to experience what life is like for all of us ordinary bastards of the world."

"Drag aristocrats like Jonathan Millgate down?"

"I sure tried my damnedest."

"Be careful. If you talk like that to the wrong person, you could be providing a motive for why you might have wanted to—"

The next obvious words—*kill him*—never came out. Abruptly Jill stopped talking as the waitress set down their orders: grapefruit, English muffins, and yogurt for Jill; hash browns, eggs, and bacon for Pittman.

"You'll never get back into shape if you keep eating that way," Jill said.

"At least I ordered whole-wheat toast. Besides, I've been using a lot of energy lately."

"Right. You're not in enough danger—you've got to order a death sentence for breakfast."

"Hey, I'm trying to eat."

Jill chuckled, then glanced around at the warm dark tone of the wood in the rustically decorated room. "I'll be right back."

"What is it?"

"Somebody just left a newspaper. *USA Today.*" She looked eager to read it, but once she returned to their table and studied the front page, she murmured, "Suddenly I'm not hungry anymore."

"Bad?"

As the waitress seated a man and a woman at the table next to them, Jill handed him the newspaper. "Some things are better left unsaid."

Pittman scanned the story, becoming more and more disheartened. The crazed obituary writer's murder spree continued, bold letters announced. Pittman was being blamed for killing Father Dandridge. He was also being charged for shooting a man who, with two associates, had supposedly been sent to Jill's apartment by Jonathan Millgate's son to pass on his thanks for the skillful attention she had given his father while in intensive care. In addition, Pittman was suspected of abducting Jill.

"It keeps getting worse," Pittman said. "Maybe I ought to just hang myself and be done with it."

"Don't say that, not even as a joke."

Pittman thought about it. "The thing is, it *was* a joke—

about suicide. I'm amazed. A couple of days ago, I wouldn't have been able to do that."

Jill looked at him harder. "Maybe some good will come out of this."

Pittman gestured toward the newspaper. "At the moment, it doesn't look that way. We'd better leave. We've got plenty to do."

"Find the library?"

"Right." Pittman stood. "There's a reference series most libraries have. The *Dictionary of American Biography*. It lists the background, including education, for almost every intellectually famous person in the United States. It'll tell me if all the grand counselors went to Grollier. Then maybe the librarian will be able to help with something else."

"What's that?"

"How to find Grollier Academy."

4

"Four hundred dollars?" Jill shook her head, skeptical.

"I know. I'm not crazy about it, either, but I think this is the best deal we're going to get," Pittman said. "Every other used car on the lot costs more than the cash we have."

The car salesman, gangly, wearing a bow tie, watched with interest from the window of his office as Pittman and Jill circled the gray 1975 Plymouth Duster. The two-door sedan had what was once considered to be a sporty outline, but the rust on the rear fenders and the cracks in the vinyl top were evidence of the hard use that the vehicle had received.

"Then let's forget about paying cash," Jill said. "I'll write him a check and get something decent."

"Can't." Pittman recalled an interview he had once conducted with a private detective who was an expert in tracing fugitives. "An out-of-state check. The salesman will probably decide to call your bank to see if the check is good. The police will have put the bank on alert about reporting any attempt to get money from your account. My guess is that the grand counselors will have used their influence to get the same information. They would all know where to focus their search. It's the same reason we can't rent a car. To do that, we need to use your or my credit card. The moment either name is in the computer, we're blown. The grand counselors would immediately figure out why we're in Vermont. They'd have men waiting for us by the time we showed up at Grollier Academy."

"Four hundred dollars." Jill bleakly surveyed the rusted automobile.

"I know. It's a fortune when the only money at our disposal is a thousand. But we don't have an option. At least we bargained the salesman down from four hundred and fifty."

"But can we be certain the car won't break down when we drive it off the lot?"

"Well, the best thing I can tell you is, this car has a Chrysler slant-six engine. It's almost indestructible."

"I didn't realize you knew about auto mechanics."

"I don't."

"Then how—?"

"I once did a story about used-car lots and ways to tell if the buyer was getting cheated."

"Remarkable. I'm beginning to realize you're the sum of all the interviews you conducted."

"Something like that."

"And if we buy this heap, you think we'll be getting a good deal?"

"Only if the salesman gives us a free tank of gas."

5

As they headed northwest from Montpelier past the mountains that flanked Route 89, the Duster performed better than Pittman expected, its slant-six engine sounding powerful and smooth.

Because his bandaged left hand made it awkward for him to steer, Jill did the driving. She opened her window. "Whoever owned this car sure liked cigars."

"On the positive side, the seat covers don't look bad. Which is more than I can say about me. I'd better get presentable for when we arrive at Grollier."

He took the battery-powered razor from his gym bag, and while he shaved, he stared at the wooded peaks. "The map the used-car salesman gave us says this range is called the Green Mountains. An odd name for a place known for skiing."

"I told you the French were the first settlers here. Analyze the name of the state. Vermont is another way of saying *mont vert*: Green Mountain."

"It seems so peaceful here. What could there possibly be about Grollier Academy that's so terrifying to the grand counselors?"

"At the library, the *Dictionary of American Biography*

sure wasn't much help,'' Jill said. ''Professor Folsom was right. Eustace Gable and Anthony Lloyd went to Grollier, the same as Jonathan Millgate. But the other two grand counselors don't have any mention of Grollier in the entries about them.''

''That still doesn't prove anything. Does it mean they didn't actually go there, or is it that they don't want to advertise?''

As the Duster rounded a curve, revealing a meadow flanked by spruce trees, wooded peaks looming above them, Pittman was so preoccupied, he barely noticed the vista. ''Maybe they realized that it wasn't in their best interests for it to be known that they all went to the same prep school.''

''Why would that hurt them?''

''Too blatantly chummy. The general public might catch on about one of the federal government's nasty secrets: how inbred it is. Certain prep schools for the elite prepare the cream of the future Establishment to go to Ivy League colleges. That future Establishment graduates from those colleges and heads toward Washington. There they dominate various branches of the government. The CIA is tight with Yale, for example. The State Department used to be dominated by people from Harvard. Clinton's administration has a close relationship with Yale Law School.

''But it gets more specific. Ivy League colleges have secret societies, and the most prestigious—Skull and Bones, for example—are almost exclusively for members of the Establishment. A President appoints his classmates, his fellow society members. They become ambassadors or serve on the cabinet or as his advisers. You know the story—the President goes out of office and his appointees move into the private sector, where as members of the boards of various corporations they use their influence in Washington to manipulate government regulations. Or else they form their own consultation businesses and cater to foreign clients who pay them extremely well to use their powerful contacts. That's the reason I wanted to bring Millgate down to my level. Because he was in thick with the weapons manufacturers. He advocated military involvement in Korea, Vietnam, Panama, and Iraq, to name the most famous instances. But the question is, Was that for the good of the country and the world, or was it for the good of the weapons manufacturers and Millgate's Swiss bank account?

"On the most basic level, one of the reasons there's so much corruption in the government is that few politicians and diplomats have the courage to question the behavior of a former classmate and club member. Good old so-and-so made a mistake by accepting bribes. But he's not really a bad guy. Why turn him in and make trouble for him? Some social commitments are more important than representing the American people. Did you ever hear about Bohemian Grove?"

"No." Jill looked puzzled.

"It's another secret society: a males-only club, the main purpose of which is a summer outing that takes place each year in a compound in the woods of northern California. Its members are among the most powerful men in the United States: senators, cabinet members, major financiers, and corporate executives. Every Republican President since Nixon has been a member. The members are allowed to bring equally powerful guests from foreign countries. And what do all these influential men do? They get drunk, sing campfire songs, put on skits, and have pissing contests."

"A boy's camp for grown-ups," Jill said.

"Right. And when the festivities are over, when all those men go back to their powerful occupations, is it likely that any of them would ever accuse any others—they pissed against trees together at camp—of improper professional conduct? No way. The ultimate consequence of Bohemian Grove is to make it seem in terribly bad taste for power brokers to accuse one another of being unethical. And that's just one example of how club rules are more important than society's rules. The whole damned thing stinks."

Except for the drone of the Duster's engine, the car became silent. Jill steered around another curve, passing cattle near a stream in another valley.

At last she spoke. "Now that you've got that off your chest, do you feel better?"

"No."

"My father went to Yale. He was a member of Skull and Bones."

"I wasn't trying to be personal."

"But it's true. My father works in international commodities. Because he belonged to Skull and Bones, he seems to have more influence than his competitors. He's able to call in better favors."

"Then imagine the influence the grand counselors have," Pittman said. "Advisers to Presidents from Truman on. Ambassadors, members of the cabinet. At one time or another, three of them were secretaries of state. Two of them were secretaries of defense. Several were chiefs of staff and national security advisers, not to mention ambassadors to the United Nations, NATO, Great Britain, the USSR, Saudi Arabia, West Germany, et cetera. Never elected. Always appointed. With influence since the Second World War. A government within the government. When their power wasn't officially granted to them by the White House—during the Kennedy and Carter years, for example—they still managed to maintain their influence indirectly by creating foreign policy as members of think tanks like the Council on Foreign

Relations, the Rand Corporation, and the Rockefeller Foundation. Three of the grand counselors went to Harvard. Two went to Yale. And at least three of them, maybe all of them, went to the same prep school. But one of them felt so troubled by that prep school, he wanted to confess something about it on his deathbed, and the others were prepared to do anything to stop him."

6

At a scenic town called Bolton, they turned north off Route 89, following a narrow, winding road that took them through a long valley filled with meadows alternating with sections of pine trees.

"If the librarian in Montpelier knew what she was talking about," Jill said, "there ought to be a village up ahead."

Pittman squinted through the windshield, wishing he had sunglasses. "There. Just above that break in the trees. See it?"

"A church steeple. Good. We're right on schedule."

The steeple was brilliant white, and as they entered the village, they saw that not only the church but every building in town was the same radiant color. The village green seemed even more green by contrast. For a moment, even allowing for telephone poles and other evidence of modern technology, Pittman had the sense that he'd been transported back in time, that he was in a slower, more peaceful century.

Then the village was behind them, and as Jill drove next to a brisk stream filled with snowmelt, Pittman felt a sudden apprehension. He opened his gym bag and took out the .45, which he'd reloaded with ammunition from the container he had stored in the bag.

Remembering a detail from a story he'd written about undercover police officers, he put the .45 behind his back, beneath his belt, at the base of his spine. It felt uncomfortable, but that didn't matter. He knew that his sport coat would conceal it far better than if he carried it in his overcoat pocket, where it would form a drooping, conspicuous bulge. He would have to get used to the feel of metal against his back.

Last Wednesday night, I had the barrel of that gun in my mouth, he thought, and now . . .

He opened Jill's purse.

"Hey, what do you think you're doing?"

"Seeing if this fits."

He reached into the gym bag again and pulled out the other pistol, the one he had taken from the gunman in Jill's apartment. The gun was almost the same size as the Colt .45, but its caliber was smaller: a 9-mm Beretta.

"You don't expect me to carry that," Jill protested. "I don't even know how to use it."

"Nor did I until a couple of days ago. Learn as you need to—that's my motto."

Jill's purse was a shoulder bag, made of leather.

"Fits perfectly," Pittman said.

"I'm telling you I'm not going to—"

"The first thing you need to know about this gun," Pittman said, "is that the ammunition is stored in this spring-loaded device—it's called a magazine—that's inserted into the bottom of the grip."

"Are you serious?" Jill squinted as the Duster emerged from a covered bridge into dazzling sunlight. "Have you any idea how many people in critical condition because of gunshot wounds I've had to try to keep alive in intensive care? I don't want to know anything about that gun. I don't want it in my purse. I don't want to have anything to do with it."

Pittman studied her, then peered ahead. "The first turn on the right past the bridge."

"I *know*. It's on the sheet of directions the librarian gave us. I *remember* what she said."

"I was just trying to be helpful."

"Look, I'm sorry. I don't mean to be snappy. It's just . . . You scared me with that business about the gun." Jill's voice was unsteady. "For a while there, when we were on the train, I was able to forget how serious this is. I wish I wasn't doing this."

"Then turn around," Pittman said.

"What?"

"We'll go back to Montpelier and put you on the train back to New York. I'll go out to the academy on my own."

"Put me on the . . . ? What good would that do? Nothing's changed. Those men are still after me. I can't go back to my apartment. You've convinced me that the police wouldn't be able to protect me forever. I certainly can't depend on my parents to get me through this. They're probably being watched. As for my friends, I don't want to put them in danger. Being with you is the safest place I can think of, and that's not saying much, but it's all I've got."

"I've already fed a round into the firing chamber. To shoot this gun, you don't need to cock it. All you have to do is pull the trigger. There's the gate." Pittman pointed toward a large elegant sign that read: GROLLIER ACADEMY.

"I love its motto," Pittman said.

TO LEAD IS TO SERVE.

7

They veered from the road, following a paved lane up a treed incline. A white wooden fence had an open gate. They passed a small building that reminded Pittman of a sentry box at the entrance to a military base, but no one was there, and Pittman assumed that the building was for deliveries.

At the top of the incline, the view was spectacular enough to make Jill stop driving. On each side, fir trees stretched along a ridge, rising toward mountains. But directly ahead and below, the trees had been cleared, replaced by an impressive expanse of grassland. In the valley, there were stables, horses in a pasture, an equestrian ring, and a polo field. Adjacent were several football fields. In the distance, an oval-shaped lake glinted with the reflection of sunlight, and Pittman remembered the importance that Professor Folsom had said the school placed on team rowing.

But Pittman's attention was mostly directed toward the buildings in the center of the valley: a traditional white-steepled church, an imposing pillared building that was probably the school's administration center, fifteen other structures made of brick, covered with ivy.

"Dormitories and classroom buildings," Pittman said.

"Solid, efficient, functional. What the Establishment considers roughing it."

Jill looked puzzled. "You really have a problem about privileged society."

"To rephrase Will Rogers, I never met a rich person I liked."

"*I'm* rich."

"But you don't *act* rich. . . . I had an older brother," Pittman said.

Jill looked as if she didn't understand the jump in topics.

"His name was Bobby. He taught me how to ride a bicycle, how to throw a baseball. When I came home with a black eye from a fight in the school yard, he showed me how to box. There wasn't anything Bobby couldn't do. He was my idol. God, how I loved him."

"You keep using the past tense."

"He died in Vietnam."

"Oh. . . . I'm sorry."

"He didn't want to go," Pittman said. "He didn't believe the war was right. But my parents didn't have any money, and Bobby didn't have the means to go to college and he couldn't get a draft deferment. I remember him cursing about how all the rich kids got deferments but he couldn't. All of his letters mentioned the same thing—how everybody in his unit was part of the *Dis*establishment. Of course, Bobby used cruder terms. He kept writing about a premonition he had, about how he was sure he wouldn't be coming back. Well, he was right. Friendly fire killed him. I used to go to the cemetery every day to visit him. I remember thinking how easy it was for rich people to start wars when their children wouldn't have to fight. Later, after I saved enough money from working on construction to go to college, I realized something else—those rich people got richer because of the wars they started. That's why I became a journalist. To go after those bastards. To get even for my brother."

"I'm sorry," Jill repeated.

"So am I." Pittman stared down at his bandaged hand. "I apologize. I didn't mean for all that to come out."

Jill touched his arm.

8

The buildings were situated along a square that reminded Pittman of a parade ground. Pavement flanked each side of the square, and Jill almost parked there, until she saw a lot next to what appeared to be the administration building. Fifteen other cars were already parked there.

Pittman got out of the Duster, conscious of the .45 under his sport coat. It dismally occurred to him that one mark of how far he had come since his suicide attempt Wednesday night was that he thought of being armed as ordinary.

Jill locked the car and came around to join him. Her sneakers, jeans, and sweater were in a small suitcase in the backseat. The brown pumps, sand-colored A-line skirt, forest green jacket, and yellow blouse that she'd bought in Montpelier fit her perfectly. Pittman still wasn't used to seeing her in clothes that weren't casual and loose. The lines of her legs were as elegant as those of her throat.

"Ready?"

Jill inhaled nervously and nodded, securing the strap of her purse to her shoulder. "It's heavy."

"Just try to forget a weapon's in there."

"Easy advice from you. I still don't see why it couldn't stay in the car."

"Because things keep turning out differently from the way I expected."

They walked from the parking lot and watched as the square, which had been deserted except for a few groundskeepers, suddenly filled with hurrying students a few seconds after a bell rang in several of the buildings.

Wearing uniforms of gray slacks, navy blazers, and white shirts with red striped ties, the boys moved with brisk determination from what seemed to be classroom buildings, crossing toward a larger building opposite the church.

"Fire drill?"

Jill glanced at her watch. "Noon. Lunchtime."

A boy of about fifteen stopped before them. Like the others, he had brightly polished black shoes and neatly cut short hair. His gaze was direct, his voice confident, his posture straight. "May I help you, sir?"

"We were wondering where the school library is," Pittman said.

The boy pointed to Pittman's left. "In building four, sir. Would you like to see Mr. Bennett?"

"Mr. Bennett?"

"The academy's director."

"No. There isn't any need to bother him. Thank you for your help."

"You're welcome, sir." The boy turned and continued quickly toward the building the other students were entering on the opposite side of the square. Although they hurried, they managed to look like gentlemen.

"He'll be a credit to Washington insiders," Pittman said.

He and Jill walked in the direction the young man had indicated, reached a brick building with the number 4 above its entrance, and left the noon's intense sunlight, entering a cool, well-lit stairwell that smelled sweetly of wax. Steps led down and up.

The building was eerily silent.

"I doubt very much that a library would be in the basement," Jill said. "Too much danger of moisture getting into the books."

Nodding in agreement, his footsteps echoing, Pittman went up to the first floor. A hallway had several doors on each side. Many of the doors were open. In one, study desks were equipped with computers. In another, the desks had tape players and earphones, probably for language study.

As Pittman approached a third door, an elderly man came out, holding a key, about to close the door. He wore the same uniform that the students had been wearing. Short and somewhat heavy, he looked to be about sixty, with a salt-and-pepper mustache and receding gray hair.

He peered over his glasses toward Pittman and Jill. "I was just going to lunch. May I help you?"

"We were told that the library is in this building."

"That's correct." The man cleared his throat.

"Is that where you keep old yearbooks, things like that?" Pittman asked.

"They would be in our archival section." The man squinted. "I don't believe I've met you before. Why exactly would you need to know?"

"My name is Peter Logan. I'm a freelance journalist, and I've decided to write the book I always promised myself I would."

"Book?"

"About Grollier Academy. A great many distinguished public servants have graduated from this school."

"You could say that we've had more than our share. But

I strongly suspect that they wouldn't want their privacy invaded."

"That isn't what I had in mind. Grollier Academy itself, that would be my emphasis. I thought it would be an example to other schools if I wrote about the superior methods of this one. This country's in a crisis. If our educational system isn't changed . . . I'm worried about our future. We need a model, and I can't think of a better one than Grollier."

The man scrunched his eyebrows together and nodded. "There is no better preparatory education in America. What sort of research did you intend to do?"

"Well, for starters, Mr. . . . ?"

"Caradine. I'm chief librarian."

"Naturally I'll devote a considerable portion of the book to Grollier's educational theory. But I'll also need to supply a historical perspective. When the academy was founded. By whom. How it grew. The famous students who passed through here. So, for starters, I thought that a general immersion in your archives would be helpful. The yearbooks, for example. Their photographs will show how the campus changed over the years. And I might discover that Grollier had many more famous graduates than I was aware of. I want to skim the surface, so to speak, before I plunge into the depths."

"A sensible method. The archives are . . ." Caradine glanced at his watch. "I'm sorry. I have a lunch meeting with the library committee, and I'm already late. I'm afraid I can't show you through the archives. If you come back at one o'clock . . . The head of the refectory will, I'm sure, be pleased to provide you with lunch."

"Thanks, Mr. Caradine, but my assistant and I had a late breakfast and . . . To tell the truth, I'm anxious to get started. Perhaps you could let us into the archives and we can familiarize ourselves with the research materials while you're at your meeting. I had hoped not to inconvenience you. I'm sure you have better things to do than watch us read journals."

Caradine glanced at his watch again. "I really have to be at . . . Very well. I don't see the harm. The archives are on the next level. The first door on your right at the top of the stairs."

"I appreciate this, Mr. Caradine. If you'll unlock the door, we'll do our best not to trouble you for a while."

"Just go up." Caradine started past them toward the stairs. "The door isn't locked. Almost none of the doors at Grollier are locked. This is a school for gentlemen. We depend on the honor system. In its entire one-hundred-and-thirty-year history, there has never been an instance of thievery on this campus."

"Exactly what I was getting at earlier. This school is a model. I'll be sure to put what you just told me into my book."

Caradine nodded, fidgeting with his hands, saying, "I'm terribly late." He hurried down the stairs and left the building.

9

The door thunked shut. Pittman listened to its echo, turned to Jill, and gestured toward the stairs that led upward. "I hope he's a slow eater."

At the top of the stairs, the first door on the right had a frosted glass window. Pittman turned the knob, briefly worrying that Caradine had been mistaken about the door's being unlocked, but the knob turned freely, and with relief, Pittman entered the room.

He faced an area that was larger than he had expected. Shelves lined all the walls and, in library fashion, filled the middle area. Various boxes, ledgers, and books were on the shelves. Several windows provided adequate light.

Jill shut the door and looked around. "Why don't you check the shelves against that wall? I'll check these."

For the next five minutes, they searched.

"Here," Jill said.

Pittman came over. Stooping toward where Jill pointed at lower shelves, he found several rows of thin oversized volumes, all bound in black leather, their spines stamped with gold numbers that indicated years, arranged chronologically, beginning with 1900.

"I thought Caradine said the school went back a hundred

and thirty years,'' Pittman said. ''Where are the other yearbooks?''

''Maybe the school only started the tradition at the turn of the century.''

Pittman shrugged. ''Maybe. Millgate was eighty. Assuming he graduated when he was eighteen, his last semester at Grollier would have been . . .''

''The spring of '33,'' Jill said.

''How on earth did you do that so fast?''

''I've always been good with numbers. All my money, you know,'' Jill said, joking to break the tension. ''Of course, Millgate might have graduated when he was seventeen.''

''And the other grand counselors aren't all Millgate's age. Let's try a few years in each direction—1929 to 1936.''

''Fine with me,'' Jill said. ''I'll take up to '32. You take the rest.''

''There's a table over here.''

Sitting opposite each other, they stacked the yearbooks and began to read.

''At least the students are presented in alphabetical order. That'll save time,'' Jill said.

Pittman turned a page. ''We know that Millgate, Eustace Gable, and Anthony Lloyd went to school here. The other grand counselors are Winston Sloane and Victor Standish. But we also have to look for someone else.''

''Who?''

''Duncan. The way Millgate said the name . . . It had the same intensity as when he said 'Grollier.' I have to believe the two are connected. The trouble is, Duncan can be a first name as well as a last.''

''Which means we'll have to check every student's name in all these books.'' Jill frowned toward the stack. ''How large a student body did Professor Folsom say Grollier had?

Three hundred at one time? We've got a lot of names to read."

They turned pages intently.

"Dead," Pittman murmured.

Jill looked at him, puzzled.

"Old photographs always give me a chill," he said.

"I know what you mean. Most of these students are dead by now. But here they are, in their prime."

Pittman thought of how he coveted every photograph of his dead son. His mouth felt dry.

"Eustace Gable," Jill said. "Found him. Nineteen twenty-nine. A freshman."

"Yes, I found him as a senior in 1933. Here's Anthony Lloyd. Nineteen thirty-three. A senior," Pittman said.

"I've got him as a freshman in '29. And here's Millgate."

"But that doesn't do us any good. We already knew they went to school here."

"Hey," Jill said. "Got another one."

"Who?"

"Winston Sloane. A freshman. Nineteen twenty-nine."

"So I was right. He did go to school here, but the son of a bitch didn't include that in biographical facts he gave to researchers. He wanted it off the record."

"Got another one," Jill said excitedly. "Victor Standish."

"Every damned one of them."

"We don't need the other books," Jill said. "The names are repeated from year to year. They entered in '29 and graduated in '33."

"But what about Duncan? I didn't come across even one student with a first or last name of Duncan. What was Millgate trying to tell me. What's the connection between . . . ?"

10

A shadow loomed beyond the door's opaque glass window. Although Pittman wasn't looking in that direction, he sensed the brooding presence and turned just as the door came open. The stranger who entered took long, forceful steps. He wore the gray slacks, navy blazer, and red striped tie that were Grollier's uniform. He was tall, rigidly straight, in his fifties, with a pointed jaw, a slender patrician nose, and an imperious gaze.

"Would you mind telling me what you're doing?"

Pittman stood. "Why, yes. I'm planning to write a book about your school, and—"

"You didn't answer my question. *What are you doing?*"

Pittman looked at Jill in feigned confusion. "Research. At the moment, we're looking at yearbooks."

"Without permission."

"Mr. Caradine, the librarian, said we could—"

"Mr. Caradine doesn't have the authority to give you permission."

"Perhaps you could tell me who—"

The man's eyes flashed. "Only *I* can. I'm the academy's headmaster."

"Ah. Mr. Bennett." Pittman remembered the name that

the boy outside had mentioned. "We wanted to speak with you, but since it was lunchtime and you weren't in your office, we thought we'd come over here in the meanwhile."

"It wouldn't have done you any good. There are procedures that must be followed, letters to be submitted, applications to be filed."

"Letters? Applications? But you just said that you're the only one who can give permission for—"

"I said I'm the academy's headmaster. I have a board of supervisors who must be consulted about the sort of breach of privacy you're suggesting."

"But my book would be for the benefit of—"

"I'm afraid I must ask you to leave."

If he cuts off one more of my sentences . . . Pittman thought.

"Whatever you want," Pittman said. "I'm sorry for the misunderstanding. Perhaps we could go back to your office and discuss the problem."

"Yes, there *is* a misunderstanding, but not the one you suspect. I did not mean leave this room. I meant leave the campus."

Bennett glared toward Pittman, pointing toward the open door.

"Very well." Pittman worked to control himself. He was suddenly conscious that Jill stood next to him. "I'll write you a letter explaining what I want."

"I doubt that the letter will accomplish anything."

"I see."

"Good day."

"Good day."

11

"Friendly place." Jill drove from the parking lot.

"Yeah, I've been kicked out of a lot of spots, but never a prep school."

Jill followed the paved section that flanked the square, passed several classroom buildings and the administration building, then headed along the lane through the valley. "Is he still watching?"

Pittman turned to look. "In front of the library building. I can feel him glaring all the way from here. Mr. Personality."

Jill steered past the stables, then reached open grassland. The lane began to rise. "What touched him off? Do you think he's really annoyed that we didn't ask permission from him instead of the librarian?"

"Something tells me it wouldn't have done any good if we'd gone to see him first. This way, at least we got into the archives. Looks like we've got company."

"I see it in the rearview mirror. A brown station wagon leaving the school. Millgate's people?" Jill tensed. "What if they were waiting in case we came here?"

"I think they'd have moved against us before now."

"Unless they didn't want to cause trouble at the school.

All those kids. Too many witnesses. Maybe a few miles down the road, they'll catch up to us and . . ."

Jill crested the hill. The lane sloped sharply toward the building that reminded Pittman of a sentry's station. He lifted the back of his sports coat and pulled the .45 from behind his back.

"What are you doing?" Jill asked nervously.

"Just in case," Pittman said.

At once Jill was past the small building, driving through the open gate, reaching the country road.

"No, don't turn left. Go the other way," Pittman said.

"But left takes us back toward Montpelier."

"That's the way they'll expect us to go. If Millgate's people are in that station wagon . . . For now, they can't see us from the other side of the hill."

Jill veered right, tires squealing, onto the narrow country road. She stepped on the accelerator so hard that Pittman was pressed against the back of his seat. He gripped the dashboard as she swung around a curve.

Pine trees lined the road.

"Take it easy."

"There's nothing wrong with my driving."

"That's not what I meant. You're doing great. But I want to get off the road. Look for a— There. Between those trees."

Faster than Pittman expected, Jill stamped on the brake, twisted the steering wheel, and jolted off the road onto a semiovergrown, wheel-rutted lane that disappeared among pine trees. Sunlight became shadows as the Duster scraped past bushes. The impact of lurching over a rock slammed Pittman harder against the seat.

He stared through the rear window. "We're hidden from the road. Stop."

The moment Jill did, Pittman shoved his driver's door

open and hurried out. Stooping, doing his best not to expose himself, he chose an angle through the pine trees that would lead him back to the curve in the road. Sensing that he was close, he slowed, stepped carefully over a log, and crept among undergrowth. Immediately he came into sunlight and sank to the ground, seeing the road.

Across from him, to his right, was the open gate that led to the academy. Beyond it, the station wagon came rapidly into sight at the top of the wooded hill. As it sped down toward the gate, Pittman saw two husky men in the vehicle. They didn't look happy.

But to Pittman's surprise, the station wagon didn't pull out onto the road and speed toward Montpelier in pursuit of the Duster. Instead, it skidded to a stop at the gate. The two men got out angrily, swung the gate shut, and secured a chain and lock to it. With the gate fully in view, Pittman noticed a sign that he hadn't been able to see before: NO TRESPASSING. VIOLATORS WILL BE PROSECUTED.

I bet they will, Pittman thought as the two men stalked back to the station wagon, slammed their doors shut behind them, and drove back up the hill, disappearing over it toward the school.

Pittman waited to make sure that no one else was coming, then slowly stood. As he turned toward the forest, he saw Jill rise from bushes not far behind him.

"I don't get it," she said. "If they were Millgate's people, wouldn't they have followed us?"

"Maybe they were ordered not to leave the campus." Pittman entered the cover of the trees.

"Or maybe that's just Grollier's physical education staff," Jill said. "The football coach. The rowing instructor. Bennett might have told them to make sure we were off the property, and if we weren't, to give us some physical incentive."

Pittman stepped over another log. "Until reinforcements arrive. Bennett was testier than he needed to be. Someone might have warned him to be suspicious of visitors."

"And now he'll make some phone calls."

"Right," Pittman said. "But maybe they'll think we've really gone."

"We haven't?" Jill frowned. "You mean you don't plan to go back to Montpelier?"

"Where would we go from there?" Ahead, through the shadows of the trees, Pittman saw the gray Duster. "What other leads do we have?"

"But what else can we do here? We found out that no one named Duncan, first or last name, went to school with the grand counselors. Millgate must have been rambling. Duncan and Grollier have nothing to do with each other."

"No. I have to be sure." Pittman reached the Duster and leaned against its side. "I'm going back. Tonight."

12

As Pittman climbed the slats in the chest-high wooden fence, a quarter moon in a cloudless sky provided sufficient illumination. He dropped to the other side and entered the darkness of trees. He wore sneakers and the dark sweat suit he had stored in his gym bag. In addition, he wore a black wool cap, jacket, and gloves that he had bought, along with the knapsack, in a village ten miles farther along the road from the school. The jacket had roomy pockets, one of which contained his .45, the other a small flashlight.

He crept through the trees and soon emerged again into moonlight, crouching on an open ridge, staring down a grassy slope toward the murky silhouettes of Grollier's buildings. The time was almost midnight, and lights were off in every structure except the administration building. Exterior lights illuminated the square and the front of every building. There wasn't any sign of activity.

Nonetheless, Pittman waited, thinking, sensing. The weather report on the car radio had predicted a low of thirty-five degrees, and Pittman believed it, seeing frost come out of his mouth. He shivered, but only partially from the temperature, mostly from fear. He couldn't help contrasting how he had felt the night he entered the estate in Scarsdale with how he felt now. Back then, he'd been nervous but fatalistic. What did a man about to commit suicide have to lose? But now . . .

Yes? Pittman asked himself. What about now?

You're scared. Which means you *do* have something to lose. Are you suddenly afraid of dying?

Why?

Jill?

The thought came unexpectedly. What are you hoping for?

Hope. Pittman realized that the word hadn't been part of his vocabulary in quite a while. And with hope came fear.

He started down the grassy slope. The night was silent, making him conscious of a subtle breeze. His jogging shoes became wet, chilling his feet with moisture from the grass. He ignored the sensation, concentrating on the shadows of the equestrian ring that he passed and then the football field. The buildings of the school were outlined against the mountains.

He'd done enough newspaper stories about the military to be aware that someone with a sniper's rifle and a nightscope would have no trouble seeing him in the dark and killing him. With each step that brought him closer and with each second of awareness that he hadn't been shot, he gained confidence. Maybe the school is safe, he thought. Maybe it won't be as difficult as I feared.

A horse whinnied from somewhere behind him, and he froze, self-conscious, worried that the noise would attract someone's attention. The second time the horse whinnied, Pittman became mobile again, hurrying forward, reaching the shadows at the back of one of the buildings.

The night became quiet once more. Moving as rapidly as caution would allow, he skirted the perimeter of other buildings, taking care to avoid spotlights. When he came to the side of the square that was opposite the ridge from where he had entered, he pressed himself against a classroom building, intensified his senses, and concentrated on every detail in the darkness around him. The fact that he'd gotten this close continued to encourage him. But fear persisted in making him tremble, and he knew he couldn't take anything for granted.

Mustering his determination, he crept from the side of the classroom building and reached the library building. He didn't dare go to the front and expose himself to the spotlights. Instead, he approached the back door, turned the knob, and discovered that the door was locked. Remembering how the librarian had bragged that the school's successful honor system made it unnecessary for doors to be locked, Pittman realized the degree to which he and Jill had made the academy's headmaster nervous. Almost certainly, Bennett had been warned to watch out for strangers. But why? Pittman thought. What are Millgate's people trying to hide?

Earlier, when he'd been in the library building, Pittman hadn't seen any indication of a security system. At least that was one thing he didn't have to worry about as he took out his tool knife and used its lock picks. The scrape of metal made him wince. It seemed terribly amplified, certain to draw someone's attention. Nonetheless, he kept working, freeing one pin, then another, continuing to apply pressure to the cylinder, suddenly feeling it turn. As the lock's bolt slipped free, Pittman turned the knob, worrying that someone might be waiting for him on the other side. He drew his pistol, lunged through the opening, aimed toward the darkness with his right hand, and quickly used his bandaged hand to shut the door.

He listened. The echoes of his rapid entrance diminished. Enveloped by silence, he held his breath, straining to see in the darkness, on guard for the slightest sound. A minute passed, and in contrast with the chill he had felt outside, his body now streamed sweat.

He locked the door behind him, felt his way upstairs to the main floor, listened, crept up to the second floor, listened again, and approached the door to the archives. Its opaque window revealed a hint of moonlight glowing into the room. It, too, was locked, but this time he wasn't surprised.

Quickly he freed the bolt on this door, as well. He entered cautiously, shut the door behind him, crouched, and waited. If gunmen were in here, they had ample opportunity to move against him. After thirty seconds, he decided to take the risk. First he twisted the dead bolt's knob, locking the door behind him. Then he crossed to the windows and pulled down blinds. Finally he crept toward the middle shelves, turned on his flashlight, made sure that its modest beam was aimed toward the floor, where it wouldn't cast a glow on the windows, and reached for the yearbooks that he and Jill had examined that afternoon.

The gap on the shelf dismayed him. The yearbooks from 1929 to 1936 were gone. Hoping that they might still be on the desk where he and Jill had left them, he spun, but the flashlight revealed that the table was bare. Bennett must have taken them away.

Jesus, what am I going to do? Pittman thought.

Sweat continued to stream from him. He shut off his flashlight and slumped on the floor, propping his back against a shelf.

Check the other yearbooks, he told himself. Look at 1937.

Why? What's the point? The grand counselors had graduated by then.

Well, what other choice do you have?

Maybe there are other records.

Earlier, when Pittman and Jill had searched the room, they had concentrated on finding the most obvious research tool—the yearbooks. Pittman hadn't paid much attention to binders and boxes. Many of them were labeled SEM REP, followed by sequential, overlapping numbers—51–52, 52–53, 53–54, et cetera—and the pressure of a time limit had prevented him from investigating the contents. Now, with no alternative, he roused himself, stood, turned on his flashlight, and approached other shelves in the room.

The box he opened, chosen at random, contained neatly arranged smaller boxes, each of which held a roll of microfilm. It occurred to Pittman that SEM REP possibly meant semester report and that the numbers referred to the fall and spring sessions of each school year—the fall of 1949, for example, and the spring of 1950. The next school year would begin in the fall of 1950 and continue to the spring of 1951, thus the overlapping numbers—49–50, 50–51. Over the years, the accumulation of documents had become difficult to store, not to mention a fire hazard, so the pages had been transferred to microfilm, convenient for the school but a major frustration for Pittman.

What am I supposed to do, steal the rolls for the years the grand counselors attended Grollier? I still wouldn't be able to read them.

Unless you take them to a library that has a microfilm reader.

But the rolls I steal might not have the information I need. I can't leave here until . . .

Wait a minute. There wouldn't be microfilm if there wasn't a . . .

Pittman recalled from his previous visit that a bulky object covered by a cloth had stood on a table in a corner to the right of the door. Its shape was distinctive. He shifted toward it, pulled off the cloth, and found, as he had hoped, a microfilm reader. When he turned it on, he didn't know which made him more nervous—the hum of the machine's fan or the glow on its screen. He went back to the boxes, checked labels, and sorted among rolls of microfilm, soon finding one for 31–32. He attached it to the spools on the machine, wound the microfilm past the machine's light and its magnifying lens, and studied what appeared on the screen.

What he squinted at was a class list and final grades for students in Ancient History I. None of the grand counselors' names was on the list. He spooled forward through individual reports about various students, reached Classical Literature I, and again was frustrated to discover that none of the grand counselors had been in that course.

At this rate, it'll take me hours to read the entire roll. There's got to be a more efficient way to . . .

Ancient History I? Classical Literature I? The numeric designation implied that there were later sections of those courses, Pittman thought—II, III, maybe IV. Heat rushed into his stomach as he understood. Grollier was a four-year prep school. The grand counselors had been juniors in 1931–1932. They would be in the class reports for juniors, three-quarters through the roll.

Pittman swiftly turned the roll forward, ignoring classes marked II, reaching III, and immediately slowing. He found a course in British History in which all the grand counselors were registered and had received top grades. He found a number of other courses—British Literature, European History, Greek Philosophy, and Latin—in which the grand counselors had also been registered and received top grades. But in none of those classes did he find anyone named Duncan.

He spooled onward to a course in Political Science, and immediately his attention was engaged: While the other courses had contained numerous students, this course contained only six—the five grand counselors, plus a student named Derrick Meecham.

Pittman hesitated. When he and Jill had separated the yearbooks, hers had been for 1929–1932, his for 1933–1936. As he had learned, the grand counselors had graduated in 1933. But it now seemed to him that when he had concentrated on the *M* category, looking for Millgate's name, he hadn't come across any reference for a student named Meecham in the 1933 yearbook.

He knew he could be wrong. All the same . . .

He spooled forward to the spring semester for that course, and now he frowned with puzzlement. The roster had dropped from six names to five.

Derrick Meecham was no longer enrolled.

Why? Had Meecham gotten sick? His grade from the previous semester had been an A, so he couldn't have found the course so difficult that he'd dropped it. Besides, Pittman had the suspicion that at Grollier, students didn't have the option of dropping courses. Rather, Grollier dropped students.

Then *why*? Pittman thought again. He became more convinced that his memory hadn't failed him, that Derrick Meecham had, in fact, not been in the yearbook for the following year. Pittman rubbed the back of his neck. His gaze wandered to the bottom of the screen, where the course's instructor had signed the grade report, and suddenly he felt as if he had touched an exposed electrical wire, for the instructor's ornate signature seemed to come into focus. Pittman tried to control his breathing as he stared at the name.

Duncan Kline.

Jesus, Pittman thought. Duncan hadn't been a student. He'd been a teacher. That was the connection with Grollier. Duncan Kline had been Millgate's teacher. All of them. He had taught *all* the grand counselors.

13

A noise made Pittman stiffen. Despite the whir of the fan on the microfilm machine, he heard footsteps on the stairs beyond the door. Angry voices rapidly approached.

Startled, he shut off the machine.

". . . can't believe you didn't leave someone on guard."

"But the two of them left. I made sure."

The voices became louder.

"Were they followed?"

"To the edge of campus."

"Stupid . . ."

"It's a good thing we flew up here."

"The outside door was still locked. That proves the records are safe."

"It proves nothing."

Lights came on in the hallway outside the door. Their illumination glowed through the opaque window. The shadows of men loomed beyond it.

"I took the yearbooks they were looking at."

"But what else might they have come back to look at?"

Someone tried to turn the knob on the door.

"It's locked."

"Yes, I secured that door, as well. I told you no one's been here."

"Just get out your key and unlock the damned door."

Pittman's chest cramped. He couldn't get enough air. In desperation, he swung toward the murky room, trying to figure out where he could hide, how he could stop the men from finding him.

But he remembered how the room had looked during daylight. There'd been no other door. There was nothing to hide behind. If he tried to conceal himself beneath a table, he'd be found at once.

The only option was . . .

The windows. As he heard a key scraping in the lock, a voice saying, "Come on, hurry," Pittman rushed to a window, raised its blind, freed its lock, and shoved the window upward.

"Stop," one of the voices in the hallway said. "I heard something."

"Somebody's in there."

Bennett's unmistakable nasally voice said, "What are you doing with those guns?"

"Get out of the way."

Pittman shoved his head out the window, staring down. He had hoped that there might be something beneath the window to break his fall, but at the bottom of the two-story drop, there was nothing except a flower garden.

"When I throw the door open, you go first. Duck to the left. Pete'll go straight ahead. I'll take the right."

Pittman studied the leafless ivy that clung to the side of the building. The vines felt dry and brittle. Nonetheless, he had to take the chance. He squirmed out the window, clung to the ivy, and began to climb down, hoping that there weren't other men outside in the darkness.

"On three."

Pittman climbed down faster. The ivy to which he clung made a crunching noise and began to separate from the bricks and mortar.

Above him, he heard a crash, the door being thrust open. Simultaneously the ivy fully separated from the wall. As Pittman dropped, his stomach soaring, his hands scrabbled against the wall, clawing for a grip on other strands of ivy. The fingers on his bandaged left hand were awkward, but those on his right hand snagged onto vines. At once those strands snapped free from the wall, and he dropped farther, grabbing still other ivy, jolting onto the ground, falling backward, desperately bending his knees, rolling.

"There!" a man yelled from the window above him.

Pittman scrambled to his feet and raced toward the cover of the rear of the next building. Something kicked up grass next to him. He heard the muffled, fist-into-a-pillow report from a sound-suppressed gunshot.

Adrenaline made his stomach seem on fire. Needing to discourage them from shooting again, he spun, raised his .45, and fired. In the silence of the night, the roar of the shot was deafening. His bullet struck the upper part of the window, shattering glass.

"Jesus!"

"Get down!"

"Outside! He can't go far on foot! Stop him!"

Pittman fired again, not expecting to hit anybody but wanting anxiously to make a commotion. The more confusion, the better. Already lights were going on in dormitory windows.

He raced past bushes, rounded the back corner of the next building, and tried to orient himself in the darkness. How the hell do I get out of here? He left the cover of the building, running toward the murky open meadow. A bullet whizzed past him from behind. He ran harder. Suddenly a shadow darted to his left, someone running parallel to him. He fired. In response, another bullet whizzed past, from his left. A car engine roared. Headlights gleamed, speeding toward the meadow ahead of him.

With no other direction available, Pittman veered sharply to his right. He zigzagged and veered again as a third bullet parted air near his head. In the darkness, he'd become disoriented. Dismayed, he found that he was running back toward the school. The rear of the buildings was still in shadow, but the commotion was causing more lights to come on all the time. Feeling boxed in, he took the only course available, charged up to the back door of the nearest building, prayed that its lock hadn't been engaged, yanked at the door, and felt a surge of hope as it opened. He darted in, shut and locked the door, felt the impact of a bullet against it, and turned to sprint along a hallway.

But he'd bought only a few moments of protection. When he showed himself outside the front of the building . . .

Can't hide in here. They'll search until they . . .

What am I going to do?

This building was evidently a dormitory. He heard students on the upper floors, their voices distressed.

Witnesses. Need more witnesses. Need more commotion.

He swung toward a fire-alarm switch behind a glass plate and hammered the butt of his .45 against the glass. The plate shattered with surprising ease. Trembling, he reached in past shards and pulled the switch.

The alarm was shrill, reverberating off walls, causing picture frames to tremble. Despite its intensity, Pittman sensed the greater commotion on the floors above him, urgent footsteps, frightened voices, a *lot* of them. A welter of shadows in the stairway became students in pajamas scurrying to get outside.

Pittman hid his weapon and waved his right arm in fierce encouragement, as if he was their benefactor, his only interest their safety.

"Hurry up! The place is on fire!"

The students surged past, and Pittman went with them, storming into the arc lights that blazed in the night. He saw gunmen to his right but knew that they didn't dare shoot with so many students in the way, and as the students dispersed in turmoil, Pittman darted toward the next building on the left, lunging inside.

There, he again broke the glass that shielded the fire-alarm switch. Activating the alarm, wincing from the ferocity of the noise, he rushed back in the direction he had come, toward the front door.

They'll expect me to go out the back. They'll try to cut me off, some of them coming through here while the others wait in the darkness behind the building.

He pressed himself against the wall next to the front door, and at once it was banged open, gunmen charging into the building. In the same instant, students came scurrying down the stairwell. Amid the confusion as the gunmen and the students collided and tried to pass one another, Pittman scrambled out the front door, students swirling around him. But instead of continuing the pattern he'd established to race toward the next building on this side of the square, he took what he felt was his best chance and sprinted directly across the square, veering among students who milled sleepily, their bare feet obviously cold, frost coming out of their mouths in the glare from the arc lights. He heard the fire alarms and students swarming out of adjacent buildings and gunmen shouting, chasing him.

Even allowing for his being out of condition, he didn't think he'd ever run so fast. His jogging shoes hit the ground perfectly, his legs stretched, his sweat suit clung to his movements as it had so many mornings when he had gone jogging before heading to work—before Jeremy had gotten sick. He felt as if his increasing effort was the distillation of every race he had ever entered, every marathon he had ever endured. Inhaling deep lungfuls of air, pumping his legs faster, stretching them farther, he surged between buildings on the opposite side of the square and kept racing into the darkness behind them.

This was the direction from which he had initially come down off the ridge and across the meadow, approaching the campus. In a frenzy of exertion, he managed to increase speed, spurred by the buzz of another bullet parting air near his side. They've crossed the square, he thought. They saw where I went and followed me.

From the square, he heard the roar of cars. They'll soon drive behind these buildings. There's no way I can outrun . . .

He changed direction just in time, almost banging into the side of a building. His eyes, stung by the glare of the arc lights in the square, were only now adjusting to the darkness, and in confusion, he took a moment to realize that he'd reached the stables.

Men shouted behind him. A bullet struck the stone side of the building. Pittman whirled, went down on his left knee, propped his right arm on his other knee to steady his trembling aim, and fired toward the men pursuing him. They cursed and dove to the ground. A car fishtailed around a building, its headlights blazing, and Pittman fired toward them, missing the headlights but shattering the windshield.

Immediately he ducked back, knowing that the muzzle flashes from his pistol had made him a target. More bullets struck the side of the building, splintering stone. From somewhere on the other side, horses whinnied in panic. Pittman swung around a corner, approaching them. He reached a fence and opened its gate, scrambling back as horses charged through, escaping into the night. The more confusion, the better. He had to keep distracting his pursuers.

Then racing across the horse pen toward the opposite fence, he heard the roar of the cars speeding toward the stables. Have to get ahead of them.

A horse had stopped on the other side of the fence. With no other choice, Pittman clambered onto the rails. He'd once written a story about the stables near Central Park. He'd taken a few lessons. His instructor had emphasized: "When afraid of falling, keep your legs squeezed as tightly as you can around the horse's sides and clamp your arms around the horse's neck."

Pittman did exactly that now, leaping off the fence, landing on the horse, startling it, clinging as it reared, but he was prepared and the horse wasn't. Compacting his muscles in desperation, he managed to stay on, and now the horse wasn't rearing. It was galloping, hoping to throw off its burden. Pittman clung harder, jolted by the horse's rapid hoofbeats. He leaned so severely forward, clutching the horse's bobbing neck, that he didn't think he provided a silhouette for the gunmen.

From behind, the headlights of several rapidly approaching cars lit up the meadow around and ahead of him. The roar of the engines and the noise of the galloping horse were too great for Pittman to be able to hear if bullets whizzed past him, but he had to assume that his pursuers were shooting at him, and he furiously hoped that the uneven meadow, its bumps and rises and dips, would throw off the gunmen's aim in the darkness.

Without warning, the horse changed direction. Unprepared, Pittman felt his grip slipping, his body shifting to the right. About to topple, he clamped his legs so tightly around the horse that the pain of the effort made him wince. His rigid arms completely encircled the horse's neck. The cars sped nearer, bumping across the meadow, their headlights bobbing, gleaming, as the horse changed direction again, but this time Pittman anticipated, and although his body shifted, he felt in control.

He was wrong. Deeper shadows loomed before him, suddenly illuminated by the headlights. The forest seemed to materialize out of nothing, a wall of trees and bushes forming an apparently unbreachable barrier that so startled the horse, it reared up, at the same time twisting sideways, and Pittman's grip was finally jerked free. As the horse's front hoofs landed heavily and the animal twisted again, more sharply, to avoid colliding with the trees, Pittman flew in the opposite direction. Frantically praying that the horse wouldn't kick backward, he struck the ground, flipped, and rolled, the wind knocked out of him, the pistol in his jacket pocket slamming against his ribs.

He rolled farther, urgently trying to avoid the panicked horse, to save himself from being trampled. Immediately the horse galloped away, and Pittman faced the headlights speeding toward him. He stumbled to his feet, struggled to breathe, and lurched toward bushes, stooping to conceal himself. Bullets snapped twigs and shredded bark from trees. He crouched lower, hurrying among the thickly needled branches of pine trees. Bullets walloped into trees and sliced needles that fell upon him. Hearing car doors being opened, he spun, saw the headlights through the trees, and fired, surprising himself that he actually shattered one of the lights.

At once his pistol no longer worked. In dismay, he pulled the trigger. Nothing happened. The .45 felt off balance in his hand. Its slide remained back, its firing chamber open. Heart sinking, he understood. He had used all his ammunition. He had more in his jacket pocket, but his pursuers were so close that there wasn't time for him to reload, and he didn't have confidence in his ability to remove the pistol's magazine and refill it in the dark.

Not while men were shooting at him.

Not while he was on the run, which he immediately began doing, scurrying uphill through the murky forest. Several times he bumped painfully against trees. In the darkness, he failed to see deadfalls and stumps and tripped, losing his balance, hitting the ground. Each time, he ignored his pain and surged upward, moving faster, harder, spurred by the noises of gunmen chasing him. Flashlights blazed. Men shouted.

Pittman strained to figure out where he was. He had entered on this side of the valley—that much he was sure of. But there the trees had stopped on a ridge, giving way to grassland that sloped toward the meadow. Here the trees were at the bottom of the slope. In which direction was the grassy hill? He had to find it. He had to get to that ridge. Because past the trees and the fence beyond it, Jill was waiting with the car.

"I hear him!"

"Over there!"

"Spread out!"

Pittman raised his right arm to shield his eyes from needled branches. Enveloped by darkness, he climbed with less energy, his legs weary, his lungs protesting. He kept angling to the right, choosing that direction arbitrarily, needing *some* direction, hoping to reach the grassy slope.

Without warning he broke free, nearly falling on the open hill. Hurry. Got to reach the top before they're out of the trees, before they see me. His only advantage was that he was no longer making noise, snapping branches, crashing through bushes, scraping past trees. But the gunmen were definitely making noise. Pittman could hear them charging through the underbrush behind him, and responding to an intense flood of adrenaline, he braced his legs, took a deep breath, then struggled up the slope, its incline becoming steeper, its wet grass slippery.

Briefly his senses failed him. The next thing he realized, he was lumbering over the top of the ridge, men were yelling below him, their flashlights silhouetting him, and then he was past the ridgeline, entering more trees, colliding with the fence, clutching it, gasping.

"Here!" a man yelled behind him, flashlight bobbing.

Pittman strained to climb the wooden fence, dropped to the other side, and staggered ahead, enveloped again by trees.

"Jill!" His voice was hoarse, his words forced. "Jill, it's me! It's Matt!"

"He's not far ahead!" a man yelled.

"Jill! Where are you? I can't see you! It's me! It's Matt!"

Flashlights reached the fence, their beams stabbing into the darkness, revealing Pittman among the trees.

A bullet nicked his jacket. Another singed his hair.

Gunshots roared among the trees. Pittman didn't understand. His pursuers had been using silencers. Why would they have taken them off? Why would they want to make noise?

They didn't. They hadn't. The gunshots came from ahead of him. The men were sprawling on the ground behind the fence, yelling to one another to turn off their flashlights, to stop making themselves targets. Bullets struck the fence. The shots continued from ahead of Pittman.

"I'm here!" Jill screamed.

Pittman saw the muzzle flashes from the pistol she fired.

"I see you!"

"Stay down!" she yelled.

Pittman dropped to his hands and knees, scurrying among bushes, reaching her.

"Hurry! Get in the car!"

He opened the passenger door and flinched as the interior light came on, revealing him. After diving in, he slammed the door shut and watched in amazement as Jill—who was already in the car and had been firing through her open window—turned the ignition key, stomped the accelerator, and rocketed from a gap in the trees onto the narrow, winding country road.

14

"Thank God, thank God," was all he could say. The words came out between his urgent attempts to breathe, his chest heaving, falling, his body shaking as sweat streamed off his face and soaked his clothes.

The Duster skidded around a sharp corner. Expertly controlling the car, Jill immediately increased speed. The car's headlights revealed the twists and turns of the tree-flanked two-lane road.

Quickly Pittman turned to see if headlights followed them.

"Not yet," Jill said. "They have to go back and use the lane from the school. The gate's two miles away. By the time they get onto this road . . ."

She reached another straightaway and again increased speed.

"Thank God," Pittman continued to murmur. "When I didn't see you, when I yelled but you didn't answer . . ."

"I didn't know what to do. I heard shooting from the school, then something that sounded like fire alarms."

"Yes." Pittman caught his breath, explaining.

"I heard car engines," Jill said. "Then there was shooting among the trees, and suddenly you came over the fence, stumbling toward me, yelling. The flashlights behind you, those men chasing you . . . All I could think of was that I had to distract them. You told me that to fire the pistol I didn't need to cock it. I only had to pull the trigger. I didn't bother trying to aim. I just leaned out the car window, pointed the gun up, and started shooting. My God, it holds a lot of bullets."

"Fifteen."

"And it jerks, and my ears are ringing from the noise. . . . When I saw where you were, I pointed the gun away from you and aimed toward the fence."

She braked, steered sharply around a curve, and pressed harder on the accelerator.

Pittman shook his head in amazement. "Where did you learn to drive like . . . ?"

"My father's a nut about Porsches. One of the few father-daughter things he ever did was teach me about racing. If this car had a clutch and a standard shift, I could really show you about gaining speed around curves."

Pittman's hands wouldn't stop shaking.

"And you're bleeding," Jill said.

"What?"

"There's blood smeared on your face, your hands, and your clothes. You must have scraped yourself on that wall or running through those trees. Or else . . ."

"Say it."

"I hope you weren't hit."

"No. I don't feel any pain."

Jill stared ahead, speeding under a covered bridge.

"I said, I don't feel any pain."

"That's not always a good sign."

"What do you mean?"

"Sometimes a wound traumatizes nerves in the area and stops them from sending messages."

Shaking worse, Pittman felt along his legs, his torso, his arms. "Everything seems to be all right." Surprising himself, he yawned and realized that he'd been doing so for quite a while. "What's wrong with me? I'm worried I might have been shot and yet I can't stop yawning."

"Shock. The adrenaline's wearing off. Your body's telling you it needs a long rest."

"But I don't feel sleepy."

"Right." Jill turned on the car's heater.

Pittman yawned again.

"Just to humor me," Jill said, "why don't you crawl in the backseat, stretch out as best you can, and close your eyes for a while?"

"The backseat. That reminds me." With difficulty, Pittman squirmed into the darkness of the backseat and zipped open his gym bag.

"What are you doing?" Jill asked.

"Reloading. Hand me your pistol. I've got other magazines from the gunmen who were at your apartment. I'd better reload yours, too."

Jill muttered something.

"I didn't hear you."

"Guns. I swore I'd never touch one of the damned things. Now here I . . ."

The Duster's slant-six engine roared as Jill drove faster.

15

The silence woke him. Pittman blinked, disoriented, realized that he was slumped in the car's backseat, and squinted ahead toward Jill behind the steering wheel. The sky was gray with false dawn. The car was stopped.

"Where are we?" Groggy, he sat up and winced from stiffness.

"A motel in Greenfield, Massachusetts. That's about ten miles south of Vermont and a hundred and fifty miles from the school. That ought to be far enough to keep them from finding us." Jill hesitated. "For now."

"You must be exhausted."

"I shouldn't be. Normally I'd be getting off my shift at the hospital in an hour. I'd work out, eat a light dinner, watch something I taped on the VCR, and go to sleep around noon."

"But this isn't 'normally.' "

"No kidding. You'd better stay in the car while I see if the desk clerk will accept cash to rent a room. With that dried blood on you, you're not exactly presentable. I'll tell the clerk we were visiting relatives in Waterford, Connecticut. We thought we could drive all night and get home, but finally we're exhausted."

Jill got out of the car, went into the motel's office, and returned with a key.

The room was on the bottom level, in back of the motel, a location Jill had requested, telling the clerk they didn't want to be disturbed by morning traffic.

No one was around when she unlocked the door and Pittman followed her in. They set the gym bag and small suitcase on the floor, assessing the unit. It was plain but clean, its air stale but not offensive.

"I asked for a nonsmoker's room." Jill locked the door. "The clerk assured me the television works. There's no one in the rooms on either side of us, so we won't be disturbed that way, either."

"Twin beds," Pittman said.

"Lucky."

"Yeah." Sex was the last thing on Pittman's mind. Nonetheless, he felt self-conscious.

"You'd better get in the bathroom and take your clothes off. We have to find out how badly you were injured." Jill reached into Pittman's gym bag and pulled out a first-aid kit that they'd bought, along with the flashlight and Pittman's wool coat, the day before.

"I bet you were a drill sergeant on the ward."

"Don't tell me you're going to get modest on me." Jill looked amused. "I didn't say I was going into the bathroom with you. Close the door, undress, rinse the blood off, and after you get a towel around you, I'll check you out. For sure, I'll have to change the bandage on your hand."

"I bet you loved poking big needles into your patients."

Pittman went into the bathroom and, feeling a strain on his right side, removed his clothes.

"And you'd better not use the shower." Jill's voice came

muffled from the opposite side of the door. "You might get weak and lose your balance. Sit in the tub."

He examined himself. "I can tell you right now, there aren't any holes in me. But I've got a nasty bruise along my right ribs."

"Soak in the tub. I'll be back in a minute."

"Where are you going?"

"There's an all-night convenience store across the street. I'm going to see what they've got to eat."

Orange juice, doughnuts, and skim milk, Pittman discovered when he finished his second bath (the first had been pink from the dried blood he'd rinsed off). He came out of the steaming bathroom, feeling awkward, knowing he looked embarrassed, holding a towel around his hips.

"I'm surprised," Jill said. "Given everything you've been doing—sleeping on park benches, pretending to be a policeman—you didn't strike me as the bashful type."

Pittman saw a blanket on a metal shelf outside the bathroom and pulled it down.

"Before you cover yourself, I need to look at that bruise on your ribs." Jill drew a finger along it.

"Ouch."

"Ouch? Grown-ups don't say ouch. Little kids say ouch. Does this rib hurt?"

"For Christ sake, yes."

"Now that's what big kids say. Inhale. Exhale. Does the pain get worse? No?" She thought about it. "An X ray would tell for sure, but I doubt any ribs are broken. Not that it matters."

"Why?"

"The treatment for broken ribs is the same as for bruised ones—nothing. You don't put on a cast for broken ribs. These days, you don't even get taped. What you get is a warning not to exert yourself and not to bump your ribs against anything."

"Swell."

"The miracles of modern medicine. The cut on your hand, those scratches and scrapes, those I can do something about." After putting on antibiotic cream and rebandaging Pittman's left hand, Jill began applying disinfectant to portions of his face. "Are you hungry?"

"Yes, but I wish you'd brought some coffee along with the doughnuts, orange juice, and milk."

"After the adrenaline rush you just went through? Haven't you had enough chemical stimulation for a while?"

"I get the feeling you don't do much without thinking of the chemical effect on your body," Pittman said.

"Better living through proper diet."

"In that case, I'm surprised you bought doughnuts."

"It's the only thing remotely acceptable the store had. Beef jerky was out of the question."

"I hate skim milk."

"Give it a chance. You'll learn to like it. Then even two percent tastes awfully rich."

"If we stay together, I suppose I'm going to have to learn to like it."

Jill looked strangely at him.

"What's the matter?" Pittman asked.

"Nothing."

"Tell me. What is it?"

"You were talking about if we stay together. Under better circumstances, I'd like that," Jill said.

Pittman felt himself blush.

"It's my turn for that bath." Looking as self-conscious as Pittman had earlier, Jill picked up her suitcase and went inside. "Turn on CNN," she suggested before closing the door. "See if there's anything about us."

Pittman didn't move for a moment, thinking about what she had said . . . about staying together. Six days ago, he'd been eager to die.

16

Jill finished a glass of orange juice and pointed toward the news report on CNN. "Nothing about what happened at the school."

"I'm not surprised."

"You think they didn't link it to us?"

"No, I'm sure they did," Pittman said.

"Then . . . ?"

"I'm also sure that some very powerful people squashed the story. They don't want any attention whatsoever directed toward that school."

"Yes," Jill said. "I see what you mean. All those Establishment parents, they don't want anything to sully the reputation of the prep school their sons graduate from. For that matter, the alumni don't want Grollier to be associated with break-ins and shooting, either. Far too vulgar."

"Maybe more than that," Pittman said. "Maybe what we're trying to learn is serious enough to destroy the school."

Jill turned quickly toward him, her gaze intense. "Yes, that would explain a lot."

"Duncan Kline. One of the men who taught the grand counselors. And Derrick Meecham, the student who dropped his class with them."

"Or got sick and had to leave school," Jill said.

"But never came back to Grollier the following year, the year he would have graduated. I wonder, how do we find out about Duncan Kline and Derrick Meecham? I'm sure as hell not going back to Grollier."

After a moment, Jill said, "I have an idea. A minute ago, we were talking about Grollier's alumni."

"Yes?"

"Grollier's students are all targeted for Ivy League colleges. In particular, Harvard, Yale, and Princeton. If we assume that Derrick Meecham finally graduated from a prep school similar to Grollier, then it's also logical to assume that he went to one of the Ivy League colleges," Jill said. "The registrar's office for each school can tell us if Meecham went to any of them. But that won't help us. What we really want to know is where Meecham is now."

"The university organizations that keep track of the current addresses of graduates are the alumni foundations," Pittman said.

"Exactly. The groups that are always asking graduates for big bucks to support their alma mater. My father graduated from Yale. He's one of the biggest donators to its athletic program. The alumni foundation is on the phone to him all the time, sucking up to him, offering special tickets, inviting him to exclusive athletic banquets, wanting more money. Believe me, for his daughter, they'll do whatever I want. And if Derrick Meecham didn't go to Yale, I'll ask them to contact the alumni foundations at the *other* Ivy League colleges."

17

"Fine, Ray, fine," Jill said to the telephone. Her blue eyes gleamed with intensity. "Yes, my father's feeling well, too. Oh, that. Sure, we have disagreements from time to time. We always patch them up. We're getting along fine." Concentrating, she drew a hand through her long, straight blond hair. "As a matter of fact, I think I might drive up and see him this weekend."

From one of the twin beds, Pittman watched her. She was wrapped in a blanket, sitting on the desk that supported the phone. A digital clock next to her showed 11:38 A.M. He and Jill had gotten four hours sleep, which wasn't nearly enough, his sore body and raw eyes told him, but there wasn't time to rest longer. The call had to be made. They had to keep moving.

"The reason I'm calling, Ray, is I'd appreciate it if you did me a favor," Jill said to the telephone. "It's easy, and it won't cost you money." She laughed. "Great. I knew you'd feel that way. I'll be sure to tell my father that you helped me out. What I'd like you to do is check your computer files for an alumnus named Derrick Meecham. What class? I'm not sure. Some time in the thirties. Yes, that does go a way back. Is it a problem? One of my elderly patients is terminal. He wants to tie up some loose ends, and evidently there's something he wants to tell this Derrick Meecham. I guess they haven't seen each other in fifty years. Don't ask me why it's important to him, but I feel sorry for the old guy and I'd like to do him a favor. Yeah, I'm a softy. On the ward, they're always kidding me about— What? You must have a hell of a computer system. Just a minute while I write down that address. The phone number. Wonderful. I've got it. Thanks, Ray. I really appreciate this. I'll be sure to tell my father. You bet, and you take care of yourself, too."

Jill set down the phone and looked at Pittman. "Boston."

Pittman studied a map he'd found in the bedside table. "That's only a hundred miles away. It looks like if we take Route Two, we can be there in a couple of hours."

"Matt?"

"What's wrong?"

"Suppose Meecham can't help us."

Pittman didn't answer.

"Suppose he can't," Jill repeated.

"Don't think like that," Pittman said. "We need to believe that he *will* help us. Otherwise, we won't be able to keep going."

Jill studied him. "Your determination surprises me."

"Why?"

"A man who's planning to kill himself normally doesn't worry about the future, about staying alive."

"Survival? That's not what this is about."

"Oh? You sure as hell could have fooled me. What *is* it about?"

"A week ago, I was sitting in my bathtub with a gun in my mouth."

Jill wasn't prepared for the change of subject. The stark sentence shocked her.

"I had settled all of my affairs. Every debt I owed had been repaid, every favor returned. Everything was in order. I wasn't beholden to anyone. I intended to leave this world with every loose end tied. Then my phone rang and a friend I thought I was even with asked me to do him a favor. He had done so much for my son that I couldn't possibly refuse him. Now I have another debt."

"To whom?" Jill asked.

"You."

"What are you talking about?"

"It's my fault that you're involved in this. If I hadn't gone to your apartment . . . I have to make sure you're safe."

Holding the blanket tightly around her, Jill walked over to him. She touched his shoulder. "Thank you."

Pittman shrugged, self-conscious.

"And if you're successful?" Jill asked.

Pittman didn't know what to answer.

"*Then* what?" Jill asked. "Do you still plan to kill yourself?"

Pittman looked away.

FIVE

1

They took longer than they had anticipated. Route 2 was under construction. It ended well before Boston, and they were forced to take an indirect route, using 495 south, then 90 east into the city, arriving only in late afternoon. Pittman's bandaged left hand felt less awkward. He did the driving this time, letting Jill nap in the backseat until he stopped at a rest area just outside the city.

She sat up, stretched, and yawned.

"These are your old stomping grounds," Pittman said. "Do you think you can find the address?"

"Sure. No problem."

"You don't need to look at a map?"

"Derrick Meecham must have a lot of money. This address is in Beacon Hill. It's a couple of blocks from where my parents live."

Rush hour slowed their progress even more, but finally, shortly after six, Jill steered from the Massachusetts Turnpike onto Columbus Avenue, from there to Charles Street through Boston Common, and then into the historic, exclusive district of Beacon Hill.

Pittman studied a narrow, tree-lined, cobblestoned street. On one side, a spiked wrought-iron fence enclosed a small park, while on the other side, nineteenth-century brick town houses cast shadows from the lowering sun. Jill turned a corner, and here gated driveways separated some of the mansions. Through the metal bars, Pittman saw courtyards, gardens, and carriage houses converted into garages.

"And this is where you were raised?"

"When I wasn't at private schools," Jill said.

"It's beautiful."

"It can also be a trap. That's why I moved away to real life."

"At the moment, I'd prefer to *escape* from real life."

Ahead, a Mercedes pulled away from a line of cars parked at the curb, and Jill eased into the space. When she got out, she straightened her tan skirt and put on her green blazer. "Do I look presentable?"

"Lovely."

"Just remember, when we knock on the door, whoever opens it is going to make an instantaneous judgment about us, based on how neatly and acceptably we dress."

Pittman reached into the car, took his tie from his gym bag, and put it on. He hoped his shirt wasn't too wrinkled. His slacks and sport coat were as clean as he could make them.

"If I understand your logic," Pittman said, "I'd better not identify myself as a reporter."

Jill nodded. "The kind of wealth we're dealing with is extremely class-conscious. The press is definitely considered beneath them."

"Then what angle are we going to use? What I tried at Grollier? That I'm writing a book about the academy?"

"Better yet, you're a *history professor* who's writing a book about the academy. Academics have privilege."

They went up a half dozen stone steps to a large, polished, weathered oak door.

"It probably dates back to the early 1800s," Jill said.

Pittman grasped an iron knocker and tapped it against a metal plate secured to the door.

They waited.

Pittman knocked again.

"Maybe no one's home."

"I don't see any lights in the windows," Jill said.

"Maybe they've gone out to dinner."

Jill shook her head. "Any respectable Boston Brahmin doesn't go out to dinner this early. Besides, Meecham's elderly. I doubt he strays far from home."

Pittman raised his hand to knock on the door again, but he was interrupted as he heard a lock being freed. The knob was twisted. The door came slowly open, revealing a short, frail-looking white-haired woman who wore a tasteful high-collared blue dress that had long sleeves and a hem that almost covered the support hose on her swollen calves and ankles. She had liver spots on her deeply creased skin.

She opened the door only partially, squinting through her thick glasses at Pittman and Jill. "Yes? Do I know you?" Her voice was tremulous.

"No, ma'am," Pittman said. "My name is Peter Logan. I'm a history professor from across the river." He referred to Harvard. "I apologize if this is an inconvenient time for me to be calling, but I was wondering if I could speak to your husband about a book that I'm writing."

"History professor? Book? My husband?"

"Yes, ma'am. I'm doing research about some American educational institutions, the classic ones, and I'm hoping that your husband can answer some questions that occurred to me."

"Questions? My husband?"

Pittman's stomach sank. She keeps repeating what I say, turning my statements into questions. We're wasting our time, he thought. She's senile. She doesn't have the faintest idea of what I'm talking about.

The woman raised her head. "I don't know what questions you have in mind, but I'm afraid my husband can't answer them. He died a year ago."

The shock of what she said and the lucidity with which she said it made Pittman realize that he'd severely misjudged her.

"Oh." He was too surprised to know what to say. He knew he should have considered the possibility that Meecham would be dead by now, but the fact that the grand counselors, except for Millgate, were still alive had made Pittman hope that those associated with the counselors would still be alive, as well.

"I'm terribly sorry," he said. "The alumni association at Yale told me that Derrick Meecham lived here. I assumed that their records were up to date."

"They are." The woman's voice became more tremulous.

"I don't understand."

"Derrick Meecham does live here."

"Forgive us, ma'am," Jill said. "We still don't understand."

"My son."

"Mother," a man's refined voice said from inside the house. "I thought we agreed that you had to save your energy. There's no need for you to answer the door. That is Frederick's responsibility. Where is he, by the way?"

The door came all the way open, and Pittman faced a distinguished-looking man in his early fifties. The man had a broad forehead, graying hair, steady eyes, and the solid expression of someone used to giving orders and expecting them to be obeyed. His three-piece gray pinstriped suit was the most perfectly tailored that Pittman had ever seen.

"Yes, may I help you?" the man asked without enthusiasm.

"This man is a professor," the elderly woman said.

"Peter Logan," Pittman added. "I teach history at Harvard. I've made a mistake, I'm afraid. I wanted to speak with your father, but as I've just learned, he passed on. I didn't mean to intrude."

"Speak to my father? What about?"

"I'm doing research on the history of Grollier Academy."

The man didn't react for a moment, didn't blink, didn't seem to breathe. "Grollier?"

"It's had such a major influence on American government, I thought it was time to investigate what makes it unique."

"Oh, it's unique all right."

Cars drove by on the street. The sun dipped lower, casting shadows. The man continued to stare at Pittman.

Then his chest moved. "Come in, Professor. . . . I'm sorry, could you repeat your name?"

"Logan. Peter Logan. This is my wife, Rebecca. She's a historian, also."

"Derrick Meecham." The man offered his hand, once more saying, without enthusiasm, "Come in."

2

The man locked the door and led the way, escorting his mother along a wide wood-paneled corridor that had landscape paintings, forests and farmhouses, on the walls. The frames looked old enough to be from the nineteenth century.

They passed a brightly polished maple staircase, its banister beautifully carved. At the end of the corridor, lights glowed in several rooms, from one of which a tall man wearing a white jacket appeared.

"Where have you been, Frederick?" Meecham asked. "I found my mother answering the door."

"I thought she was upstairs," the man in the white jacket said. "I apologize, sir. I didn't hear the door. I was down in the wine cellar, looking for the Rothschild you requested."

"Did you find it?"

"Yes, sir."

"The '71?"

"Yes, sir."

"Good. Mother, why don't you rest until dinner? Frederick will take you up to your room. Perhaps you can watch one of your television shows." Meecham's tone implied that he himself did not watch television.

"*Victory Garden* is about to begin, Mrs. Meecham," Frederick said.

"Yes," the elderly woman said with enthusiasm, allowing herself to bc escorted into a small elevator.

As the cage rumbled and rose, Meecham turned to Pittman and Jill. "In here, please."

They entered one of the many rooms that flanked the wide corridor. There were bookcases with leather-bound volumes on them, mostly law books. The furniture was subdued, correct, and, Pittman assumed, more expensive than he would have dreamed. An Oriental rug stopped three feet short of the walls on each side, revealing a rich oak floor.

Meecham gestured. "Sit down. May I have Frederick get you anything?"

Pittman and Jill each took a chair across from where Meecham stood by the fireplace.

"Thank you, no," Pittman said.

"I was just about to have a cocktail," Meecham said, his hospitality surprising Pittman.

I don't get it, Pittman thought. He was ready to give us the bum's rush until I mentioned Grollier. Now he invites us in and wants us to have cocktails. Either *he* needs the drink, which it doesn't look like, or else he hopes a little booze might get us to talk more candidly than we normally would have.

"A cocktail would be nice," Jill said. "Whatever you're having."

"Vodka martinis."

"That would be fine."

Meecham walked to the door, opened it, spoke to someone, then shut the door again and sat on a Chippendale chair next to the fireplace.

He looked steadily at Jill and then Pittman. "Grollier Academy."

"That's right. Your father went there, I believe," Pittman said.

"Oh, indeed he did. But I don't quite understand. Of all the students who went to Grollier, why would you have chosen my father for an interview?"

"Because he was a classmate of the so-called grand counselors. Jonathan Millgate, Eustace Gable, Anthony Lloyd . . ."

Meecham's features hardened. "I know who the grand counselors are. My father had no relationship with them after he left Grollier."

"But evidently he was close to them at the time."

Meecham spoke quickly. "What makes you think that?"

"In his junior year, your father enrolled in a course in political science. The number of students was quite small. Only six. The five grand counselors—"

"And my father."

It was the first time that Meecham had volunteered any information. Pittman tried not to look surprised.

"Yes," Jill said. "Naturally in so close an environment, especially on the subject of political science, your father would have heard ideas exchanged that might have explained the direction the grand counselors took in their political careers."

Meecham studied them. "My father never discussed that with me."

The room became silent. Meecham was through volunteering information.

"Then perhaps he said something about the grand counselors themselves," Pittman said, "some kind of reminiscence when he read about them in the newspapers, something that would give insight into their formative ideas."

"He never discussed that with me, either," Meecham said flatly.

"No comment at all when he read about something controversial that they did?"

"Only that he'd gone to school with them."

Yes, Meecham had definitely stopped volunteering information.

The room became silent again.

Someone knocked on the door. Frederick came in carrying a tray that held glasses and a martini pitcher.

"Frederick, we won't have time for cocktails after all. I just remembered that the San Francisco office is going to be phoning me in five minutes," Meecham said.

Frederick paused where he was about to set the tray on a sideboard.

Meecham stood, approaching Pittman and Jill. "I don't like conducting business in the evening. That's probably why I forgot about the telephone call. Let me escort you to the door. I regret I couldn't be of more help, but my father was a private man. He seldom talked to me about personal matters. Grollier was a long time ago."

Pittman stood, as well. "One last question. I wonder if you have any idea why your father didn't graduate from Grollier."

Meecham, whose gaze had been steady, blinked twice.

"He dropped out of the political science course that he was taking with the grand counselors," Pittman said. "And then he stopped attending Grollier altogether."

"I've changed my mind, Frederick," Meecham said. "The San Francisco office can talk to me tomorrow. When the phone rings, tell them I'm unavailable."

"Very good, sir."

"Please, serve the martinis."

"Certainly, sir."

Meecham sat again, looking uncomfortable. Pittman and Jill lowered themselves back into their chairs. Frederick poured the martinis and brought a tray to each of them, offering a choice of olives or pearl onions.

Pittman sipped, enjoying the cold, smooth taste, suddenly realizing how little alcohol he had had to drink since he'd followed Millgate to the Scarsdale estate five nights earlier. Prior to then, he'd been really putting it away, guzzling it. He hadn't been able to face the day—and especially the nights—without it. He had needed to distance himself from reality. Now he couldn't allow anything to keep him from facing reality.

The situation became awkward. No one said anything, waiting for Frederick to leave.

3

As the door was finally closed, Meecham said, an edge in his voice, "What do you really want?"

"Just what we told you—to know your father's attitude toward Grollier and the grand counselors," Pittman said.

"If you're aware that my father never graduated from Grollier, that he dropped out in his junior year and went to another school, it must be obvious to you that he had ambivalent feelings."

"Did he ever say anything about one of his teachers? Duncan Kline?"

Meecham's gaze became piercingly direct. "This has nothing to do with a book about education."

"I beg your pardon?"

"You're not here because you're doing a history of Grollier." Meecham stood abruptly. "You know about Grollier. You keep talking around the subject, hinting about it, but you know."

"I don't understand," Pittman said.

"Otherwise, you wouldn't have mentioned Duncan Kline."

"He taught the political science class that your father dropped out of."

"The man was perverted."

Pittman had taken a sip from his martini. Surprised by Meecham's comment, he swallowed hard. "Perverted?"

"You mean you actually don't know?" Meecham looked threatened, as if he'd let down his defenses.

"We know something happened there," Pittman said. "Something traumatic enough to make Jonathan Millgate obsessed about it, even all these years later, on his deathbed."

"I can't speak for Jonathan Millgate. All I know is what my father told me when I suggested that I send my own boys to Grollier. It was one of the few times he ever showed open emotion. He told me that under no circumstances was I to send his grandsons there. I was to send them to a decent school, a place like Groton, from where my father had eventually graduated and then gone to Yale."

"But why did he dislike Grollier so much?" Jill asked.

Meecham scowled at the floor, debating with himself. "Maybe it's time." He looked up. "Maybe Grollier hasn't changed. Someone should have done something long ago to make sure it stopped."

"To make sure *what* stopped?"

Meecham nervously tapped his fingers against his martini glass. "This is all off the record."

"If that's the way you want it."

"It's the way it *has* to be." Meecham seemed to struggle with himself in order to say the words. "Duncan Kline was a pedophile."

Pittman stared.

After further painful hesitation, Meecham continued. "A boy's prep school was a perfect environment for him. From what my father told me, I gather that Duncan Kline was a brilliant instructor, quick, amusing, encouraging, the sort of charismatic figure who attracts the brightest of students. Apparently he was also an athlete, particularly when it came to rowing. His policy was to assess each incoming class, to select the most promising boys, a very small group, a half dozen or so, and then to nurture them throughout their four years at Grollier. I suspect that he also chose them on the basis of how emotionally distant they were from their parents, how keenly they needed a substitute father. Certainly my father was never close to *his* father. Duncan Kline encouraged them to take small private seminars from him. He trained them to be oarsmen and to outdistance the best official Grollier team. He gradually became more and more intimate with them, until by their junior year . . . As I said, one group from each incoming class. That way, as one group graduated and went on to college, another was there to take that group's place."

Pittman felt sick.

His face tight with emotion, Meecham took a long sip from his martini. "My father rejected Kline's advances. Kline backed off. But soon he came back and *persisted* in making advances. This time, when my father rejected him, Kline was either so indignant or else frightened of being exposed that he made academic life intolerable for my father, giving him impossible assignments, ridiculing him at every opportunity. My father's grades declined. So did his morale. And his health. Apparently he had some kind of collapse at home during the Easter break of his junior year. He never went back to Grollier."

Pittman couldn't keep dismay from his voice. "But didn't your father's parents do anything about Duncan Kline?"

"Do what?" Meecham shook his head, puzzled. "What would you have had them do?"

"They should have reported Kline to the authorities. They should have reported the whole mess to the headmaster of the school."

Meecham looked at Pittman as if he'd gone insane.

"Reported . . . ? You obviously don't grasp the situation. This happened in the early 1930s. The time was repressive. I assure you that topics such as child molestation were definitely not considered fit for conversation. Not in polite society. That type of sordidness existed. Everyone tacitly knew that. But surely it didn't occur often, and when it did, it happened to other people, lesser people, unrefined, crass people who were economic and moral inferiors."

"Dear Lord," Pittman said.

Meecham looked more disturbed as he took another long sip from his martini. "That was the prevailing opinion of the time. Grollier boasts governors, senators, congressmen, even a President of the United States among its distinguished alumni. For a student to claim that sexual abuse occurred on a regular basis at that school would have been unthinkable. So many reputations would have been at stake that the authorities would never have treated the charge seriously. They would have been forced to conclude that the student was grievously mistaken, that he was making such an outrageous accusation because he needed to blame someone for his poor grades. As a matter of fact, when my father told *his* father what was happening at Grollier, his father slapped him, called him a liar, and told him never to repeat such filth again."

Pittman was astonished.

"So my father kept it a secret and never told another person until I suggested to him that Grollier might be a good prep school for my sons."

"But surely the other students would have supported your father's claim," Pittman said.

"Would they have? Or would their parents ever have allowed them to be subjected to questions of such a gross nature? I wonder. In any case, it's a moot issue. The matter never got that far."

Her blue eyes intense, Jill leaned forward. "Are we to assume that Duncan Kline made advances to the grand counselors, also? That those advances were accepted?"

Meecham stared at his martini glass. "They were Duncan Kline's chosen few, and they did continue to take his seminars. By the time my father told me this—my sons went to prep school in the mid-seventies—it was too late to do anything about Kline himself. He died in the early fifties. By then he'd retired from Grollier and had a place here in Boston. My father said that one of the happiest days of his life was when he read Kline's obituary. Believe me, my father had very few happy days."

Meecham finished his martini and frowned toward the pitcher as if he could use another drink. "I don't know what you've set out to prove, but if there were other instructors like Kline at Grollier and if their counterparts still teach there and if your book exposes them, we've both done some good."

Suspecting something, Pittman asked, "Would you be willing to be quoted?"

Meecham reacted sharply. "Of course not. Do you think I'd want that kind of public attention? I told you before, this conversation is strictly off the record. I'm just pointing you in the right direction. Surely someone else would be willing to substantiate what I've told you. Ask the grand counselors." Meecham looked bitterly amused. "See how willing *they'd* be to go on record."

"When Jonathan Millgate was in intensive care, he told his nurse, 'Duncan. The snow. Grollier.' What do you suppose he meant by the reference to snow?"

"I have no idea. Certainly my father never mentioned anything that linked Duncan Kline with snow."

"It's a slang expression for— Could it be a reference to cocaine?"

"Again, I have no idea. Was that expression even used back in the early thirties? Would someone as distinguished as Jonathan Millgate reduce himself to that type of language?"

Pittman shrugged in discouragement, then turned, hearing a knock on the door.

Frederick stepped in. "Mr. Meecham, two policemen are at the door."

4

Pittman felt a hot rush of adrenaline.

Meecham looked surprised. "Policemen?"

"Detectives," Frederick said. "They want to know if you've had any contact with someone named Matthew Pittman. He's traveling with a woman and . . ." Frederick's gaze settled on Pittman and Jill.

Meecham frowned.

"Where does that door lead?" Pittman stood unexpectedly and crossed the room toward a door in a wall that faced the rear of the house. The door was the only other way out of the room, and since Pittman had no intention of using the door through which Frederick had come, of going out to the corridor where the detectives might see him, he had to take this route. He heard Jill's footsteps behind him.

"What do you think you're doing?" Meecham demanded.

By then, Pittman had pulled the door open and was lunging into a narrow hallway, Jill hurrying to follow. Pittman's breathing quickened.

"Stop!" Meecham said.

On the left, Pittman passed the entrance to the mansion's kitchen. He had a glimpse of a male cook in a white uniform, who opened his mouth in surprise. Then Pittman, flanked rapidly by Jill, was out of sight, running farther down the hallway, reaching a door, the window of which revealed a cobblestone courtyard.

Pittman jerked the door open and felt pressure in his chest as he realized that the dusky courtyard was bordered by a high barred gate, an even higher wall, and a carriage house turned into a garage. We'll never get out of here!

Dismayed, he swung to look behind him. Frederick appeared at the opposite end of the hallway. The cook appeared at the entrance to the kitchen. Heavy footsteps pounded toward the hallway from the front of the house.

To the right of the door, stairs led upward. Pittman suddenly thought of a way to escape and charged up, tugging Jill behind him. At a landing, the stairs veered up on another angle, and Pittman bounded higher, reaching a hallway on an upper level of the house.

Closed doors lined the hallway. Meecham was making indignant demands to someone downstairs. He flinched as a door came open across from him.

Meecham's elderly mother appeared, deceptively frail. "So much noise. I can barely hear the television."

Pittman made a soothing gesture. "Mrs. Meecham, does your bedroom have a lock?"

"Of course it has a lock. Doesn't every bedroom have a lock? Do you think I want people barging in on me? What are you doing up here?"

"Thanks." Pittman hurried with Jill, who didn't understand what Pittman was doing.

"You can't go in there," Mrs. Meecham said.

Pittman slammed and locked the door. From a television in the corner of the well-appointed lace-curtained room, complete with a four-poster bed, the opening theme music for a nature program almost obscured Mrs. Meecham's feeble pounding on the door.

Jill swung toward Pittman. "What are we *doing* in here?"

A look of sudden understanding crossed her face as Pittman rushed toward a window. It faced the back of the house, above the peaked roof of the garage. Pittman opened it. "Come on."

Inexplicably Jill seemed frozen.

"What's wrong?"

Jill stared toward the door. She turned her head and stared at Pittman.

"Come on!" Pittman said.

At once Jill became animated, taking off her pumps. "Of all the times to be wearing a skirt."

The hem tore as she raised her legs and climbed out the window. The pounding on the bedroom door became louder. Angry male voices were on the other side. The door shuddered as if shoulders were being heaved against it.

Wincing from pain in his injured ribs, Pittman squirmed out the open window after Jill. The garage roof sloped down on each side, and Pittman tried to stay balanced while running along the peak. Behind him, something crashed in the bedroom. Jill reached the end of the roof and jumped down onto something, appearing to run on the shadowy air as she disappeared around the corner of another house.

When Pittman came to the end of the garage, he saw that what Jill had jumped down onto was the foot-wide top of the high wall that enclosed the courtyard. That wall continued to the left, bordering the courtyards of other houses, bisecting the block. Hearing a shout behind him, Pittman climbed down as well and followed her, breathing so deeply and quickly that his lungs felt on fire.

Then he, too, was out of sight from the window. He concentrated not to topple from the wall as he hurried after Jill, who clutched her shoes in one hand, her purse in the other, and scrambled in bare feet across the peak of another carriage house turned into a garage.

A shingle gave way beneath Jill, skittering off the roof, clattering onto cobblestones. She fell on her shoulder, beginning to roll. Pittman grabbed her arm. She dropped her shoes, which hit the cobblestones next to the shingle.

Pittman charged ahead with Jill and halted unexpectedly.

The wall didn't continue beyond the garage. The courtyard was framed only by buildings. Below them, a red Jaguar was parked outside the garage.

Pittman jumped down onto the car, feeling the roof protest but hold. Jill didn't need encouragement; she leapt down after him, the metal so smoothly waxed that her bare feet nearly slid out from under her. Pittman clutched her, kept her from falling, held her arms, lowered her toward the cobblestones, then jumped down next to her.

The Jaguar's owner must have been planning to leave soon. The gate to the street was open. Racing along the driveway, they reached a narrow, quiet, tree-lined, twilit street around the corner from Meecham's address.

Their gray Duster was parked three spaces to their left.

"Drive." Jill threw him the keys, then climbed into the backseat, ducking below the windows.

As Pittman sped away from the curb, he heard her rummaging in the back. "What are you doing?"

She was scrunched down out of sight, fumbling with something.

"Jill, what are you—?"

"Getting out of this damned skirt and into my jeans. This skirt is ripped up to my backside. If I'm going to be arrested, there's no way it's going to be with my underwear showing."

Pittman couldn't help it. He was frightened, and he couldn't catch his breath, but she sounded so embarrassed, he started laughing.

"I've had it with skirts. And those useless pumps," she said. "I don't care who I have to make an impression on. All this running. From now on, it's sneakers, a sweater, and jeans. And how the hell did the police know we were at Meecham's? Who could have . . . ?"

Pittman stared grimly ahead. "Yes. That's really been bothering me." He concentrated. "Who?"

"Wait a minute. I think I— There's only one person who had that information. The man I phoned."

"At the alumni association?"

"Yes. This evening, he must have called my father to suck up to him by bragging how he'd done me a favor."

"That's got to be it. Your father knows that the police are looking for you. As soon as he heard from the alumni association, he phoned the police and sent them to the address the man gave you."

"We've got to be more careful."

Pittman steered onto Charles Street, trying to keep his speed down, not to be conspicuous. As other cars switched on their headlights, so did he.

"Exactly," Pittman said. "More careful. What were you doing back there?"

"I told you, putting on my jeans."

"No. I mean back at the house. In the bedroom. You looked as if you weren't going to leave with me."

Jill didn't respond.

"Don't tell me that's true," Pittman said. "You actually thought about staying behind?"

"For a second . . ." Jill hesitated. "I told myself, I can't keep running forever. The police don't want *me*. It's Millgate's people who want to kill me. I thought I could end it right there. I could stay behind and give myself up, explain to the police why I've been running, make them understand you're innocent."

"Yeah, sure. I bet that would have been good for a few laughs at the precinct." Although Pittman could understand Jill's motives, the thought that she would have left him caused his stomach to harden. "So what made you keep going? Why didn't you stay?"

"The story you told me about how you'd been arrested when you were trying to get an interview with Millgate seven years ago."

"That's right. Two prisoners, probably working for Millgate, beat me up while I was in a holding cell."

"The police weren't quick enough to help you," Jill said.

"Or maybe the guards were bribed to take a long coffee break." Pittman continued to feel bitter that she might have left him. "There's no way the authorities could guarantee your safety. So that's why you came with me? Your common sense took over? You listened to your survival instincts?"

"No," Jill said.

"Self-preservation."

"No. That's not why I came with you. It had nothing to do with worrying whether the police could protect me."

"Then . . . ?"

"I was worried about you. I couldn't imagine what you'd be like on your own."

"Hey, I could have managed."

"You don't realize how vulnerable you are."

"No kidding, every time somebody shoots at me, I get the idea."

"*Emotionally* vulnerable. Last Wednesday, *you* were going to do the shooting."

"I don't need to be reminded. It would have saved a lot of people a lot of trouble."

Jill squirmed from the back into the passenger seat. "You just proved my point. I think the only reason you've managed to get this far is you had somebody cheering for you. I've never met anybody more lonely. Why would you want to keep going if you didn't have anything to live for, anybody to care?"

Pittman felt as if ice had been placed on his chest. Unable to speak, he drove through the shadows of Boston Common, reaching Columbus Avenue, using the reverse of the route Jill had taken.

"The reason I decided to stay with you," Jill said, "is that I didn't want to be apart from you."

Pittman had trouble speaking. "You sure did a lot of thinking in a couple of seconds."

"I've been thinking about this for a while," Jill said. "I want to see how we get along when life gets normal."

"If," Pittman said. "If it ever does get normal. If we can ever get through this."

"This is a new feeling for me," Jill said. "It kind of snuck up on me. When you introduced me as your wife . . ."

"What?"

"I liked it."

Pittman was so amazed that he couldn't react for a moment. He reached over, touching her hand.

A car horn blared behind him as he steered from traffic and stopped at the curb. His throat feeling tighter, he studied Jill, her beguiling oval face, her long corn-silk hair, her sapphire eyes glinting from the reflection of passing headlights.

He leaned close and gently kissed her, the softness of her lips making him tingle. When she put her arms around his neck, he felt ripples of sensation. The kiss went on and on. She parted her lips. He tasted her.

He felt a swirling sensation and slowly leaned back, pleasantly out of breath, studying her more intensely. "I didn't think I'd ever feel this way again."

"You've got a lot of good feelings to catch up on," Jill said.

Pittman kissed her again, this time with a hunger that startled him.

Shaking, he had to stop. "My heart's beating so fast. . . ."

"I know," Jill said. "I feel light-headed."

Another car horn blared, passing them. Pittman turned to look out his side window. Where he'd stopped was in a no parking zone. "The last thing we need is a traffic ticket."

He pulled from the curb.

Immediately he noticed a police car at the corner of the next street. He tried to keep his speed constant, to peer straight ahead. It seemed to take him forever to pass the cruiser. In his rearview mirror, he saw the police car move forward—not in his direction, but along the continuation of the side street.

He loosened his tight grip on the steering wheel. His brow felt clammy. He was more afraid than usual.

5

"Where are we going?"

Pittman shook his head, squinting at the painful glare of headlights on the crowded Massachusetts Turnpike. For several minutes, he'd been pensively quiet, trying to adjust—as he assumed Jill was—to the powerful change in their relationship. "We're heading out of Boston. But where we're going, I have no idea. I don't know what to do next. We've learned a lot. But we really haven't learned anything. I can't believe that Millgate's people would want to kill us because we'd found out what happened to him in prep school."

"Suppose he wasn't molested."

"The circumstantial evidence indicates—"

"No, what I mean is, suppose he'd been willing," Jill said. "Maybe Millgate's people believe that the old man's reputation would have been ruined if—"

"You think *that's* what his people were afraid of?"

"Well, he confessed something to you about Grollier, and they killed him for it. Then *you* had to be stopped. And me because they have to believe you've told me what you know."

"Killed him to protect his reputation? I just can't . . . There's something more," Pittman said. "I don't think we've learned the whole truth yet. Maybe the other grand counselors are trying to protect *their* reputations. They don't want anyone to know what happened to *them* at Grollier."

"But what exactly? And how do we prove it?" Jill asked. She rubbed her forehead. "I can't think anymore. If I don't get something to eat . . ."

Glancing ahead, she pointed to the right toward a truck stop off the turnpike, sodium arc lamps glaring in the darkness.

"My stomach's rumbling, too." Pittman followed an exit ramp into the bright, eerie yellow light of the gas station/restaurant, where he parked several slots away from a row of eighteen-wheel rigs.

After they got out of the car and joined each other in front, Pittman hugged her.

"What are we going to do?" She pressed the side of her face against his shoulder. "Where do we go for answers?"

"We're just tired." Pittman stroked her hair, then kissed her. "Once we get something to eat and some rest . . ."

Hand in hand, they walked toward the brightly lit entrance to the restaurant. Other cars were pulling in. Wary, Pittman watched a van stop ahead of them. The driver had his window down. The van's radio was blaring, an announcer reading the news.

"I guess I'm needlessly jumpy. Everybody looks suspicious to me," Pittman said. He made sure that he was between Jill and the van when they came abreast of the driver's door. The beefy man behind the steering wheel was talking loudly to someone else, but the radio was even louder than his gruff tone.

Pittman turned toward the van. "My God."

"What's the matter?"

"The news. The radio in that van. Didn't you hear it?"

"No."

"Anthony Lloyd. One of the grand counselors. *He's dead.*"

6

Dismayed, Pittman ran with Jill back to the Duster. Inside, he turned on the radio and switched stations, cursing impatiently at call-in shows and country-western programs. "There must be a news station *somewhere*."

He turned on the car's engine, afraid he would weaken the battery while he switched stations. Ten minutes later, an on-the-half-hour news report came on.

"Anthony Lloyd, onetime ambassador to the United Nations, the former USSR, and Britain, past secretary of state as well as past secretary of defense, died this evening at his home near Washington," a solemn-voiced male reporter said. "One of a legendary group of five diplomats whose careers spanned global events from the Second World War to the present, Lloyd was frequently described—along with his associates—as a grand counselor. To quote the reaction of Harold Fisk, current secretary of state, 'Anthony Lloyd had an immeasurable influence on American foreign policy for the past fifty years. His wisdom will be sorely missed.' While the cause of death has not yet been determined, it is rumored that Lloyd—aged eighty—died from a stroke, the result of strain brought on by the recent apparent murder of his colleague, Jonathan Millgate, another of the grand counselors.

Authorities are still looking for Matthew Pittman, the former reporter allegedly responsible for Millgate's death."

The news report changed to other topics, and Pittman shut off the radio. In silence, he continued to stare at the dashboard.

"Died from a stroke?" Jill asked.

"Or was *he* murdered, too? It's a wonder they didn't blame *his* death on me, as well."

"In a way, they did," Jill said. "Their story is that the first death caused the second."

"Died from strain." Pittman bit his lip, thinking. He turned to Jill. "Or from guilt? From worry? Maybe something's happening to all of them. Maybe the grand counselors aren't as strong as they thought."

"What are you getting at?"

"We'll have to eat on the road and take turns sleeping while the other drives. We've got a lot of miles to cover."

7

Shortly before 7:00 A.M., in dim morning light, Pittman parked near the well-maintained apartment building in Park Slope in Brooklyn. Traffic increased. People walked by, going to work. "I just hope she hasn't left yet. If she has, we could end up sitting here all day, thinking she's still in the apartment." Pittman used his electric razor to shave.

"You're certain she works outside the home?"

"If you'd ever met Gladys, you'd know she'd definitely prefer to be away while her husband works at home and takes care of the baby." He sipped tepid coffee from a Styrofoam cup.

"Do we have any more of that Danish left?" Jill glanced around, peered at her Styrofoam cup of stale coffee on the dashboard, and grimaced. "I can't believe I'm doing this to myself. I hardly ever drink coffee, and now I'm guzzling it. Yesterday morning, I was eating doughnuts. Last night, chili and French fries. Now it's the gooiest Danish I ever . . . And I can't get enough of it. After years of eating right, I'm self-destructing."

"There." Pittman gestured. "That's Gladys."

A prim, sour-faced woman stepped out of the apartment

building, tightened a scarf around her head, and walked determinedly along the street.

"Looks like she runs a tight ship," Jill said.

"Talking to her makes you think of mutiny."

"But we *won't* have to talk to her."

"Right." Pittman got out of the car.

They walked toward the apartment building. In the vestibule, Pittman faced a row of intercom buttons and pretended to study the name below each button as if looking for one in particular, but what he really did was wait for the man and woman leaving the building to get out of his sight in time for him to grab the door as it swung shut. Before it could lock itself, he reopened it and walked through with Jill, heading toward the elevator.

When the door to 4 B opened in response to the knock, Brian Botulfson—who still wore his pajamas, had rumpled hair, and looked exhausted—slumped his shoulders with discouragement the moment he saw Pittman. "Aw, no. Give me a break. Not you. The last thing I need is—"

"How *are* you, Brian?" Pittman asked cheerily "How have you been doing since I saw you last?"

In the background, Pittman heard an infant crying harshly, not the usual baby cry, but a hurt cry, a sick cry. Pittman remembered it well from when Jeremy had been an infant.

"Uh-oh, sounds like you've been up all night." Pittman entered.

"Hey, you can't—"

Pittman shut the door and locked it. "You don't seem very happy to see me, Brian."

"The last time you were here, I got in so much trouble with . . . If Gladys was here . . ."

"But she isn't. We waited until she left."

Jill was preoccupied by the cries from the baby. "Boy or girl?"

"Boy."

"He doesn't sound well. Has he got a fever?"

"I think so," Brian said.

"You didn't check his temperature?" Jill asked.

"I didn't have time. I was too busy getting him clean after he threw up."

"Seems like you could use some help. Where's your thermometer? Let me see the baby supplies you got."

Pittman raised his hands. "Almost forgot, Brian. This is my friend Jill."

"Hello, Brian. I'm a nurse. I used to work in pediatrics. I'll take good care of your son. The thermometer?"

"On his bedside table." Brian pointed.

As Jill went toward a room to the left of the kitchen, Pittman said, "See, it's your lucky day."

"Yeah, I feel lucky all to hell. Look, you've got to stop coming here. The police are searching for you."

"No kidding."

"I can't get involved in this. I can't—"

"I won't come around again. I swear, Brian. Scout's honor."

"That's what you said the last time."

"Ah, but I didn't swear on Scout's honor."

Brian groaned. "If the police find out . . ."

"I'm a dangerous criminal. Tell them I terrified you so much, you had to help me."

"The newspapers say you killed a priest and a man in somebody's apartment and . . . I'm losing count."

"Not my fault. All easily explainable."

"You still don't get it. I don't want to know anything you're doing. I'd be an accessory."

"Then we're in agreement. I don't want you to know what I'm doing, either. But if you refuse to help me, if I get caught, I'll convince the police that you *are* an accessory," Pittman lied.

"Don't think like that. I'd go to prison again."

"And imagine what Gladys would say. On the other hand, I never turn against my friends, Brian. The quicker we do this, the quicker I'm out of here. I want you to give me a crash course in hacking."

Jill leaned out from the baby's room. "His fever's a hundred and one."

"Is that bad?" Brian asked nervously.

"It isn't good. But I think I can lower it. By the way, Brian, those children's aspirins are a no-no for a baby's fever. They can cause a serious condition called Reye's syndrome. Have you got any Tylenol?"

"See?" Pittman said. "In good hands. Now come on, Brian, pay us for the house call. Show me how to do a little hacking. Or we'll hang around the house until Gladys comes home."

Brian turned pale. "What programs do you want to get into?"

"Unlisted telephone numbers, and the addresses that go with them."

"What city?"

"I don't want to tell you, Brian. You're going to have to show me how to get in without knowing what city I want. Then you're going to sit in a corner while I play with your computer."

"I feel like crying."

8

"Will the baby be all right?" Pittman drove from the apartment building.

"As long as Brian keeps giving him a children's dose of Tylenol on schedule. And liquids. A sponge bath doesn't hurt. I told him to get the baby to a doctor if the fever gets worse or the vomiting persists. Cute kid. I think he'll be okay."

"And maybe Brian will get some sleep tonight."

"Unless Gladys decides to make trouble. Did he let you have what you wanted?"

Pittman held up a sheet of paper. "I learned from the mistake we made with the guy from the alumni association. Don't let anybody know our next move. Brian showed me how to get unlisted phone numbers and addresses. But he doesn't know whose or what city."

"Washington."

Pittman nodded.

"The grand counselors."

Pittman nodded again.

"Long drive."

"We can't fly. You'd have to use a check or a credit card to buy our tickets. Your name would get in the computer. The police will be looking for it. We've got to keep driving."

"You really know how to show a girl a good time. I think I'll pull a blanket over my head and assume a fetal position."

"Good idea. Get some more rest."

"You, too. We'll need it if we're going to try to get close to the grand counselors."

"Not just yet."

"But I thought you said we were going to Washington."

"Right. But I need to see somebody else there."

"Who?"

"A man I interviewed a long time ago."

9

It was after dark when they reached Washington's Beltway, headed south on I-95, then west on 50 to Massachusetts Avenue. Despite his exhaustion, Pittman managed to drive skillfully through the dense traffic.

"You seem to know your way around the city," Jill said.

"When I was working on the national affairs desk, I spent a lot of time down here." Pittman rounded Dupont Circle and took P Street west into Georgetown.

"Reminds me of Beacon Hill," Jill said.

"I suppose." Pittman glanced at the narrow wooded street. The paving was cobblestone. Ahead, it changed to red brick. Federal and Victorian mansions were squeezed next to one another. "Never been here?"

"Never been to *any* place in Washington. New York was about as far from my parents as I felt I needed to get."

"Georgetown's the oldest and wealthiest district in the city."

"The remaining grand counselors live here?"

Pittman shook his head. "This is too ordinary for them. They live on estates in Virginia."

"Then who did you come here to see?"

"A man who hates them." Pittman headed south on Wisconsin Avenue. Headlights and streetlights made him squint. "The guy I've been trying to phone every time we stopped along the road. Bradford Denning. He's elderly now, but in his prime, he was a career diplomat. A mover and shaker in the State Department during the Truman administration. According to him, he would eventually have become secretary of state."

"What happened that he didn't?"

"The grand counselors. They didn't like him being in competition with them, so they got him out of their way."

"How on earth did they manage that?"

"To hear Denning tell it—this was during the McCarthy witch-hunt era—they spread persistent rumors that Denning was soft on communism."

"In the early fifties, that would have ruined a diplomat."

"It certainly ruined Denning. He found it impossible to undo the damage, was given less and less responsibility in the State Department, and finally had to resign. He claims that his isn't the only career the grand counselors ruined by claiming that somebody was a Communist sympathizer. The grand counselors then ingratiated themselves with the incoming Eisenhower administration, replaced the diplomats they'd attacked, and went on to control the highest diplomatic offices. That lasted until 1960 when the Democrats regained the White House with Kennedy. Kennedy wanted to work with friends and family rather than career diplomats. For three years, the grand counselors stood on the sidelines. But after Kennedy was assassinated, Johnson, who had disliked Kennedy, was eager to assert himself by getting Kennedy's people out of the State Department and the White House staff. He welcomed the grand counselors back into diplomatic power. For the second time in their careers, they had managed the trick of being accepted by different political parties. In fact, by then they seemed to transcend the two-party system, so that when Nixon and the Republicans came back into power at the end of the sixties, the grand counselors had no difficulty in continuing to maintain their influence. So it went. In periods of intense international strain, various later Presidents continued to ask for their advice."

"And Denning?"

"Had what to most people would have seemed a productive life. He taught college. Wrote for political journals. Contributed editorial columns to the *New York Times* and the *Washington Post*. But he always felt cheated, and he never forgave the grand counselors. In fact, he devoted most of his spare time to researching a book about them, an exposé of their ruthlessness."

"Is that how you know about him? Because of the book?"

"No. The book was never published. Near the end of his research, his house caught fire. All his notes were destroyed. After that, he was a defeated man. Seven years ago, when I was preparing to write a story about Millgate, one of the few people who agreed to talk to me told me about Denning. I came down here to Washington to see him. But he'd been drinking, and what he had to say was all innuendo—he'd once had proof, he insisted, but it went up in the fire—and I finally realized I couldn't quote him. I never wrote the story, anyhow. After I was arrested and my jaw was broken by those two prisoners in jail, my editor assigned me to something else."

Driving, Pittman brooded. Thinking of his reassignment had reminded him of Burt Forsyth, not only his editor but his closest friend. The fight in the construction area off Twenty-sixth Street was brutally vivid in Pittman's memory, Burt stepping back as the gunman came into the shadows, the gunman shooting at Pittman, then at Burt.

Grief felt like arms around his chest, squeezing him breathless. They didn't need to kill Burt, he thought. The bastards.

"You look awfully angry," Jill said.

"Don't you think I've got reason to be?"

"Without a doubt. But it's surprising."

"How so?"

"When you came to my apartment Sunday, the emotion you communicated was desperation. Your motive was passive—a reaction to being threatened. But anger's an active emotion. It's . . . Let me ask you a question. If somehow a truce could be arranged and the police wouldn't be after you and the grand counselors would leave you alone, would you walk away?"

"After everything those bastards have put me through? No way."

Jill studied him. "Yes, you've definitely changed."

"You have no idea how much. This is Wednesday. Remember, a week ago tonight, I was ready to kill myself."

Jill didn't react, just kept staring at him.

"Say something."

"I keep forgetting how deeply upset you were," Jill said.

"Still am. None of this changes my grief for Jeremy."

"Yes. You'll continue to grieve for the rest of your life."

"That's right."

"But if you wanted to die as much as you say you did, why didn't you let the grand counselors do the job for you? No. In the last week, something happened to you to make you want the rest of your life to go on as long as possible."

"You."

Jill touched his shoulder with affection. "But you'd been on the run for a couple of days before you showed up at my apartment. You had plenty of opportunity to give in to your despair. You know what I think?"

Pittman didn't answer.

"Fear made you feel alive again. While we've been driving, you told me how you sometimes have the sense that Jeremy's with you, that he talks to you."

Pittman nodded. "You think it's foolish to believe that?"

"On the contrary, I'll go you one better. I think Jeremy's been pushing you into fighting back. I think he wants you to decide to live for something."

Pittman's voice was husky with emotion. "That would be nice to believe." His throat ached as he squinted ahead toward the bright lights and congested traffic in the area of Wisconsin Avenue and M Street.

Jill sounded puzzled. "What's the problem ahead? An accident?"

Affected by the intensity of what they'd been discussing, Pittman was grateful to change the subject. "No, it's always this crowded. Wisconsin Avenue and M Street are where the action is in Georgetown—bars, restaurants, nightclubs, shops selling everything you can imagine as long as it's expensive."

"Denning lives around here?"

"Not at all. He couldn't possibly afford it. He lives on his college pension, which isn't very much. No, when I finally got in touch with him on the phone, I told him I was a journalist doing a story on Anthony Lloyd's death. I told him so many diplomats and politicians were canonizing Lloyd that I thought a dissenting opinion would give my story depth. I asked him if I could take him to dinner. He was more than happy to accept. He said he planned to go to a memorial service for Anthony Lloyd"—Pittman hesitated—"and then sit down to eat a big meal with me to celebrate."

10

The restaurant, Il Trovatore, was spacious and soothingly lit, the tables far enough apart that politicians and personalities could discuss delicate topics without being easily overheard. As Pittman walked in with Jill, he glanced to the right toward the bar and recognized a well-known senator. A network news anchorman was eating dinner with an important-looking man at a table to the left. From somewhere, a piano was playing soft jazz. The clink of silverware against plates and the murmur of voices blended with the subtle level of the music, cloaking individual conversations.

"Yes, sir?" The maître d' had pinched nostrils, wore a white dinner jacket, and looked disapprovingly at Jill's sweater, jeans, and sneakers.

"We have a reservation in Bradford Denning's name." Pittman had phoned to make the reservation during one of their stops along the interstate en route to Washington.

The maître d' glanced at a list of names. "Yes, Mr. Denning has already arrived. He's been seated at the table."

"Good."

But the maître d' continued to look with disapproval at Jill's clothing.

"If there's a problem with the restaurant's dress code . . ."

Pittman discreetly handed the maître d' twenty dollars from their diminishing supply of cash.

"No problem at all, sir. Come this way."

The maître d' led them toward the back of the restaurant, where a short, thin, elderly but intense man was seated alone in a booth. The man had sparse white hair that contrasted with the fierce brown of his eyes and the red of his cheeks. He wore a gray suit that was somewhat out of date. He was drinking whiskey on ice. A second lowball glass, empty, had been placed to the side.

"Here you are, sir," the maître d' told Pittman.

"Thank you."

"Enjoy."

Pittman turned to the man in the booth. "Bradford Denning?"

"Lester King?"

"That's right." Because the police now knew that Pittman was using the pseudonym Peter Logan, he had decided that the change was necessary. He was nervously aware that he risked being recognized by Denning, but he had to take the chance. He and Denning had met only once before, seven years ago, and Denning had been so drunk that Pittman didn't think it likely he would remember that long-ago evening. "This is my assistant, Jennifer."

"A pleasure." Keeping a careful grip on his whiskey glass, Denning half got out of his seat in a polite gesture of greeting.

"Please, there's no need to be formal." Jill sat next to him.

Pittman took the seat across from him. "It's kind of you to agree to join us."

"Kind?" Denning found the comment amusing. "I haven't been able to afford to eat in a place like this since . . . too long."

"I'm glad you approve of my choice."

"It reminds me of another Italian restaurant that used to be up the street. What was it called?" Denning sipped from his whiskey and shook his head. "Can't remember. This was back in the fifties. Elegant. Used to eat there all the time. Everybody who mattered did." He finished the whiskey. "Of course, it's out of business now. They come, and they go." He squinted. "Like people. . . . By the way, I hope you don't mind." He gestured toward the empty glasses. "I got here a little early and started ahead of you."

"Why would I mind? You're our guest. As I said, I'm grateful that you could join us."

"It's not every day that someone pays for me to celebrate the death of an enemy." Denning motioned for a waiter to come over. "Two enemies. I'm still not finished celebrating Millgate's death." He nodded to the waiter. "Bring two more of these. Jack Daniel's. Not so much ice this time."

"Certainly, sir. And for your friends?"

"Heineken," Pittman said.

"Your house Chardonnay," Jill said.

"May I tell you about our specials so you can think about them while you're enjoying your cocktails?"

"Later," Denning said. "There'll be plenty of time for that. We're not hungry yet."

"Very good, sir."

As the waiter left, Pittman wondered if Denning's haughty take-charge manner typified his diplomatic style when he was in the State Department. If so, gossip spread by the grand counselors might not have been the only reason he was forced to resign.

"Two down," Denning said. "Three to go. I intend to drink a cocktail for every one of those sons of bitches. A liquid prayer that the other three'll be dead soon, too."

Pittman noticed that Denning's voice had a subtle slur. "Your attitude toward the grand counselors is well known. Obviously you still haven't stopped hating them."

"Never."

"Do you mind if we talk before we eat?"

"About *them*?" Denning's emphasis implied numerous obscenities. "That's why I came here. You wanted something compromising to offset the righteous bullshit people are saying about Millgate and Lloyd. I'll give it to you. I'll give you plenty."

Pittman took out a pen and a notepad, maintaining the pretense that he was writing a newspaper story. "What's the worst thing you can say about them?"

"They burned my house."

"Excuse me?" Pittman had expected more of the unsubstantiated charges that he had heard from Denning seven years earlier. But this was a new accusation.

Denning frowned at him. "You look familiar. Have we met before?"

"Not that I'm aware of," Pittman said, tensing.

"You remind me of . . ."

"Washington can be a small town. Maybe we ran into each other at a diplomatic reception or—"

"I haven't been invited to a diplomatic reception in thirty-five years," Denning said bitterly.

"They burned your house."

"I was writing an exposé about them. They must have found out. They set fire to my house and destroyed my research."

"But can you prove that?" Jill asked.

"Of course not. They're too clever to leave evidence."

"Then can you tell us what you were going to expose?"

"They murdered hundreds of thousands of people."

This is as bad as the last time, Pittman thought. He's going to rant and rave, and I won't learn anything.

"Hundreds of thousands?"

Denning scowled at Pittman again. "Are you certain we haven't met before?"

"Yes." Pittman tried to assure himself that he didn't look the same as when he had first met Denning. He strained to hope that Denning wouldn't make the connection.

Denning brightened as the waiter set down their drinks. "Cheers."

The three of them raised their glasses.

"To that bastard Eustace Gable and the rest of them." Denning took a deep swallow of Jack Daniel's.

He must have been drinking this hard for many years, Pittman thought. Otherwise, as old as he is, he wouldn't have a tolerance for this much alcohol. "You said they murdered hundreds of thousands of people."

"In Korea. In Vietnam. To make themselves important. They never cared about those countries. They never cared about rebuilding Europe after the war. The Marshall Plan and all that. They cared about themselves. McCarthy."

He's rambling, Pittman thought in despair. Damn it, we came all this way for nothing. Pittman's side ached from when he'd injured it escaping from Grollier Academy. His legs, back, and neck ached from having spent nearly twenty-four hours in the car. He was tired and desperate, and he wanted to lean across the table, grab Denning's suit coat, and shake him until he made sense.

"What about McCarthy?" Jill asked. "You mean back in the early fifties? Joe McCarthy? The anti-Communist witch-hunter?"

"That's how the bastards got me out of the State Department. They convinced everybody I was red."

"Were you?"

Denning laughed to himself. "Yes."

"What?"

"Not card-carrying. A sympathizer."

Pittman tried not to show his surprise. Seven years earlier, Denning hadn't given so much as a hint that the grand counselors might have been correct.

"If *I'd* stayed on track, if the grand counselors hadn't gotten rid of me, if I'd managed to become secretary of state . . . it was too late to do anything about Korea, but maybe I could have stopped Vietnam. Hey, so what if I thought the Soviets had points in their favor? Did that make me a criminal? I wasn't going to sell out our country. But I could have done my damnedest to make sure we didn't nearly destroy ourselves because of Vietnam."

Pittman listened more intensely. "I had an older brother who died in Vietnam."

"Then you know what I'm talking about."

"Spell it out," Pittman said.

"The grand counselors based their careers on taking a hard line against communism. After the Second World War, they helped formulate the Marshall Plan to rebuild Europe . . . but exclude the Soviets. And they helped formulate the Truman Doctrine—that America had an obligation to defend the world . . . against the Soviets, of course. I fought them on their anti-Soviet bias, but I lost. That's when they began thinking of me as an enemy. In 1950, it was partly because of their urging that we sent troops into South Korea to stop the North Korean invasion . . . to stop the spread of communism. What was eventually called the domino theory. Never believed in it. I didn't think we had any business being over there, and history proves I was right. We didn't make a difference. So I fought them about going into Korea, and I lost. Then I fought them about several other issues to do with the Soviets. I didn't believe it was wise to bully the Soviets with our atomic weapons capability, for example. I was sure it would lead to a deadly arms race. I was right on that score as well, but Millgate and the others prevailed. By 1952, they'd made everybody believe I was soft on communism. I was out. The heightening of the Cold War during the fifties—they had plenty to do with that. The Vietnam War—they had even more to do with *that*. Because of them, hundreds of thousands died. And all the while, they were in deep with the arms manufacturers. They let their bank accounts determine foreign policy."

The accusation about kickbacks was the same one that Denning had made seven years earlier. It was what Pittman had been investigating back then, the reason he had gone to Denning in the first place. But Denning hadn't been able to provide substantiation for the charges. Perhaps he could now.

"I'm sure you already know this," Pittman said. "A little less than a week ago, the night Jonathan Millgate was taken from the hospital, someone leaked a secret Justice Department report that Millgate was suspected of being involved in buying nuclear weapons from the former Soviet Union."

"Another illegal arms deal." Denning smiled bitterly. "You can't teach an old dog new tricks."

"Do you have anything that would prove your accusations?"

"Not after the fire."

Pittman shook his head in frustration. Unable to think of another way, he decided to go directly to the primary question that he'd come here to ask, but the waiter's sudden reappearance at their booth made him stop.

"Are you ready to hear about our specials for tonight?" the waiter asked.

"Didn't I tell you to wait awhile?" Denning complained. "We're not hungry yet."

"Very good, sir," the waiter said dourly, and left.

Pittman noticed that Denning raised his cocktail glass, then seemed to make a decision and set it down without drinking.

"Let's talk about another matter," Pittman said. "Have you ever heard of someone named Duncan Kline?"

Denning studied him, his elderly face developing lines of strain. "Who?"

"Duncan Kline."

"Are you sure we haven't met before?" Denning asked unexpectedly.

Pittman tried not to look worried. "Quite sure."

"Then maybe it's something in the news. Talking about Millgate, Lloyd, and the others makes me associate you with . . ."

Damn it, Pittman thought. I was wrong. He doesn't remember me from seven years ago. I don't have to worry about *that*. No, what I have to worry about is something worse. When Millgate died, Denning would have devoured every speck of news on the subject. Needing to gloat, he would have read and *re*read every story. He's seen *my photograph* dozens of times. But because I'm using a different name and I look different than I looked seven years ago, he hasn't realized who I am.

But I'm afraid he will. And what'll happen when he does?

"I don't know how to explain it," Pittman said.

"Duncan Kline." Jill interrupted, obviously wanting to distract Denning and get the conversation back where they wanted.

Denning gave Pittman one more puzzled look, then turned to Jill, frowning in concentration. "I can't say the name is familiar. Perhaps if I had a context."

"He was a teacher at Grollier Academy. That's the prep school the grand counselors attended. He was their main instructor."

"Ah," Denning said.

"Then the name *is* familiar?"

"No, but . . . Odd."

"What?"

"As I get older, events from thirty and forty years ago can be vivid, and yet I have trouble remembering things that happened last month."

"Forty years ago?"

"Nineteen fifty-two. The summer. July. I remember so well because that was the turning point in my life. The Republicans had their convention that month. Eisenhower was nominated to run for President. In fact, he won the nomination on the first ballot. Eisenhower and Nixon. Given the national mood, it was obvious to me that Eisenhower would defeat Stevenson in the upcoming election. Evidently it was even more obvious to Millgate and the others. Immediately after the convention, they intensified their efforts to ingratiate themselves with those Republicans who mattered. It's a measure of their ability to manipulate that they succeeded, convincingly crossing the line from Democrat to Republican."

Pittman noticed that Denning's cheeks had become more flushed with agitation, that a film of glistening sweat had formed on his upper lip.

Denning picked up a glass, not his whiskey glass, but instead, one filled with water. He sipped quickly and continued. "July of 1952 was also the month in which they brought their campaign against me to its peak. I was so thoroughly branded as a Communist sympathizer that I became ineffectual as a diplomat." Denning squinted at Pittman. "In self-defense, I spent most of my time keeping myself informed about everything Millgate and the others did. I had to be on the alert against their next offensive. And that's when I noticed that something had made them slightly panicky. A man had arrived at the State Department near the end of July. I never saw him, but I was given a description of him. A man with a deeply tanned face and a solid frame, big shoulders, an athletic appearance, but a man who had gray hair and seemed to be in his sixties. My informant told me that for all the signs that the man was physical and preferred the outdoors, he had a refined, almost effete manner, a patrician pseudo-British accent. He asked to see Jonathan Millgate. Well, of course you don't just walk into the State Department and expect to be allowed to see one of the deputy secretaries without an appointment. The visitor gave his name and Millgate's assistant put it at the bottom of a long list. In frustration, the visitor then asked to see Anthony Lloyd. Same reaction. With greater frustration, the visitor asked to see Eustace Gable. Winston Sloane. Victor Standish."

"All the grand counselors," Pittman said.

"The same reaction in each case. The visitor's name was put at the end of a long list. At that, the visitor lost his patience, stopped asking to see them, and *demanded* to see them. For a moment, it appeared that a security officer would have to be summoned. But instead, Millgate heard the commotion, came out of his office, and . . . Well, according to my informant, Millgate turned pale. His usual domineering manner disintegrated. He immediately ushered the visitor into his office, told his assistant to cancel his next appointment, then sent for Anthony Lloyd and the rest of them. Most unusual. I have never forgotten the incident. It has puzzled me to this day. I've always suspected that if I had understood the subtext of the event, I would have had ammunition with which to defend myself."

"Was the visitor's name Duncan Kline?" Pittman asked.

"I remember some things so vividly and . . . Unfortunately my memory for names . . . The fire destroyed my records. I don't recall."

"Then why would you have told us about this?"

"Because I do recall managing to learn the visitor's connection with Millgate and the others. He had been one of their teachers at their prep school."

"Then it *was* Duncan Kline," Jill said. "The big shoulders you mentioned. Kline was an expert rower. It's the kind of build that a rower would—"

"Why is Duncan Kline so important to you?" Denning frowned and wiped sweat from his upper lip.

"Someone else I interviewed mentioned him," Pittman said. "The implication is that there may have been a secret about Kline that would have threatened the grand counselors' reputations if it were known."

"What type of secret?" Denning's gaze was disturbing.

"That's what we're trying to find out. We're reasonably certain that as teenagers at Grollier Academy, all the grand counselors were sexually molested by Duncan Kline."

Denning slammed a hand on the table. "If I'd known that, I might have been able to fight back, to defend myself against them."

"In what way?" Jill asked. "How could being victims of a child molester have hurt their careers? Wouldn't it have made people feel compassion?"

"In the fifties? Take my word, there wasn't a lot of compassion going around during the McCarthy period. Guilt by association. But what if Millgate and the others *weren't* victims? What if they consented? In the political climate of the fifties, they would have been dismissed from the State Department at once." Denning breathed rapidly.

"Did you ever hear even a hint that . . . ?"

"No. But there's someone who—" Denning's hands shook.

"Someone?" Pittman leaned forward. "I don't understand. Who? What are you talking about?"

"Nothing. I meant, there must be someone who could prove it." Denning spoke with effort.

"Are you feeling all right?" Jill asked.

"Fine. I'm fine." Denning swallowed deeply from his glass of water.

"Perhaps you can help us with something else," Pittman said. "Apparently, one of the last things Jonathan Millgate said was, 'Duncan. The snow.' Does the reference to snow make any sense to you?"

"None whatsoever. Even supposing that the incident was traumatic enough . . ." He paused for breath. ". . . traumatic enough for Millgate to refer to it when he was close to death . . ."

"Are you sure you feel all right, Mr. Denning?"

"The teacher who showed up at the State Department and startled Millgate . . . arrived in the summer, not the winter. . . . The snow. I have no idea what it means. I wish I did. Anything to punish them."

The waiter reappeared at the booth. "For our specials tonight—"

"I don't have an appetite." Denning groped to stand. "I don't feel well."

Jill hurried to stand, allowing him to lurch from the booth.

"All this excitement. Millgate, then Lloyd. Too much excitement. Too many questions."

"Do you need a doctor?" Pittman asked quickly.

"No."

"Can we give you a ride home?"

"No." Agitated, Denning wiped his face with a handkerchief. "I'm fine. I can manage by myself." He stumbled past the waiter, almost bumped into another waiter carrying a tray of food, then veered past crowded tables.

Pittman and Jill tried to go after him, but a group being seated blocked their way for a moment. Past a woman in an evening dress, Pittman saw Denning reach the front lobby. Then the group was out of the way and Pittman and Jill hurried toward the front exit.

11

On the busy sidewalk outside the restaurant, amid the noise of traffic and the glare of headlights as well as street-lights, Pittman studied the pedestrians to his left, then those to the right, while Jill studied the opposite side of the street.

"What the hell was *that* about?" Pittman asked.

"I was hoping *you'd* know. He looked as if he might be ill, but . . ."

"Or maybe what he said was true—that the conversation overexcited him."

"The thing is, what's he going to do about it? Where was he going in such a rush?"

"Come on, let's split up and see if we can find him."

"*There they are,*" a man said accusingly behind them.

When Pittman turned, he saw their waiter and the maître d' glowering at them from the restaurant's open door.

"We needed to see if our friend was all right," Pittman said.

The maître d' fumed. "This is what happens when I make an exception to our dress code."

"We were coming back."

"Certainly. But in case you're detained, I'm sure you

won't mind paying for your cocktails before you look for your friend."

"Jill, run down to the corner on the right," Pittman said. "Maybe you'll see him on the next street. If we get separated, I'll meet you at the car. . . . How much do we owe?" Pittman quickly asked the maître d'.

"Four Jack Daniel's, a Heineken, and—"

"I don't need it itemized. Just tell me how much."

"Twenty-eight dollars."

Pittman shoved thirty dollars at the waiter, seriously depleting their money supply, and hurried in the opposite direction from Jill, wincing from cramps in his legs after having been in the car for so long.

At the corner to the left of the restaurant, he gazed intensely toward pedestrians on the next street. Immediately he straightened at the sight of Denning, a quarter of the way along the block, lurching from between parked cars to hail a taxi. The elderly man looked more agitated as he got into the taxi, blurting instructions to the driver before he closed the door.

Pittman ran to try to reach the taxi, but it pulled away, and at once Pittman raced back toward Jill, his cramped legs protesting.

"I didn't see him." Jill was waiting where they'd parked the car across the street from the restaurant.

"*I* did. Hurry, get in."

Pittman started the engine and steered impatiently from the curb, narrowly missing a BMW. A horn sounded behind him. He ignored it and turned left, reaching the street where he'd seen Denning get into the taxi.

"Where do you suppose he's going?" Jill asked.

"I don't know. But this is a one-way street headed north. Denning wouldn't have waited until he was around the corner before he hailed a taxi unless he intended to go in this direction. There's a good chance that the taxi is still on this street."

"You've already passed two taxis. How will you know which one is Denning's?"

"I got the license number." Pittman kept driving. "I don't see . . . Damn it, do you suppose we lost him?"

"There."

"Yes! That's the taxi."

Pittman immediately hung back, keeping a reasonable distance between his car and the taxi so the driver wouldn't realize he was being followed. Fifteen seconds after he obeyed the speed limit, a police car passed them.

"It's your lucky night," Jill said.

"I wish I *felt* lucky. Where on earth is he going?"

"Back to where he lives?"

"In the heart of Georgetown? No way. He doesn't have enough money."

Elegant town houses gave way to mansions.

Pittman followed the taxi, turning left onto a street paved with worn bricks, streetcar tracks embedded in them. The taxi stopped in front of one of the few mansions set back from the street. The brightly lit building was on top of a slight hill and had a large landscaped yard, its shrubs enclosed by a waist-high wrought-iron fence.

Denning got out of the taxi and hurried up concrete steps toward a spacious porch, its pillars reminding Pittman of a Greek temple.

"I wonder who lives here," Pittman said.

"And why was he in such a rush to get here?"

They watched Denning knock repeatedly on the mansion's front door. A uniformed male servant opened it. Denning gestured, talking insistently. The servant turned to request instructions from someone inside, then allowed Denning to enter.

"Now what?" Jill asked.

"I'm tired of sitting in this damned car. Let's make a house call."

SIX

1

The uniformed male servant opened the door in response to Pittman's knock. "Yes, sir?" He was middle-aged and somewhat portly. So much unexpected activity evidently puzzled him.

"A minute ago, a man named Bradford Denning came here," Pittman said.

"Yes, sir?" The servant looked more puzzled.

"Did he mention that he was expecting us?"

"No, sir." The servant's brow developed deep furrows.

"Well, we're with him. It's important that we see him."

"George?" a woman asked from inside. "Who is it?"

"Someone who claims to be with your visitor, ma'am."

Pittman peered inside toward a tall, slender woman in her late fifties. Her hair was short and frosted. She wore a scoop-necked designer dress made of silk, the blue of which brought out the sparkle in her diamond earrings. Although attractive, her features had the severe tight-skin-against-prominent-cheekbones look of someone who'd had numerous face-lifts.

The woman stepped forward, her high heels clicking on the mirrorlike finish of the vestibule's hardwood floor. "You know Bradford?"

"We were supposed to have dinner with him tonight."

"The last time we saw him, he didn't look well," Jill said. "Is he all right?"

"Actually he looks dreadful." The woman's expression became tighter. "But he didn't mention anything about you."

Pittman tried to remember the false names he'd given to Denning. "Tell him it's Lester King and Jennifer."

"Don't listen to them, Vivian." Denning appeared suddenly at a doorway on the left. With a wrinkled handkerchief, he continued to wipe glistening sweat off his face. "They're reporters."

The woman's gaze darkened, her voice deepening with disapproval. *"Oh?"*

"But we're not here to make trouble," Jill said quickly. "We're here to help."

"How?"

"We suspect Bradford Denning came here to tell you what we spoke to him about earlier. You might want to get the story directly from the source."

The woman's severe face didn't develop lines of emotion. Instead, suspicion and confusion were communicated by the rigid tilt of her head and the hardness of her gaze. "Come in."

"No, Vivian," Denning said.

The woman ignored him. "It's all right. Come in."

"Thank you," Pittman said.

"But if it turns out that you *are* here to make trouble, I'll have George summon the police."

The threat caused a further surge of adrenaline to roil Pittman's stomach. He fought not to show his concern.

As the servant shut the door behind them, the woman led Pittman and Jill toward Denning. They went through the doorway on the left.

Pittman had expected antiques and a Colonial atmosphere.

On the contrary, the large room was furnished in a glinting glass-and-chrome modern style. Abstract Expressionist paintings hung on the walls, splotches of colors communicating a welter of emotions. Pittman thought he recognized a Jackson Pollock.

"May I offer you anything?" the woman asked.

"No, thank you."

"Jack Daniel's," Denning said.

"Bradford, you reeked of alcohol when you arrived. You know how I feel about overindulgence. You've had enough."

Denning continued to wipe his flushed, glistening face.

"Since none of the rest of us wants anything, why don't we sit down and discuss why the three of you came here?"

"Yes," Pittman said, "I'd like to hear Bradford's version of the conversation we had with him. If that's all right with you, Mrs. . . . ?"

"Page."

The name meant nothing to Pittman. His lack of appreciation must have shown on his face.

"Mrs. Page is one of Washington's leading socialites," Denning said, his boastful tone suggesting that he thought he gained stature by knowing her.

"Obviously our guests still don't recognize the name," Mrs. Page said. "Or else they have the wisdom not to be impressed by society." Her lips formed a tight, bitter smile. "But perhaps another name will be significant to them. It's the only reason Bradford ever comes to see me, so I assume that your visit has some connection with it. I'm Eustace Gable's daughter."

2

The woman's announcement that she was a daughter of one of the grand counselors was so surprising that Pittman inhaled sharply. He sensed Jill become tense beside him.

"I didn't realize," Pittman said.

"Obviously. But now that you know, do you intend to continue the conversation?"

"That's up to you, Mrs. Page," Jill said. "Some of what we need to talk about may be indelicate."

Pittman frowned toward Denning, wondering why the man had felt compelled to come here. Was Denning's claim to hate the grand counselors merely a ploy that allowed him to gain the confidence of their enemies? Was Denning a spy for the grand counselors and the first person he'd decided to report to was Eustace Gable's daughter?

"When it comes to my father," Mrs. Page said, "*every* subject is indelicate."

"I'm not sure I follow you," Pittman said.

"I'll speak freely if you speak freely."

Still confused, Pittman nodded.

"I hate my father."

Again, Pittman was caught off guard.

"Loathe him," Mrs. Page continued. "If it was in my power to hurt him . . . truly and seriously hurt him . . . destroy him . . . I wouldn't hesitate for a second. He's repugnant." The ferocity in her eyes was appalling. "Is that clear? Have I communicated my attitude?"

"Perfectly."

"I assume that what you and Bradford spoke about tonight is something that he believes I can use as a weapon against my father," Mrs. Page said. "That's why I invited you in. Am I correct? Do you have biases as a reporter? Do you regard my father as an adversary?"

Pittman nodded again, not sure whether he was being set up.

"Good." Mrs. Page turned to Denning. "Bradford, I'm disappointed in you. If you felt that these people could help me, why did you tell me to turn them away? Did you want all the credit, is that it? After so many years, are you still behaving as if you're in the State Department?"

Denning fidgeted and didn't answer.

Despite Mrs. Page's earlier invitation to sit, they had all remained standing. Now Pittman eased down onto an unusual-looking chair that had severe angles and edges and was made from wood embedded in shiny metal. It reminded him of experimental furniture that he had seen in New York at the Museum of Modern Art. Unexpectedly, he found that the chair was comfortable.

The others sat also.

"How did . . . ?" Pittman felt awkward, not sure how to ask the question. "What made you . . . ?"

"Speak directly. My father taught me always to get to the point," Mrs. Page said bitterly. "Why do I hate my father? He killed my mother."

Pittman was conscious of his heart beating.

"Since you've started, tell them, Vivian," Denning said. "Tell them everything."

Mrs. Page narrowed her eyes and shook her head. "It's not something that outsiders can regard with sympathy, perhaps. You see a house of this magnitude—my mother's was even more grand—and you ask yourself how can anyone possibly be unhappy living in such luxury. Someone working on the assembly line at an automobile factory in Detroit would be more than pleased to trade places. But every circumstance has its unique liability. My mother was beautiful. She came from a traditional southern family that still remembered and retained affectations of genteel society from before the Civil War. In that world, a woman wasn't meant to do anything. My mother was taught that she gained her value simply by existing. She was raised as if she were an orchid, to be admired. Then she met my father on one of the last ocean cruises to Europe before the outbreak of the Second World War. The surroundings were romantic. She foolishly fell in love with him. The match was approved. They were married. And to her surprise, she discovered that she was indeed expected to do something—to be perfect in every regard. To give the most perfect dinner parties. To provide the most perfect conversation. To be perfectly dressed. To create the most perfect impression."

Mrs. Page's voice quavered. She hesitated, then continued. "Again, that hypothetical factory worker I mentioned wouldn't have any sympathy for a society woman who claimed to be suffering while living in splendor. But what if that factory worker had a foreman who criticized every task he did, day after day, month after month, year after year? What if that foreman had a way of getting into the worker's heart, of making every insult feel like the cut of a knife? The worker's nerves would be affected. His dignity would be wounded. His spirit would be destroyed. Oh, you might say that the worker would have the option of resigning and finding another job. But what if that option wasn't available to him? What if he had to endure that foreman's abuse forever?"

Mrs. Page swallowed dryly. "My father is the cruelest man I have ever encountered. His need to dominate was so excessive that he browbeat my mother at every opportunity. He ridiculed. He demeaned. He degraded. I grew up in constant terror of him. Nothing I could do was good enough for him. And certainly nothing my mother could do was good enough. I used to cry myself to sleep out of pity for my mother. Divorce? For a career diplomat with immense ambitions? In those days? Unthinkable. My mother raised the subject only once, and my father's reaction so terrified her that she never mentioned it again."

Mrs. Page thought for a long moment. Her perfectly poised shoulders weakened. "So my mother began to drink. Neither my father nor I realized that she had a problem with alcohol until her addiction was far advanced. At the start, she evidently did most of her drinking when my father was out of the house and I was at school. She drank vodka, so the alcohol would be less detectable on her breath. A vicious cycle developed. Her drinking impaired her ability to strive for the perfect standards that my father required. Dinner parties weren't organized to his satisfaction. My mother's behavior became indifferent. She no longer helped organize, let alone appeared at, required society charity events. At diplomatic receptions, she showed the boredom she'd been hiding. Naturally my father criticized her. The more he criticized, the more she drank, and that of course further affected her performance, causing him to be more furious with her, and in turn causing her to drink more.

"Eventually my mother's slurred speech gave her away.

In the days before the wives of public figures had the courage to admit their problems with alcohol and other substances, this had the capacity to be a major scandal. For a man of my father's strict standards and boundless ambitions, the situation was horrifying. Not because my *mother* had a problem, but because *she* had given *him* a problem. She couldn't be allowed to embarrass him and compromise his image. The first thing he did was search the house and find every bottle that she had hidden. The second thing he did was hire someone whose sole responsibility was to make sure that my mother didn't get near alcohol. The tactics worked, but they didn't achieve what my father intended. My mother didn't return to her former ways and strive to match his image of perfection. Instead, with no escape, feeling even more repressed, my mother had a nervous breakdown.

"This was equally horrifying to my father. If the diplomatic community discovered that his wife was emotionally and mentally unstable, he feared that he would be tainted. He worried that his colleagues would feel he was too distracted to perform his duties to the maximum. His career would be ruined. After my mother managed to break out of the house and caused what my father called a drunken scene at a nearby tavern, he decided to remove her from Washington.

"In those days, there wasn't any such thing as the Betty Ford Clinic, of course, or its equivalent—places where a problem could be dealt with openly and thoroughly. But there *were* clinics of a different sort, where problems that the wealthy had were treated with utmost discretion. My mother's alcoholism, the instability caused by her nervous breakdown, these were addressed through drug therapy—sedatives. It was felt that my mother needed a rest, you see. Fatigue had to be the cause of her problems. After all, no woman with my mother's advantages of wealth and prestige could possibly be unhappy. For three months, as a consequence of the sedatives, she was in a stupor, little better than a sleepwalker. She needed help to go to the bathroom. She didn't recognize me when I came to visit. When the clinic decided that the alcohol was fully out of her system, gradually the sedatives were taken away. She came home. She seemed to be more satisfied.

"Then one day she disappeared. After a frantic search, the servants found my mother drunk, collapsed, mumbling next to the furnace in the basement. After that, my father's attitude became quite different. The excuse he'd given Washington society for my mother's three-month absence, her stay in the clinic, was that she had been visiting relatives in Europe. Now he concocted a different excuse. This was during July of 1953. He rented a summer estate on Cape Hatteras. He sent away all the servants. He bought my mother several cases of vodka. To this day, I vividly remember the sneering tone with which he told her, 'You want to avoid responsibilities? You want to have a drink now and then? Here. You're on vacation.'

"He poured her a drink, poured her another, and another. When the supply of vodka diminished, he bought more. He made sure that her glass was always full. If she appeared to be losing her taste for it, he would berate and humiliate her until she again felt the urge to drink. Sometimes in the night, I would hear noises and sneak from my room, to discover that my mother was sprawled in the bathroom, where she had vomited. My father would be kneeling beside her, calling her disgusting names, pouring vodka down her throat. When my father realized that I was noticing too much, he arranged for me to visit his parents at their summer estate on Martha's Vineyard. I hated to be near him, but I was afraid for my mother, and I begged not to go."

Mrs. Page had been staring toward a violently colored Abstract Expressionist painting across from her all the while she spoke in a monotone, her flat, bleak voice communicating no hint of the intense turmoil that her eyes indicated she was feeling. Now she paused, her normally rigid shoulders drooping as she turned her attention to Pittman and Jill. "I never saw my mother again. She was dead by the end of the summer. I was told that the medical examiner's explanation for the cause of death was alcohol poisoning. My father talked to me in detail about what had happened. He tried to make me interpret what I had seen in such a way that his behavior was understandable. 'Your mother had a greater problem than you can imagine,' he said. 'I encouraged her habit because I hoped that if she got sick enough, she would stop drinking. I made her drink after she'd vomited in the hopes that she would associate nausea with alcohol.' My father hired an expert on alcoholism who claimed to have advised my father to try this approach."

The room became silent.

Pittman spoke softly. "I'm very sorry."

Mrs. Page didn't reply.

"But there's something I don't understand," Pittman said.

"And what is that?"

"If your father was afraid of scandal because of your mother's alcoholism, if he tried to hide it initially, why did he suddenly change his attitude and cause her death, especially in that particular way? That certainly would have attracted attention and caused a scandal."

"My father is an immensely devious man. He came to realize that if he made *himself* appear the victim, he would gain his colleagues' sympathy. He told them that the problem had been going on for quite a while, that he had done everything possible for her, that his life had been a nightmare. He pretended to be inconsolable, distraught from the effort of having tried to control her all summer. He'd done everything possible, he kept insisting. And the diplomatic community believed him. Then, in his greatest piece of hypocrisy, he created the impression that with great pain he was overcoming his grief to devote himself to his profession. Each day his colleagues admired him for his strength. His reputation grew. He became ambassador to Great Britain, and after that, ambassador to the Soviet Union, and eventually, of course, secretary of state. But I know him for what he is. He killed my mother, and I'll never forgive him."

"Because we both hated him, Vivian and I joined forces," Denning said. "In an effort to help her, I managed to obtain a copy of the medical examiner's report. Vivian's father had lied to her. The cause of death was alcohol poisoning *in tandem with the use of Seconal.*"

"Seconal?" Jill straightened. "But that's a tranquilizer."

Mrs. Page nodded. "The type of sedative that my mother was given while she was away for three months in the clinic."

"Wait a minute," Pittman said. "Are you suggesting that your mother wasn't dying fast enough to suit your father, so he helped her along by adding sleeping pills to the vodka?"

"That is correct." Mrs. Page tightened her lips.

"Either way, it's murder," Jill said. "But the second way, using the sleeping pills might be easier to prove."

Mrs. Page shook her head. "My father somehow discovered that I'd read the medical examiner's report. He anticipated my accusation and confessed that there was a secret he hadn't been able to bring himself to tell me. He said that when my mother was in the clinic, she had apparently stolen a container of the tranquilizers that she was being given. The container—with a label that indicated where she had obtained them—was discovered after her death. The night she died, she had swallowed so many of the Seconal capsules that he had no other choice except to conclude she had committed suicide."

Pittman's stomach soured.

"You believe he was lying," Jill said.

"What I believe makes no difference. Proof is what matters. And there is no way to discount my father's story. I want to destroy him, not throw my own integrity into question. Unless I have indisputable evidence, he will simply use the reports from the mental hospital and the medical examiner to disparage my claims. Any further accusations I make won't be treated seriously. I will have only one chance. For most of my life, I have struggled to find a way to punish him for what he did to my mother, with no success. And now, as other grand counselors"—she said the words with contempt—"have died, I am forced to consider the possibility that my father is old enough that he, too, might die before I succeed in punishing him."

Denning stood. "That's why I came here tonight. I may have found a way."

Mrs. Page focused her intense gaze upon him.

"There's a chance we can prove that your father and the others may have allowed their sexual orientation to compromise their work."

"Sexual orientation?"

"Were they homosexuals? It never occurred to me until my discussion with these reporters tonight. Did you ever have any suspicion that—?"

Mrs. Page widened her eyes.

The sound that came from her throat made Pittman's skin prickle. At first he feared that Mrs. Page was choking on something. Then, as the sound became louder, he recognized it for what it was: laughter, full-throated, contemptuous laughter.

"Bradford, you are a fool. Is *that* what you rushed here to tell me? Even if my father *had* engaged in homosexual conduct, what use would that be to me? You keep behaving as if you're still in the State Department in the late forties and early fifties. Socially, those were the dark ages, Bradford. These days, only religious fanatics care if a person is a homosexual. It seems as if celebrities are standing in line waiting to proclaim that they are gay."

"Diplomats aren't celebrities," Bradford said indignantly.

"Of late, some behave as if they are. That isn't the point. What one does in private is no longer a matter upon which one's reputation is judged. It's how one performs one's public duties that matters. To accuse my father and the others of being homosexuals would serve no other purpose than to make *me* look bigoted. It's a distasteful, pointless charge."

"But what if their sexual orientation compromised them in some way?" Denning insisted. "In the fifties, it would have been a serious charge. What if they were blackmailed?"

"By whom? The Soviets? If so, the attempt at extortion didn't work. No diplomatic group was harder on the Soviets than my father and his associates. And on anyone suspected of being sympathetic to the Soviets. *You* above all should appreciate that."

Denning's face became redder.

"But even if I thought that it was a ruinous matter to accuse someone of being a homosexual," Mrs. Page said, "I wouldn't make that accusation against my father."

"Why not?"

"Because my father is an asexual being. In his prime, he had no interest in sex of *any* kind. My mother once confided to me that the only time they'd engaged in what my mother called the marital act was the night I was conceived. I'm convinced that he was too worried about his career to risk taking on a mistress—and given the repressive nature of the 1940s and '50s, he wouldn't have risked consorting with men. His ambition was all he cared about. *That* was his mistress. Henry Kissinger said it best for all men like my father: 'Power is the ultimate aphrodisiac.' " Mrs. Page glared at Pittman and Jill. "Surely *you* know how valueless it would be to attack my father on the basis of sexual conduct."

"Yes," Pittman said. "All the same, there's something that makes him feel vulnerable. We know the grand counselors have a secret that they're prepared to do anything to keep hidden."

"A secret?"

"About the prep school they went to. Grollier Academy."

"That's another matter I wanted to tell you, Vivian," Denning said. "It's been suggested that one of their teachers made advances to them."

"But this is the same subject we just dismissed," Mrs. Page said sharply.

"It goes beyond that," Pittman said. "We're not sure in what way, but . . ."

"Mrs. Page, did you ever hear anything about a man named Duncan Kline?" Jill asked.

"Duncan Kline?" Mrs. Page cocked her head, searching her memory. "No, I don't believe so."

"He taught your father and their friends at Grollier Academy."

Denning interrupted. "A man who was probably Duncan Kline showed up at the State Department in the summer of 1952. Your father and the others were shocked by his arrival.

They met him behind closed doors, reacting as if to a grave situation."

"What type of grave situation?"

"I don't know, but I thought that *you* might."

Mrs. Page concentrated, tightening the already-tight skin on her face. "Not if it's about Grollier Academy. My father was extremely loyal to the school. Throughout his career, he contributed generously to the alumni fund. When did you say this man came to see my father? The summer of 1952? That was an important year for my father. I remember his mood well. After Eisenhower was nominated at the Republican convention that summer, my father was convinced that he would win against Stevenson."

"I already explained that to these reporters," Denning said.

Mrs. Page glared. "Let me finish. My father and the others focused all of their energy on ingratiating themselves with Eisenhower's people. And then of course, Eisenhower won in November. Having declared their loyalty *before* Eisenhower's victory, my father and his friends had an advantage. Throughout November and December, up to the inauguration in January, they increased their attempts to impress Eisenhower. The tactic succeeded and made possible their various promotions. Within a few years, the group controlled every major diplomatic position within the government. It was the beginning of the myth about the grand counselors. That's why—given the importance of their need to impress Eisenhower after the November election—I was surprised that they took time off to go to a December reunion at Grollier Academy. It's a measure of how much affection they felt for the school. Obviously if they were sexually molested there as students, they wouldn't have wanted to go back."

"Unless they consented to Duncan Kline's advances," Denning insisted.

"Bradford, I refuse to hear any more of these sexual accusations," Mrs. Page said. "They're a waste of time to consider. My father is so skilled a diplomat that if anyone accused him of this type of activity at his prep school, he would turn it to his advantage and make himself appear a victim of a molester. He'd attract sympathy, not blame."

"That's what we told Bradford earlier tonight," Jill said. "But there *is* some kind of secret that the grand counselors are determined to go to any lengths to hide, and it has something to do with that school."

"Any lengths to hide?" Mrs. Page sounded pensive. "How do you know this?"

Jill hesitated.

Pittman answered for her. "Reliable sources we've interviewed."

"Who?"

"I'm not at liberty to reveal their names," Pittman said. "They spoke to us on condition of anonymity."

Mrs. Page gestured in frustration. "Then they're useless to you. *And* to me. How can I add to what you know and how can it help me punish my father if I don't understand the connection that your sources have with him?"

"Does the expression 'the snow' mean anything to you?" Pittman asked. "One of the last things Jonathan Millgate said was 'Duncan. The snow.' "

"Before he was murdered," Mrs. Page said.

Pittman nodded, waiting.

"No," Mrs. Page said. "I haven't the least idea what Jonathan Millgate would have been talking about." She studied Pittman, Jill, and Denning. "And that's all? These are the important subjects that you came here to tell me? This evening has been worthless."

"Millgate," Denning said unexpectedly.

They looked at him in surprise.

"I beg your pardon?" Mrs. Page said.

"Millgate." Denning stared at Pittman. "You mentioned *Jonathan Millgate*."

"Bradford, have you lost your senses?" Mrs. Page asked.

Denning suddenly pointed at Pittman. "Now I remember where I've seen you before."

Pittman felt a chill.

"Your name isn't Lester King or whatever you said it was! It's Matthew Pittman! I met you several years ago! I've seen your photograph a dozen times in the newspaper! But you had a mustache and— You're the man the police want for killing Jonathan Millgate!"

"Bradford, this is outrageous. Do you realize what you're saying?" Mrs. Page demanded.

"I'm telling you this is the man!" Denning said. "Do you have a newspaper? I'll prove it to you! I'll show you the photographs! This man killed Jonathan Millgate!"

"Don't be absurd," Pittman said. "If I killed him, what would I be doing here?"

The door opened. The uniformed servant appeared, his brow deeply furrowed. "Mrs. Page, I heard loud voices. Is anything wrong?"

"George, phone the police!" Denning said.

"The police, sir?" George looked puzzled, glancing toward Mrs. Page for an explanation.

"Bradford, what do you think you're doing?" Mrs. Page demanded.

"Hurry! Before he kills all of us!"

Pittman stood, making Denning cower. "Bradford, I'd stop drinking if I were you. It affects your behavior and your judgment." He turned to Mrs. Page. "I regret that this happened. We're sorry for the inconvenience. Thanks for agreeing to talk with us."

Jill stood as well. "We appreciate your time."

Pittman shifted toward the doorway. "With Bradford in this condition, obviously it's pointless for us to continue this conversation."

Mrs. Page looked bewildered.

"Good evening," Pittman said. "And thanks again."

"Call the police, George!" Denning insisted. "Before they get away!"

"No," Mrs. Page said. "I don't understand this at all. Bradford, what on earth has gotten into you?"

Pittman and Jill passed the servant, left the room, crossed the shiny hardwood floor of the vestibule, and opened the door to the porch, its pillars casting shadows from lights among shrubs.

3

"We'd better hurry," Jill said.

In the cool night air, she and Pittman started down the brick steps from the porch, about to reach the murky area beyond the lights on the lawn, when Pittman faltered, touching Jill's arm. "More trouble."

Jill tensed, seeing what he meant. "Our car."

It was parked in front of the mansion. Revealed by streetlights, two rugged-looking men in windbreakers were staring at the front license plate on the Duster.

Pittman backed up. "They must have been watching the house."

"Why would they . . . ?" Jill retreated quickly up the steps toward the porch. At once she realized. "Eustace Gable knows his daughter is a threat. He must have arranged for the house to be watched in case we came here."

"And the Vermont license plates on our car," Pittman said. "They're probably the only ones on the street. They connect us with our visit to Grollier Academy."

As Pittman and Jill hurried toward the mansion's front door, one of the men shouted, "Hey!" Pittman turned, seeing the man point at him. Simultaneously Pittman saw a dark

Oldsmobile appear beyond the cars parked in front of the house. It skidded to a stop. Men scrambled out.

Pittman gripped the doorknob, praying that the servant hadn't locked the door after they'd left. Exhaling with relief when he made the knob turn, he shoved the door open, lunged inside behind Jill, slammed the door, and locked it.

The noise caused startled voices in the room to the left. As Pittman swung toward that doorway, the servant loomed into view, Mrs. Page and Denning behind him.

"What are you doing?" Mrs. Page asked. "Why did you come back?"

"I'm afraid we brought you trouble," Pittman said. "There isn't time to explain. We have to figure out how to—"

"Six of them." Jill stared past the lace curtain of a high, narrow window next to the front door.

"Six?" Mrs. Page veered past Denning and the servant. "I don't know what you're—"

"They're coming up the sidewalk," Jill said.

Pittman stepped closer to Mrs. Page. "You're in danger. What's in back? How do we get out of here?"

"Danger?" Denning's voice shook.

"They're separating." Jill strained to look out the window. "Two in front, two going along each side of the house."

"Mrs. Page, those men are from your father," Pittman said.

"My . . . ?"

"The two in front just pulled out handguns," Jill said.

"Mrs. Page, I think they intend to kill all of us," Pittman said. "They'll make it look as if I did it."

"Kill us?" Mrs. Page looked horror-stricken. *"Why?"*

"Because your father's afraid of what you might have told me. We have to get out of here."

"Some of them will go to the back," Jill said. "They've got the house sealed off."

"My father would *never* try to kill me."

"He killed your mother, didn't he? Why wouldn't he kill you?"

Mrs. Page's eyes widened with shocked understanding.

"The two in front are coming toward the porch," Jill said.

Pittman turned to the servant. "Did you do what Denning wanted and call the police?"

"No. Mrs. Page told me not to."

"Then you'd better call them *now*."

"There isn't time!" Denning whined. "The police won't get here before—"

Glass shattered at the back of the house. Denning whirled toward the sound.

Pittman reached beneath his sport coat and pulled out the .45, the sight of which made Denning's face become the color of cement.

From the porch, someone tried to turn the doorknob.

"Jill," Pittman warned, "get back."

She hurried toward Pittman as he told the servant, "Switch off the lights in the hallway."

The vestibule became dim, illuminated only by lamps in the room that they had left.

More glass shattered at the back of the house.

"Jill, if anybody tries to come through that door, do you think you can use the gun in your purse?"

"I'm so scared."

"But *can* you?"

"Yes, if I have to."

"Good." Pittman rushed from the vestibule toward the rear of the house. "Find a place to hide," he heard Jill saying.

"The car," Mrs. Page said.

At the rear of the house, Pittman crouched in shadows, clutching his .45, concentrating to hear the sounds of someone climbing through a window.

"Yes, the car," Denning said.

From the porch, shoulders slammed against the front door.

"The car? Forget it," Jill said. "Some of those men are outside in the back. They'll shoot us if we try to get to the garage."

"You don't understand," Mrs. Page said. "It's in the basement."

Shoulders kept slamming against the front door.

"What are you talking about? The basement?" Jill sounded hoarse, her throat dry from fear. "What's a car doing in the basement? What good would—?"

From a room at the back of the house, Pittman heard footsteps scraping on broken glass. He clutched his pistol tighter, aiming.

"The *garage* is down there," Mrs. Page said. "The garage is under the house. If we get to the car, we'll be safe."

"No!" Jill said. "We'll be *trapped*. If we try to drive away, they'll shoot through the windows and doors and—"

"Why must you be so stupid? Listen to me. Listen to what I'm telling you."

Pittman heard Mrs. Page's high-heeled shoes on the vestibule's hardwood floor. A door opened, echoing.

"Stop," Jill said.

"Down here," Mrs. Page insisted.

"I'm going with you," Denning said.

A man's footsteps scurried across the vestibule, joining the urgent rapping sound of high-heeled shoes descending stairs.

"Wait for me!" The servant quickly followed.

"Matt!" Jill shouted.

From the back of the mansion, Pittman heard other footsteps scraping on broken glass. A shadow moved. Pittman fired, his ears ringing from the .45's fierce blast. The recoil threw him off balance. From the darkness at the back of the house, he saw what seemed to be a spark. Simultaneously he felt more than heard a bullet strike the wall next to him. For a frenzied moment, he feared that thc blast from his .45 had deafened him. In a greater frenzy, he realized that he hadn't heard the shot from the back of the house because the gunman had used a silencer. The ringing in Pittman's ears had obscured the muffled spit. He fired again, squirming backward, flinching from the impact of four soundless bullets striking the wall where he'd been crouching.

"Matt!" Jill screamed.

We don't have a chance, Pittman thought, scurrying faster backward. We can't possibly kill all six of them.

"Jill, come on!"

"Where!"

"The basement!"

As Jill rushed past him, hurrying down the stairs that the others had used, Pittman fired once more toward the back of the house, spun and fired toward the front door, then charged into the stairwell and slammed the door shut.

Not that thc closed door would do him any good, he suddenly realized. It did have a lock, but the knob for the bolt was on the opposite side. He couldn't possibly keep the gunmen from coming through.

Fear made him nauseated. Lights in the stairwell revealed stone steps that led to a concrete floor. Jill had already reached the bottom. Pittman backed down, aiming toward the closed door. He saw the knob being turned and fired, his ears ringing worse as the powerful bullet splintered the door, walloping through, a man on the other side screaming.

The two men at the front door had been a diversion, Pittman thought. They had pounded on the door to drive everyone toward the back of the house, where the men who'd broken in waited with silenced pistols. The slight commotion at the front probably hadn't attracted much attention from the street. The silenced pistols couldn't be heard outside the mansion.

No one knows what's happening in here! Pittman thought. The servant was supposed to have phoned the police, but Pittman hadn't seen him do it. Had the servant been distracted by fear? Nobody realizes we need help! We're trapped down here! The only way someone outside can know we're in danger is . . .

The blast from Pittman's .45. *That* could be heard outside. As he continued to stare up toward the door to the basement, he saw the knob being turned, and he fired again, his ears suffering from the pistol's torturous blast, the confines of the basement magnifying the roar.

Someone outside is bound to hear, Pittman told himself. Although the ringing in his ears was excruciating, he prepared to fire yet again. But suddenly a warning instinct told him that he was almost out of ammunition. How many times had he fired? He strained to remember. Six. He had only one round left. If they try to rush us . . .

Jill, he thought. She hasn't fired yet. Her pistol's still fully loaded. He spun toward her, wanting to trade weapons, and froze in surprise at the sight of the car in the basement. Its length and height were totally unexpected. It was a silver Rolls-Royce, its paint and chrome gleaming from obvious daily care. Someone had backed it in. A pulley in the ceiling led to a garage door that could be raised electronically.

Pittman's surprise was offset by dismay when he saw how panicked Mrs. Page, Denning, and the servant were. They had scurried into the car, slamming the doors, evidently locking them. Jill was straining to open the driver's door while Mrs. Page struggled to shove a key into the car's ignition switch.

"Mrs. Page, unlock the door! Let me in!" Jill's shout was muffled by the ringing in Pittman's ears.

Pittman redirected his attention toward the door at the top of the stairs. Again the knob turned. Again he fired. The ejection slide on top of his pistol stayed back, indicating that the weapon was empty.

No! He shoved the .45 into his coat pocket and ran toward Jill. "I need your gun!"

She was so preoccupied, pounding on the driver's door, trying to get into the Rolls-Royce, that she didn't seem to notice when Pittman took the pistol.

It held more ammunition than the .45. As a consequence, Pittman felt briefly confident. But then he realized that he was still trapped. If Mrs. Page started the car, opened the automatic garage door, and sped away, it wasn't possible for Jill and himself to defend themselves against six gunmen.

The door at the top of the stairs opened slightly. Pittman fired, the recoil from the 9 mm less violent than that from the .45. It was obvious what the gunmen were doing—holding back, staying on either side of the door, taunting Pittman by moving it, trying to entice him into wasting all his ammunition.

Sickeningly, his heartbeat surged as he wondered why the police hadn't arrived. Surely a neighbor must have heard the shots and phoned for help. Why were the police taking so long?

Jill kept pounding on the driver's door. "Let me in!"

Abruptly Mrs. Page pushed a button that caused the locks to disengage, making a thunking sound. She opened the door. "I can't get the car to start!"

"My father owns one of these! Let *me* try! Move over!" Jill shoved at her, squirming behind the steering wheel.

Pittman ran to the car and saw that Denning was scrunched next to Mrs. Page and Jill. He yanked opened the passenger door, dragged Denning out, and shoved him into the backseat with the servant.

As Pittman dove into the back with them, he yelled to Jill, "Let's get the hell out of here!"

Jill slammed her door and turned the ignition key. "It doesn't work!"

"Try again!"

"It doesn't want to turn all the way!"

Pittman scurried from the car and aimed toward the stairs. "Hurry!"

"The key!" Jill said. "This isn't the right key!" Hands shaking, she sorted through other keys on a ring.

Even with his protesting ears, Pittman heard sounds on the stairs. Shadows, then shoes came rapidly into view. He fired. Splinters from concrete spattered the shoes. The gunmen scrambled back out of sight.

Jill shouted, "Got it!"

The Rolls-Royce's engine roared.

"Hurry!" Pittman fired once more at the stairs and dove back into the car. "Lock all the doors!"

Jill pressed a button that engaged the locks. She pressed another button. With a rumble, the garage door began to rise.

Pittman glanced in dismay through the car's rear window. The gunmen were charging down the stairs.

"They'll shoot out the windows!" Pittman yelled. "Stay down!"

"They can't!" Mrs. Page shouted.

A bullet struck the rear window, ricocheting.

"My husband was afraid of terrorists!"

"What?"

Jill revved the Rolls-Royce, speeding forward as the garage door rose above the hood. With a crunch, the car's roof struck the rising garage door. But the Rolls kept hurtling from the garage. It soared up an incline and jounced down onto ground level. Through the windshield, Pittman saw three of the gunmen crouched in a shadowy lane behind the house. They were waiting, aiming toward the car. He couldn't hear the shots from their silenced weapons, but the upward jerk of the pistols showed that the gunmen were firing. Bullets struck and deflected off the hood and the windshield.

"What the—?"

"The windows are bulletproof!" Mrs. Page said. "The whole car is! That's what I've been trying to tell you!"

Jill swerved, increasing speed, veering past the gunmen, who now fired at the side of the car.

Pittman felt the vibrating impact of the eerily muffled bullets hitting the Rolls.

Jill struggled with the steering wheel. "This thing handles like it's a tank!"

"At the time, I thought my late husband was insane to want an armored car!"

A gunman appeared ahead of them, firing directly at the windshield, diving for cover as Jill sped past. She swerved from the narrow tree-lined lane and reached the side of the house, aiming the Rolls along the brick driveway toward the street. There hadn't been time to turn on the headlights, but the glare of lights in the shrubbery at the front combined with the glow of streetlights, showing that the dark Oldsmobile the gunmen had arrived in was parked directly in front of the exit from the driveway. There wasn't any way past it.

Other cars were parked everywhere along the curb, preventing the Rolls from veering off the driveway, across the sidewalk, and onto the street.

"Brace yourselves!"

Jill tightened her grip on the steering wheel, directing the Rolls toward the front fender of the Oldsmobile blocking the driveway. "I hope this *is* a tank!"

In the backseat, preparing himself for the collision, Pittman felt the Rolls increase speed. The Oldsmobile grew alarmingly, seeming to fill the windshield. The Rolls struck it with such force that the Oldsmobile jerked sideways.

Pittman felt as if his chest had been punched. His head snapped back. Next to him, Denning slammed onto the floor. As the Rolls kept heaving forward, ramming the Oldsmobile farther sideways, the servant groaned. In the front seat, Mrs. Page shoved her hands against the dashboard to absorb the shock.

Even though Pittman's ears kept ringing, he couldn't help hearing the crunch of metal and the crash of glass. The Oldsmobile had been jolted sufficiently sideways that the Rolls slammed past it, scraping an Infiniti parked at the curb but hurtling forward, reaching the street and streaking across it. Jill stamped the brake pedal. But the heavily armored car barely slowed. Jill swung the steering wheel to avoid the cars parked on the opposite side of the street. But the Rolls—never meant to be so heavy—responded sluggishly. One of the cars across the street seemed suddenly huge. The Rolls struck it, more glass shattering, metal crumbling. The Rolls rebounded, its distinctive winged woman hood ornament and thickly slatted, shiny grill falling onto the pavement.

From the backseat, jolted by the two collisions, Pittman watched Jill in dismay as she tugged the car's gearshift into reverse and stared behind her. Working the steering wheel, she tried to maneuver the car so that it wasn't positioned diagonally across the street, blocking both lanes. Too late. Pittman was suddenly knocked sideways by the jolt of another collision. A car coming along the street hadn't been able to stop in time to avoid hitting the Rolls. Headlights glaring, a car coming in the opposite direction squealed to a stop before it struck the other side of the Rolls.

No! Pittman thought. We're boxed in!

Drivers got out of the cars. Alarmed by the din of the multiple collisions, men and women hurried out of houses on both sides of the street. Pedestrians watched in shock. The sidewalks became rapidly crowded. Horns blaring, cars lined up in each direction, blocked by the accidents.

"What are we going to do?" Denning whimpered.

"One thing's sure. We're not going anywhere in the Rolls," Jill said.

"Get out of the car," Pittman said.

"They'll shoot us," the servant said.

"We can't stay here. Hurry. Everybody out." Pittman helped Denning rise from where he'd been thrown to the floor. "Are you all right? Mrs. Page, what about you?" Pittman shoved his door open. *"Mrs. Page, I asked if you're all right."*

Stunned, slumped in the front seat, Mrs. Page groaned.

Jill leaned over, examining her.

Outside the car, Pittman rushed forward and opened the passenger door. "How is she?"

The drivers of the cars that blocked the Rolls crowded toward Pittman.

"What the hell did you think you were doing?" a man yelled. "You came out of nowhere."

"She's shaken up," Jill said. "But I don't see any bleeding."

"We have to get away from here!" Denning wailed.

Pittman spun to study the driveway next to the mansion. Past the commotion of numerous onlookers, he saw solemn-faced men wearing windbreakers running down the shadowy driveway, dispersing into the crowd.

"Jesus, buddy!" a bystander said, stumbling back in terror, pointing toward Pittman's right hand.

Pittman didn't understand why the man behaved as he did. Then, squinting down at his right hand, Pittman saw that he still clutched the pistol he had taken from Jill.

The panicked man who'd seen the pistol bumped against the driver of one of the cars that had struck the Rolls. Now the driver, too, saw the pistol and reacted the way the first man had, stumbling to get away.

"Jesus, he's got a gun!" somebody yelled.

A woman screamed.

The crowd around Pittman bumped into one another in a frenzied effort to get away from the gun.

Pittman kept darting his gaze past them, toward the driveway and sidewalk at Mrs. Page's mansion. The solemn-faced men wearing windbreakers were no longer in view. He scanned the panicked bystanders, afraid that the gunmen might be using them for cover, stalking nearer.

"She's all right," Jill said abruptly behind him.

Pittman spun, seeing Mrs. Page next to Jill.

"Let's get out of here!" Denning yelled.

"The Duster." Pittman ran toward the front of the mansion where he had parked it. He pulled out his car keys and unlocked the driver's door, frantically opened it, then pulled the passenger seat forward, wishing that the Duster had four doors.

Denning scurried into the front. Jill and the servant helped

Mrs. Page into the back, throwing Pittman's gym bag and Jill's suitcase onto the floor. Pittman pushed the passenger seat back into place, hurried behind the steering wheel, slammed his door, started the car, and sped away from the curb. In the opposite lane, ten cars were backed up, headlights gleaming, drivers and passengers leaning out in confusion. But Pittman's lane was completely empty, the Rolls and the car that had hit it blocking traffic behind him.

"Stay down!" Pittman yelled to Jill and the others. "If those gunmen are still in the area . . . !"

He sped through a murky intersection, steered sharply to avoid a pedestrian, shuddered, and turned on his headlights. In the sudden glare, flat-faced brick town houses with cars parked along curbs were a blur on either side of the Duster.

"We got lucky!" Denning blurted. "The crowd scared them away!"

"Maybe," Pittman said.

"What do you mean *maybe*?" Denning peered behind him. "I don't see any headlights! No one's following us!"

"I agree with you. I think we got away," Pittman said. "At least for now. What I meant was, I'm not sure they were scared by the crowd."

Denning shook his head in confusion.

"I have a hunch that if it suited their purposes," Pittman said, "they'd have shot us right there in the street. In the dark and the panic, who'd be able to identify them?"

"Then why didn't they?"

Tires protesting, Pittman swerved the Duster around a corner, speeding south on Thirty-fourth Street. Slow down, he warned himself. You can't let the police stop you. Sweating, he reduced speed and blended with traffic.

"You didn't answer my question," Denning complained.

"If you don't think they were frightened by the crowd, why didn't they shoot us when we got out of the Rolls? What do you mean, it didn't suit their purpose?"

"The idea wasn't just to kill us all," Pittman said. "You're right. I am Matthew Pittman. The police want me for murdering Jonathan Millgate. But I swear to you, I didn't do anything to him. If anything, I was trying to help him." Pittman explained what had happened at the Scarsdale estate. "I've been on the run ever since. What Millgate told me is dangerous enough to all of them that they're desperate to kill me before I figure out what it means."

Driving, Pittman stared nervously ahead, seeing the lights and traffic of Pennsylvania Avenue. "To prevent me from finding out, they also killed several people I went to for information. They made it look as if *I* had killed those people. That's why the newspapers create the impression I'm on a homicidal rampage. But I haven't killed *anyone*. No, that's wrong. I have to be totally honest with you. God help me, I did kill. I had to defend myself against a man in my apartment, against a man who tried to shoot me on a street in Manhattan, and against a man who threatened Jill in *her* apartment."

"That's my real name," Jill told Mrs. Page. "Those men think *I* know something, too."

"But the rest of us," Mrs. Page said. "Why would they want to—?"

"Those men work for your father and presumably the other grand counselors," Pittman said. He reached Pennsylvania Avenue and turned to the right onto brightly lit M Street. Traffic was dense. "Your father knows how much you hate him. He knows you want to destroy him. You're a logical person for us to go to and ask for help."

Denning objected. "You weren't aware of her. If it hadn't been for me . . ."

"But Eustace Gable doesn't know that," Pittman said. "What he does know is that I'm a former reporter. He might have been afraid that I'd use my sources to learn about Mrs. Page and go to her—which is exactly what happened tonight. My guess is, he had a man watching the house in case we showed up. When we did, the man telephoned for help."

Ahead, Pittman saw the gleaming lights of Francis Scott Key Bridge and steered left onto it, following traffic across the Potomac into Virginia. "I'm supposed to be on a killing spree, some kind of vendetta against the grand counselors. They'd have made it seem that I'd killed you. Why would I have done it? Who knows? The authorities think I'm insane, after all. Maybe, because I couldn't find Eustace Gable, I vented my rage on his daughter. But Eustace Gable was worried about his daughter. He sent men to see if she was safe. They caught me after I'd killed her. Shots were exchanged. Jill and I didn't survive. End of story. End of the threat to the grand counselors. And with no one to prove otherwise, the police would have gone along with that explanation."

"The police," Mrs. Page said. "We have to go to the police."

"*You* can," Pittman said. "I think they'll listen to you. With your money and prestige, they'll do their best to protect you. But your father will do everything in his power to discredit you, to make people think *you're* insane. Which is more acceptable to the authorities, that *I'm* a maniac or that your distinguished father was so determined to keep a secret that he didn't care if his daughter was killed?"

"My distinguished father," Mrs. Page said with disgust.

"And there's always a risk that your father will arrange to have an accident happen to you while you're in protective custody," Pittman said. "Seven years ago, Jonathan Millgate arranged to have the Boston police arrest me for suspicion of burglary while I was investigating him. Two men working for him broke my jaw while I was in jail."

"That's why we haven't given ourselves up," Jill said. "If Matt surrenders to the police and tries to tell his story, he doesn't think he'll be safe. He won't be believed."

"The evidence is against me. My chances are a whole lot better if I stay free and do what I can to prove I'm innocent."

"How?" Mrs. Page asked.

"I've been thinking about that. But I can't do it alone. Will you help?"

"Tell me what you need."

"I'm still figuring out all the details. But I know this much right now. At your house, people saw the gun in my hand. They saw us put you in our car. They'll almost certainly have seen our Vermont license plates. What happened can be interpreted as a kidnapping. The police will be looking for us, and they'll be counting on our Vermont license plates to make it easy for them." Across the Potomac, opposite Washington, Pittman drove along Fort Myer Drive in Rosslyn, Virginia. "I need to find a nice big bar with a crowded parking lot."

"Yes," Denning said. "I could use a stiff drink."

"That's not exactly what I had in mind," Pittman said. "I want to steal somebody's Virginia license plates. After they're on, we're going to a pay phone. I want you to call your father, Mrs. Page. There are several things I want you to say to him."

"But I don't have his private number. He refuses to give it to me."

"No problem. *I've* got the number," Pittman said.

"*You* do? How?"

"Someone I once interviewed gave it to me."

4

The phone booth was outside a brightly lit convenience store. Pittman parked with other cars in front, and as people went in and out of the store, he remained in the Duster, coaching Mrs. Page on what he wanted her to say.

"Can you remember all that? Do you think you can do it?"

"I'm going to enjoy this," Mrs. Page answered grimly, the tautness of her face emphasized by shadows in the car. "It's exactly what I *want* to say to him."

"I hope I'm not misleading you. You understand that this can put you in danger."

"I'm already in danger. I need to protect myself. But I don't see why we have to use a pay phone. Why can't we rent a hotel room and use *its* phone? We'd be more comfortable."

"If your father's as obsessed about security as I think he is, he'll have equipment to trace the phone calls he receives. It's not that hard to do anymore. Look at Caller ID. It can be done instantly," Pittman said. "In that case, he'd send men to the hotel. Our room would be a trap."

"Of course," Mrs. Page said. "I should have thought."

"But *you* thought of it," Denning told Pittman.

Pittman rubbed his brow, troubled. "The precaution just

seemed obvious to me.'' He was beginning to realize that he had a talent for being on the run. His head throbbed as he wondered what *else* he didn't know about himself.

Jill came back from the store, handing Pittman coins from a five-dollar bill that she had changed. ''We'll soon be out of cash.''

''I know. Thanks for the coins.'' He pointed. ''What's in the paper bag?''

''Coffee and doughnuts for everybody.''

''You'll never eat right again.''

''I just hope I get the chance to try.''

Pittman touched her hand, then turned to Mrs. Page. ''So what do you think? Are you ready? Good. Let's do it.'' He escorted Mrs. Page to the phone booth, which was situated where they wouldn't be disturbed, a distance from the store's entrance. He pulled out a sheet of paper with the list of telephone numbers that he'd gotten from Brian Botulfson's computer. After putting coins into the box, he pressed the buttons for Eustace Gable's home and handed Mrs. Page the telephone.

She stood in the booth and glared through the glass wall before her as if she was seeing her father. In a moment, she said, ''Eustace Gable. . . . Oh, in this case, I think he'll want to be disturbed. Tell him it's his loving daughter.'' Mrs. Page tapped her pointed fingernails impatiently against the glass of the phone booth. ''Well, hello, Father dear. I knew you'd be concerned, so I thought I'd call to tell you that in spite of the goons who came to my house, I'm safe.'' She laughed bitterly. ''What goons? The ones you hired to kill me, of course. . . . Stop. Don't insult my intelligence. Do you actually expect me to believe your denials? I know I've disappointed you in a number of ways, not the least of which is that I'm not perfect. But you can take pride in this. You did not raise an idiot. I know what's happening, Father, and I'm going to do everything in my power to guarantee that you're stopped. . . . What am I talking about? Duncan Kline, Father. . . . What's the matter? All of a sudden, you don't seem to have anything to say. When I was young, you always interrupted everything I tried to tell you. Now you're finally listening. My, my. Duncan Kline, Father. Grollier Academy. The snow. You murdered Jonathan Millgate to keep it a secret. But I'm going to let your secret out. And damn you, I hope you spend the rest of your life suffering. *For what you did to Mother*."

Mrs. Page set the telephone on its receptacle, stared at it, exhaled, and turned to Pittman. "That was extremely satisfying."

"You'll have plenty of other chances. I want to put pressure on your father, on *all* of them," Pittman said. "But right now, we need to get back to the car and drive out of this area—in case your father did trace the call."

Twenty seconds later, Pittman watched the lights of the convenience store recede in his rearview mirror. "We'll drive for a couple of miles, then use another pay phone."

"Right. Now it's *my* turn to make a call," Jill said. "To Winston Sloane. I can't wait. It feels so good to be confronting them."

5

At last it was Pittman's turn. He stopped the car at a phone booth on the edge of a shopping mall's deserted parking lot in Fairfax, Virginia. Standing in the booth's light, he studied the list of phone numbers, put coins in the box, and pressed numbers.

The phone on the other end rang only once before a man answered, his deep voice somewhat strained. "Standish residence."

"I need to speak to him."

The voice hesitated. "Who's calling, please?"

"Just put him on. I'm certain he's still awake, because I'm certain he just received calls from Eustace Gable or Winston Sloane, probably both of them."

"How do you know that, sir?"

It wasn't the type of question that Pittman expected a servant to ask. Just as the voice had hesitated a short while earlier, now Pittman hesitated. His plan depended in part on the likelihood that the grand counselors would feel pressured by the phone calls, that they would contact one another and feel even more pressure when they learned that each had been called in a similar manner but by different people. The message to them was clear: You failed to keep your secret;

more and more people know what you did in the past and what you've done to hide it. With luck, the grand counselors would overreact, make mistakes, and . . .

The deep, strained voice interrupted Pittman's thoughts. "Sir, are you still there? I asked, how did you know that Mr. Standish received telephone calls from Eustace Gable and Winston Sloane?"

"Because I want to talk to him about the same matter *they* wanted to talk to him about," Pittman said.

"And what is that?" The voice sounded more strained.

"Look, I'm tired of this. Tell him *Duncan Kline*, *Grollier Academy*. Tell him he can talk to *me* about it or he can talk to the police."

"I'm afraid I don't understand. Duncan Kline? Grollier Academy?"

In the background on the other end of the line, Pittman heard other voices, the sound of people moving around.

What the hell's going on? Pittman thought.

"Who am I speaking to?" the voice insisted.

"I get the feeling you're not a servant."

"Mr. Standish won't speak with you unless he knows who's calling. If I could have your name . . ."

In the background, Pittman heard a man call out, "Lieutenant."

"You're with the police," Pittman said.

"The police, sir? What makes you think that? All I need is your name and I'll ask Mr. Standish if—"

"Damn it, what's happened?"

"Nothing, sir."

"Of course. That's why you're having a police convention at his house."

"Just a few guests."

"Stop the bullshit! I assume you're trying to trace this call.

Don't bother. I'm going to hang up if you don't answer my questions. *What's happened?''*

''I'm afraid there's been an accident,'' the voice on the phone said.

6

"Victor Standish is dead?" Jill leaned forward, startled, as Pittman drove quickly from the pay phone in the shopping mall's deserted parking lot.

"How?" Mrs. Page asked in astonishment.

"The policeman wouldn't say." Pittman merged with traffic on Old Lee Highway. "I'm surprised he told me even that much. Obviously he hoped to keep me on the line until he had the number I was calling from and could send a cruiser there."

Behind him, Pittman heard a fast-approaching siren. He peered tensely toward his rearview mirror and saw the flashing lights of a police car speeding through the glare of traffic. "Maybe I didn't hang up soon enough."

The cruiser switched lanes, taking advantage of a break in traffic, increasing speed. Unexpectedly, it veered off the highway.

Pittman's cramped hands were sweaty, slicking the steering wheel. "I think I've had enough adrenaline for one night."

"I'm glad to hear I'm not the only one who feels exhausted," Mrs. Page said. "I could use a chance to lie down."

"Isn't it wonderful," Denning exclaimed.

"What?"

"Three dead. Two to go," Denning said gleefully. "They're dropping like flies, Vivian. It's everything I dreamed of. They're finally getting what they deserve. Stop," he blurted to Pittman. "We have to find another pay phone."

Pittman didn't know how to respond to Denning's outburst.

"Do what I tell you," Denning insisted. "There. At that service station. Quickly. Pull over."

Puzzled, compelled by Denning's emotion, Pittman obeyed. He stopped the Duster next to the air pump at the side of the gas station. Confused, he stood with the others next to the phone booth as Denning made his call.

"Answering your own phone these days, are you, Eustace? Feeling that nervous, are you? . . . An old enemy. I'm calling to tell you how pleased I am to hear that Victor Standish died tonight. Thrilled. Ecstatic. The bastard deserved it. So do you. It's enough to make me believe in God. Tell me, Eustace, do you suppose Victor's death had anything to do with your secret? When people learn about Duncan Kline, you'll be ruined. You'll die in disgrace. I'll dance on your grave, you son of a bitch."

Denning slammed down the phone, his eyes fierce, his frenzied expression made stark by the harsh fluorescent lights that glared from the gas station's large window.

The attendant came out, wiping grease from his hands. "Need some gas?"

Pittman was so gripped by the hateful expression on Denning's face that it took him a moment to respond to the attendant. "No. We just needed to use the phone."

"Your friend doesn't look well."

"You're right," Pittman said. "He doesn't." Pittman was alarmed by Denning's sudden pallor.

"Need some rest." Denning's knees bent.

Pittman grabbed him.

"Too much has been happening," Denning said. "Need to lie down."

"Oh God, should I call an ambulance?" the attendant asked.

"No." Pittman's urgent thoughts were complicated. He wanted to make sure that Denning was all right. At the same time, he needed to get away from the gas station in case Gable had managed a trace on Denning's call and sent men here. "My friend's a nurse. We'll get him into the car. She'll check him. If I have to, I'll take him to a doctor."

They rushed to put Denning into the backseat. The next thing, Pittman was behind the steering wheel. He slammed the door, started the Duster, and steered back into traffic. "How is he?"

In the backseat, Jill was examining him. "His pulse is rapid but weak. Unsteady."

"What does that mean? Is he having a heart attack?"

"I don't know. He says he isn't having sharp pains in his chest or down his left arm. It's more like a hand on his chest. Sounds like angina. If I had some instruments, a blood-pressure cuff, I could . . . I don't think you should take any chances. Get him to a hospital."

7

They sat in the Emergency waiting room, squinting from the stark reflection of strong lights off white walls. Pittman squirmed on a metal chair, his bruised side aching, his legs continuing to feel stiff from having spent so much time in the car. Next to him, Mrs. Page looked considerably older, her taut face almost skeletal from fatigue.

Pittman scanned the haggard faces of other people waiting for word about patients. It occurred to him that under different circumstances, being in a hospital would have intensified his preoccupation with Jeremy's death. But now so much had happened, there was so much for him to brood about, Jeremy was only part of the welter of thoughts and feelings that he endured. He was amazed that he did not see this as a betrayal of Jeremy. If Jeremy wasn't constantly in his thoughts, that had nothing to do with a reduction of love for his dead son, he realized. Rather, it meant that he knew he couldn't grieve if he was dead. In contrast with his morass of despair a week ago, he understood that his primary responsibility was to remain alive—to keep Jeremy's memory alive, to continue loving him. He had to do everything to survive.

Jill was coming through a swinging door beside the nurse's station. Her jeans and sweater looked rumpled. Her blue eyes were glazed with weariness as she tugged fingers through her long blond hair and came over.

"Any news?" Pittman asked.

"They're still doing tests, but so far it doesn't look as if he had a coronary." Jill slumped in the chair beside him. "For the moment, the theory is exhaustion. The doctor wants to keep him overnight for observation."

"He'll be safe here. No one will think to look for him in a Fairfax hospital."

"Provided he keeps his mouth shut."

"Oh, I think he feels helpless enough that he won't want to make more phone calls. He won't advertise where he is."

Mrs. Page roused herself, her voice dry. "But he's not the only one who's exhausted." She turned to her servant. "George, you've been good to stay with me. I think, however, that it's time you looked after yourself. You need to rest. Your family will be wondering where you are. Call them and reassure them. Then go home."

George hesitated. "Do you think that's wise, ma'am? To go home? The men looking for you might be watching where I live. They might interrogate me to find out where you are."

"But you won't know where I've gone," Mrs. Page said.

"George has a point," Pittman said. "Even if he doesn't know where you are, they'd still have to torture him to find that out. He'd be in danger the same as the rest of us."

"I'd like to come along, ma'am. From the looks of things, you need my help more than ever."

8

The Holiday Inn was west of Fairfax, off Route 29. Pittman chose it because it was close to where the two remaining grand counselors had their estates. For a moment, he'd been confused about how he was going to pay for the rooms. He and Jill had very little money left. He couldn't use his or Jill's credit card. Similarly, the group couldn't use Mrs. Page's—her name was familiar in the Washington area and was almost certain to attract attention. The police and Eustace Gable would have alerted the credit card companies, stressing that they needed to be informed if and where anyone used her card.

The difficulty had appeared insurmountable until Pittman realized that the one person most likely to be invisible was Mrs. Page's servant. It would take the police and the remaining grand counselors quite a while to discover George's name. In the meantime, the group absolutely needed to rest.

They waited in the shadows of a parking lot while George went into the motel's brightly lit lobby and made the arrangements. The rooms were on the outside, on the second floor, in back, and after Pittman trudged up a flight of concrete steps, an arm around Jill, he turned to Mrs. Page and George.

"It isn't a good idea to be in one place too long. We ought to be out of here by seven tomorrow morning."

Mrs. Pagc looked surprised by the schedule, obviously not used to getting up that early, but she didn't say a word, only braced her shoulders and nodded.

"Remember, we can't make any phone calls from here," Pittman said.

This time, both George and Mrs. Page nodded.

"Sleep well," Pittman added.

"How I wish," Mrs. Page said.

After watching George and Mrs. Page go into their rooms, Pittman unlocked the one he and Jill had requested. They carried in the gym bag and suitcase, set them on the carpeted floor, then shut and locked the door, not bothering to examine the clean and functional room. Instead, they turned to each other, studied each other's weary features, and tenderly embraced.

They held each other for what seemed a long time. As tired as he was, Pittman felt as if he could stand and hold Jill all night long.

But then his knees became unsteady. Taking Jill's hand, he sat with her on the side of the bed. "The worst part is that I'm actually beginning to think we can get out of this," he said. "To hope. The last time I hoped for something, really hoped, with all my heart, it didn't work out."

Jill stroked the side of his face. "We'll get out of this. It'll happen. We'll *make* it happen."

"Sure." But Pittman's tone was less than positive. He kissed her softly on the cheek, then stood and removed his sport coat. His .45, which he hadn't had time to reload, was in his gym bag. But the 9 mm that he had taken from Jill was wedged behind his belt at his spine. With relief, he pulled it free and set it on the counter that supported the television.

His back hurt from where the sharp edges of the weapon had pressed into his skin.

Jill pointed toward the television. "Maybe we should have a look at CNN. There might be some news about what happened to Victor Standish."

"Good idea." Pittman turned on the set, inspected a list of television stations that was taped to the top, and used the remote control to switch to CNN. He watched thirty seconds of a story about a child being rescued from a well.

"That boy looks as dirty as I feel," Jill said.

"How would you like to use the shower first?"

"You certainly know the right things to say." After briefly rubbing Pittman's back, Jill took some things from her suitcase and went into the bathroom.

Pittman listened to the scrape of shower curtain hooks, the spray of water into the hollow-sounding tub. He took his .45 and its box of ammunition from his gym bag, returned to the bed, and reloaded the pistol, continuing to watch CNN. An announcer summarized the day's stock market activity. A commercial followed. Then there was a story about a seventy-year-old woman who was getting a Ph.D. in political science.

Human-interest stuff, Pittman told himself, glancing at his watch. Almost midnight. The hard news won't come on until the top of the hour.

He took off his shoes and kneaded his stockinged feet against the carpet, feeling his rigid soles begin to relax.

He must have dozed off. The next thing he knew, he was on his back on the bed and Jill was gently nudging him.

"Uh."

"Sorry to wake you." Jill tightened the towel wrapped around her. "But I think you'll be a lot happier if you shower before you go to sleep."

"If I don't fall asleep under the water and drown."

For the first time in a long while, Jill's blue eyes twinkled. "Want some help?"

"It's a tempting offer. But I bet we'd slip in the tub and crack our heads."

"You sure are having visions of doom."

"Wonder why." Pittman mustered the energy to stand, grabbed his gym bag, and went into the bathroom. He tried to remember the last time he'd been clean. The sharp hot water lancing at him was exquisite. Shampooing his hair, he felt as if he could never equal this luxury. For a moment, he remembered how he had hated the comfort of a shower after Jeremy's death. Exhausted, he shut out the thought, allowing the shower to relax him.

At last, after he'd toweled himself until his skin felt pleasantly irritated, he brushed his teeth, wrapped the remaining dry towel around him, and stepped out of the bathroom.

After the steam in the bathroom, the comparatively cool air of the bedroom made his bare chest tingle. Unexpectedly, self-consciousness replaced his weariness. He was suddenly very aware that the room had only one bed, that Jill was sitting up in it, pillows propped behind her, covers pulled up to her bare shoulders, and that she looked self-conscious also. Her gaze flicked nervously from him to the droning television set.

"Anything on the news?" Pittman tried to sound casual.

She shook her head.

"Nothing about Standish? Nothing about us?"

"No."

Pittman approached the bed, and Jill visibly tensed.

"Are you okay?"

"Fine." She stared at the television.

"You're sure?"

"Why wouldn't I be fine?"

Pittman sat on his side of the bed. "Hey. Come on, talk to me."

"I . . ."

"If we can't be honest with each other, I guarantee we'll never survive this."

"I made a mistake before you went into the shower," Jill said.

"Oh?" Pittman shook his head in confusion. "What was that?"

"I joked about going in with you to help you shower."

"Yes. I remember. So what?"

"Bad joke."

"Why?"

"I don't want to be a tease. I don't want to lead you on."

"I'm confused."

"You're not the only one," Jill said.

The television kept droning. Pittman vaguely understood that the announcer was talking about an economic conference that was taking place in Geneva. But he didn't take his gaze off Jill.

"In Boston, we said certain things to each other. I love you." Pittman felt as if he was being choked. "I don't say that easily. I treat those words very seriously. To me, they're a commitment."

"I couldn't agree more."

"Then you regret making the commitment, is that it?" Pittman asked. "It was a mistake? You confused depending on each other under stress with being in love? You want to correct the misunderstanding? You want to set the record straight?"

"No, not at all."

"Then I really don't . . ."

"I don't want to take anything back. I love you," Jill said. "I've never been more certain of anything in my life."

"Then what's the problem?" he managed to ask. When he touched her shoulder, he felt her sinews harden.

"This room. This bed." Her voice dropped. "I told you I don't want to be a tease."

"Ah. I think I'm beginning to understand. This is about whether or not to have sex."

With disturbing intensity, Jill focused her eyes upon him.

"You're tired," Pittman said. "I understand."

Pittman had never been looked at so directly.

"Everything's been happening too fast," Jill said.

"It's okay. Really," Pittman said. "No pressure. I figured things would happen when they were supposed to."

"You mean that?"

When Pittman nodded, Jill visibly relaxed.

"Making love shouldn't be an obligation," Pittman said. "It shouldn't be something you feel you have to do because the circumstances put pressure on you. We'll wait. When we're both relaxed, whcn the time feels right . . ."

"You want to know how confused I am?"

Pittman didn't understand.

She took his hand, and immediately he did understand. He leaned toward her as she raised herself up toward him. His blanket fell at the same time the sheets that covered her slipped away. Their lips touched. Their bodies pressed against one another. Feeling her smooth breasts against his skin, Pittman thought that his heart had never pounded so hard and fast. At once he didn't think about anything except how much he loved her.

Much later, when time began again, Pittman became conscious that he lay beside her, that his arms were around her and hers around him, that his love gave him a reason to live.

His buoyant mood was canceled as a man's voice made him frown. "The television."

"Yes," Jill murmured. "We forgot to turn it off."

"That's not what I mean." Pittman sat up abruptly. "Listen. It's about Victor Standish." His heart pounded fast again but this time making him nauseated with shock, as he stared toward the chaotic scene of an ambulance and police cars in front of a mansion, emergency lights flashing while policemen made way for attendants bringing out a body bag on a gurney.

A somber announcer was saying, ". . . verified that the distinguished diplomat Victor Standish died from a self-inflicted gunshot wound."

SEVEN

1

No matter how desperately Pittman wanted to, he couldn't sleep. The shock of learning about Standish's suicide kept him and Jill awake, watching CNN for further details until after 2:00 A.M. A summary of Standish's long, distinguished career was punctuated by photographs of him and the other grand counselors, first as robust, steely-eyed, ambitious-looking young men, later as elderly icons of diplomacy standing with bolt-straight dignity despite their frail bodies, some of them bald, others with wispy white hair, their faces wrinkled, skin drooping from their necks, but their eyes communicating as much ambition as ever.

When it became clear that the report wouldn't be updated until the morning, Pittman reluctantly turned off the television. In the darkness of the hotel room, he lay tensely in bed, his eyes open, directed toward the murky ceiling. Beside him, Jill's eventual slow, shallow breathing made him think that at least she had finally managed to shut off her mind and get some rest. But Pittman couldn't stop the announcer's words from echoing through his frantic memory: ". . . *died from a self-inflicted gunshot wound.*"

The suicide was totally alien to Pittman's expectation. He strained to analyze the implications. The grand counselors had killed one of their own, Jonathan Millgate, in an effort to keep him from revealing information about them. The cover-up, which had involved using Pittman as a scapegoat, had gotten so out of hand that another grand counselor, Anthony Lloyd, had died from a stroke. Now a third grand counselor, Victor Standish, had shot himself, presumably because of fear. Earlier, Denning had said gleefully, "Three dead. Two to go." But Pittman didn't share Denning's manic enthusiasm. True, Pittman was encouraged that a fissure of weakness had developed in what he had assumed was an armorlike resolution among the grand counselors. But if the tension was affecting them so extremely, there was every danger that the remaining two grand counselors, Eustace Gable and Winston Sloane, would succumb to age and desperation.

Damn it, Pittman thought, I have to do something. Soon.

When he and Jill had arrived in Washington that evening, one of his primary emotions had been rage, the urge to get even with the grand counselors for what they had done to him. But his encounter with Bradford Denning had made him realize the consequences of rage. The emotion had so distorted Denning's approach to life that he had *wasted* his life. Indeed, tonight he had worked himself into such a frenzy that his rage had nearly killed him.

As Pittman continued to lie wearily, rigidly on the bed in the dark hotel room, it occurred to him that Denning's rage and the grand counselors' fear were mirror images, that Denning and the grand counselors were unwittingly destroying themselves because of their obsession with the past.

But not me, Pittman thought. What I'm doing isn't a disguised version of a death wish. It isn't a version of the suicide I attempted a week ago. Indeed he was struck by the irony that suicide, which had seemed reasonable and inevitable to him, now was shocking when someone else committed it. I want to live. Oh God, how I want to live. I never believed I'd feel that way again.

Pittman's thoughts were suddenly interrupted as he felt Jill move beside him. Surprising him, she sat up. He was able to see her shadowy silhouette in the darkness.

"What did you say?" she asked.

"Nothing."

"Sure you did. You were mumbling."

"Mumbling? . . . I thought you were asleep."

."I thought *you* were asleep."

"Can't."

"Me, either. What were you mumbling? Something about you want to live."

"I must have been thinking out loud."

"Well, I applaud your motivc. In a week, you've certainly come a long way from putting a pistol into your mouth to wanting to live."

"I was thinking about Denning."

"Yes. We ought to phone the hospital and find out how he is."

"I was thinking how thrilled he was to know that three of the grand counselors were dead."

"That's what put him in the hospital."

"Exactly. And there's no guarantee that the two remaining grand counselors won't wind up in the hospital or worse because of this also. I was thinking that *I* might as well be dead if Eustace Gable and Winston Sloane don't survive. Because, in that case, I won't have any way to prove that

I'm innocent. Everything's happening so fast. I don't know if I've got enough time. I have to . . ."

"What?"

"I used to be a reporter. It's what I do best—interviewing people. I think it's the only way to save us."

2

Shortly after dawn, feeling a chill in the air, seeing vapor come out of his mouth, Pittman parked next to a pay phone outside a coffee shop. Sparse traffic sounded eerie as he got out of the car, Jill following, and stepped into the booth. After studying the list of telephone numbers that he had used last night, he put coins in the box and pressed numbers.

A male voice, with the haughty obsequiousness of a servant to the powerful and rich, answered after two rings. "Mr. Gable's residence."

"Put him on."

"Who may I say is calling, sir?"

"You're supposed to say it's too early to disturb him."

"I beg your pardon, sir?"

"It's barely six in the morning, but you didn't take long to answer the phone. It's like you've been on duty for quite a while. Are things a little frantic over there?"

"I really don't know what you're implying, sir. If you wish to speak with Mr. Gable, you're going to have to tell me who you are."

"The man he's been trying to have killed."

The line became silent.

"Go ahead," Pittman said. "Let him know."

"As you wish, sir."

Pittman waited, looking at Jill, whose lovely face normally glowed with health but now was wan from stress and fatigue.

Thirty seconds later, a man's voice, aged and frail, like wind through dead leaves, came on the line. "Eustace Gable here."

"Matthew Pittman."

Again the line became silent.

"Yes?" Gable sounded as if he was having trouble breathing. "I've been reading about you in the newspapers."

"You don't seem surprised that I'm calling."

"At my age, I'm not surprised by anything," Gable said. "However, I don't understand the way you identified yourself to my assistant."

"I can see where it might be confusing, depending on how many other people you're trying to have killed."

Gable stifled a cough. "I don't know what you're talking about."

"Not over the phone at least. I can understand that. It's what I'd expect from a diplomat famous for conducting secret meetings. All the same, I do think we ought to talk, don't you?"

"Perhaps. But how, if not on the phone?"

"In person."

"Oh? Given that you murdered my friend and colleague, I'm not certain that I'd feel safe in your presence."

"The feeling's mutual. But as you know, I didn't murder him. You did."

"Honestly, Mr. Pittman. First you fantasize that I'm trying to have *you* killed. Now you're fantasizing that I killed my friend."

"No one else is on this line, so you can save the disinformation."

"I *always* assume that someone else is on the line."

"Does that prevent you from negotiating?"

Gable stifled another cough. "I'm proud to say that in my entire career, I have never turned down a request to negotiate."

"Then listen. Obviously things have gotten way out of hand. You never expected me to stay alive this long. You never expected so many other people to become involved."

The only sound was Gable's labored breathing.

"You've destroyed my life," Pittman said. "But I know enough to be able to destroy yours. Let's call it a stalemate. I think it's in our mutual best interests if I disappear. With a retirement fund. A million dollars and a passport that gives me a safe name."

"That's a substantial retirement fund."

"But that's my price. Also a safe passport for Jill Warren."

"Passports are difficult."

"Not with your contacts in the State Department. Think about it. I disappear. Your cover-up works. No more problems for you."

"If I agree to the meeting you propose, I want it completely understood that I don't admit any involvement in your false accusations about cover-ups and murders. We're discussing hypothetical matters."

"Whatever makes you feel good, Mr. Gable."

"I'll need time to consider the implications."

"And I've been on this line too long. I'll call back at ten A.M."

3

Mrs. Page opened the door the moment Pittman knocked on it. Her designer dress was wrinkled and looked out of place in a motel early in the morning. Otherwise, she appeared alert and determined, her skin-tucked face severe with intensity. "Did you watch the morning news?"

"About Standish's suicide?" Pittman nodded.

"He was always the weakest of the five. My father was the strongest. We have to keep putting pressure on him."

"This morning, I started again."

"How?" Mrs. Page asked quickly.

Pittman explained.

"Be careful. My father is a master of manipulation."

"And arrogant about it. I'm counting on that," Pittman said. "I'm hoping that it's inconceivable to him that someone could outmanipulate him."

"But *can* you? You're taking a tremendous risk."

"If I could think of another way, I'd do it. We can't just hide. We have to keep pushing them. We have to go back to Washington. I've got several stops to make. In particular, I need to see two other people I once interviewed."

"Who?"

"A security expert and a weapons specialist. I'll explain as we drive."

"But what if they remember you?" Mrs. Page asked. "If they connect you with the newspaper stories and television reports . . ."

"I interviewed them at least five years ago. I was heavier. I had a mustache. There's a good chance they won't recognize me. But even if the risk was greater, I'd still have to take it. I can't make this plan work without their help."

As they spoke, Pittman walked to the next door and knocked on it. When George came out, they went down concrete steps to where Jill was waiting at the car.

"Give me your room keys. I'll leave them at the desk and check everybody out," George said.

"Fine. We'll meet you at the restaurant down the street," Jill said.

"Restaurant?" Mrs. Page looked horrified. "That's not a restaurant."

"Okay, it's a Roy Rogers. Think of it as a broadening experience. We're so pressed for time, we'll have to eat takeout as we drive."

"Time. Yes. We have to make time for something else," Mrs. Page insisted. "We have to see about Bradford. We have to go to the hospital."

4

Amid the drone of fluorescent lights and the pungent odor of antiseptics, Pittman frowned in response to Jill's frown as she came back from speaking to a nurse at the counter outside the cardiac-care unit.

"What's the matter?" Pittman's hands suddenly felt cold. "Don't tell me he died."

"He's gone."

Mrs. Page stepped forward, ashen. "He *is* dead?"

"I mean he literally isn't here. He's gone. He left," Jill said. "The nurse looked in on him at five A.M. His bed was empty. He'd pulled an IV needle from his arm. He'd turned off his heart monitor so it wouldn't sound a warning when he pulled the sensor pads from his chest. His clothes were in a cupboard in his room. He put them on and snuck out of the hospital."

"It's a wonder he had the strength," Pittman said. "What the hell did he think he was doing?"

George shook his head. "Last night, it was exhaustion. But if he's not careful, he'll give himself a heart attack."

"Obviously he believes the risk is worth it," Jill said. "To get back at them. The remaining two grand counselors. I can't imagine anything else that would have made him act so obsessively."

"Damn it, now we've got a wild card out there," Pittman said. "He's so out of control, he scares me. God knows what he might do to interfere with our plan."

"But we can't let him worry us," Mrs. Page said. "We have to go ahead. Why are you looking at me like that?"

Pittman stepped forward. "Mrs. Page, how are your connections with the *Washington Post*? Do you think you can get someone in the obituary department to do us a favor?"

5

Eight hours later, in midafternoon, Pittman was back in Fairfax, Virginia, quickly passing through it, taking 29 west, then 15 north toward Eustace Gable's estate. During his second telephone call to Gable, which Pittman had made exactly at ten as promised, using a pay phone in Washington, Gable had given him instructions how to get to the estate. As Pittman drove toward the rendezvous, squinting from the sun, he glanced toward his rearview mirror and was reassured to see that despite congested traffic, the gray Ford van remained behind him, Jill visible behind the steering wheel. The van and the equipment inside it had been rented using George's credit card, and Pittman thought morbidly that George certainly deserved a bonus, the trick being for all of them to stay alive so he could receive it. Pittman passed farms and strips of woods, the sunlight making them seem golden, and he prayed that he would have a chance to see them again, to see Jill again. He thought about Jeremy, and as much as he missed his son, he felt strangely close to him, as if Jeremy were with him, helping him. Give me strength, son.

As instructed, Pittman came to a sign—EVERGREEN COUNTRY CLUB—then headed to the left, trees casting shadows from the sun. A mile later, he went right, along an oak-lined gravel road. This time when he glanced toward his rearview mirror, he saw Jill stopping the van, parking it among bushes at the side of the gravel road. She was doing what they had agreed upon. Nonetheless, he wished she didn't have to. Until now he hadn't felt alone.

He rounded a curve and proceeded up a gentle rise flanked by April-lush fields, and he couldn't help contrasting his increasing fear with the peaceful setting. More, he couldn't help contrasting his apprehension as he approached Gable's estate with the indifference to his safety that he had felt a week earlier when he had snuck into the estate in Scarsdale to find out why Jonathan Millgate had been removed from the hospital.

Back then, Pittman's only motive had been to get a story for Burt Forsyth, to relieve his obligations to his friend. Obsessed with the need to commit suicide, Pittman had felt liberated from apprehension as he had crept through the rainy darkness, circling the Scarsdale mansion, finding Millgate surrounded by a nurse, a doctor, and the grand counselors in a makeshift hospital room off a deck above the five-stall garage. The effort had been easy, the sense of danger nonexistent, because Pittman hadn't cared what might happen to him. Prepared to kill himself, he had felt immune to any risks.

Not anymore.

6

At wide intervals, mansions were set back from the road. White wooden fences enclosed horses. Ahead on the left, Pittman saw a high stone wall. He came to a closed metal gate and stopped within view of a security camera mounted to the left on top of the wall. As instructed, he leaned out his driver's window so that the camera could have a good look at him.

Immediately the gate whirred open. Pittman drove through, checking his rearview mirror, noting that the gate closed behind him while he followed a paved lane through spacious grassland. The lane went over a hill, and on the other side, snuggled into the slope, just below the crest on the right, was a distinctive, sprawling one-story complex that reminded Pittman of homes designed by Frank Lloyd Wright. The main impression was of limestone, terraces, and beams, and the way it conformed to the landscape, aided by plentiful trees and shrubbery, would make it invisible from the golf course below, Pittman guessed.

From the moment that the gate had opened, allowing him onto the estate, Pittman had noted the absence of guards. To anyone who might be watching from the road, there was nothing out of the ordinary. To all appearances, Pittman was an unremarkable visitor who knew Eustace Gable well enough that the gate had been opened without delay. The closer Pittman came to the house, taking a downward curve in the lane, proceeding to the right, passing fir trees, the more Pittman was struck by the lack of activity on the property. Given the size of the estate, he would have expected gardeners at least, maintenance personnel, someone to take care of the horses that came into view below him in a paddock next to a long, low stable rimmed by more fir trees and made from limestone, matching the house. But the place seemed deserted. There weren't any cars, which presumably had been placed in a garage on the opposite side of the house.

Perhaps the lack of guards was intended to make him feel unthreatened, Pittman thought. To encourage him not to change his mind. To lure him into a trap. But if the purpose was to lull him, the opposite effect had been achieved. Instead of lowering his defenses, the eerie solitude intensified Pittman's apprehension, sending warning signals throughout his body, compacting his muscles.

He reached a circular driveway in front of the house, stopped the car, and got out, surveying the apparently deserted area. He heard water trickling from somewhere, presumably a fountain. He heard a breeze whispering through the fir trees. A horse whinnied.

A door opened, and Pittman, who had glanced toward the stable on the slope below him, whirled toward the house. An elderly man, narrow-faced, with white hair, spectacles, and wrinkle-pinched features, stepped from a polished wooden doorway onto a stone terrace. Tall and slender, he wore a dark blue three-piece suit that conformed to his rigidly straight posture. Pittman recognized him from photographs and the incident at the Scarsdale estate. Eustace Gable.

"Four P.M. precisely. I admire punctuality." Even at a

distance, it was obvious that Gable's chest heaved. "We have much to discuss. Come in, Mr. Pittman."

Pittman took one last look around and, seeing no threat, climbed steps to the terrace. He frowned when Gable offered his hand.

"This won't do, Mr. Pittman. Rudeness is a poor way to begin a negotiation."

"I'm not used to civility from people who want to have me killed."

"The formalities matter," Gable said. "Even when negotiating with the most bitter enemy, it is essential to be respectful and courteous."

"Sure. Right. But it sounds like hypocrisy to me."

Gable coughed, raising a handkerchief to his mouth. The ripple of pain that crossed his wrinkled features made Pittman realize how much effort it took for the old man to stand as straight as he did, to maintain the diplomatic bearing that had made him famous in his prime.

Composing himself, Gable again held out his hand. "Ritual controls emotion. It encourages order."

"Is that what you told yourself when you arranged for Jonathan Millgate to be murdered?"

Gable's expression hardened, his wrinkles becoming like cracks in the deep grain of weathered wood.

"And Burt Forsyth?" Pittman said. "And Father Dandridge? I wouldn't call their murders controlling emotion and encouraging order."

Gable inhaled with effort. "Order dictates necessity. I'm still waiting."

Pittman finally shook his hand with exaggerated indifference, but the slight gleam in Gable's wizened eyes told Pittman that the old man thought he had won an advantage. Gable gestured for Pittman to enter the house.

Pittman's unease deepened. He almost turned away, wanting to get back to the car, to drive from the estate as fast as he could. But he told himself that if Gable meant to have him killed here, an expert marksman with a sniper's rifle could have done it easily when Pittman was in the open, climbing the steps to the terrace in front of the house.

The plan, he thought. I have to go through with it. I can't keep running. I've used up nearly all my resources. This might be the only chance I get.

"You know my terms," Pittman said.

"Ah, but you haven't heard mine." Gable's thin lips formed a grimace that may have been a smile. "After you."

His veins swelling from increased pressure, Pittman entered the house.

7

Hearing Gable shut the door behind him, Pittman noted that the inside had walls and beamed ceilings made from various tropical woods of varying colors, mahogany and teak among others. The lighting system was recessed but remarkably bright. The temperature was unusually warm. Passing a thermostat in a stone-floored corridor, Pittman saw that it was set at eighty degrees. Even on the coldest winter day, he would have considered that temperature excessive. But given that this was a mild day in late April, Pittman had to conclude that Gable was using the heat to combat his evident illness. Similarly, the bright lights suggested that Gable's vision might be fading. To Pittman's fear and anger, the unexpected emotion of pity was added, and Pittman urgently subdued it, knowing that Gable would take every advantage he could. For all Pittman knew, the bright lights and the excessive temperature were part of a carefully designed stage setting that would allow Gable to manipulate him.

Proceeding along the hallway, heading left, the direction that Gable indicated, Pittman listened to the old man's labored footsteps. An open door led to a spacious room with a wall-length window that provided a view of the ponds and sand traps of the golf course at the bottom of the slope.

But Pittman's attention was primarily directed toward two men who waited for him. One of them he recognized. A gaunt-cheeked elderly man sitting nervously on a sofa had a neatly trimmed white mustache, wore a dark three-piece suit almost identical to Gable's, and was recognizable from photographs, particularly because of a distinctive cleft in his chin that had deepened with age: the other remaining grand counselor, Winston Sloane.

The second man was in his thirties, six feet tall, well built, with strong features emphasized by his short haircut. His gray suit looked less carefully tailored than Gable's and Sloane's. Indeed, the jacket seemed slightly too large and had a bulge on the left side. As Pittman studied the man, who stood in the middle of the room, it occurred to him that he knew this man also, or at least had seen him before. Last night, the man had been with the group who had attacked Mrs. Page's house.

Pittman turned to Gable. "I didn't know that we wouldn't be alone."

"It doesn't do to negotiate unless all interested parties are in attendance. May I present my colleague—Winston Sloane."

With effort, Sloane tried to stand.

"No need," Pittman said.

Gable pointed toward the second man. "And this is my assistant, Mr. Webley."

Pittman nodded, giving no indication that he recognized the man.

"I'm sure you won't mind if Mr. Webley performs a security check," Gable continued.

For a moment, Pittman wasn't sure what Gable was talking about. "You're saying you want this man to search me?"

"We're here on good faith. There shouldn't be any need for weapons."

"Then why is your assistant armed?"

Webley's eyes narrowed.

"Because his duties require him to be armed. I do hope this isn't going to be a problem," Gable said.

Pittman raised his arms.

Webley reached for something on a chair behind him and came over with a handheld metal detector, tracing its wand along the contours of Pittman's body.

It beeped when it came to the base of Pittman's spine. Webley groped behind the sport coat and removed Pittman's .45.

Gable made a tsking sound. "How can we negotiate on a basis of trust when you bring a weapon to our meeting?"

"Force of habit. For the last week, I've gotten used to needing protection."

"Perhaps after this afternoon, you won't need it anymore."

"I certainly hope so."

Webley continued to scan Pittman's body with the metal detector. It beeped several more times. "Keys and coins. His belt buckle. A pen," Webley told Gable.

"Examine the pen. Check him thoroughly. Be certain that he isn't wearing a microphone."

Webley did so. "Nothing unusual."

"Very well. Be seated, Mr. Pittman. Let's discuss your proposal."

"Why?" Winston Sloane asked. "I don't see what purpose this so-called negotiation will serve. Our best course is to telephone the police and have this man arrested for murdering Jonathan."

"A week ago, I would have agreed with you," Gable said. "In fact, I did agree. We all agreed." He cleared his throat and turned to Pittman. "As you must have concluded by now, our original intention was to blame you for what we were forced to do to Jonathan. Your history of animosity toward Jonathan and your suicidal impulses made you an excellent candidate. No one would believe your denial, for which you would have no proof. Not that we wanted you to have a chance to deny anything. We made arrangements to have you killed before the police could take you into custody."

"The man in my apartment," Pittman said.

Gable nodded. "We bribed a policeman to let our own man take his place and wait there."

Sloane's cheeks became alarmingly flushed. "You're telling him too much."

"Not at all," Gable said. "If we're to accomplish anything, we have to be candid. Correct, Mr. Pittman?"

"That's why I'm here. To be candid. To find a way out of this."

"Precisely."

"What I don't understand," Pittman said, "is why you needed to blame *anyone* for Jonathan Millgate's death. He was old. He was sick. He was on oxygen. If you'd taken away his life-support system, let him die, and then hooked him up to the support system again, his death would have seemed natural. No one would have been the wiser."

"That's what *I* wanted," Sloane insisted, his cheeks even redder.

"And at the start, you were right," Gable said patiently. "Try to remember the sequence. As Jonathan's health dwindled, he became more afraid of dying. He'd been flirting with religion for the past several years. That priest, that damnable priest. I never understood Jonathan's attitude toward Father Dandridge. The priest hounded us during the Vietnam years.

He organized demonstrations and called press conferences to criticize every policy we made about Vietnam. It was because of Father Dandridge that Jonathan left public life. The priest's interference made it impossible for Jonathan to function effectively in the government. And yet two decades later, Jonathan asked the priest to be his personal confessor."

"Father Dandridge felt that Jonathan Millgate needed a confessor who wouldn't be intimidated by him, a spiritual adviser who would stand up to him about ultimate matters," Pittman said.

Gable's gaze turned cold. "Ultimate matters. I forgot that you spoke to the priest briefly."

"I was there when you had him killed."

"He shouldn't have gotten involved. He shouldn't have made trouble."

"He would never have revealed what he heard in confession," Pittman said.

"So *you* claim. But in my career, I have known diplomats who conveyed all sorts of confidential information to trusted associates, only to have that information repeated back to them by third parties. God only knows what Jonathan had already confessed to the priest, but I know for certain that what he *intended* to tell the priest on his deathbed would have been ruinous. I was visiting him in the hospital, and all he could do was keep telling me that he had to see Father Dandridge. He had to clear his conscience. He had to save his soul." Gable said the last word with contempt. "Then the Justice Department leaked its report that it was investigating rumors about a covert plan to buy nuclear weapons from the former USSR. Jonathan was implicated as having acted as an intermediary."

"Intermediary? Stop hiding behind words. What you mean is, Millgate was functioning as an *arms dealer*," Pittman said with disgust. "The *worst* kind of arms. What possible reason could justify—?"

"The safety of the world," Gable said indignantly.

"Yeah, right. That's the excuse you and your buddies always came up with. The safety of the world. It doesn't matter how self-serving the idea is, you always justify yourselves by saying it's good for everybody."

"Are you so naïve as to think that the fall of communism and the dissolution of the USSR mean the end of a threat from that region?"

"Of course not," Pittman answered. "The bloodbath in Bosnia shows that any damned thing can happen over there. After decades of being repressed, the provinces of the former USSR might *all* go in the opposite extreme. Soon they might *all* be out of control."

"With access to nuclear weapons about which neither the former government nor the disbanding military is responsible." Gable gestured for emphasis. "If a *new* government, a *rogue* government comes into power, there's a very real danger that those nuclear weapons will be used to allow that new government to *consolidate* its power. What's unscrupulous about trying to stop that from happening?"

"The way you put it, nothing. But I've been a reporter too long not to be able to read between the lines."

"What are you talking about?"

"The Justice Department's accusation was specific: Jonathan Millgate was implicated in *buying* nuclear weapons. Not paying to have them destroyed in Russia, nothing wrong about that, but *buying* them. What the hell was he going to do with them once he owned them? Bring them all the way to the United States to have them destroyed? Sounds a lot more expensive than it needs to be, not to mention dangerous, all those warheads being moved around. And who's paying for these nuclear weapons, anyhow? The U.S. government? Not damned likely. It would be political suicide for anyone in the government to get involved in such an outrageous scheme. So you've got two problems: how to pay for the weapons and what to do with the weapons once you own them. Those problems bothered me ever since I heard that Millgate was under suspicion. And then the solution came to me. Of course. The way you get rid of the nuclear weapons enables you to pay for them in the first place—*you sell them to someone else*."

Gable squinted. "I'm impressed, Mr. Pittman."

"The compliment doesn't sound sincere."

"But I *am* impressed. You see to the heart of the issue. You understand the brilliance of the operation."

"Brilliance?" Pittman asked in disbelief.

"The threat of the nuclear weapons in the former USSR is eliminated," Gable said righteously. "At the same time, it's possible to maintain the balance of power in other troubled regions. For example, it's no secret that North Korea has been working furiously to develop a nuclear capability. What do you think will happen when its nuclear weapons are functional? It'll control Southeast Asia. But if *South* Korea also gains nuclear capability, there'll be a stalemate. They'll balance each other."

"Wrong. They'll destroy each other. And maybe get the rest of the world involved," Pittman said.

"Not necessarily." The emotional strain of the conversation was having an evident effect on Gable. His breathing was more labored, his posture less erect. He lowered his voice. "To save the world, sometimes risks have to be taken."

"And bank accounts fattened? You hypocrite. You and your friends pretended to be selfless public servants, and all along, from the forties onward, from the postwar anti-Soviet policy to the Iran-Contra arms-dealing scandal, you've been making a fortune in kickbacks from the weapons industry. How much money did you earn arranging to use American funds to arm Iraq so it would act as a counterweight against Iran? And then we went to war against Iraq, and you received kickbacks from the arms industry because you recommended that war."

Anger made Gable regain his rigid posture. "I refuse to discuss the nuances of foreign policy with a mere reporter. You are not privy to classified information. You are not in a position to judge the delicacy of various negotiations that I have successfully concluded for the good of the United States and the world."

"Right. The old excuse. There's always secret information that justifies becoming rich by starting more wars and selling more weapons."

"These matters are beyond your understanding," Gable said. "You are here for one purpose only—to try to settle our differences, to undo the disastrous effects of your blundering into matters that do not concern you. After the leak implicating Jonathan in the purchase of Russia's nuclear weapons, it was only a matter of hours, perhaps minutes, before reporters would have shown up at the hospital in hopes that Jonathan would be strong enough to make a statement. We had to get Jonathan out of the hospital to keep him from telling reporters what he intended to tell the priest. You were there when my men took him from the hospital. You followed them to Scarsdale. Damn it, what were you doing in his room? If only you hadn't gone into his room."

"His IV tubes had slipped out. His oxygen prongs weren't attached to him. He was having some kind of seizure. I was sure he was going to die."

"That was the idea," Gable said with barely subdued irritation. "My colleagues and I said good-bye to him. Everyone except his nurse and doctor left the room. They removed his life supports. Then *they* left. He was supposed to die. But *you* had to get into the room and reattach the supports. And he finally had a chance to confess. If the nurse hadn't come back into the room at that moment, we never would have known that Jonathan had betrayed us."

"If only we'd stopped right there," Sloane said.

"We *couldn't*," Gable said. "Because as far as we knew, *this* man"—Gable pointed toward Pittman—"saw our first attempt to kill Jonathan. And *this* man"—Gable pointed harder toward Pittman—"had information that could ruin us. One of our security team riding in the escort car noticed a taxi following the ambulance. As soon as he reached the estate and told me about the taxi, I sent him to locate it before it disappeared from the area. The driver's passenger was gone. But the driver could identify the passenger because of a check that the passenger had written to cover the expense of the ride. Imagine our concern, Mr. Pittman, when we researched your background and discovered that you were a reporter. What were we to do? Allow you to write a story about our attempt to kill our friend and about the information he revealed to you? Certainly not. But we did have another option. Our investigation revealed that you'd harassed Jonathan seven years ago, that you were currently having an emotional collapse. It wasn't any effort to make it seem that *you* killed Jonathan. We had the check you'd given to the taxi driver. We had your fingerprints on the door to Jonathan's room and on his life-support equipment. In a twisted personal vendetta, you killed Jonathan, then continued with your plans to kill yourself."

"And when your men caught me, they were going to help me along."

Gable spread his hands. "Unless the police caught you first, in which case I had the resources to arrange for you to commit suicide in jail."

"You're awfully confident that you can manipulate the system to make it do anything you want."

"I'm a diplomat. I helped *design* the system. I guarantee that the plan would have worked."

"Then why didn't it?"

Gable glanced at the floor.

"Well?" Pittman asked.

"I congratulate you. You're far more resourceful than your profile led me to believe. If you weren't so resourceful, I wouldn't have agreed to this conversation, I assure you. For a man determined to commit suicide, you have a remarkable talent for survival."

"You see, I changed my mind."

Gable looked puzzled.

"I don't want to kill myself any longer. Because of you."

"Explain."

"What you did to me made me so afraid that I had to ask myself, If I was so eager to die, why was I running? Why not let you do the job for me? I rationalized by telling myself that I wanted my death to be my idea, not yours. But the truth is, you forced me to reconsider where I was in my life. I love my dead son. I miss him desperately. But you distracted me enough that I think I can accept my grief now rather than fight it."

Gable studied him as if he had no understanding of the emotions Pittman referred to. At last, he sighed. "It would have been so much easier if my men had been able to shoot you when you were running from the Scarsdale estate."

Sloane fidgeted. "First Jonathan. Then Anthony. Now Victor. No more. I want this settled. I want it stopped."

"That's why we're here," Gable said. "To settle things."

Throughout, the man known as Mr. Webley stood against the wall to Pittman's right, watching the group, holding Pittman's .45.

"For a negotiation to be successful," Gable said, "each side must have something to gain. So tell me, Mr. Pittman, what do *we* gain in exchange for the million dollars and the two passports that *you* gain?"

"Security. Peace of mind."

"All very well. Desirable conditions. But vague. How *exactly* are you going to give us security and peace of mind?"

"By disappearing."

"Be specific."

"I'll make it look as if I carried through on my intention to commit suicide. I'll do it in such a way that my body can't be identified."

"Again, be specific."

"I thought perhaps I'd arrange for your men to trap me on one of your yachts. I'd blow it and myself up. My body would never be found. Presumably sharks and other scavengers would have eaten what was left of me. Of course, I wouldn't actually have been on the yacht. But your men, having watched the explosion from another yacht, would testify that they'd seen me go aboard."

Sloane's voice trembled with enthusiasm. "It might work."

"One of my yachts?" Gable squinted. "You imagine expensive ways to disappear."

"Another factor that makes it convincing. Given the magnitude of your property loss, the police wouldn't think that you were involved."

"He has a point," Sloane said quickly.

Gable scowled at his fellow grand counselor, then redirected his calculating gaze at Pittman. "Forgive my colleague's outbursts. He's forgotten one of the primary rules of negotiation. Never let your opponent know your actual opinion of his argument."

"I thought we were here to be candid," Pittman said.

"Then why haven't you yourself been completely open? You expect me to believe that after you pretend to commit suicide you'll disappear forever and we'll have nothing to fear from you."

"That's right," Pittman lied.

"What guarantees do we have?"

"I told you. I want to live. I don't want to be hunted anymore. I want to be left alone."

"Under an assumed name."

"Yes."

"With Ms. Warren."

"Yes."

"Perhaps in Mexico. Perhaps farther south. In a country where the economy is such that a million dollars is worth considerably more."

"Yes."

"And after the barrage of telephone calls last night," Gable asked with irritation, "how do you intend to protect us from the *other* people who—thanks to you—have acquired knowledge of our private affairs?"

"Your daughter, for example?"

"In particular."

"Those phone calls were staged to get your attention," Pittman said. "To put pressure on you so you'd agree to this meeting. To make you want to end this before it spreads any farther. The truth is, your daughter doesn't know anything for certain. If you agree to my terms, I'll go back to her and—"

From somewhere in the house, a phone rang, the faint sound echoing.

Pittman glanced past Webley toward the hall as the phone rang a second time.

"It's not important," Gable said. "The fax machine in my home office is on a line that's separate from the main telephone line. That's what you heard, the fax machine. Two rings and it answered."

Pittman nodded. "If you agree to my terms, I'll go back to your daughter and behave irrationally enough that she'll lose faith in my credibility. My apparent suicide will make her even more skeptical about me. She'll be forced to conclude that her accusations, based on what I told her, are the nonsense you say they are."

"I like it," Sloane said eagerly. "It makes sense. It can get us out of the mess we're in."

"Winston." Gable's aged eyes flashed. "Your persistent outbursts force me to violate protocol. I have never before done this in a negotiation. But you leave me no choice. I must ask you not to interrupt me again."

"But—"

"Winston!" Gable's chest heaved, the effort of emotion having an obvious weakening effect on him.

Sloane looked abashed and lowered his gaze toward his hands.

Gable's breath rate subsided. He composed himself and studied Pittman, frowning. "So you restricted the information that you gave to my daughter."

"That's right."

Gable shook his head in disagreement. "I suddenly have doubts about you."

"Doubts?"

"To enlist my daughter's aid, it isn't logical that you would have held back. To make your strongest case, you would have told her everything you know. I'm beginning to worry that all of this has been needless. What exactly *do* you know? What are we buying? What precisely is worth one million dollars and two passports?"

"Duncan Kline was an instructor at Grollier Academy."

Gable raised his bushy white eyebrows and gestured for Pittman to continue.

"He liked to gather the brightest students around him," Pittman said. "He persuaded them to join him in small study groups. He nurtured them."

"Of course. Nurturing is something that a good teacher does automatically."

"But good teachers don't molest their students," Pittman said.

Gable's face became rigid, his wrinkles deepening.

"Duncan Kline carefully prepared his few chosen students," Pittman said. "It took time and devotion, painstaking kindness and delicate reassurance. At last he made himself so necessary in their lives, so essential to their emotional well-being, that they found themselves incapable of resisting his advances. You and the other grand counselors, all of you were molested by him. It's affected you ever since."

Gable kept staring, his wrinkled features reminding Pittman of a crust of mud that was cracking.

"Molested?" Gable asked. "You honestly think I'd go to all this trouble to hide the fact that we were molested as students at Grollier? Which we were, by the way." Gable raised his face to the beamed ceiling and burst out laughing, his feeble Adam's apple bobbing, his bony throat sounding as if gravel were stuck in it. At once he seemed to strangle on his laughter. In pain, he lowered his face, tugged out his handkerchief, and coughed repeatedly into it. His pale face turned red from effort. The spasms slowly subsided. "Of course we were molested." He swallowed and put away his handkerchief. "If you revealed that information, I could easily turn it to my advantage, eliciting sympathy from the media. In America today, there is no such thing as shame, only prurience and pity. You know nothing that threatens me, Mr. Pittman. You're wasting my time."

"You didn't let me finish."

"Oh? Are you suggesting that you have information of more substance to share with us?"

Pittman's chest ached, swollen with pressure. His heart pumped faster. He had hoped that Gable would take for granted that Pittman had discovered his secret. An open discussion, in which Gable revealed details that he assumed were shared knowledge, had been part of Pittman's strategy. What he hadn't counted on was that Gable, the lifelong negotiator, wasn't about to acknowledge *any* information unless Pittman volunteered it first.

8

Sweat rolled down Pittman's back. Paradoxically cold, the sweat stuck his clothes to his skin, making him shiver, although he fought not to show it. Okay, he told himself nervously, you came here because you felt your best weapon was your ability to interview somebody. Well, it's time to prove how good you are. Let's see you interview a world-class negotiator.

He turned toward the wall-length window, straining to concentrate, composing his thoughts. Sunlight gleamed into the room, making him squint. Nonetheless, he was able to focus on the fir trees beyond the window, amazingly green and clear, preciously beautiful, given his proximity to death. At the bottom of the wooded slope beyond the house, distant golfers took advantage of the pleasant April day. A man in a golf cart drove past a sand trap, toward where his ball had landed near the wall that separated Gable's estate from the golf course.

Pittman stared at the sand trap, and again he couldn't help being aware of the bitter irony that a week ago his nightmare had begun near a golf course and now was about to end near another one.

"Mr. Pittman," Gable said, "if you have substantive information to share with us, do so. Otherwise, I'm afraid that Mr. Webley will have to ensure that you never share anything with anyone again."

Continuing to squint, Pittman turned to Gable.

"You're sweating," the grand counselor said. "Look at your forehead. It's pouring off you. Surely you're not nervous. In a negotiation, you should never allow your emotions to show. Certainly *I* never do."

"It's the temperature in this room. It's too hot in here." Pittman wiped his forehead.

"My doctor has given me instructions that the temperature must be kept at eighty. To remedy a mild health problem of mine. Take off your sport coat if the temperature is making you uncomfortable. You're wearing a sweater also."

"I'm fine." Pittman refocused his attention, concentrating on the view through the window. The man in the golf cart had disappeared behind the wall at the bottom of the slope. "That fax, the one that arrived a few minutes ago."

"What about it?" Gable asked.

Pittman looked directly into Gable's steel gray eyes. "It was for me."

Gable didn't respond immediately. "For you?"

"What does he mean?" Winston Sloane asked.

Ignoring his colleague, Gable told Pittman, "That's absurd. Why would anyone send a fax to you here? *How* could anyone do that? The fax number is confidential."

"The same as your telephone number is confidential," Pittman said. "But I arranged for your daughter to phone you last night. And for Jill to phone *your* confidential number, Winston. And then we phoned Victor Standish's confidential number. Too late in that case. He'd already blown his brains out. Because he couldn't stand hiding the secret you shared. But if I had no trouble using my contacts to learn *those* numbers, I assure you it was just as easy for me to find out your fax number. The message is Duncan Kline's obituary. I'm sure we'll all find it interesting."

Gable frowned with suspicion. "Mr. Webley, see that my visitor remains exactly where he is while I get the fax message from my office."

Webley raised Pittman's .45. "Don't worry. He isn't going anywhere."

Pittman watched Gable stand with difficulty and proceed from the room. His back as regally straight as he could make it, Gable disappeared down a corridor.

9

Pittman was uncomfortably aware of more sweat slicking his brow. His anxiety, combined with the heat in the room, made him nauseated. Avoiding Webley's intense gaze and Sloane's nervous expression, Pittman turned again toward the wall-length window. It took him a moment to adjust his vision to the painful glare of the sun. The fir trees were even more beautiful. The green of the spring grass was made exquisite by his terror. In the distance, golfers passed trees near a pond.

Abruptly a motion caught Pittman's attention. At the bottom of the slope on Gable's estate. Close to the wall. *This* side of the wall. The man who'd driven the golf cart toward the opposite side of the wall was now in view, climbing the slope toward Gable's mansion. Pittman didn't know how he had gotten over the wall, but it was the same man, Pittman could tell, because the man in the golf cart had worn a white cap and a red windbreaker, the same as this man. Despite the sheltering cap, it was now possible to see that the man was elderly. But he moved with slow determination, climbing, holding something in his right hand. And as he trudged higher, beginning to show the physical cost of his effort, just before pine trees obscured him, Pittman realized with hastily subdued shock that he recognized the grimacing elderly man.

Pittman had bought a drink for him last night. He'd followed him to Mrs. Page's mansion. He'd taken him to a hospital when the elderly man collapsed. *Bradford Denning*. This morning, Denning had snuck from the hospital's cardiac ward, and now he looked totally deranged as he stumbled into view again, leaving the fir trees, struggling higher toward the house. With equal shock, Pittman distinguished the object in Denning's right hand—a pistol held rigidly to his side.

No! Pittman thought. If Gable sees him, if Webley notices, they'll decide that I've tricked them, that I can't be trusted, that everything's out of control. The moment they realize Denning's armed, they'll shoot him. And then they'll finish *me*.

10

The echo of faltering footsteps on a stone floor alerted Pittman. He straightened, turned from the window, hoped that no one else had seen what he had, and directed his full attention to Eustace Gable, who entered the room, looking considerably frailer and older than when he had left. Ashen, the grand counselor regarded the single sheet of fax paper that he had brought from his office.

"How did you obtain this?" the old man asked.

Pittman didn't answer.

Gable assumed as imperious a stance as he could manage. "Answer me. How did vou obtain this?"

Not knowing the substance of the message, knowing only that it was what he had asked Mrs. Page, using her contacts at the *Washington Post*, to send to him, Pittman hoped that he sounded convincingly casual. "Surely you haven't forgotten that lately my assignment has been obituaries." Pittman stood, approached Gable, and attempted to take the fax from Gable's rigid grip.

Gable resisted.

Damn it, if I don't get a chance to read this . . . Pittman thought in hidden panic.

Unexpectedly, Gable released his grasp.

As if he'd seen it numerous times, Pittman glanced offhandedly down at the text. It was from the obituary page of the *Boston Globe*, December 23, 1952. The death notice for Duncan Kline.

Pittman's temples throbbed, sickening him. "I'm sure it was a difficult matter for you to decide—whether to arrange for a small discreet notice about Duncan Kline's passing or whether to allow the larger obituary that one might expect for a remarkable teacher who had taught many remarkable students. In the first case, Duncan Kline's former colleagues and students might have been suspicious about the indignity of giving him only a few words. They might have sought out more information. But in the second case, they might have unwittingly learned too much if the circumstances of his death were elaborated. As it is, you struck a prudent compromise."

The room became deathly silent. Thinking with furious speed, Pittman imagined Bradford Denning struggling higher up the slope. The old man would not yet be close enough to be a danger. But Pittman had been disturbed by his resolve. He remembered how Denning had pressed his left hand to his pained chest while his right hand clutched his pistol.

"The obituary tells you nothing," Gable said. "It's been a matter of public record for more than forty years. If there was anything incriminating in it, someone would have discovered it long ago."

Pittman raised his voice. "But only if someone knew what to look for." The faster his heart rushed, the more his lungs felt starved for oxygen. His reporter's instincts had seized him, propelling his thoughts, thrusting them against one another, linking what he already knew with what he had just now discovered, making startling connections.

"Duncan Kline died in 1952," Pittman said. "That was the year he suddenly appeared at the State Department, demanding to see all of you. July. Eisenhower had won the Republican nomination for President. All of you were busy ruining the reputations of your competitors while you prepared to jump ship from a Democratic administration to one that you were sure would be Republican. Your conservative, anti-Soviet attitudes were in tune with the times. The future was yours. Then Kline showed up, and he scared the hell out of you, didn't he?"

As yet, Pittman had no idea why the grand counselors had been afraid of Kline, but the intensity with which they listened to Pittman's insistence that they had indeed been afraid of Kline gave Pittman the incentive to follow that line of argument.

"You thought you'd buried him in your past," Pittman said. "But suddenly there he was, making a very public appearance, and yes, he scared the hell out of you. In fact, he scared you so much that in the midst of your determined efforts to convince Eisenhower and his people to bring you on board, you took time out—all of you—to go to a reunion at Grollier. That was in December. Kline must have put a lot of pressure on you since July, when he showed up at the State Department. Finally you had no choice. You all went back to the reunion at Grollier because it was natural for Kline to be there, as well. It wouldn't have seemed unusual for you and Kline to be seen together. While you tried to settle your differences without attracting attention."

Pittman's nervous system was in overdrive as he studied Winston Sloane's reactions, the old man's facial muscles tightening in a stressful acknowledgment of what Pittman was saying. For his part, Eustace Gable's expression provided no indication as to whether Pittman was guessing correctly.

"Duncan Kline had retired from teaching," Pittman continued. "He was living in Boston, but this obituary says he died at a cottage he owned in the Berkshire Hills. I don't need to remind you they're in western Massachusetts, just south of Vermont. In December. Why the hell would an elderly man who lived in Boston want to be at a cottage in the mountains during winter? Under the circumstances, the best reason I can think of is that he made the relatively short drive to the cottage after he attended the reunion at Grollier. Because his business with all of you wasn't finished. Because you needed an isolated place where he and you could continue discussing your differences."

Pittman stopped, needing to control his breathing, hoping that his inward frenzy wasn't betraying him. As frightened as he was, he felt elated that neither Gable nor Sloane contradicted what he had said. Imagining Bradford Denning climbing the slope outside, not daring to risk a glance toward the window to see how close Denning had staggered to the mansion, Pittman shifted toward a wall of bookshelves at the side of the room, desperate to prevent his audience from facing the window and seeing what was happening outside.

Pittman pointed toward a section of the obituary he held. "Duncan Kline was English. He came to the United States in the early 1920s, after teaching for a time at Cambridge."

Pittman's stomach tensed as he made another connection. British. If only I'd known earlier that Kline was British, that he came from Cambridge.

"I'm sure it must have been quite a coup for an Anglophile school like Grollier to have acquired an instructor from Cambridge as one of its faculty members. Ironic, isn't it? Over the years, Grollier's students have gone on to be congressmen, senators, governors, even a President, not to mention distinguished diplomats such as yourselves. But for all its effect on the American political system, the school's philosophical ties have always been to Britain and Europe. I've seen the transcripts of the seminars you took from him. Kline's specialty was history. Political science."

Winston Sloane's face turned gray.

Pittman continued. "So a political theorist from Cambridge bonded with five special students and trained them for their exceptional diplomatic careers. The five of you provided the philosophical underpinnings for almost every administration since Truman. The theories Duncan Kline instilled in you—"

"No! When we were young maybe," Winston Sloane objected. "But we *never* carried through on Duncan's theories!"

"Winston, enough!" Gable said.

"But listen to what he's saying! This is exactly what we feared! He'll destroy our reputations! We were *never* Communists!"

And that was it. What Pittman had fervently hoped, that one of the grand counselors would unwittingly volunteer information, had finally happened. The word *Communists* seemed to echo eerily. At once the room became disturbingly silent just as everyone in it seemed frozen in place.

Slowly Eustace Gable took out his handkerchief. He coughed into it in pain. Winston Sloane peered down at his gnarled hands, evidently ashamed of his lapse, realizing how severely he'd declined from having once been a great negotiator renowned for keeping his counsel.

For his part, Webley showed no reaction. He just kept pointing the .45 at Pittman.

Gable cleared his throat and put away his handkerchief. Despite his problems of health and age, he looked so dignified that he might have been conducting a meeting in the White House. "Complete your thought, Mr. Pittman."

"In 1917, the Russian Revolution electrified anti-Establishment British intellectuals. Liberal faculty members at British universities, especially at Cambridge, became enchanted with socialist theory. The eventual results of that enchantment were the British spy rings—former students who'd been recruited by their professors at Cambridge—working for the Soviets to undermine England and the United States. Guy Burgess. Donald Maclean. Kim Philby. In fact, now that I think of it, Burgess and Maclean defected to Russia in 1951. Philby was suspected of having warned them that they were about to be arrested as spies. The next year, Duncan Kline made his threatening appearance outside your offices at the State Department. I guess you could say that he was more advanced than Philby and the others. After all, Philby had been converted in the thirties, whereas Kline had become a Communist sympathizer a decade earlier, in the twenties. He must have been an exceptional seducer—sexually, politically. And after all, you and your friends were so young, so impressionable. You graduated from Grollier in 1933. You attended college, some of you at Harvard, others at Yale. Meanwhile, the Depression worsened. Kline's Communist theories presumably continued to be fascinating to you, given the chaos of the country. But eventually you stayed loyal to the capitalist tradition. Did it finally occur to you that if you followed Kline's theories and undermined the Establishment, you'd be undermining yourselves, inasmuch as you were the next leaders of the Establishment?"

Pittman stared at Gable and Sloane, but neither man responded.

"I think you're opportunists," Pittman said. "If communism had taken control of the United States, you'd have insinuated yourselves into the highest levels of the new system. But once the Second World War started, communism lost its limited appeal here. The Soviets appeared to be as huge a threat as the Nazis. So you insinuated yourselves into the upper echelons of the State Department. There, you not only jettisoned your former Communist attitudes; you also gained more power by eliminating your competitors, claiming that *they* were Communist sympathizers.'' Pittman thought nervously of Bradford Denning clutching his pistol, struggling up the slope past fir trees, toward the mansion. ''In the anti-Communist McCarthy hysteria of the early fifties, you built your careers on the sabotaged careers of other diplomats. Then Duncan Kline showed up and threatened to ruin everything. What did he do? Hold you up for blackmail? Unless you paid him to be quiet, he'd reveal that you were as vulnerable as the men you accused of being Communists, is that it?''

The room became so still that Pittman could feel blood pounding behind his eardrums.

Eustace Gable forlornly shook his wizened head. His tone was a blend of discouragement and disappointment. ''You know far more than I expected.'' The old man exhaled wearily. ''You've demonstrated remarkable journalistic skills. That's why I permitted you to come here—so that I could judge the extent of your knowledge. But you're wrong.''

''I don't think so.''

''Duncan didn't attempt to blackmail us. He didn't want money,'' Gable said.

''Then what *did* he want?''

''For us to be true to the principles he'd taught us. He was appalled that we'd formulated such stern government policies against the Soviet Union. He wanted us to undo those policies and recommend cooperation between the two countries. It was nonsense, of course. The Soviets had been made out to be such monsters that there wasn't any way to change America's official attitude toward them. Any politician or diplomat who tried would be committing professional suicide. No, the only way to build a career was to be more anti-Soviet than anyone else."

"And after all, your careers mattered more than anything," Pittman said.

"Of course. You can't accomplish anything if you're out of the loop."

"So you balanced Duncan Kline against your careers and . . ."

"Killed him," Gable said.

Pittman tensed, his instincts warning him. It wasn't Gable's habit to reveal information. *Why was he doing so now?* To hide his unease, Pittman frowned toward the obituary he held. "It says here that Duncan Kline died from exposure during a winter storm." Dear God, Pittman thought. He finally understood. Involuntarily, he murmured, "The snow."

"That's right, Mr. Pittman. The snow. Duncan was an alcoholic. When we met him at his cabin, he refused to be budged by our arguments. He insisted that if we didn't soften our policy toward the Soviet Union, he would expose us as former Communist sympathizers. A blizzard was forecast. It was late afternoon, but the snow was falling thickly enough already that we couldn't see the lake behind Duncan's cabin. He'd been drinking to excess before we arrived at the cabin. He drank heavily all the while we tried to reason with him. I suspect that if he'd been sober, we might have had more patience with him. As it was, we used the alcohol to kill him. We encouraged him to keep drinking, pretending to drink with him, waiting for him to collapse. Or so we hoped. I have to give Duncan credit. After a while, even as drunk as he was, he finally suspected that something was wrong. He stopped drinking. No amount of encouragement would persuade him to swallow the scotch we poured for him. In the end, we had to force him. And I have to give Duncan credit for something else—all those years of rowing had made him extremely strong. Drunk and in his sixties, he put up quite a struggle. But he wasn't any match for the five of us. You helped hold his arms, didn't you, Winston? We poured the scotch down his throat. Oh yes, we did. He vomited. But we kept pouring."

Pittman listened, repelled. The scene that Gable described reminded Pittman of the way in which Gable had murdered his wife.

"At last, after he was unconscious, we picked him up, carried him outside, and left him in a snowbank," Gable said. "His former students and faculty members knew how extreme his alcohol problem was. They thought that the reference to exposure was discreet, since privately many of them were able to learn the true nature of his death. Or what they thought was the true nature—that he'd wandered drunkenly outside in his shirt sleeves and passed out in the snowstorm. No one ever discovered that we had helped Duncan along. We removed all evidence that we'd been in the cabin. We got in our cars and drove away. The snow filled our tire tracks. A relative of his became worried when Duncan didn't return to Boston after the reunion at Grollier. The state police were sent to the cabin, where they saw Duncan's car, searched, and found his bare foot sticking out from under a snowdrift. An animal had tugged off his shoe and eaten his toes."

"And almost forty years later, Jonathan Millgate began having nightmares about what you'd done," Pittman said.

"Jonathan was always the most delicate among us," Gable said. "Strange. During the Vietnam War, he could recommend destroying villages suspected of ties with the Communists. He knew full well that everyone in those villages would be killed, and yet he never lost a moment's sleep over them. But about that time, his favorite dog had to be destroyed because it was suffering from kidney disease. He wept about that dog for a week. He had it buried, with a stone marker, in his backyard. I once saw him out there talking to the gravestone, and that was two years after the fact. I think that he could have adjusted to what we did to Duncan, a bloodless death, falling ever more deeply asleep with snow for a pillow, the corpse preserved in the cold, if only the animal hadn't eaten Duncan's toes. The mutilation took control of Jonathan's imagination. Yes, he did have nightmares, although I assumed that after a time the nightmares stopped. However, a few years ago, I was surprised, to say the least, when he began referring to them again. The Soviet Union had collapsed. Instead of being jubilant, Jonathan reacted by saying that the fall of communism only proved that Duncan's death had been needless. The logic eluded me. But the threat didn't. When Jonathan began pouring his tortured soul out to Father Dandridge, I felt very threatened indeed."

"So you killed him, and here we are," Pittman said, "trying to come to terms with your secrets. Was it really worth it, everything you did to me, the people who died because of the cover-up? You're elderly. You're infirm. The odds are that you would have died long before the investigation led to a trial."

Gable rubbed his emaciated chin and assessed Pittman with eyes that seemed a thousand years old. "You still don't understand. With all that you've been through and with all that we've discussed this afternoon, you still somehow fail to understand. Of course I'd be dead before the matter even got as far as a grand jury. I don't care about being punished. Indeed, as far as I'm concerned, I did nothing for which I deserve to be punished. What I care about is my reputation.

I won't have a lifetime of devoted public service dragged into the gutter and judged by commoners because I eliminated a child molester, a drunkard, and a Communist. Duncan Kline was evil. As a youth, I didn't think so, of course. I admired him. But eventually I realized how despicable he was. His death was no loss to humanity. My reputation is worth a hundred thousand Duncan Klines. The good I have done for this country is a legacy that I refuse to allow to be smeared because of a desperate act of necessity that protected my career."

"Your career."

"Precisely," Gable said. "Nothing else matters. I'm afraid that I brought you here under false pretenses. The million dollars, the two passports, I regret to say that I never intended to provide them. I wanted to discover what you knew. Quite a lot, it turns out. But without proof, it's all theory. You're hardly a threat to my security. But you are very much a threat to my reputation. Winston's behavior this afternoon shows that he, too, is a threat to my reputation. He can't guard his tongue. Fortunately both problems have a common solution. Mr. Webley."

"Yes, sir."

Webley proceeded toward Pittman and stopped behind him. Pittman's bowels turned cold when he heard the hammer on his .45 being cocked.

"No!"

The barrel of the .45 suddenly appeared beside him. The shot assaulted his eardrums. Across the room, Winston Sloane gasped, jerking back, blood erupting from his chest and from behind him, spattering the sofa upon which he sat. The old man shuddered, then collapsed as if he were made of brittle sticks that could no longer support one another. His head drooped, tilting his balance, sending his body sprawling onto the floor. Pittman was sure he heard bones scraping together.

The shocked expression on Pittman's face communicated the question he was too horrified to ask. *Why?*

"I told you, I need to eliminate problems," Gable said. "Mr. Webley."

The gunman stepped from behind Pittman and walked toward the entrance to the room. He stopped, turned, set the .45 on a table, and pulled a different pistol from beneath his suit coat.

"Perhaps you're beginning to understand," Gable told Pittman.

Terrified, Pittman wanted to run, but Webley blocked the way out. The instant Pittman moved, he knew he'd be killed. His only defense was to keep talking. "You expect the police to believe that I came in here, pulled a gun, shot Sloane, and then was shot by your bodyguard?"

"Of course. The .45 belongs to you, after all. Mr. Webley will wipe his fingerprints from it, place the weapon in your hand, and fire it so that nitrate powder is on your fingers. The physical evidence will match what we insist happened."

"But the plan won't work."

"Nonsense. Your motive has already been established."

"That's not what I mean." Pittman's voice was hoarse with fear. He stared at the pistol Webley aimed at him. "The plan won't work because this conversation is being overheard and recorded."

Gable's wrinkle-rimmed eyes narrowed, creating more wrinkles. *"What?"*

"You were right to be suspicious," Pittman said. "I did come here wearing a microphone."

"Mr. Webley?"

"You saw me search him thoroughly. He's clean. There's no microphone."

"Then shoot him!"

"Wait." Pittman's knees shook so badly that he didn't know if he could support himself. "Listen to me. When you searched me, you missed something."

"I said shoot him, Mr. Webley!"

But Webley hesitated.

"My gun," Pittman said. "The .45. Before I came here, I went to a man I interviewed five years ago. He's a specialist in security, in electronic eavesdropping. He didn't recognize me, and he didn't ask any questions when I said I wanted to buy a miniature microphone-transmitter that could be concealed in the handle of a .45. I knew the gun was the first thing you'd take from me. I was counting on the fact that you'd be so pleased to get it away from me, you wouldn't stop to realize it might be another kind of threat. You checked my pen, Webley. But you didn't think to check the gun."

Webley grabbed the .45 off the table and pressed the button that released the pistol's ammunition magazine from its handle.

Pittman kept talking, nauseated from fear. "I have a friend waiting in a van parked in the area. It's loaded with electronic equipment. She's been recording everything we said. She's also been rebroadcasting the conversation, directing it to the Fairfax police. Her signal is designed to block out normal police transmissions. For the last hour, the only thing the police station and all the police cars in Fairfax have been able to hear is our conversation. Mr. Gable, you just told several hundred police officers that you killed Duncan Kline, Jonathan Millgate, Burt Forsyth, and Father Dandridge. If

I'd had time, I'd have gotten you to admit that you also killed your wife."

"Webley!" Gable's outrage made his aged voice amazingly strong.

"Jesus, he's right. Here it is." Webley looked pale as he held up a bullet-shaped object that was obviously intended for another purpose.

"Damn you!" Gable shouted at Pittman.

"I'll wait in line, thanks. *You're* damned already."

"Kill him!" Gable roared toward Webley.

"But . . ."

"Do what I say!"

"Mr. Gable, there's no point," Webley said.

"Isn't there? No one subjects me to ridicule." Spittle erupted from Gable's mouth. "He's ruined my reputation." Gable's face assumed the color of a dirty sidewalk.

As Webley continued to hesitate, Gable stalked toward him, took the gun from his hand, aimed at Pittman . . .

"No!" Pittman screamed.

. . . and fired.

The bullet struck Pittman's chest. He groaned in anguish as he felt its slamming impact. It lifted him off his feet at the same time that it jolted him backward. In excruciating pain, he struck the floor, cracking his head, graying out for a moment, regaining consciousness, struggling to breathe.

From where he lay, his chest heaving spastically, he watched in panic as Gable coughed, faltered, then lurched toward him.

Gable's shriveled face towered above him. The pistol was aimed toward Pittman's forehead.

Paralyzed from shock, Pittman couldn't even scream in protest as Gable's finger tightened on the trigger.

The roar of the gunshot made Pittman flinch. But it didn't come from the pistol in Gable's hand. Rather, it came from behind Pittman, from the direction of the wall-length window as glass shattered and gunshots kept roaring, Gable's face bursting into crimson, his chest shuddering, obscene red flower patterns appearing on it. Five shots. Six. Gable lurched against a chair. The pistol fell from his hand, clattering onto the floor. A bullet struck his windpipe, blood gushing, and suddenly Gable no longer had the stature of a diplomat, but the gangly awkwardness of a corpse toppling onto the floor.

Through gaps in the window that had been shattered by gunshots, Pittman heard Denning shout in triumph.

Denning's grotesquely manic face was framed by a jagged hole in the window. The old man's skin seemed to have shrunk, clinging to his cheekbones, making his face like a grinning skull.

Hearing a noise from the other side of the room, Pittman twisted in pain and saw Webley stand from behind a chair, where he had taken cover. He raised the .45, aiming toward Denning.

The pistol that had fallen from Gable's hand lay on the floor next to Pittman. Sweating, wanting to vomit, mustering resolve, Pittman reached, grasped the weapon, and fired repeatedly at Webley, too dazed to know if he was hitting his target, merely pulling the trigger again and again, jerking from the recoil, concentrating not to lose his grip on the pistol, and then the gun wouldn't fire anymore, and it was too heavy to be held any longer anyhow, and Pittman dropped it, his chest seized by agonizing pain.

He waited for Webley to retaliate. No response. He listened for a sound from Webley's direction. Nothing. He fought to raise himself, squinting past Gable's corpse, still seeing no sign of Webley.

What difference does it make? Pittman thought. If I didn't kill him, I'm finished.

But he had to know. He squirmed higher, clutching a chair, peering over it, seeing Webley lying motionless in a pool of blood.

Pittman's painful elation lasted only a second as he heard a groan from beyond the shattered window. His chest protesting from the effort, he turned and saw Denning clutch his own chest. The old man's elated grin had become a scowl. His eyes, which a moment ago had been bright with victory, were now dark with terror and bewilderment. He dropped his pistol. He sagged against the windowsill. He slumped from view.

By the time Pittman staggered to the window, Denning was already dead, collapsed in a flower garden, his eyes and mouth open, his arms and legs trembling, then no longer trembling, assuming a terrible stillness.

Pittman shook his head.

In the distance, he heard a siren. Another siren quickly joined it. The wails became louder, speeding nearer.

Bracing himself against a chair, Pittman peered down, fumbling to open his sport coat. The bullet that had struck his chest protruded partly from his sweater. When Gable had commented that the two garments were the reason Pittman reacted badly to the eighty-degree temperature in the room, Pittman had been afraid that Gable would become suspicious about the sweater. After all, the sweater was the reason Pittman had needed to contact someone else he had once interviewed before he came to the mansion to confront Gable.

The person he'd gone to see was a security expert. The sweater was a bullet-resistant vest whose state-of-the-art design made it look like ordinary clothing.

I'm the sum of all the people I ever interviewed, Pittman

thought morosely as he stared again out the shattered window toward Denning's corpse.

He turned away. The effort of breathing made him wince. The security expert had explained that the woven fibers of the bullet-resistant vest could stop most projectiles but that it offered no protection against the force of their impact. Bruises and injured ribs were sometimes unavoidable.

I believe it, Pittman thought, holding himself. I feel like I've been kicked by a horse.

The sirens, joined by others, sped nearer and louder.

Pittman staggered across the living room, passing Gable's corpse, then Sloane's, then Webley's. The stench of cordite and death was cloying. He had to get outside. He had to breathe fresh air. He stumbled along the stone-floored hallway, his legs weak from the effects of fear. As he reached for the main door, he heard tires squealing on the paved driveway outside. He opened the door and lurched onto the terrace, breathing sweet, cool air. Policemen scrambled from cruisers. Weapons drawn, they didn't bother slamming their car doors. They were too busy racing toward Pittman. He lifted his arms, not wanting them to think he was a threat. But then he saw Jill among them, racing even harder to reach him, shouting his name, and he knew that for now at least he didn't have to be afraid. He held her, clinging to her, oblivious to the pressure against his injured chest. She was sobbing, and he held her tighter, never wanting to let her go.

"I love you. I was so afraid that I'd lose you," she said.

"Not today." Pittman kissed her. "Thank God, not today."

EPILOGUE

Love is an act of faith, Pittman thought. People get sick and die, or they die in traffic accidents, or they eat food that hasn't been properly cooked and they get salmonella and they die, or they fall from a ladder and break their necks, or they get tired of you and they don't want to see you anymore and they don't answer your phone calls, or they divorce you. There were so many ways to be tortured by love. Indeed, eventually all love, even the truest and most faithful, doomed the lover to agonizing loss—because of death. Love required so much optimism, so much trust in the future. A practical person might say that the possible immediate benefits did not compensate for the ultimate painful result. A cautious person might deny his or her feelings, closet the temptation to love, smother it, and go through life in a safe, emotionless vacuum. But not me, Pittman thought. If love requires faith, I'm a believer.

These thoughts occurred to him as he held Jill's hand and walked between rows of tombstones toward his beloved son's grave. It was Thursday again, a week after the events that had taken place at Eustace Gable's mansion and two weeks after Pittman had tried to save Jonathan Millgate's life at the Scarsdale estate. Following the arrival of the police and the discovery of the corpses in Gable's blood-spattered living room, Pittman and Jill had been held in custody. But as Pittman had hoped, the damning conversation that had been broadcast to the police was his salvation. After he and Jill had been questioned at length, after Mrs. Page corroborated those portions of their story about which she had personal experience, after the police in Boston and New York verified other details (with help from the Vermont State Police, who went to Grollier Academy), Pittman and Jill were eventually released.

Now in New York, they stopped before Jeremy's grave, and the warm sunshine-filled spring afternoon made Pittman's heart ache worse from love for his absent son. It was terrible that Jeremy would never again see and experience weather so beautiful.

Pittman put his arm around Jill, drawing comfort from her, while he studied the amazingly green grass that covered Jeremy's grave. As his tear ducts stung his eyes, he was reminded of something that Walt Whitman had written, that grass was the hair of graves. Jeremy's hair. The only hair he has now. Except that isn't true, Pittman thought. A hundred years ago maybe, when coffins were made of wood and weren't surrounded by a concrete sleeve and lid. In the old days, the coffin and the body would decompose, become one with the earth, and generate new life. Now the way bodies are hygienically sealed within the earth, death is truly lifeless, Pittman thought. If his ex-wife had agreed with Pittman's wishes, their son's body would have been cremated, his ashes lovingly scattered in a meadow where wildflowers could bloom from him. But Pittman's ex-wife had insisted so strongly and Pittman had been so emotionally disabled, Jeremy's body had been disposed of in a traditional manner, and the sterility of it made Pittman want to cry.

The thought of death, which for the past year had preoccupied him, now weighed heavier on his mind. Since his escape from the Scarsdale estate, he had seen his best friend killed, and Father Dandridge, and that didn't include several men whom he himself had killed, and it certainly didn't include the slaughter at Gable's mansion. The more Pittman brooded about it, the more he wondered if the other grand counselors—Anthony Lloyd dead from a stroke, Victor Standish dead from suicide—should also be included. And of course, Jonathan Millgate. I set out to do an obituary on a man who wasn't dead, Pittman thought. In the process, I inadvertently ended up causing the death of that man and of all his associates.

The grand counselors were evil. Of that, Pittman had no doubt. But they would have died soon anyway, he told himself, and maybe that would have been better than exposing their obscene secret and causing so many other deaths along the way. Would any of this have happened, Pittman wondered, if he hadn't believed that the public truly had a right to know about the abuses of power? If he'd been less determined, he would never have gone after Jonathan Millgate seven years previously. Burt would never have chosen him to go after Millgate again two weeks ago. Do *I* bear some responsibility for what happened?

Pittman couldn't believe that. No, I was right to go after them, he told himself with force. Those bastards did think they were above everyone. They didn't care who suffered and died as long as their careers prospered. They deserved to be punished—not killed, too easy for them, but exposed, condemned, ridiculed. In the old days, they would have been put in a cage in the town square and people would have spat upon them. And maybe other diplomats would have been discouraged from abusing power.

This "what if" type of thinking, this "if only" second-guessing had been typical of Pittman's mind-set after Jeremy's death. He had kept imagining an alternate reality in which if only this or that had happened, everything would have turned out for the best. But the "if only" hadn't happened. "If only" wasn't the case. Reality was the case. And reality was painful.

As a consequence, he had not been prepared for the love that he had found in Jill. He held her close to him. He treasured her. Yes, love was doomed to end in pain, he thought, but in the meantime it was an anodyne against other kinds of pain, the tragic imperfections of life. He still could not adjust to the realization of how close he had come to killing himself two weeks earlier. He had been in such black despair because of grief, the pain had been intolerable. Now grief still weighed upon him, unrelieved by the tears that streamed down his cheeks as he blinked through them at Jeremy's sunbathed grave, but he had been shocked into dealing with the present rather than dwelling on the past, and with Jill beside him to share the weight of his grief, he knew that he could now persist, just as he would gladly share the weight of whatever despair would eventually seize her.

And to be sure, a few good things had happened. The day after the massacre at Gable's mansion, the newspaper for which Pittman had worked and which had been scheduled to go out of business had found a financial white knight willing to keep it in business. The dying paper had been reborn, and the publicity that Pittman's story had received had prompted the paper's new owner to rehire Pittman as a lead reporter—in exchange for an exclusive series about what had happened to him and what he had discovered about the grand counselors, although his prestigious new position didn't matter to him as much as the chance to continue telling the truth about the abuses of power.

If only Jeremy was alive to cheer me on, Pittman thought.

If only.

But "if only" was to look backward, and at the moment, watching Jeremy's grave, tightening his arm around Jill, he knew that he had an obligation to himself and Jill to look to the future.

An act of faith, Pittman thought.

He turned to Jill, who wiped his eyes and kissed him.

"I'm sorry you're hurting," she told him.

"Hey, I'm alive. You're here with me." His voice broke. "Tears don't always mean a person's sad."